FADE IN

Also by Kyle Mills

The Immortalists
Lords of Corruption
Darkness Falls
The Second Horseman
Fade
Smoke Screen
Sphere of Influence
Burn Factor
Free Fall
Storming Heaven
Rising Phoenix

For Vince Flynn's Mitch Rapp Series

Code Red
Oath of Loyalty
Enemy at the Gates
Total Power
Lethal Agent
Red War
Enemy of the State
Order to Kill
The Survivor

For Robert Ludlum's Covert One Series

The Patriot Attack
The Utopia Experiment
The Ares Decision

FADE IN

KYLE MILLS

Authors Equity
1123 Broadway, Suite 1008
New York, New York 10010

Copyright © 2025 by Kyle Mills
All rights reserved.

Cover design by Gregg Kulick
Cover art by Getty Images
Book design by Scribe Inc.

This is a work of fiction. Names, characters, places and incidents either are products of the author's imagination or are used fictitiously.

Most Authors Equity books are available at a discount when purchased in quantity for sales promotions or corporate use. Special editions, which include personalized covers, excerpts, and corporate imprints, can be created when purchased in large quantities. For more information, please email info@authorsequity.com.

Library of Congress Control Number: 2025934722
Print ISBN 9798893310399
Ebook ISBN 9798893310429

Printed in the United States of America
First printing

www.authorsequity.com

The dreams in which I'm dying are the best I've ever had.

—Tears for Fears

Prologue

AT FIRST, the sound didn't seem like much—a quiet crunch penetrating curtains flowing across an open window. One of the local raccoons that had devised ways to defeat even his most secure trash cans? No. The sound, though nearly inaudible, had an unmistakable heft to it. A member of the resurgent black bear population roaming the Virginia mountains? Maybe. But only if the local bruins had taken to wearing combat boots.

Salam al-Fayed remained motionless on his bed, clad only in a pair of *Looney Tunes* boxer shorts and with his blankets relegated to the floor. Every night, the darkness took on more weight. Pressing him into the mattress. Making it hard to move. Hard to breathe.

The men quietly surrounding his house could solve that problem. They could solve all his problems.

He'd once read a book by a man who could manipulate his dreams. Just as the author entered the twilight between consciousness and unconsciousness, he would conjure whatever universe suited him. It was a trick al-Fayed had been working on for years. He'd succeeded in creating the world—a pleasantly mundane one in which there was no bullet fragment in his spine slowly paralyzing him. Only a vaguely neurotic wife and three uncontrollable kids. Transportation was handled by a minivan, and excitement was provided by spectating peewee sports and attending suburban dinner parties.

But he'd never managed to inhabit it.

A thick clunk reached him, confirming his suspicions. Based on considerable experience, that particular attack and decay was caused by only one thing. Rubber on stone.

He knew he should just lie there and let them make the weight of the darkness permanent, but instead, he found himself rolling silently out of bed. He'd spent so much time training for scenarios like these during his time as a SEAL, he wasn't capable of surrender. What was it his BUD/S instructors had been so fond of saying?

You will not die until I give you permission to die!

They'd turned him into a cockroach. A creature that instinctively fought to prolong a life that had no meaning. There was no mission anymore. No fight for God and country. Not even fear. Just a knee-jerk reaction programmed by his former superiors and a million years of evolution. Keep going until you drop.

And so there he was, standing in his dark bedroom, accompanied only by Daffy, Bugs, and the rest of the gang, preparing to take out as many of the men who had come for him as possible. To delay for a few more minutes the futile and violent end to his futile and violent life.

The man sloppily creeping up to his window was getting close enough to force a decision. Al-Fayed had a pistol on the nightstand, and the temptation was to just shoot half-heartedly at whatever face appeared. But then his week of planning and the draining of the last few dollars from his bank account would be wasted.

He kept the fluttering drapes in his peripheral vision as he reached up to a small door that led to the attic. It opened smoothly on recently oiled hinges, and he pulled himself inside.

The cut-rate command center he'd built didn't have the aesthetic grace he normally strived for, but time had been short, and sacrifices had to be made. He closed the door and lay down in something that looked disturbingly like a lidless steel coffin. A bank of tiny monitors was installed in front of him, but he had to feel around in the darkness to find the power button. Once pushed, a muted glow illuminated the tight, mold-scented space.

He connected a ground wire to a series of switches and powered up a controller lying next to him. After checking the neatly arranged compact AR-15, combat knife, and SIG P226 pistol, he focused his attention on the screens in front of him.

The images were surprisingly detailed. It was uncanny what you could get off the internet these days. Most of it was measurably better than the supposedly state-of-the-art stuff he'd used during his brief stint with the CIA.

Honestly, he was surprised they worked at all. It had seemed almost certain that the team sent for him would jam the wireless cameras he'd set up, but running cables had just felt like too much trouble. Stranger yet was that the generator he'd hidden in the basement was still idle. The power hadn't been cut. Maybe all this was a figment of his paranoid imagination. Maybe he was getting ready to unleash hell on a squirrel.

That hypothesis survived only a few seconds before a black-clad man with an M4 rifle darted past a camera above the front door.

A few moments later, there was motion on nearly every screen as men settled into the obvious positions he'd created with rusting appliances, car parts, and broken tree branches. Once they were comfortable, two more appeared on his back patio.

Al-Fayed brought his nose a little closer to the monitors, trying to see if anyone was covering his workshop but lost interest when he realized that he'd forgotten one obvious piece of gear: clothes. It looked like he was going to make his last stand in his underwear. At least it was clean.

The screen depicting a perfect sniper position was still empty, which seemed odd. Did they have a new gizmo that made that vantage point redundant? Something didn't feel right.

He managed to shrug despite being propped on his elbows. Based on the ultimate objective of this operation, it wasn't really worth getting in a twist over details. Besides, he'd never been one to worry about next-gen technology. Sure, it had its place in large theaters, but in situations like these, it just tended to be a distraction. Assuming of course that whatever gadget they were relying on hadn't gotten a little dust in it and stopped working.

In truth, he'd bought the cameras entirely for their fun factor. If he'd known they were actually going to work, he'd have put a few farther afield. Was Matt Egan out there personally directing this little pageant? If so, was he within reach?

Al-Fayed tried to imagine lining up his scope on Egan's forehead and pulling the trigger but found the image hard to summon. He tried again but couldn't get past centering the crosshairs. Faced with the opportunity for real, though, he'd damn well take the shot. One hundred percent.

A man passed through the unlocked front door just as one of his teammates did the same in the back. Al-Fayed switched to interior cameras and watched them do an initial sweep of the living area and kitchen before giving the okay for the entry of two comrades. The rest stayed outside, all committed to positions al-Fayed had made irresistible.

He continued to toggle through the interior cameras as the four men moved cautiously around his house. After finishing a thorough inspection, they relaxed a bit and began to turn on lights. Two members of the team remained in the living room while the other two stood at the foot of his bed. Interestingly, neither had checked to see if it was warm. One was speaking into his throat mic, but the cameras didn't have audio, so there was no telling what was being said.

Al-Fayed had physical access to both rooms—the bedroom through the attic door and the living room through a panel he'd cut in the ceiling. The question was what he should do with that access. He assumed they'd studied the architectural details of the house, so it seemed likely that they'd suspect he was up there. Were they trying to draw him out? Of course. It was clearly a trap, but what kind of trap? They were just standing around with guns dangling. What was that sneaky bastard Egan up to?

One of the men in the living room walked over to examine a heavy piece of steel plate lying on the floor in front of the fireplace. He didn't seem to know what to make of it. In the bedroom, the chitchat continued.

Al-Fayed smiled and silently admonished himself. This was all ego. He didn't want to be outsmarted. Better to stay focused on the result he was after: lots of gunfire, a few cool explosions, and his own death. If he stayed up there much longer, the only thing he was going to die of was curiosity.

Grabbing his rifle, he lifted himself out of what was apparently not going to be his final resting place and threw open the door.

Both men spun at the sound, and one actually managed to get off a couple hastily aimed shots before each took a single round to the face. Al-Fayed hung partially out of the attic, squinting through electric light at the pulverized flesh contained in the men's helmets. What the hell was going on? Why was that so easy?

The sound of running feet caused him to pull back just before a series of bullets tore through the ceiling.

"Attic! Attic!" he heard someone shout as he yanked the door shut and fell back into his armored coffin.

A moment later, the air was full of wood, plaster, and the deafening ring of rounds impacting steel.

On one of the dusty screens in front of him, he could see a man spraying the ceiling from the living area while his comrade moved into the bedroom and concentrated fire on what was left of the attic door. Their teammates outside were yelling pointlessly into their throat mics but didn't seem anxious to get any more involved than that.

Al-Fayed watched the man in the living room walk more or less directly beneath him, still firing upward. Then, suddenly, he was down. It took a moment to figure out that he'd been hit by one of his own ricochets.

"You've got to be kidding me," he said aloud, though he couldn't hear himself over the ringing in his ears and the shooter in the bedroom.

The monitors captured three men breaking cover and sprinting across his yard. One came alongside the house, produced a set of bolt cutters, and finally cut power to the building. The backup generator kicked on automatically, causing his screens to flicker, restart, and then die again. He fiddled with the connections to no effect. Hard to complain. Given his wiring skills, the system had held together a lot longer than he'd expected.

When the gun in the bedroom went silent, al-Fayed donned a pair of night vision goggles, hung the rifle and homemade controller across his bare chest, and dropped into the living room through the panel he'd cut.

The house was old but still solid. That, combined with a threadbare area rug, kept the noise of his landing to a minimum. He held his knife in his teeth as he slithered to the man lying on the floor, confirming he was dead. The ricochet had penetrated his neck just above his flak jacket. Bad luck.

He continued to crawl, finally coming alongside the open door to his bedroom. After a quick glance over his shoulder, he rolled inside and found the shooter fumbling with a fresh magazine in the darkness. The man died blissfully unaware of the bullet that killed him.

When al-Fayed slipped back into the living room, everything was still. He used the respite to take the radio from the body bleeding all over his landlord's carpet. After inserting the earpiece, he started toward the fireplace.

"Entering through the kitchen!" a voice crackled.

That wasn't ideal.

He dodged just in time to avoid a series of rounds raking the oak planks next to him.

"We have a man down in the living room! And I can see at least one more down in the bedroom," he heard over the comm. "The suspect is armed and heading toward the south end of the living area!"

It seemed likely that any guys still outside would be moving around to the windows. If they made it there faster than he could get to the fireplace, he was going to find himself at the center of a nasty cross fire. Time to shit or get off the pot. He hurled himself over the sofa, hitting the floor with the back of his neck and rolling onto all fours. The sound of breaking glass behind him prompted another burst of speed that sent him sliding toward a brick wall that was being chipped away by gunfire.

He felt a slight sting in his hip as he crammed himself into the fireplace and pulled the steel plate up after him. It covered the hole, offering protection from a volley that pounded the metal. Painfully loud, but better than the equally familiar sound of bullets pounding his flesh.

He removed his goggles and used a red penlight to examine the slightly-worse-for-wear remote control hanging around his neck.

"Kill 'em all!"

He was initially startled by the familiar voice but then looked down at his thigh to see Yosemite Sam staring at him with guns smoking.

"That's the plan, Sammy."

He rubbed his fingers together for a moment and then ceremoniously pressed buttons labeled *Kitchen* and *Living Room* on the remote.

Nothing happened.

"Use your space modulator, Fade!" Marvin the Martian suggested.

Fade.

He hadn't been called that in a long time. His navy buddies had found *Salam al-Fayed* a bit of a mouthful and slightly disconcerting during their Middle East escapades. They were the ones who'd created the more pronounceable and culturally palatable nickname.

"No dice, Marv. Amazon was out of stock."

He switched off the penlight and eased his grip on the chunk of steel protecting him. After sliding the remote's antennae through the resulting gap, he pressed the buttons again. The resulting explosion slammed the plate back hard enough to sever the antenna and shove him into the bricks behind.

Much more satisfying.

"What about thh-thh-thuh tunes?" Daffy asked.

"Shit! I forgot!" Fade felt around for a stereo remote and hit the power button.

His speakers had taken some damage, but the staticky sound that reached him was still recognizable as the Go-Go's "We Got the Beat."

He waited a few more seconds, bobbing his head to the rhythm and feeling the heat creep into the handle he was gripping. Finally, he lowered the shield far enough to take in his new operating environment.

The entire north wall was gone, and he assumed most of the kitchen with it. There were numerous small fires burning on the floor and on what used to be his furniture. The smoke was on his side—thick enough to confuse eyes, but not thick enough to asphyxiate him. Yet.

"Report!" came a woman's voice over his commandeered earpiece.

"Tom's down," someone responded. "I can see him from my position, but I can't see Jim. He was in the kitchen, and the kitchen's fucking gone."

"Maintain your position and stay cool! Any sign of the suspect?"

"No. He's gotta be dead. Half the house blew up."

"Craig! What have you got?"

"The south two-thirds of the structure is pretty much intact, but the fire looks like it's spreading. I have no movement, but there's a lot of smoke. If he is alive in there, he isn't going to last long."

Probably true, Fade knew. But if his remote still had decent signal with its broken antenna, he'd be around longer than they would.

He let the steel plate fall and laid himself out on the floor, holding the device as high as he could to get maximum range.

"I've got movement!"

"Stay where—"

The explosions—produced by grenades buried beneath the exterior men's positions—were more muted than the ones that had brought down his house.

"I'm hit. I'm hit!" he heard over the radio. The statement was followed by a fit of wet coughing. Obviously, the guy had moved out of position in the excitement. He should have been lying right on top of that charge.

An unfortunate complication. Where was he? And was he still capable of handling a gun?

"Hold on, I'm on my way." That woman again. Where the hell was Matt Egan in all this? Since when did he let other people direct his ops?

Fade leaped to his feet, dancing clumsily through the hot debris to Belinda Carlisle's soundtrack. Despite the flames, north seemed to be the path of least resistance, so he chose that direction. Once clear of the building, he started sprinting for the woods, but then immediately slowed. Where was he going? There was no long-term component to this plan. He was broke, homeless, and had just taken out an American black ops team charged with either recruiting or burying him.

The trees ahead began spewing light, and a moment later, a van appeared with high beams gleaming like the sun. He stood motionless as it accelerated, everything going blank white around him.

Then it went black.

1

KRISTEN WHITAKER reached for the light switch, flooding the room with the same fluorescent glare as the rest of the hospital. It always seemed a little sacrilegious. A violent attack on the peace that reigned in a place that had become a chapel to her.

The lone inhabitant looked more or less like he always did. The long dark hair and unlined face. The Buddha-like calm of his expression, now partially obscured by a goatee that was undoubtedly the work of Tim Pace. Unlike the other nurses, he was drawn to the bad-boy look. Fitting, perhaps, but also vaguely disturbing. A little too much demon in a man she'd spent more than a year transforming into a saint.

The machine monitoring his vital signs had been generating weird data all night, most notably a series of heart rate fluctuations that were virtually unheard of in long-term coma patients. The electronics were likely the culprit, but looking down at him, it was hard not to fantasize about it being something more.

The thought of Salam al-Fayed waking unleashed a mix of emotions that were both much stronger and more confusing than they should have been. Over her time caring for him, he'd become a confidant, priest, and therapist. An endlessly generous listener who never interrupted or judged. He afforded the same infinite gravity to her struggles with rude baristas as he did her mother's recent cancer diagnosis.

After a hard reset, the dull beep of the monitor began again, tracking his heart with none of the anomalies that had registered earlier. She dimmed the lights and gazed down at him. Maybe Tim was right. With the softer illumination, the goatee kind of worked. The yin and the yang. No one was completely good or completely evil. And no one was a better example of that than the man lying in front of her.

Like most longtimers on the floor, she knew everything about him. Before a police sniper had left a hole in his chest, Salam al-Fayed had written heartbreakingly about his creeping paralysis, his isolation, and the loved ones who had betrayed him.

He'd been accused of more crimes than she could count, including the murder of nearly the entire SWAT team sent to arrest him on charges trumped up by the government. There had been the expected emphatic denials from Washington, but in the end, they'd turned out to be the usual lies.

That, mingled with his physical beauty and the fact that his last act was to trade his life for the life of an innocent young woman, had turned him into something of a folk hero. One that the politicians had worked hard to sweep under the rug.

Now al-Fayed had been forgotten by virtually everyone except the people on this ward. For those lucky few, he'd become whatever they needed. An antihero who had given everything to fight the corrupt powers that be. A loyal warrior who had spent his life defending honor, freedom, and the American way. But for her, he represented something more intimate. A fellow human being who had shared her struggles with depression, loneliness, and doubt. Someone who'd fought to find a path and, when it disappeared from in front of him, sought redemption in one last meaningful act.

He was a monument to courage. But not in the battle against terrorists, enemy combatants, and American traitors. Those were nothing but fleeting skirmishes. No, where he'd really distinguished himself was in the battle against life itself. The insidious things that wore you down hour after hour. Day after day.

She turned back toward the monitor and checked the screen. All normal.

"Looks like you're good to go," she assured him quietly. "Coffee later? What do you think?"

When she glanced down to take in his familiar nonresponse, he was staring right at her.

2

THE ANGLE of the sun turned the lake's surface obsidian. Surrounding mountains were low and heavily forested, but farther afield, they rose rocky and majestic. Late spring snow clung to the summits of many despite unusually warm temperatures.

The armored SUV completed a sweeping turn, aligning with a canyon to the blinding west. Matt Egan and the man behind the wheel lowered their visors and continued scanning the empty landscape.

An identical vehicle in front slowed, and they did the same to keep their interval. Behind, a third SUV closed slightly. They were badly exposed despite his precautions and the number of men he had with him. This part of Kazakhstan was sparsely populated and attracted only the most adventurous tourists. Their half-assed motorcade would be easy to spot, easy to track, and easy to isolate. If something went wrong, help wouldn't arrive for at least an hour. Which was as good as not arriving at all.

During Egan's days with the Agency, he'd gotten bogged down in a nearly identical landscape in Chechnya. Same blinding sun. Same narrow road and steep embankments. Same dense trees and shimmering water.

The sound and smell of the Spetsnaz ambush were still burned into his mind, but the rest of the details were blurred by the fog of war. He'd survived the initial assault partially due to his youth and spec ops training, but mostly because of luck. The bullet that penetrated his right thigh had passed through without hitting anything vital. But it wasn't like the movies. In the real world, you didn't just grit your teeth and walk off an injury like that. Mostly you bled and prayed and questioned your life choices.

He'd lost two men that day and would have died with them if his former best friend wasn't a complete freak of nature. He'd managed not only to dispatch half the Russian team but also to drag Egan's stumbling carcass up a mountain pass and into a blizzard that stymied pursuit. That part of the memory was still surprisingly sharp. His friend's silhouette. The snow clinging to his hair, eyelashes, and beard. The sound of him humming the same Go-Go's tune over and over as they climbed relentlessly upward.

Now all those advantages were gone. Egan's youth had slipped away. His luck had turned to shit. And his friend . . . His friend had come to hate him and been transformed into a useless bag of meat by the horrors of modern medicine.

"Beautiful, isn't it?" Jon Lowe said from the back seat.

Egan agreed reflexively but didn't turn to look at the man. "Yeah."

Lowe was an obscenely wealthy venture capitalist who had his hands in everything from cutting-edge technology to energy, media, defense, and health care. Despite that, he operated very much under the radar. No yachts or young supermodels. No interviews or political affiliations. And despite having founded the largest nonprofit in history, he somehow never appeared on any *Forbes* lists.

Not that it didn't make sense to stay out of the public eye. The idea that Lowe and his overachiever cronies could use their wealth and expertise to tackle society's problems wouldn't be as well received now as it would have been a few decades ago. Neither would his impatience with hippy do-gooders and political correctness. In his mind, if the modern world was going to be saved, it would have to be done with the same cold calculation and brute force that had built it.

Making that theory a reality, though, was a heavier lift than even Lowe had counted on. A lift that had finally led him to Egan's door.

He'd initially turned down the offer to become the foundation's director of security. What the hell did he know about security? He'd been trained to kill people on the battlefield by the army and then to stab them in the back by the CIA. In the end, though, Lowe had made him an offer he couldn't refuse. Something that caused him to wonder if the man was more than just another egomaniac billionaire with delusions of grandeur. Maybe he was different. Maybe he was willing to do what it would take to actually move the needle.

Somehow, all that had led them here. To bumfuck Kazakhstan to meet some guy named Bóchéng. Who he was, why he was important, and what the hell he was doing out here weren't details that Lowe had shared. What was obvious, though, was that this wasn't a normal power lunch. Lowe had requested the armor and security personnel himself. Not that it was strictly necessary, he'd explained. But just in case.

Bullshit. If there was one thing Egan had learned in his time working with the man, it was that he never did anything without a reason. So a lot of red flags on the play, but none he could do anything about.

"Did you know that Kazakhstan is the least populated country in the world?" Lowe asked.

"No."

"Only seven people per square kilometer. Easy to believe when you're driving through it."

Egan just nodded.

The road—a lane and a half wide at best—straightened, and they found themselves driving dead into the descending sun. A steep slope loomed above and to the left, bisected by a dirt track that disappeared into the terrain's undulations. To the right was a gentler, boulder-strewn gradient that led to the lake.

It was such a picture-perfect location for an ambush that Egan felt no surprise at all when his earpieces came to life.

"We have a problem." The accented voice belonged to the driver of the lead car—a talented former operator from Germany.

"What kind of problem?"

"A dead cow blocking the road."

Egan twisted around to watch their chase car pass the dirt track that intersected the road from above. Lowe immediately read his expression.

"Matt? Are you okay? This is an agricultural area, right? Cows do die in them."

Egan faced forward again. "Are you familiar with the saying *the oldest trick in the book*?"

"Of course."

"A dead farm animal blocking the road at a choke point might actually be it."

"Really? How interesting."

Ahead, the lead car stopped, and Egan's driver did the same.

"Orders?"

There was no way to go around. It was too steep to the left and too rocky to the right. Straight through was the obvious option—the SUV's suspension was certainly capable. But the second oldest trick in the book was to booby-trap the dead farm animal you used to block the road at a choke point. That left a hasty retreat, but he suspected the dirt track behind was going to put an end to that possibility before he could even utter the command.

And as was customary in these kinds of situations, he was right. A Soviet-era transport truck appeared above and began barreling toward the road. It would intercept the asphalt about fifty yards behind their chase car, hemming them in.

What would come next was equally easy to predict.

"Get down!"

Throwing himself over the seats, he landed on top of Lowe just as armed men appeared from behind the boulders to the north. A shouldered RPG caught his eye, causing him to immediately duck down beneath the glass. The expected explosion didn't materialize, but the impacts of small arms fire did.

An analysis of the situation was already running through Egan's head when the sound of the Russian Ural ramming their chase car reached him. The fact that the RPGs hadn't been fired yet might be a positive sign. Lowe wasn't worth much dead, and their attackers might not be a hundred percent sure which vehicle he was in.

On the other hand, the pounding their SUV was taking didn't suggest a lot of concern for the man's safety. Miraculously, though, the armor seemed to be holding. Egan glanced up at the rear passenger window and saw that it was spiderwebbed and billowing with the force of the rounds hitting it. Still, no sign of penetration. It was as though the movement was intentional—a strategy to absorb kinetic energy.

The rate of fire waned enough for him to risk rising to the level of the window. There was no question that he was in the last minutes of his life, and he'd be damned if he was going down without looking in the eyes of the men who killed him.

What he saw was rare in a combat situation: something he hadn't predicted. His attackers—beautifully positioned, optimally armed, and previously dug in like ticks—were now in disarray. A few were still shooting in their direction, but the rest appeared to be in the midst of a panicked retreat. One, running toward the lake, suddenly went down as though he'd been swatted by the hand of God. The others took note and adjusted their trajectories away from him.

There was no time to think. As much as his life had been one of careful analysis and meticulous follow-through, sometimes you just had to leap.

"Everybody out! South side. Stay low. Kill anything that moves!"

"No!" Lowe shouted. "Stay in the cars!"

Egan ignored him, rolling back into the front seat and grabbing one of the MP7s mounted to the floorboard. He thought about his wife and daughter as he followed the driver out the door. No second guesses. No hesitation. But also no targets. Or shooting. He lined his weapon up on the six-wheeled Ural. The sun was reflecting off the windshield but not with enough intensity to obscure the fact that the interior was spattered with blood.

The driver of the chase car exited in the same manner he had, landing in a crouch and moving his rifle in a confused arc. No contacts. The man on the passenger side followed, ignoring Egan's orders and coming out to the north. He was barely through the door when he was hit.

"What the hell did that?" Egan's driver said from behind.

"I don't know," he replied before tapping one of his earpieces. "Form up on me. Watch for snipers in the high ground."

As his men approached, Egan broke cover and moved toward the lake, sweeping his weapon across the increasingly shadowed landscape. Various bodies were visible—many still dug in, lying peacefully over their weapons as if they'd gotten bored during the op and fallen asleep. A few had made it a bit farther and now lay sprawled in low foliage or sunk into the soft lakeshore. One had actually made it to the water and was now floating face down in it.

Egan heard a shout from beneath a van-sized boulder in front of him, and he trained his submachine gun on it. A man began crawling out, hands in front of him to demonstrate that he was unarmed. It was impossible for Egan to understand what he was saying, but based on the desperate calm of his tone, it probably translated to a lengthy list of reasons not to kill him: *I have a family. I was just following orders. I can provide you with whatever information you need* . . . Arguments that likely wouldn't have been given much weight if the shoe was on the other foot.

He was still talking when a sizable hole appeared in his chest. Egan dropped to his stomach, scanning the south ridge. Nothing.

The sound of footsteps caused him to jerk his barrel left, but he found himself aiming at Jon Lowe. The man was walking toward the chase car, looking down at what appeared to be their only casualty.

"Check if any of the vehicles are still operable," Egan shouted. "If not, we'll see if we can swap some parts to get one moving. And someone go put some rounds in that fucking cow!"

The men dispersed, leaving Lowe staring silently at the dead man. His hands were buried in his pockets against the dropping temperatures.

"You can lead a horse to water, but you can't make him drink," he said as Egan came alongside.

"What?"

Lowe motioned with his head toward the corpse. "I can give advice. I can explain what's in a person's best interest. I can even bark orders. But unless you force people to comply, it doesn't do any good." He looked over at Egan. "What do you think, Matt? Should people be forced to do what's good for them at the barrel of a gun? Or should they just be left to drown?"

"What happened here, Jon?"

"Could you be more specific?"

"What killed all these men?"

"An antipersonnel drone built by a company I'm involved with."

"You had it lingering above us?"

He nodded.

"It was probably the bad light," Egan said, speaking through the same lump in his throat that he always felt when he lost a man. "The operator couldn't see clearly."

"There was no operator."

"What?"

"Artificial intelligence. It's completely autonomous."

"I thought that taking humans completely out of the loop was frowned upon."

"Why? Because we're so good at telling right from wrong? Its processor can make millions of decisions a second, integrating information from HD cameras, LIDAR, and radar, as well as calculating wind speed, temperature, and air density. It doesn't make mistakes. Certainly not because of the sunset. Its only problem is that it's too expensive and delicate to be put into widespread use. Too much money for too narrow a mission."

Egan pointed to the man lying on the asphalt. "It doesn't make mistakes?"

Lowe indicated the watch Egan was wearing and then the empty wrist of the man at their feet. The touchscreen timepieces had been passed out just before they'd landed in Kazakhstan with orders that they be worn in-country.

"The drone uses them to discern between friend and enemy," Lowe explained.

Machine gun fire erupted somewhere up the road, followed by an explosion. Undoubtedly the booby trap in the cow being set off. A moment later a motor started, quickly followed by another.

"We look good on the vehicles," a voice said over the comms. "Lead and center are both operable."

"Let's go then," Lowe said. "We're behind schedule."

"Behind schedule for what?"

"My meeting with Bóchéng."

"Hold on, now, Jon. Has it occurred to you that he's one of the only people who knew we were coming? This could have been his doing."

"Oh, I can almost guarantee it," he said, starting back toward the pummeled SUV they'd arrived in. "But that's no excuse for being late."

3

MATT EGAN'S headlights washed across a treelined driveway that smelled of pine and winter only recently vanquished. The house at its end was overly large, overly modern, and illuminated only by the gloom of a few dirty security lights. He pulled up to one of the garage bays, killed the engine, and sat motionless. Above, clouds were spitting frozen raindrops that swirled through his open window and stung his cheek.

The home's design had been a concession to his wife, Elise, while the large, wooded lot had been a rare win in his column. In an opposites-attract marriage, everything was a negotiation. When he'd left the government, she'd wanted out of DC and suggested a flat in New York or San Francisco. He, in contrast, had advocated for fifty acres in Idaho.

Park City, Utah, had been another of the many compromises that made their unworkable marriage work so shockingly well. Decent schools for their daughter, Kali; proximity to Salt Lake's quirky urban cool; and a dash of natural beauty. Tolerable for everyone involved.

The early morning storm was intensifying, but instead of reaching for the remote on the visor, he rolled up the window and stepped into the rain. The garage had become a repository for his wife's car and the other memories he'd cleared from the house in a fifteen-hour alcohol-fueled frenzy. It had been more than two years since he'd set foot inside.

Egan started toward the front door, triggering a somewhat-better-maintained porch light that gave the place a strange quality. Like a photo of a home instead of the real thing. A movie set propped up by two-by-fours hidden just out of sight.

He went straight to the kitchen, fishing a beer from a refrigerator stacked with them. A quick search of his phone for news relating to Kazakhstan turned up nothing but an article on wild horses. Apparently, a bunch of heavily armed corpses rotting in its hinterland didn't make it above the fold.

Despite the ambush and subsequent condition of their vehicles, they'd managed to make their meeting with Bóchéng with a few minutes to spare. Lowe despised being late. Unlike most men in his economic strata, he considered wasting people's time an unforgivable offense. Even when they had just tried to kill him.

Not surprisingly, their arrival had been unexpected. In the end, that might have been what saved them from another confrontation. Or maybe news of Lowe's little airborne toy had traveled faster than their shot-up SUVs. Either way, the hour-long closed-door meeting had gone off with no fireworks, and the two men had emerged smiling and backslapping. It almost always went that way. While it was true that Lowe was a genius in a number of disciplines, all paled when compared to his ability to figure out what people wanted and give it to them.

Egan had no idea what was discussed, what was accomplished, and what was gifted. And frankly, he didn't want to know. His soul was sold. All that was left to do was go through the motions like he still had possession of it.

After downing the beer, he grabbed a half-full bottle of Jack Daniel's and descended into a basement full of musical instruments and electronics he didn't understand. On one wall, a whiteboard displayed a colorful drawing by his daughter and music notation scrawled in a somewhat more sophisticated hand. The erasable substrate had been his wife's insistence. In her mind, art was transitory. An excuse for constant reinvention.

He used a remote to start a slideshow on her computer monitor. It opened with a photo from the day they'd adopted Kali, followed by them skiing at Alta. Then Elise onstage, screeching into a microphone and doing her best to destroy a guitar he'd gone into hock to buy her.

How long ago had that been? He took a pull from the bottle. So long that it didn't seem real anymore. In truth, it had never seemed real. How had a dipshit like him married a woman that *Spin* magazine once called America's most visionary songwriter? She'd been only twenty-five when they'd first met, playing in no fewer than three bands to make ends meet. He, on the other hand, had been a thirty-three-year-old CIA contractor fresh out of the army.

On-screen his wife's hair whipped through a swirl of colored lights. Speakers on the desk pumped out a song that he still thought sounded like cats being dipped in boiling oil. The crowd didn't see it that way, though. They bounced joyfully, and someone climbed onstage to immediately dive back off.

The room went silent as the video was replaced by a photo of his daughter at the beach. She would have been six when it was taken. Six years, three months, and twelve days, to be more precise. He examined the sand stuck to her knees and elbows. The sunglasses oversized for her face. The white globs of lotion clinging to her ear. And then she was gone. Replaced by the broad face of a bison in Yellowstone National Park.

He redirected his gaze to the tangle of wires, consoles, and laptops that had turned out to be a way better investment than he'd anticipated. In one of her stranger about-faces, Elise had suddenly decided that as a new parent, she needed to start contributing financially to the family. Soon after, she backed away from performing and maxed out their credit cards to acquire the equipment surrounding him.

He'd protested, but it had proved pointless in the face of her unwavering belief that famous artists would pay a lot of money for songs that brought to mind the torture of domestic animals. Fortunately, he hadn't gone to the mat, because she'd turned out to be right. Apparently, her talents weren't limited to writing stuff that would make Kurt Cobain's ears bleed. She could do dance, rap, country, and a number of genres that he'd never even heard of. So while he'd coughed up for the gear, Madonna had covered the house that contained it.

In fact, the money had rolled in so fast, it allowed him to walk—run, really—away from his gig at Homeland Security. Suddenly he was a full-time father and kept man. All he had to do was play golf and keep his girls safe so their lights could keep shining. A complete moron could do it.

He began to lift the bottle again when an unknown number rang through on his phone. Instead of rejecting it, he picked up. Why not? He had precisely nothing better to do than talk with someone trying to sell him insurance or get him to reveal his bank account number. Not a single thing.

"What?"

"This is the number I was given to call." A woman's voice. Nervous. Educated. Not the timbre of someone who wanted to sell him a time-share.

"By who?"

"The hospital."

"Hospital," he repeated. "What hospital? Why?"

"Salam al-Fayed is showing signs of coming out of his coma."

A burst of adrenaline hit hard enough to bring some Jack back up into his throat. "Who is this?"

"Dr. Smith. I'm overseeing his care."

"Does anyone else know?"

"Just me and two nurses."

"Can we keep it that way? I can be on my way to the airport in ten minutes."

The answer would undoubtedly be no. While the passage of time had blurred his history, Fade hadn't exactly slipped into a coma unnoticed. He'd wiped out a SWAT team, shot up a medical facility, kidnapped a cop, given an entire division of Homeland Security catastrophic diarrhea, and tortured a serial killer to death. And that was leaving aside the former recon Marine he'd killed with an ejector seat fitted in his classic Cadillac. If he was awake, an army of cops, government flunkies, and reporters were already inbound.

"Of course."

"Sorry? What?"

"No need to be concerned. It's all been taken care of."

4

THE FEW people visible in the street seemed to have no purpose other than to kick up dust that then hung in air that smelled like antiseptic. Most were dressed entirely in white, some with faces obscured by surgical masks and others with no faces at all. The overwhelming impression was silence punctuated by a dull beep that kept perfect time with Fade's heartbeat.

He skirted along a rock wall, finally squatting in the shade near a section shattered by mortar fire. The winter sun was like an ice pick, providing glare but little in the way of warmth or comfort. He pulled a waterskin from beneath his robe, watching the phantoms around him adjust their trajectory to keep their distance. Maybe they saw him like everyone else did—another dangerous man using any means necessary to enforce his suffocating vision of Islam.

Instead of goat and dirt, the water had a weird fruit-punch quality that stung his cracked lips and set him to calculating exactly what he'd pay for a tube of ChapStick. And a shower. And a glass of Cierto reposado. He managed to stop a thin smile from spreading far enough to cause bleeding. Not even thirty years old, and he was already getting downright delicate.

A rare combination of perfect weather, overly pessimistic intelligence, and good fortune had allowed him to add four more ghosts to the thousands already haunting the countryside. And two hours ahead of schedule, no less. Unfortunately, the region was a bit short on Starbucks—a situation America was undoubtedly anxious to remedy—so he couldn't go wash off in a tidy little bathroom and then linger over a toffee-nut latte. That left him with nothing to do but squat in the shade and pick goat hairs from his teeth.

Join the Navy, the recruiting pamphlet said. *See the world*. He'd thought they meant Hawaii.

Join the CIA, the creepy guys with matching John Lennon glasses said.

See the world. He'd thought they meant a Monaco casino full of Russian honeypots.

A woman passed about fifty yards ahead, and he thought he recognized her. A girl he'd had a crush on in high school, but with a burqa clinging to her like pale mist. Suddenly all the people around him were characters from his past. Familiar, but not immediately unidentifiable. Like a name that was on the tip of his tongue but refused to proceed further.

Where was he again?

Afghanistan. Or was it Libya?

Why?

To kill some assholes for Uncle Sam.

Not exactly anything new, so what made everything around him feel so unnatural? Was it doubt? Despite his solo mission going off without a hitch, it had the feel of one too many. Like his luck had peaked and was now in decline.

Or maybe that quiet sense of dread was just nature's way of hinting that he wasn't quite as fast or strong as he once was. A million-year-old survival reflex speaking to him in a language his modern mind could understand. On the other hand, it could have been nothing more than the grinding futility of it all.

Fade was no longer under the illusion that America would be any safer because of the four men he'd left blackening beneath the empty sky. They would have already been replaced. And so it would go, until the American people and politicians got bored enough to call it quits.

He'd come to believe the problems plaguing the world were ingrained to the point that there really were no solutions. Only quixotic attempts to delay the inevitable. At the dawn of the twenty-first century, people were no different than they had been thousands of years ago. Humanity was destined to be a twitchy, mean-spirited species bent on self-destruction. Why? He had no idea. But it was true.

He took another sip of water and scanned the broken buildings in front of him. Despite being built of hardened mud and ancient stone, they had a strange aura of nonpermanence. Ancient bulwarks that were hopelessly inadequate when faced with modern war. Whether they'd succumb to America's bombs, a sudden flare-up of factional fighting, or just decay and despair, was hard to predict. The only certainty was that they would succumb. Everything did eventually.

He leaned his head against the cool stone behind him and stared up at the sky. For a man whose education ended with a whimper in the twelfth grade, he was becoming quite the philosopher. Not exactly a useful trait for someone in his profession. Some might even say counterproductive.

He started up the dirt road again, making it barely a hundred yards before a high-pitched scream broke the oppressive quiet. By the time he got a hand on the AK-47 beneath his robe, the street was empty. Even the widely scattered livestock had gone up in thin air.

The terrified cry sounded again, this time long enough to pinpoint its source as a narrow alley between buildings to the north.

His planned route was in the other direction, but there was something in the sound that drew him. He jogged toward it, eyes sweeping shadowy corners and rooftops as he turned into the alleyway. Screams turned to begging, high pitched and slurred in a way that suggested a young girl.

When he reached a sharp corner, his suspicions were confirmed. The black scarf that should have covered the girl's face had been torn off, making it possible to estimate her age at around sixteen. She was on her back in the dust, kicking and punching violently at two men trying to control her. One had a knee on her chest, keeping her pinned but making it harder for his compatriot to remove the shroud that covered her from neck to toe. The operation was a bit disorganized, but overwhelming force was on the men's side, and with the aid of a knife, they were able to expose her dirty T-shirt and the remnants of a wool skirt. Fade looked on silently as the man on top removed his knee and began using it to pry her legs apart.

She managed to free a hand and was about to claw him, but lost focus when she spotted Fade. The pleas for help began again as her struggle refocused on maintaining eye contact with her would-be savior.

One of the men looked back and taunted him, but Fade remained planted where he was. There was something wrong with the girl. Her eyes were too dark. A black that couldn't be fully explained by the deep contrast of the shadows. Maybe they'd been turned that way by the reality she'd been relegated to. Her parents were likely victims of the chaos that had erupted in the area and that didn't leave much for her but violence, poverty, and hunger. A precarious position that demanded a bit more caution than she'd apparently shown.

Fade had never taken religion all that seriously. Evolution, though, was a philosophy he could get behind. From what he'd been unfortunate enough to see, the strong survived and the meek weren't going to inherit shit. This girl had been stupid to let herself get pulled into that alley. The men he'd killed the day before hadn't been smart or strong enough to defend themselves. And on a larger scale, North America thrived while much of the Middle East wallowed. Life had an oddly comforting simplicity once you exorcised all the mysterious deities.

The man temporarily gave up on the girl's legs and was now concentrating on holding her wrists above her head. He looked back at Fade again. "Do you want to save her? Are you a godly man? I think not. Now go!"

Good advice. This girl had no future. It wasn't anybody's fault in particular, and it wasn't worth crying over. She was just born in the wrong place at the wrong time. Whether she died today, tomorrow, or next week didn't matter. Not to him. Not to her. Not to anyone.

Her pleas were now coming as gasps. At this pace, it would be less than a minute before her fight was over.

With his companion firmly in control of their prey, the other man began to move in Fade's direction. His face was nearly invisible behind a thick beard that grew almost to his eyes. He shouted something that came out like a record run backward, then reached behind him to retrieve some kind of weapon.

Fade took a step forward, pinning the man's arm long enough to retrieve his knife and shove it through the impressive beard and into the throat behind. He seemed surprised. His gaze angled downward in time to watch the knife slide back out and blood fan across his chest. Then he crumpled to the ground.

The girl's muted grunts turned into a piercing scream that tipped off the other man that something had gone wrong. He was faster than he looked and managed to retrieve an ancient pistol as he spun.

Fade threw the knife, hoping to distract his aim. In keeping with his stellar luck on this mission, it hit blade-first and stuck in his chest. Not deep enough to seriously injure him, but plenty deep to cause his bullet to miss its target.

The man was on his knees when they collided. Fade jerked right and closed his eyes against the flash of gunpowder, feeling it burn as a round screamed past his left temple. He ignored the pain, palming the man's face and shoving his head back into the depressingly soft dirt. His AK was trapped between them, so he had no choice but to begin the difficult task of working his blade out of the man's breastbone.

It was almost free when an intense ache in his lower back robbed him of his strength. He twisted, throwing his body weight into one final yank. The knife came free with a wet crunch, and Fade swung it behind him in a clumsy arc. He caught the girl across the neck, missing critical arteries but doing enough damage to make her lose her grip on the bloody shiv she'd stuck him with.

They hit the ground simultaneously, and Fade used his momentum to roll to all fours. When he tried to stand, his body wouldn't respond. He turned his head toward the girl, watching her choke and vomit blood that then fell back into her face.

He heard movement behind him and managed to crane his neck far enough to see the surviving man rise to his feet and take aim. The bullet struck Fade in the lower back, causing him to collapse into the dirt.

The girl was motionless now. Not dead but staring blankly upward, waiting for death to come. She let her head loll to the side, fixing her black eyes on him.

Can you hear me?

The sun suddenly became blinding, turning everything into an overexposed haze.

"*Mr. al-Fayed! Can you open your eyes?*"

For some reason, the voice prompted a reel of his not-so-greatest hits. Giving up countless athletic scholarship offers to become a SEAL. Walking away from the woman he loved to go it alone. Mistakenly killing a bunch of innocent cops but failing to kill the man who sent them.

Then he was back in the crumbling village. The place where his life had gone from crap to total shit.

"Can you look at me?"

The blinding sun again. But not the village. A white ceiling framing a face hovering over him. A coat that matched the room. A stethoscope. Fuck. He was alive.

Again.

He tried to sit up, but nothing happened. Attempts to speak produced similar results, but it was possible that his lips were moving. He wasn't sure.

"Relax," the man above him said. "You were shot. You've been unconscious. Give it time."

He held Fade's eyelids open and flashed an even brighter light into them. "Incredible. You were dead for almost a minute. This is the third time, isn't it? That you died and were brought back? You must be the luckiest man alive."

Fade would have laughed if he were capable.

5

THE CONFERENCE room Jon Lowe entered was as generic as the glass cube of a building that housed it. Situated just outside of Salt Lake City, the location was a low-profile compromise between the power centers of the coasts. Matt Egan's idea, and a good one, as it turned out.

Having said that, it didn't feel like home. Nothing did. Not for a long time. Lowe had no surviving family of note and no one he could realistically classify as a friend. His forty-seven years had been spent more as an observer of human society than an active participant. Of course, he knew how to operate the levers, but that's all they were to him. Levers. The complex and often malfunctioning controls of an extremely dangerous machine.

The depressing fact was that the people sitting around the table in front of him were perhaps the closest he'd ever get to companionship. Members of his tribe, he supposed. Captains of industry, entrepreneurs, tech gurus, and politicians. Men and women who had already succeeded wildly but weren't finished making their mark on the world.

Some were sincerely altruistic. Others were in search of community and status. A few sought to quench their insatiable thirst for power. And finally, there were those who desired darker things. Experiences, privileges, and possessions that were denied to everyone but the ultra-elite.

All things he'd learned to provide in return for their contribution to the greater good.

It was ironic that his difficulty connecting emotionally with his species made him so effective at manipulating it. With a few notable exceptions, he didn't feel other people; he calculated them. To him, every individual was an equation to be solved. Or maybe a series of equations would be more accurate. What did they want to hear? When was the optimal moment to smile, groan, or laugh? What did he need to offer or withhold in order to bend them to his will? Flattery, humiliation, reward, punishment. Even love. All applied in just the right amount and at just the right moment.

It was a strange skill, but it was one that had taken him a long way in life. To that very conference room, in fact.

The young woman giving a presentation on an African water project fell silent as Lowe settled into an open seat, but he waved a hand dismissively. "Please continue. And apologies for being the last to arrive. I couldn't avoid it."

She began speaking again, raising her voice to be heard over the greetings murmured by the twelve people around the table. Lowe feigned attention, but he'd read the analysis of her proposal on the way over.

The country she wanted to operate in was becoming increasingly unstable as its aging dictator lost his grip. When he died or was overthrown, a civil war would likely erupt. And then there was the issue of cattle. Adding wells to the area tended to supply drinking water less for the residents than to the herds favored by young men as a display of wealth. In an environment already inadequate to provide for its human population, contributing to the growth of those herds would be counterproductive at best. Deadly at worst.

The presenter finished, thanked them, and exited, closing the door behind her. A lengthy silence ensued, finally broken by one of only two women on his board. The founder of a medical technology start-up, she was still in her mid-thirties. Idealistic and in possession of the purest heart in the group. "Beyond water being the most essential commodity for survival, the amount of time women in this area spend hauling it is fundamental to them not being able to develop."

Greg Madison, the man who responded, was almost forty years her senior. Despite that, he still had a full head of dark hair and a musculature that would have been impressive at any age. He'd made his billions in the financial industry and still measured all expenditures through the icy lens of return on investment. "Come on, Samira. That place is about to explode. We all know it. Best-case scenario, any infrastructure we manage to get in place lasts a year. When the war starts, the wells get poisoned, and the people dig up the pipes and machinery to sell on their way out."

"I understand the challenges, Greg. But we know that the liberation of women—both from menial tasks and the inability to plan their families—is the best tool for increasing prosperity."

"But is that even what we'd be doing? Would women actually get to use those wells? Or would they be blocked by a bunch of men from surrounding villages trying to put together enough cattle to attract a good wife? This is exactly the kind of thing this organization was set up not to do, right? Throw money at projects for the feel-good component. I mean, my understanding is that they've got a pretty good start on some sustainable agriculture. Do we want to be the people behind it being trampled by a bunch of out-of-town livestock?"

The argument that ensued drew in almost everyone and wasn't particularly productive.

"I think we're going to have to pass on this," Lowe finally interjected, causing everyone to fall silent. "Samira. We all understand that you experienced situations like this as a child and acknowledge that you see them from a perspective we can't. But in this instance, Greg's right. We have limited resources, and we have to focus on producing results. I don't believe we have the power to do that here. Someday, maybe. But I'm afraid not now."

"I understand, Jon, but I wonder if our criteria are too strict. At this point, we're in danger of never handing out a dime."

He nodded. Giving away money that didn't end up in the pocket of a dictator, financing weapons, or just backfiring in some unforeseeable way was harder than it looked. Sometimes just avoiding doing harm was a win.

It was a problem that bothered many high-net-worth people—even as they were being increasingly villainized for their wealth. Frustration and donor fatigue were exploding around the world, accompanied by a rising sense of superiority and disassociation with the other ninety-nine percent. *Let them wallow in the mud and kill each other*, he'd heard on more than one occasion. *They seem to like it.* It was an extraordinarily dangerous attitude. Particularly in light of the fact that people like him and the others in that room were gaining power and wealth at a rate never seen in history.

"Okay," Lowe conceded. "Let's keep this project on the drawing board.

Maybe we could plumb spigots to individual houses and bury the infrastructure at a depth that makes it uneconomical to pull up. Certainly more than we'd budgeted, but theoretically doable. Samira? Is that acceptable?"

She nodded.

"Good. Then let's move on to the next order of business..."

THE ROOM that Lowe entered later that day was even more utilitarian than the one before. This space was smaller, windowless, and completely soundproof. It was swept for listening devices regularly, and no electronics were allowed inside. A place where thoughts and ideas could be debated without fear of reprisal.

The five people present were a select group carved from the one before. These were the men and women who had been with him since the organization was little more than an informal discussion group exploring the dizzying pace of change in the modern world.

Originally, the meetings had focused on protecting investments and seeking opportunity. Later, they became more abstract and somewhat darker. It seemed that society was on a path that would provide opportunities to absolutely no one. That realization shifted the conversation toward wishful thinking—solutions that were technically workable but politically, culturally, or psychologically impossible. Entertaining, but of little real-world value.

Governments were increasingly run by dictators, sociopaths, and geriatric half-wits—men and women who fanned the flames of radicalism in their followers and then found themselves slaves to it. Instead of solving problems, they were rewarded for inventing, exaggerating, or exacerbating them. The line between truth and lies had already become hopelessly blurred, and as artificial intelligence advanced, it would be erased entirely.

These changes were prompting the elites to circle their wagons. More and more, they separated themselves from the masses, constructing bunkers, investing in private health care, and hiding their wealth in every corner of the globe. The education of their children was handled by handpicked tutors and their friends were curated from families with the same privileged background. It was the beginning of a slow slide to an era of omnipotent rulers who knew no more about their desperate subjects than the royalty of old.

But was the elite's retreat the result of nothing more than laziness and lack of imagination? Certainly, the people at the table with him knew they were powerful, but none had yet internalized exactly *how* powerful.

Throughout modern history, ultimate authority had largely rested with governments. But was that still true? Without Lowe and his companions, those governments would have no rockets to enter orbit. No satellites for communications, nor munitions and spare parts for their war machines. No computing power. No media platforms to reach their followers, attack their enemies, and disseminate their lies.

The list got longer every year. As politicians became ever more fixated on the task of securing their positions, they had no choice but to leave the day-to-day operation of the world to the private sector.

The question was whether his companions had the courage and vision to take advantage of this unprecedented opportunity. And if so, for good or for evil? He and the other people in that room saw the former as a much more compelling proposition. Creation was painful, exhausting, and occasionally brutal, but also beautiful. Destruction, on the other hand, was nothing more than a shiny toy for idiots and megalomaniacs.

"Tracker Six," Lowe said, choosing to remain standing. "Does it live up to the hype?"

He was referring to a self-driving car start-up helmed by a brilliant Russian engineer who had emigrated to the US a number of years ago. Reports of his progress were nothing short of extraordinary.

"I'm afraid it does," Henri Laurent responded. A French investor with significant ties to the automobile industry, he was the foundation's transportation expert.

"Meaning?"

"It works, Jon. And I mean *well*. He let me tell the car where I wanted to go with no constraints. We drove through the middle of rush-hour San Francisco, out to the highway, and back again. I diverted it into construction and traffic backups, put it alongside cyclists, and gave it last-second instructions... It never hesitated, and I never felt the need to touch the wheel."

"Did you make him our offer?" Lowe asked.

He nodded. "A nine-figure investment."

"And?"

"He told me he didn't need it. That's always been the weakness in our plan. What he's done is create a computer simulation for his system that's as good as real time out on the road. It runs the equivalent of a million test miles every day."

"That's a lot of practice," Greg Madison commented.

"Worse. It's *enough* practice. Against human drivers, his cars are already safer in all imaginable scenarios, speeds, and weather conditions. But Yuri says that in order to gain public acceptance, they have to be an order of magnitude safer."

"There's no question that the technology is under a microscope," Lowe commented.

"Exactly."

"So how far from that level of safety is he?"

"About six months. At that point, he'll start pitching the major manufacturers. Based on what I saw, adoption will be almost immediate in commercial areas like trucking and cabs. A little slower with the general public but still fast. Particularly in the younger generations."

Lowe sat and let out a long breath. "Susan?"

The only politician on their board, Nevada Senator Susan Kane was unusually intelligent and policy driven when compared to her congressional colleagues. Qualities that made her despise the people she worked with and recognize that there was no hope of ever accomplishing anything meaningful. She'd been days from announcing her retirement from government service when Lowe convinced her to reconsider.

"Six months . . ." she repeated. "For all the reasons we've talked about in the past, this is a potential disaster. The only thing the government's contemplated at all relates to safety. But that's the least important aspect of an advance like this. It's the economic consequences that are the real danger. Driving—in whatever form—is the number-one employer of American men at a time that they're already struggling. Putting millions of them out of work over the course of a few years is a recipe for disaster. History has a lot to say about what happens when you have too many idle young men in search of purpose and identity."

Lowe nodded. "I just don't see the benefit of this technology. Sure, implement it as a safety measure like lane assist or adaptive cruise control.

In that role, it could save a lot of lives. But there's no reason not to continue the illusion that drivers are a necessary link in the chain."

"Agreed," Laurent said.

"So unlike the Africa project, this is *exactly* what we've been talking about," Jeffrey Barnes said. He'd made his first billion in internet retail and then used the money to revolutionize online payment systems. Having sold off his companies, his focus now was on the world he was going to leave his grandchildren. "It's the kind of move that we're capable of making and the government isn't."

"Are we capable?" Susan said. "It sounds like Yuri doesn't want our money."

Everyone fell silent and looked to Lowe.

"We are," he said finally.

"How?"

"Matt Egan's team has looked into Yuri's hasty departure from Russia and found out there was a reason for it. A reason that he wouldn't want made public."

"Are we talking about blackmail?" Susan said.

"Since I'm sitting at a table with four billionaires and one politician, can I assume this wouldn't be the worst thing any of us ever did?"

The quiet laughter that ensued was a sufficient answer.

"Let me be clear here. I don't have any interest in shutting him down. He can sell this as the safety feature we talked about and make billions saving lives. Cracking self-driving is just ego. Not worth the price I can make him pay."

"All right, then," Madison said. "Should we bring it to a vote? We agreed that any action taken needs to have unanimous approval."

The hands were a bit hesitant, but all rose.

"Then I suppose we're finally up and running," Lowe said.

"For better or for worse," Susan added.

"I believe the former" was his somewhat honest response. A better way of putting it would be that he *chose* to believe the former. Driverless cars were a relatively trivial matter compared to technologies like quantum computers, AI, social media, and bioengineering. But it was a good start. A toe in the water.

"Then we're adjourned?" Madison said.

"No. One more item. China."

"That's a big item," Barnes commented.

"I'm afraid it is."

"I'm intrigued," Susan said. "I have regular security briefings on China, but there hasn't been anything out of the ordinary."

"I'm not surprised," Lowe said. "I initially found out about this through a medical research partnership I'm involved with there."

"A legal one?" she asked. Despite her position and intelligence, Susan Kane couldn't help clinging to the naive belief that the law applied equally to everyone.

"The money flows through a Belarusian company."

He ignored her disapproving frown and continued. "We've recently seen a large number of scientists being questioned by authorities. Some have been jailed with no clear charges. Others have just disappeared. And all this is happening at the same time as a purge of government officials that oversee the country's scientific research."

"In China, that kind of thing usually relates to corruption," Madison said.

"Normally, I'd agree with you," Lowe said. "But all these people are involved in biology or genetics, and some are at the very top of that field. The speed and scale of the crackdown worry me. So does the fact that I suddenly can't get any of my contacts there to return my calls."

"And?" Madison said.

"As Susan mentioned, the US intelligence community doesn't seem to be tracking on the problem, so I turned to another source. A former Chinese intelligence operative living in exile in Kazakhstan. For a very high price, he was able to provide an interesting piece of information. The catalyst for all this seems to be the suicide of a biology professor who worked at the Wuhan lab from 2017 to 2021. Rumor has it that she released a trove of documents to the internet before her death. The Chinese government's recent activities are centered around eradicating those online documents and silencing anyone who might know anything about what's in them. But there's some question as to whether that's possible."

"Why do I feel like the other shoe is about to drop?" Susan said.

"Because it is. According to my contact, the documents contain proof that COVID wasn't first seen at a wet market in Wuhan in 2019, but a year earlier in a small village almost a thousand miles to the south. The scientists at the Wuhan lab were doing research on it when it escaped containment."

Susan pressed her palms to her forehead, eyes widening. "That's not good, Jon. We've spent a lot of time trying to keep a lid on the lab leak hypothesis, and if it blows up in our faces, the conspiracy theorists are going to have a field day. Particularly when they see the Chinese government covering it up. No one's going to believe it was an accident. They're going to see a bioweapons lab and call people like me complicit for not pursuing it. And then there's Beijing. If we can be sure of anything, it's that when they get their backs against the wall, they turn to nationalism as a distraction. In the current environment, that tends to mean forced reunification with Taiwan. I mean, I don't want to be melodramatic here, but this could be a recipe for World War III."

"I don't think that's melodramatic," Madison said. "Is there any way this could die down without it going public?"

Lowe shook his head. "I'm not hopeful. I bring this up here primarily as a warning. Do what's necessary to protect your political and financial interests. But do it quietly."

6

MATT EGAN jogged across the hospital parking lot, ignoring the rain soaking the dress shirt he'd just spent the last twenty-three hours sweating through. Finally, he'd made it to DC. The last place in the world he wanted to be.

A physician met him in an entry hall strangely devoid of angry cops and overexcited reporters.

"Mr. Egan?" he said, extending his hand. "I'm Dr. Smith." He was fit for middle age, with close-cropped hair and utilitarian glasses. Almost certainly former military.

Egan clasped his hand a little too hard, trying to make up for the fact that he looked and smelled as though he'd just rolled off a barge. "What's his condition?"

"Conscious, but I want to warn you that the chances of him slipping back into a coma are high. These kinds of situations are unpredictable."

"Has he said anything?"

"No. It's possible that he can't, but he seems to be tracking on what's happening around him. So I think it's more likely that he just doesn't want to."

"Brain damage?"

"There's no indication of it, but we can't be certain."

"What about his legs? Do they work? He had a bullet fragment in his back that was paralyzing him."

"Unknown. He underwent an experimental surgery more than a year ago to remove it."

"Surgery? Who authorized that?"

Smith just shrugged.

"And the fact that he's awake is still under wraps?"

"Yes. But it won't last. A lot of people are involved in the care of a patient like this."

Egan wasn't sure why everyone was being so cooperative. Or why they'd called him and not the authorities. Did hospital management think he still worked for the government? Had Fade fallen so far through the cracks that no one remembered what he'd done? Both unlikely scenarios.

"Can I see him?"

Smith led him to an unremarkable door at the end of an equally unremarkable hallway and then withdrew. Egan watched him until he disappeared, took a few deep breaths, and pushed through.

Oddly, the face he remembered so well had become more youthful. Probably the time expressionless and without exposure to the elements. Fade's hair was shoulder length, better groomed than he'd ever seen it, and with an incongruously healthy sheen. The goatee was new. A gift from the staff, he supposed.

Most remarkable, though, were his eyes. Open and locked, statue-like, on the ceiling. Was he dead? It'd be better for everybody involved, but the machine monitoring his heart suggested that no one was getting off that easy.

Fade's head turned, and there was a hint of recognition. So at least a few neurons were still firing. Egan didn't approach. But he also didn't allow himself to retreat. He'd known Fade since their early days in the military. The man had been like a brother to him. The best friend he ever had. But those were better times. Much better.

"I can't sleep." Fade's voice came out a hoarse whisper. "Funny, huh?"

Egan wiped the sweat from around his mouth. "Yeah. Funny."

"Am I paralyzed?"

"They did surgery on your back and took out the bullet."

"Not an answer." The effort of speaking started a weak coughing fit, and Egan finally approached. He reached for a cup next to the bed and held it so Fade could take a few sips from the straw.

It was hard to watch. Egan's most intense memories of the man were from their operations together. The great and terrible Salam al-Fayed. The golden boy who was just flat-out better than everyone else. Faster, stronger, more durable, more accurate, more fearless. But above all, more joyful. No situation was bad enough that he couldn't crack up himself and everyone around him. To this day, no one knew how he'd managed to have a compressed air pie cannon designed, built, and delivered to one of the most remote outposts in Afghanistan. Range had been directly related to the firmness of the pastry, with pecan having the best ballistic properties. His team had two confirmed hits on the enemy at three hundred yards. Even at that distance, the sugary projectiles carried enough momentum to take a Taliban fighter right off his feet.

But that wasn't the man in front of him. Not anymore.

"When do the cops show up?" Fade whispered.

"Soon, I suppose. So you remember what happened? How you got here?"

"The SWAT team."

"No. You killed them. Walked out without a scratch."

He looked confused. "The girl. The one in the alley."

Egan shook his head. "That was a long time ago, Fade. A good Samaritan took you in and saved your life. I spent two weeks finding you."

Fade seemed to lose himself. For a moment, Egan thought he might have relapsed.

"The hospital. The cops . . . They were outside."

The hospital he was referring to was on the other side of town. Fade had walked to a window and thrown the curtains open, presenting the police snipers with the target they'd been waiting for all day.

"Bingo."

"Why am I here?"

"Because of that famous Salam al-Fayed luck. Do you remember those Marines who were pinned down outside of Chitrāl? Your team got all but one of them out."

Fade nodded almost imperceptibly.

"Well, guess what one of those guys did when he left the military?"

Fade closed his eyes before answering. "Police sniper."

"You got it. He purposely pulled the shot."

A weak breath escaped the former SEAL. "The party's over, man. And I'm the guest who won't leave."

Egan didn't respond. He didn't know what to say. None of it had been Fade's fault, but no one was going to listen to that argument. No one would care about what he'd sacrificed for his country or how it had betrayed him. No, they'd want their pound of flesh. Their circus and outrage.

Denied the dramatic exit he deserved, Fade would spend the rest of his life rotting in a prison hospital bed. Or, if he was lucky, being pushed around the exercise yard in a wheelchair. And a lot of the blame for that was Egan's.

He turned to leave but paused halfway through the door when Fade spoke again.

"How are Elise and Kali?"

"Dead."

EGAN DIDN'T make it far, ending up in the hospital's cafeteria watching his coffee get cold. The mysterious Dr. Smith had never reappeared. No hospital staffer had tracked him down with a clipboard full of paperwork. No cops or reporters demanding answers had shown up. No more calls from unknown numbers had lit up his phone. But it was only a matter of time.

What the hell was he supposed to do now? Forget all about it and go back to Salt Lake? Bust him out? Tape him upright in the passenger seat of his Avis rental and go on the run? Fade would say it was the lamest sequel to *Thelma & Louise* imaginable. But with a similarly inevitable ending.

"May I join you?"

Egan started and looked up to see Jon Lowe standing at the other end of the table.

"Uh, okay," he stammered gracelessly.

The man took a chair close enough for them to speak in low tones. "How's your friend?"

"Why? What do you know about him?"

"Just what I've read. A man who goes on a multistate rampage in a classic Caddy is hard to forget. But also a legendary SEAL, right? And then there's his incredible gift for resurrection. A unique combination, don't you think? And how many unique people do you know?"

"He is that," Egan conceded.

"So what are you going to do? My understanding is that no one knows yet."

"*You* know."

The man just smiled.

"The answer is that I have no idea, Jon."

Lowe took a sip of what appeared to be somewhat warmer coffee. "Maybe I can help."

7

EGAN DIDN'T bother to turn on the lights. Despite being just past three in the morning, the shades were bleeding enough illumination for him to do what he was there to do. Fade was lying motionless on his back, head turned toward the windows. The goatee was gone, exposing even more skin robbed of its history.

"What do you want, Matt?"

Fade had always possessed a freakish sense of smell, but in this case, it likely wasn't necessary. Despite having been on the ground in DC for almost twenty-four hours, Egan still hadn't found time to shower.

The sense of déjà vu was as powerful as it was uncomfortable. He'd been present when his old friend had stepped in front of a sniper's rifle in a similar room. Somehow it seemed like both yesterday and a thousand years ago. The sudden flood of sunlight. The sound of puncturing glass. Fade jerking back and collapsing on the floor.

"I read what happened to your family," he said when Egan didn't respond. The voice was noticeably stronger than it had been the day before. "I'm sorry."

"One day, you're on top of the world. The next day, the world's gone."

"I don't know what the top of the world feels like. But I know rock bottom pretty well, and I wouldn't wish it on anyone. Even you."

"I'm sorry things got so complicated between us."

Fade's head swiveled toward him. "What do you want, Matt?"

Egan pulled a syringe from his pocket and held it up in the tenuous light. "To offer you a solution to your problems."

Fade focused on it for a moment and then nodded.

The needle slid into the crook of his elbow easily, adding to the damage made by prior ones. Not enough that anyone would notice, though.

"See you in the next life," Fade said.

"Maybe it'll work out better."

The monitor tracking Fade's heart rate slowed and then turned erratic. Egan backed away as an alarm began to sound. A few seconds later, he heard shouts and running feet in the hallway. His old friend stiffened, gripping the sheet in a fleeting display of the strength he'd once had. Then he went limp.

8

THE THUNDERSTORMS plaguing West Virginia were gone, leaving an unbroken sky and oppressive humidity. Through the ambulance's passenger-side window, Matt Egan could see haze hanging in canyons gouged through heavily forested mountains. With DC and the rest of civilization hours behind, it seemed like he should be able to rebalance. But today—like every other day—that trick eluded him.

The driver hit the siren and accelerated past an old pickup that veered obligingly onto the shoulder. Christoph—no last name—hadn't spoken since their brief introduction earlier that morning. His accent, two hundred and twenty pounds of solid muscle, and flattop made him seem like some kind of East German calisthenics instructor. According to Jon Lowe, he was actually a former military nurse, but it didn't really matter. All Egan wanted to do was complete this task, go back to Salt Lake, and work on forgetting. His favorite pastime.

He reached out and searched the static-ridden radio again, finding nothing more interesting than an NPR quiz show. That left him with no choice but to continue doomscrolling on his phone. The signal was weak, but still functional.

It wasn't completely unexpected that Fade's death hadn't made the national outlets, but the muted reaction of even the local ones was surprising. It turned out that in a world with an attention span shorter than that of a goldfish, even Salam al-Fayed was a relic. A few articles had appeared on obscure websites, but the text all seemed to be drawn from the same skimpy, inaccurate source. No mention of his association with the CIA or Homeland Security—something that had created significant headaches for the government at the time. Nothing about Egan or their relationship, thank

God. No quotes from the cop who had hunted Fade and then subsequently championed him.

As he continued to search, something started to feel a little off. While Fade was unquestionably yesterday's news, his story had just the kind of lurid appeal that the modern press loved. Government conspiracies, violence, physically attractive protagonists, and even a dash of humor. In light of that, the silence seemed deafening.

He abandoned the news feed and went to Fade's Wikipedia page—something he'd read, and even edited, in the past. It didn't take long to scroll through. What had once been multiple pages of information, fleshed out with pictures and links, now consisted only of eight lines of bland facts.

Jon Lowe.

The man's ability to do and get whatever he wanted was at the same time confidence-inspiring and terrifying. But was he really capable of wiping the internet?

The answer was yes. In fact, it probably wasn't even that heavy a lift. He and his cronies controlled probably three-quarters of the country's news outlets and eighty percent of its social media. The syringe and whatever it had contained would have come from one of the pharmaceutical companies he was invested in. And finally, there was the matter of the death certificate and the continued silence of the hospital staff. In a month or two, Egan expected to read about the facility receiving an anonymous eight-figure donation.

But what was the point of it all? Jon Lowe was unquestionably deserving of his reputation as a visionary, but sometimes his motivations were murky to the point of opacity.

Egan scrolled back to a link that he'd read earlier that morning about Fade's military service.

The page you're looking for can't be found.

"TURN RIGHT in one-quarter mile, and your destination will be on the left."

With information about Fade disappearing from the public sphere minute by minute, Egan had repurposed his phone for navigation. The well-maintained dirt road was marked with a shiny new sign that read *Thompson Training and Rehabilitation*. Another couple of minutes took them to a freshly painted farmhouse flanked by a renovated barn. A pool with a small crane to get people in and out had been installed between, along with a modest parking area containing a single Subaru Outback. Egan pointed to the house, and Christoph eased the ambulance up to its porch.

The woman who appeared was easily recognizable from the dossier Egan had been sent. Late thirties, five foot seven, dirty-blond hair pulled back in a ponytail that went to the bottom of her shoulder blades. More interesting was the snug fit of her jeans and the places where sweat was causing her T-shirt to cling to her torso. He didn't remember his therapist looking like that when he'd gotten too close to an IED in Afghanistan. But then, he wasn't the golden boy, was he?

Lisa Thompson was a former biathlete whose Olympic dreams had been cut short by a botched knee surgery. Not one to be kept down, she'd gone back to get a master's degree in physical therapy, followed by a PhD in exercise physiology. About a year ago, she'd left a prestigious gig with the Baltimore Ravens and settled here—a property that had been in her family for two generations. After a costly renovation, she'd hung out her shingle. The mission was to save other elite athletes from the soul-crushing fate she had suffered.

Despite her undeniable qualifications, the enterprise had gotten off to a rocky start. She'd burned a few bridges with her unwavering commitment to the well-being of athletes whose teams saw them as livestock to be used up and discarded. Bills were piling up, and loan payments were getting later and later. Problems that Jon Lowe could make disappear with a wave of his well-manicured hand.

Her limp was barely perceptible as she came down the steps. The worried expression, though, was there for everyone to see. She was accustomed to her clients arriving in a somewhat more dignified and upright manner.

"Dr. Thompson," Egan said, jumping from the ambulance and striding toward her with a hand outstretched. "I'm Matt."

"Please call me Lisa."

Behind him, Christoph opened the vehicle's rear door and was helping a balding, potbellied Indian man climb out. Lisa walked up to them and introduced herself.

The Austrian remained silent, but his minuscule companion bowed politely. "It's a pleasure to meet you. I'm Dr. Smith."

Egan frowned. There seemed to be a lot of Dr. Smiths in this operation.

"And that's Christoph," Egan said as the man wrestled a wheeled stretcher onto the asphalt. "He's a little shy, but a lot of fun once you get to know him."

She ignored his lame attempt at humor and instead gazed into the serene face of Salam al-Fayed. His hair had been cropped short, and combined with smooth unblemished skin, he was unrecognizable as the man he'd once been.

"Why is he unconscious?" she asked.

"It was a long trip, and we felt that he would be more comfortable sedated," Smith responded. "He's spent quite some time in a coma."

"I know. I have his file. And I want to say again that I'm not a medical doctor. And I don't have the training to give him the psychological support that he's likely to ne—"

"It'll be fine," Egan said. "We're going to leave Christoph with you for the medical side, and his emotional state is what it is. All you need to do is get his body working again. If he loses his mind, slips back into a coma, or drops dead, that's not your responsibility."

Egan helped the Austrian manhandle a machine that weighed the better part of three hundred pounds to the ground. Fortunately, the tanks that would eventually be connected to it were somewhat lighter.

"What's all that?" she asked.

"It's to administer his medication," Smith said. "Christoph will handle it."

Egan took one side of the gurney and began pushing Fade up a ramp to the right of the steps. "Where to?"

She led, padding quietly through the incongruously modern interior of the farmhouse. Tight rooms and old wood had been replaced by a more open floor plan, tile floors, and a beam ceiling. A hallway at the back had been widened and provided access to three rooms that were a well-thought-out balance between medical necessity and homey comfort. Fade's leaned more toward the former but benefited from two large windows that looked onto the pool and barn. A large en suite bathroom was designed from the ground up for accessibility, with a shower, walk-in bathtub, and safety rails sprouting from every surface. They unloaded Fade into bed, and Christoph disappeared back down the hall with the gurney.

Thompson chewed her thumbnail for a moment before speaking. "Now you understand that this kind of a recovery, even under the best circumstances, is going to be long and probably incomplete. Most coma patients like this have permanent limitations. A lot of times, serious limitations."

"We absolutely understand that," Egan said as Christoph dragged in the machine they'd retrieved from the ambulance. "Just do what you can and keep me informed."

She didn't respond.

The Austrian disappeared again, returning a few minutes later with a tank and the doctor. Together they hooked it up and completed a diagnostic. Smith pulled up Fade's shirt to expose two metal ports in his side. The skin was puckered and red around the new installations, but that didn't seem to pose a problem when Christoph connected two narrow tubes to them. A moment later, the machine was on and humming along happily.

"What's it doing?" Thompson asked.

"Providing him with hydration and medicine," Smith said.

"That's a lot of hydration and medicine."

"He's been ill for a very long time."

She watched silently as the two medical men retreated back down the hallway. Christoph would get his gear and choose a bedroom while the doc would close himself up in the cab of the ambulance. He was clearly anxious to get the hell out of there.

But nowhere near as anxious as Egan was.

"Anything else I can help you with before I go, Lisa?"

Her eyes narrowed noticeably as she returned her attention to Fade.

She wasn't an idiot and knew there was something fishy here. But did it matter? They weren't asking her to do anything illegal. Even the secrecy they'd demanded wasn't particularly unusual. Medical confidentiality wouldn't exactly be a new concept to her.

More important, they'd rented the entire place out at her full rate, putting down three months in advance and making it clear that there was more where that came from. Suddenly, she'd gone from being in danger of losing her ancestral home to being flush with cash. And perhaps even more important, she'd been given someone to rescue. Everything she wanted and needed in life.

Jon Lowe's specialty.

9

GO TOWARD *the light!*

Weren't those the instructions from *Poltergeist*? Or was it *Bill & Ted's Bogus Journey*? Both films full of useful advice. Don't build your house on an Indian burial ground, and don't play Twister with Death.

Along with the glare came heat and a notable subsiding of his numbness. A few seconds or minutes or hours later, he discovered that he could pinpoint the sensation. His face. His eyelids. Why did he still have those things?

As the awareness of his body returned, he felt something smooth and cool pressing down on him. Sheets. No. This couldn't be happening. Not again. Not a fourth time.

Eventually, he had no choice but to open his eyes. The scene was initially encouraging: A vague human figure, glowing white in the distance. As his vision began to clear, though, it did so on a crew cut and bulging pecs.

Matt Egan had fucked him again. Fade was going to carve his heart out with a spoon. Over the course of weeks. Maybe months if he could find one dull enough. And rusty. Smeared liberally with undercooked pork and habaneros.

His bargain-basement angel approached and leaned over him for a moment before disappearing. Time continued to be hard to account for, but eventually a new face appeared. Better this time. Green eyes. Blondish hair. A T-shirt emblazoned with the Swix logo. Still no wings or harps, though.

"Hi, Fred. Can you hear me? How are you feeling?"

Fred?

An alias. That bastard Egan again.

A loud clicking started next to his bed, and his mind began to clear. He looked in the direction of the sound and saw a couple of hoses connecting him to a machine he didn't recognize.

"Fred," she prompted again. "Are you—"

"Alive?" he barely got out.

"You're definitely alive." Her expression turned improbably earnest. "And you're going to be fine."

"I don't feel fine."

"I'll bet. You've been through a lot. You understand that, right?"

Better than she did, he imagined. Fred likely had a much less interesting backstory than his evil twin, Fade.

"I was in a . . ." His voice faltered. "A coma."

"That's right. And now you're here."

"Where?"

"My rehab facility. So we can get you back on your feet."

He managed to shake his head. "They don't work."

She sat on a stool and began flipping through a thick file. "Do you mean because of the wound in your back? The bullet?"

"Yes."

"It was successfully removed, and there's no evidence of permanent nerve damage. In a way, you were lucky to have been in a coma. The surgery they did demands that the patient be completely immobile for months after. Not normally very practical."

"Yeah. Lucky," he said.

"Let's have a look, shall we?" She pulled a pen from her pocket and jabbed it into the bottom of his left foot.

"Ow!"

An identical attack on his right foot elicited a similarly sharp pain.

"Excellent," she said. "Now wiggle your toes."

He did.

"Even better. The main problem I see is excuses. Are you going to have any?"

She was trying to be cheerful, but cracks were visible. The between-the-lines message was that this resurrection was going to suck just as bad as the others.

"Are you?" she prompted.

"What?"

"Going to make excuses?"

"Yes."

"Okay. Well, while I don't like laziness, I do admire honesty."

The white polyester-clad monster in the corner shifted, drawing her attention.

"Have you two met? No? Christoph, this is Fred. Fred, Christoph."

They locked eyes, but neither spoke.

"He's on loan from your friend Matt, and he's going to help get you back shipshape."

Oh God. Not nautical idioms. They really took the wind out of his sails.

She turned her attention back to his file. "I have a lot of physical data on you from when you were younger. Impressive. I've worked with Olympians who would kill for your genetics. Add some time and effort, and you've got a winning combination."

She stared down at him, seeking a reaction and making it clear she was willing to wait. A sickly smile was the best he could manage, but it seemed to satisfy her.

"I see that you've had a lot of injuries over the years. On paper, they don't look like they'll be an obstacle. Is that the case in reality?"

He managed to shrug but only barely. Whenever he moved, it felt like he was doing it through wet cement.

"I'll take that as an enthusiastic yes. Anything else I should know?"

He turned his head and gazed out the window.

10

THE FARMHOUSE appeared on the left, but Egan opted to pull his rental car onto the side of the dirt road instead of continuing to the parking area. A humid breeze amplified the ninety-degree heat as he stepped out and covered the remaining distance on foot. The goal had been to put this visit off as long as possible. Maybe even indefinitely. But the night before, Jon Lowe had offered him a ride on one of his jets that just happened to be flying empty from Salt Lake to DC. Sugarcoated for sure, but clearly not a suggestion.

Christoph was sitting in the shade of the porch, tilted back in a chair, contemplating the horizon. Neither offered a greeting to the other as Egan climbed the steps and entered the air-conditioned building. Lisa Thompson appeared a moment later to provide a somewhat warmer reception.

"You were right," she said, giving his hand an awkward up-and-down jerk.

"About?"

"Your friend's recovery. So far, it's been . . ." Her voice faltered for a moment. "Well, the only word I can think of is *miraculous*."

There was more than a hint of suspicion and disapproval in her tone, but he ignored it. Undoubtedly, she'd tried to research the machine pumping God-knew-what into Fade and come up empty. She wasn't going to do anything about it, though. Once someone made a deal with Lowe, they tended to be reluctant to jeopardize it. Anything could be rationalized if you tried hard enough.

"He's always been a freak of nature. Takes a licking and keeps on ticking."

She frowned.

"Is he in his room?"

The question was rewarded by a short nod.

"Thanks. I think I can find my way."

He could feel her eyes on him as he moved reluctantly down the hall and stopped in front of Fade's open door.

He was wearing only a pair of sweatpants, sitting up in bed, eating grilled chicken smothered in vegetables and rice. The news was playing on a television bolted to the wall, and he remained focused on it as he shoveled in food with a slightly shaky hand. His hair had grown out noticeably, but he remained clean-shaven. The tubes leading from Dr. Smith's machine were connected, and one had leaked enough blood to create a thin streak down the soft, pale skin of his side.

"How are you feeling?" was the only thing that came to Egan's mind.

"Fuck you, Matt."

His voice was still weak but far stronger than the strangled whisper from before.

"I didn't say the syringe would kill you. Just that it could solve your problems."

"Do my problems look solved?"

Egan turned his attention to the television, where two pundits were spewing nonsense about the Middle East.

"Catching up on what you missed?"

Fade swallowed with difficulty. "Turns out some woman named Taylor Swift rules the world, no one knows if they're a boy or a girl anymore, and a pandemic killed seven million people, but no one wanted to wear a mask."

"That about covers it."

"What do you want, Matt?"

"I don't understand the question."

"I'm guessing my health insurance lapsed and none of this is free."

"I don't know. Probably not. Nothing's free."

Egan stayed in the doorway. Even in his weakened state, getting too close to a pissed-off Salam al-Fayed didn't seem wise.

"Did you forget what happened last time you tried to recruit me back into the government? I made the mistake of letting you walk away. It won't happen again."

"I don't work for the government. I work for a charity."

Fade laughed before shoving a stalk of broccoli in his mouth and speaking around it. "CIA front?"

"No. Head of security for a legit NGO."

"Don't make me ask again, Matt. What do you *want*?"

"I wanted you to die. It was time. You'd reached the end of your road."

"And yet here I am."

"The man who runs the organization I work for is picking up the tab."

"Why?"

"I honestly have no idea. It's hard to predict what he's going to care about, and you seemed to have made the list."

"The internet says I'm dead. That is, if it says anything at all."

"You are dead. I have the certificate and a jar full of ashes to prove it. Frederick Darwish, on the other hand, is alive and getting the best medical attention money can buy. Think about that."

"I have thought about it. But now you're here bullshitting me that some charity faked my death, put my name on some homeless guy's toe tag, and built me a new identity. Let me guess. The Children's Initiative Advocacy? That acronym works out about right."

"I admit that we're not exactly the United Way. Not by a long shot. But we're also not the Agency. Look, man. You're breathing, you're not in jail, and Lisa seems to be fixing you up. There aren't any decisions to be made right now. Just take advantage of what you're being given."

Fade raised his middle finger and returned his attention to the TV.

When Egan emerged from the building, Christoph was gone. And so was the car Egan had parked at the side of the road. In its place was a black Yukon XL. There was no sign of life through the heavily tinted windows, but he opened the door and climbed in the back seat anyway.

"How's your friend?" Jon Lowe asked.

"Doing well, apparently."

"I'm happy to hear it."

"Why?"

"For a lot of reasons. The first is that he's important to you. Your best friend, right?"

"A thousand years ago."

"Those kinds of friendships have their ups and downs. But they're the ones that survive."

"With all due respect, Jon, you didn't do this for me."

"No. I have to admit, I find him fascinating. And impressive. Not just the fact that he was considered the very best at what he did, but that he took on an entire division of Homeland Security and won."

"Until he stopped a bullet."

"On his own terms. The end he wanted."

"But didn't get."

"No."

"So this is just for fun? A pet project?"

Lowe turned to contemplate Egan's profile. Thick, opaque glass separated them from the driver, so he could speak freely. At least as freely as he ever did.

"The world has problems, Matt. Some are simple and isolated. Others are complicated and global. The former used to be the space where NGOs operated, and the latter were the responsibility of governments. But that's not the case anymore. Governments—both democracies and dictatorships—aren't able to handle the challenges the modern era poses."

"Are you suggesting that you can?"

"I don't know. But what I *do* know is that someone has to. Politicians have never been particularly impressive, but now we're reaching levels of incompetence and corruption that would have been hard to imagine just twenty years ago. Even in America—one of the most successful countries in history—elected officials have gone from being shockingly average to being mental and moral defectives. And in more authoritarian states like Russia and China, it's even worse. Major nuclear and economic powers are controlled by people who are only interested in crushing anyone who doesn't worship them. Media companies aren't any better. They spend their time convincing people that their lives are a disaster and that they're in constant mortal danger. Fanning people's insecurities, tribalism, and envy in pursuit of ratings."

Egan kept staring straight forward. Such a calm conversation. Almost matter-of-fact. Everything was like that with Lowe—wildly understated in both delivery and substance. What did he mean by all this exactly? How far was he willing to go? Because capability never seemed to be an obstacle to him. He and the people he surrounded himself with tended to accomplish whatever they set out to do.

"And where does Fade fit into all that?"

"The carrot is important in motivating people," Lowe said, sounding uncharacteristically hesitant. "But I wonder how useful it is without the stick."

"You're talking about building some kind of paramilitary force?"

"Something like that. Over the past decades, the human race has created a lot of tinder. I'm afraid that a spark is coming. Maybe sooner than we think."

"You sound like you're talking about something specific."

"It's possible. In the next few weeks or months, I expect documents to leak that prove COVID escaped the Wuhan lab and not a wet market."

"I can see how that could be a problem," Egan said, trying to match Lowe's calm but not feeling it.

"Potentially even worse than you think. Based on the way the Chinese are rounding up scientists and mid-level government officials, I'm starting to wonder if we have the whole story."

"Then I can assume you don't have a copy of the documents that you think are going to go public."

"I don't."

"Can you get one before it blows up?"

"Me? No. But I'm confident that you and your team can."

"My team?"

Lowe handed him a piece of paper with an address in Salt Lake. Despite—or perhaps because of—his incredible grasp of technology, he was a connoisseur of the sticky note. Untraceable and typically vague due to the limited space for explanation.

"I made some initial staffing decisions, but you can modify them if you want. They're expecting you first thing tomorrow."

"And Fade?"

"I see him as part of the other project I'd like you to take on. Putting together a small group of people who can respond to emergencies."

"Respond?"

"I think you understand what I mean."

Egan tucked the paper in his shirt pocket. "Mercenaries. High class, but mercenaries just the same."

"Call them what you want."

"Fade won't make the cut."

"No?"

"No. He's pushing forty, he has a grudge against the world, and even before the coma, he was half nuts. Also, he can barely sit up in bed."

"Surmountable problems."

"Maybe. But why? I can find you top-notch, squared-away operators in their prime. Fade's a liability. In a way, he always has been."

"Top-notch, squared-away operators," Lowe repeated. "You mean strong, fast robots who follow orders."

"Don't underestimate what you can accomplish with strong, fast robots who follow orders."

"Are you sure they're not one of the reasons for the mess we're in?"

Egan didn't have an answer to that question, so he kept his mouth shut.

"I'm looking for something more, Matt. I found it in you. And I think I might find it in him."

"I disagree."

Lowe smiled. "The only commodity that means anything is talent. If I can find just one person a year who's worth anything, I count it as a victory. So let's give him a chance. The worst thing that can happen is that you turn out to be right."

"No," Egan said, shaking his head. "With Fade involved, it'll definitely be worse than that."

11

THE SUN was penetrating the window full force, burning into Fade's cheek and washing out his computer screen. With no way to shut the blinds, he used a button to lift the back of the bed into a sliver of shade. The sensation of heat subsided, and the search screen became legible again. But to what end? Despite being one of Google's best customers, there was no search term that could give his life any meaning. Or, for that matter, even provide significant evidence that it had ever happened.

So now he had proof that his suspicions were dead-on. All the shit he'd done—the people he'd killed, the ones he'd saved, the relationships started and ended, the medals earned—had added up to a nice round zero. If he'd never been born, it wouldn't have mattered at all.

He used a fork to examine the omelet in front of him. Cheese that was probably actually tofu, pureed vegetables, and a basil leaf. He took a bite, chewed it dutifully, and then washed it down with a smoothie the color of pond scum.

Not exactly a dry-aged rib eye with a side of fries and a glass of Patrón, but at least he could keep it down. For medical reasons he didn't see any reason to understand, his famously bulletproof GI tract had become downright delicate.

He switched browser tabs and toggled a Jordanian soap opera. Hassan, the next in line to be family patriarch, had been mysteriously attacked and ended up in a coma that he was just waking from. In contrast to Fade, he'd regained consciousness surrounded by family and other loved ones. The exception was his best friend, Amir. That guy was trouble. The way he looked at Hassan's wife. The shady business deals. The scraggly beard and beady eyes . . .

Fade leaned forward with difficulty as Hassan's eyes fluttered dramatically open. Then came the tears and hugs. The thanks to Allah. His mother fainting, and his young sons trying to maintain the expected manly control of their emotions. At the back was Amir, wearing an enigmatic expression and exchanging furtive glances with his brother.

"Careful," Fade said in Arabic. "It's always the best friend who puts a knife between your shoulder blades."

His memories were pretty much fully back online, but he still felt like an outsider when he reeled through them. Be that as it may, there was no denying that Matt Egan loomed large. The ops they'd done together. The camaraderie that had grown into something that felt more like family.

But that was then, and this was now.

The CIA had changed them both. While Egan had moved up in the ranks, Fade drowned in them. The politics. The futility. The slow realization that the people in charge had no idea what they were doing. It had been like a dark, distorted reflection of the military. All of the killing, none of the brotherhood.

And then there was Egan's wife and kid. Fucking hell. Fade switched tabs again, bringing up an article about their deaths. Not that he needed to read it again. Instead, he just stared at the picture of their wrecked SUV and the brick house it had collided with.

They'd gotten lost in the wrong DC neighborhood at the wrong time. Based on eyewitness accounts, two men started shooting at each other from opposite sides of the street just as Elise was driving past with Kali in a booster seat. The theory was that Elise hadn't been hit in the initial volley, but instead swerved and lost control, putting them into the building. Seat belts and airbags had worked as intended, so a bad day, but not yet a disastrous one.

One of the men involved made the sensible decision to take off running. The other, for reasons impossible to understand, walked up to the vehicle and emptied his TEC-9 into the windshield. Reports were that the still unidentified perpetrator was laughing when he finally disappeared down an alley.

What would that do to someone like Matt? What would it do to anyone?

After carefully swallowing the rest of his breakfast, Fade lowered the mattress and stared up at the exercise bands that Lisa had been torturing him with. Next to him, the Mystery Machine hummed along reassuringly, causing a now familiar itch where its hoses connected to his side.

He closed his eyes and was trying to force himself to sleep when he was interrupted by the sound of approaching sneakers. Two pairs.

"Good morning!" Lisa exclaimed a moment later.

He didn't answer. She was the most irritatingly chipper woman he'd ever met. Some of it had the feel of a facade, though. A meticulously white-washed wall hiding something more intriguing.

The owner of the other pair of sneakers was Christoph. With him, what you saw was what you got.

"Beautiful outside, isn't it?"

He remained silent.

"Don't be so gloomy. Today's your big day! No more lying around and no more bands. We're going to get you out of bed and into the barn."

He sucked air between his teeth. "I'm not sure that's a good idea, Lisa. I woke up with my back really hurting. Why don't we pencil it in for tomorrow?"

"Why don't we pencil it in for today?" she countered. "There's nothing wrong with your back. That excuse ship sailed a long time ago."

Again with the nautical expressions.

A vague pressure in his side prompted him to open his eyes and look at the man disconnecting him.

"Y tú, Gunter?"

"My name is Christoph."

Fade loved it when he said that. The thick accent and humorless expression reminded him of the old bodybuilder sketch from *Saturday Night Live*.

We want to pump . . . you up!

Lisa held a set of crutches just out of reach. "Come on. Get up. See if you can do it yourself."

"Seriously, I don't want to mess up my back again. You have no idea what it's like."

All bullshit, of course. His back felt fine, and his good friends Google, Twitter, and Instagram had informed him that she knew exactly what it was like. The Olympic dreams. The knee. The desperate search to find something to fill the hole that was left when her life was ripped from her. All that carefully contained behind a big, toothy smile.

"Let me rephrase," she said, her expression losing some of its radiance. "Get up, or Christoph will drag you out of bed and throw you through the window."

A quick glance in the man's direction suggested that he was pretty excited about the prospect.

"COME ON, man..."

It was hard to speak with his cheek pressed into the lawn. Fade spit out a few blades of grass that immediately sprang back between his lips. "Help a guy out."

It was the second time he'd collapsed, and the barn was still twenty-five yards away. Lisa was hovering over him, devoid of anything resembling sympathy. "You're not even trying."

Finally, she was showing her true colors. The sadistic dominatrix behind the sparkly curtain.

"I am too."

Partially true. He'd tried to avoid falling and all the indignities that entailed, but the simple act of walking felt nearly impossible.

Christoph grabbed him by the shirt and yanked him up while Lisa shoved the crutches back under his arms.

"Okay, you two have made your point. Good first workout. But this is enough sunshine and fresh air for one day."

"There's no such thing," she responded.

"I can tell you from experience that there is."

"What are you going to do, Fred? Lie around and watch Arab soap operas for the rest of your life?"

"They're dramas."

"Do you have any idea how lucky you are? Do you know how many coma patients there are who would give anything to be here right now?"

"I'd be happy to switch pl—"

"To be standing in the grass, surrounded by beautiful mountains? To have another chance to be with their families and friends?"

"I don't have any f—"

"And you're not really even showing signs of long-term effects. You actually have a chance at a full recovery. Show God some appreciation."

"I'm pretty sure God doesn't have anything to do with this."

"Then how about you show *me* some appreciation? A little less attitude and a little more sweat?"

It was clear that she wasn't going to let this go. And since he was no longer capable of stuffing her and her henchman's lifeless bodies in a sewer pipe, he didn't have a lot of options. The battle was hers. But the war would be long and bloody.

"I KNEW you could do it! Amazing! Great job!"

It had taken an eternity, but he'd managed to make it to the barn without eating any more turf. That was the good news. The bad news was that as his eyes adjusted to the interior light, all he could see was exercise equipment. Weight racks, Swiss balls, a treadmill big enough to fit a car, and something that looked suspiciously like a medieval rack.

"Pretty inspirational, isn't it, Fred?"

"Huh?"

"Inspirational. With the help of these machines, there's nothing you can't accomplish."

"Oh. Right. Yeah."

His confusion had stemmed less from her message than his new name. In its entirety, Frederick Abdel Darwish. More evidence of Matt Egan's obsession with detail. If someone accidentally called him Fade within earshot of the wrong people, it could be argued that they'd just misheard Fred. And if that didn't work, they could say it was a play on his initials: F. A. D.

It seemed like a lot of effort for a charity gig.

"Fred?" Lisa said, sounding a bit concerned. "Are you okay? Say something."

"I'm okay."

"Are you sure? You kind of zoned out on me there."

"I'm sure."

"Pretty inspirational," she repeated, still seeking affirmation.

"You think?" he said, looking at a pull-up bar that he probably couldn't even reach up to take hold of.

"Don't let it intimidate you. According to your file, you had a VO_2 max of 74, which puts you into the professional athlete category. Your PR in a one-and-a-half-mile run is seven minutes forty-three. Five-hundred-yard breaststroke in seven minutes forty-six. Best effort in pull-ups was thirty-eight."

"Is that supposed to make me feel better? Because my mile-and-a-half time now would be more like seven days, forty-three hours. And my five hundred breaststroke would be drowning."

She ignored him. "What was your sport?"

In truth, all of them. Every high school coach had wanted him. Track, baseball, football, wrestling. Soccer had been where he really shined, though. If he'd been born fifteen years later, he might have had a shot at playing in Europe. Then his life would have been all limousines and Spice Girls.

She looked down at her clipboard. "I measure you at just over five foot ten, and based on your bone structure, I figure the ideal weight for you is around one hundred and seventy pounds, with nine percent body fat. Sound about right?"

"Whatever you say."

"That's what I like to hear! But no pull-ups, swims, or runs today. We're going to focus on stretching. Flexibility is something they work on in the hospital, so I'm hoping it won't be a major problem. And why don't we do it outside? Knock some of the pasty off you . . ."

12

A DROP of sweat fell from Matt Egan's forehead and splashed across the text in front of him. He wiped it away and kept reading, finally finishing the ten-page executive summary of a much longer document freshly translated from Chinese.

Finally, he lifted his eyes to examine his new office, still devoid of personal items or creature comfort. Just the desk, chair, and computer that Lowe had provided. A place that he suddenly wasn't sure if he wanted to escape or to barricade himself inside.

Beyond his closed door was the entire top floor of a building in an anonymous industrial park at the edge of the Salt Lake metro area. It consisted of two hallways in the form of a cross, with windowless offices clustered in the middle and glass walls ringing the exterior.

Security was an oppressive combination of carefully designed procedures, compartmentalization, and next-gen technology. Cell phones weren't allowed on the floor, and even if someone managed to smuggle one in, it would be immediately jammed and located. Communication between offices was by hardwired internal intercom. Computers had virtually no ability to send information to the outside world, and what little passed through the firewall was examined for sensitive information. Everyone entering or leaving walked through a scanner, ensuring that they weren't carrying anything unauthorized.

The personnel were Lowe's doing. All top talent raided from America's various three-letter agencies, most notably the CIA, FBI, and NSA. It probably hadn't been difficult. Like the rest of the government, those agencies were becoming increasingly dysfunctional and ineffective. Or maybe it would be more accurate to say that they were in a transitory state. The focus was shifting from protecting America from external enemies to protecting Washington's elite from anything that could loosen their grip on power. Not surprisingly, this had created a hostile environment for the few people who still gave a shit and a target-rich recruiting environment for private industry.

The doors he strode past were all closed, unlabeled, and exactly the same. He had to count to find the one he was looking for. After a quick knock, he entered, closing it behind him as a dark-haired woman in her early forties spun in her chair.

"The translations," Egan said. "Are you confident in them?"

"Reasonably," she responded with a stunned expression softened by exhaustion. "I mean, David only found those documents around thirty hours ago. With that kind of time frame, we had to rely pretty heavily on a translation app. Any sections that didn't make sense, we sent to human translators. But for security reasons, we had to split it up in a way that removed context. Also, a lot of it's pretty technical. Specialized medical vocabulary, charts, graphs..."

"But you feel good that you captured the overall gist."

She nodded. "Definitely. We'll keep refining over the next few days, but we're talking about minor details at this point."

He took in a deep breath and let it out slowly. "Okay. Thank you."

"Can I ask what you're going to do with it?"

"Hand it over to the powers that be."

"I assume you're not going to tell me who that is?"

"Maybe that's a question for you, Jan. You were at the CIA until a few weeks ago. Should I give this to your old boss?"

The current director of the Agency was a former lawyer who had been given the position as a reward for his fanatical party loyalty and sizable political donations.

"No."

"How about our local congresswoman?"

Known widely as Botox Barbara, she was a woman with a room-temperature IQ who believed she'd been abducted—and thoroughly probed—by aliens as a teenager.

"No."

"How about the White House?"

President Dominique Wayland was a tireless antidemocracy crusader who used the power of her office to crush anyone who dared to do anything but kneel. Halfway through her second term, the entire focus of the administration was finding a way for her to stay permanently in power.

When Jan's face fell, he realized that he wasn't asking her opinion as a person who had recently worked for the government but instead venting his own frustration and anger. Leadership at its shittiest.

"Excellent work. You live up to your reputation."

"Team effort," she responded. "And you've put together a hell of a team."

THE HEADQUARTERS of Jon Lowe's operation was somewhat less austere than Egan's but still not what one would expect of a man who'd achieved his level of success. The moderately stylish steel and glass structure comprised six stories and was situated closer to central Salt Lake than Egan's shop. Practical with a few modest touches of elegance. Like the man who inhabited it.

The badge hanging around Egan's neck allowed him to bypass the security scanner and head straight for the executive elevator at the back. There was no need for buttons, as he was immediately recognized by the building's mainframe and whisked to his preprogrammed destination.

Interestingly, there was no mechanical method for reaching the top floor. Instead, he exited onto the penultimate level and took an arcing staircase to a sparsely populated space above. No reception area existed, and none was necessary. His badge knew who he was and held all the information relating to his appointment. Access would be granted based on that, and he had no idea what would happen if he deviated from the predetermined course.

Egan found Lowe's door wide open at the building's southwest corner. The man had no human assistants or secretaries that Egan knew of, but the electronic ones would have undoubtedly notified him of his security chief's approach.

The office encompassed over a thousand square feet and contained nothing that could be labeled as business furniture, only tables stacked with folders and scattered chairs that were always more comfortable than they looked. The few walls that weren't made up of glass were hung with abstract artwork that Egan assumed was expensive but looked like it had been created by throwing paint into the tail rotor of a helicopter.

"Matt," Lowe said, extricating himself from a deep sofa. "Come in. And close the door behind you."

Egan did as he was told and then accepted a warm handshake from the man. It was hard not to notice the muscles of his forearms where they extended past rolled-up sleeves. He looked significantly younger than his forty-seven years, with an athletic physique and thick sandy hair that seemed to defy what were probably considerable efforts to tame it. The skin around his eyes had some damage from a sun-drenched youth, but for some reason, the crow's-feet subtracted years instead of adding them. White teeth weren't quite as perfectly aligned as was the custom in his social circles, hinting at parents who hadn't cared about such things and couldn't have afforded to do anything about them if they had.

"Your text sounded urgent," Lowe said, pointing to a couple of squat bouclé chairs pushed close to one another.

Egan sank into one and handed over the leather portfolio he'd been carrying. "We found the leaked documents about Wuhan."

"Really? Well done, Matt. On a Chinese server?"

"No. An obscure thread on 4chan."

"So it's in the wild."

"Yeah. And where there's one copy, there are more. Right now, it's just part of the background noise of conspiracy theories floating around the net. But that's not going to last. It's too detailed and too credible."

"Have you translated it?"

He nodded.

"And? Is it what Bóchéng told us? The virus originated in the south and was being studied in Wuhan when it escaped containment?"

"No."

Lowe didn't look particularly surprised. "What then?"

"It appears that an internal investigation by Chinese authorities turned up evidence that COVID was engineered. The documents are basically a suicide note by a woman who worked on the project. They describe her involvement and the fact that the release was an accident."

"So you're telling me that an independent group of biologists engineered and inadvertently released a virus that killed millions of people worldwide. All without the knowledge or participation of the Chinese government."

"That appears to be accurate."

"Why?"

"There's no discussion of motive. What she does say is that the effort was led by a geneticist named Yichén Zhu. My people have started doing background on him, but we won't have anything comprehensive until later today."

Lowe turned his attention to windows shimmering with the outlines of distant mountains.

"Are you all right, Jon?"

"Yichén Zhu."

"That's right. He got a fair amount of press a few years back for—"

"I know who he is."

"You do?"

"I financed a number of his research projects."

"Before he went to prison?"

Lowe nodded and then sat silent for almost a minute before speaking again. "Yichén got his PhD from Stanford before going back home to Beijing. He is, by far, the most brilliant geneticist in the world. You could call him the Steve Jobs of biology. He's young and charismatic, knows how to work a crowd, and he's always pushing limits. Sometimes too far."

"Which is what got him in trouble, right?"

"Yes. That, and the fact that he's sometimes more politically outspoken than he should be. Not an ideal trait for someone living in mainland China, and he made enemies of a lot of government officials. But not enough for them to clamp down on someone with so much potential."

"Until the IQ blowup."

"Exactly. Yichén manipulated a number of human embryos in an effort to increase the intelligence of the children that were produced with them. And that was a eugenic bridge too far not just for the Chinese government but the worldwide scientific community. He ended up spending three years in a reeducation camp. When he was released, he went to work for a government-funded biotech firm that's working on therapies for diabetes. As far as I know, that's all he does now. I'm not aware of anyone in the West who's been in contact with him since his release. The general consensus is that he's being watched around the clock and under the constant threat of being imprisoned again."

"It doesn't seem like it worked."

"He's a clever one," Lowe said, putting the file he'd been given on a side table. "The idea that Chinese bureaucrats would be able to control him over the long run always seemed far-fetched. Can I assume he escaped the authorities' dragnet?"

"That appears to be the case."

Lowe went back to staring through the windows.

"Do you have any idea why he'd do something like this, Jon?"

"It could be something as innocent as an interest in coronaviruses and how to best prevent a pandemic like the one that, ironically, he just caused. But it's hard to say. What would three years in a Chinese gulag do to a man like him? I mean, the Yichén Zhu I knew was arrogant and reckless, but he wasn't insane. Is that still the case? Minds like his can be delicate."

"So you think it's possible that he and his people were developing a bioweapon?"

"Anything's possible."

"To use against who?"

"I don't know. But what I do know is that he would have planned for the possibility of being discovered. If he's escaped, the Chinese government won't find him."

"And if he actually is trying to create a bioweapon, it's possible that he's made provisions to continue that research."

"Oh, absolutely. There's nothing he'd need that isn't available on the open market. Unfortunately, that's the world we live in now."

"Well, what I can tell you for certain is that this is going to go public. Probably not tomorrow. Maybe not even next month. But it's inevitable. And then the shit's going to hit the fan."

Lowe closed his eyes and let out a long breath, lips moving subtly as he did. The words came out as barely a whisper. "Yichén, what am I going to do with you?"

13

THE MASSIVE doors on either side of the barn were open, and the sun seemed to be defying physics by flooding both sides. Fade entered and stopped in front of a slightly overhanging climbing wall. He was wearing only running shorts, shoes, and a pair of sunglasses that protected his still light-sensitive eyes. It was a side effect of the coma that he hadn't been able to shake. But admittedly, one of the few.

His skin had darkened to a shade more natural for someone of his heritage. The many scars were still evident but had softened in appearance over the three months he'd been there. Beneath his newly tanned hide were even more improvements. Not that he'd transformed himself into someone Michelangelo would have bothered to sculpt, but he had managed to gain five pounds and drop his body fat percentage from a cringeworthy thirty-one to an only mildly embarrassing twelve. His one-pack was now a two-pack.

He stepped onto the wall's low footholds, leaving the safety rope hanging unused. There was no undue discomfort or numbness radiating from his spine as he climbed. When his body received an order, it complied. Not like the old days, but not a thousand miles off either.

He reached up and did something he hadn't yet attempted in his time there—skip the easiest move in favor of something more challenging. The edge his fingers fell on was tiny and painfully sharp, but not so much so that it spit him off.

He remembered how much he'd once enjoyed climbing. Now, like everything else, it didn't feel like anything. The best moment of his day was going to sleep. But even that had been stripped of its color and flavor. He'd once been a spectacular dreamer. Crazy adventures, magical creatures, happy families. As he aged, the subject matter had gotten darker but no less vivid. Dead comrades and enemies. Wrong turns and opportunities missed.

Now there was just silent darkness. Not necessarily a bad thing. In fact, it had become almost comforting.

He continued upward with some semblance of grace, starting to feel the buildup of lactic acid in his forearms.

Who was he now? What was he? Not the obedient soldier. That was a long way in the rearview mirror. Not the clinically depressed woodworker or rocket-propelled suicide machine who had failed in his one goal.

A cremated corpse with a singed toe tag carrying his name.

A murderer.

A man stuck on a road to the unknown built by someone he'd never met.

The burning in his muscles increased, accompanied by the sensation of his hands becoming slick with sweat.

He got to the top but didn't stop, instead grabbing a rafter and moving along it hand over hand, foot over foot. His shadow tracked his progress twenty-five feet below, floating weightlessly over the equipment that had been so successful at putting Humpty Dumpty back together again.

"*Stop!*"

He glanced over his shoulder at the source of the shout, spotting a panicked Lisa Thompson running toward the wall he'd left behind. She grabbed the thick foam pad at its base, struggling to drag it beneath him.

"Climb back toward the rope! I'll keep this under—"

With his grip on the verge of failing, he just let go.

The impact was a little anticlimactic. Like the rest of the gear in the barn, the mat was top-of-the-line. He didn't even get the wind knocked out of him.

With no real reason to rise, he just lay there looking into Lisa's angry face.

"Are you insane? If I hadn't been here and you'd fallen, you could have died!"

"Doesn't matter. I always come back."

Her jaw clenched, but the glare he'd become so familiar with lost its intensity. "Why don't you let me buy you lunch? It's time we talked."

IT TURNED out that the bought food was exactly the same as the free food. Fade used a pair of chopsticks to pick at his Buddha bowl while Lisa poured him sparkling water.

He'd never had any reason to enter her office, but it confirmed what he'd come to believe about her. The tidy veneered desk. Shelves full of yawn-inducing titles like *Kinesiology of the Neuromuscular System*. A poster of a kitten clinging to a rope and the slogan *Hang in There* printed beneath.

"How *are* you, Fred?"

It was a question that came up often, but this time, it had a strangely desperate undercurrent. Maybe she was just starved for human interaction. Christoph had moved on a while back and now only appeared once a week or so to service the Mystery Machine that Fade spent his nights plugged into. Not that he'd ever been a barrel of laughs, but then neither was anyone else involved in this shit show.

"Fine," he responded, turning his attention to a guitar lying on a sofa that looked original to the house. He heard her playing it every once in a while. She was working on "Sound of Silence" and almost had it dialed.

"That's not really an answer."

There was a barely perceptible hum coming from the right side of her desk. The tone was familiar and accompanied by a mysterious power cord that snaked behind a fern. Intriguing.

"Really good," he said, popping a chunk of raw salmon in his mouth. She did the same, displaying similarly muted enthusiasm. There was something dark stuck between her front teeth. He'd written it off as a speck of black bean, but it didn't have quite the right sheen. Oreo? Was Lisa Thompson a woman with things to hide?

"I've been wanting to talk to you about your recovery. Actually, I've been putting it off. But I can't do that anymore." She paused dramatically. "Your progress has been incredible."

He shrugged. "You're doing a great job, Lisa. I appreciate it."

"I'm not using that word to mean 'amazing.' I'm using it to mean 'not credible.'"

"You've lost me."

"I think this has less to do with me being a miracle worker or you being gifted and more to do with the machine you're hooked up to."

Another shrug. "I don't know much about medical stuff."

"I do. And medical machinery has brand names, model numbers, manuals . . . Those kinds of things. This one has nothing."

"Your point?"

"Whoever brought you here is pumping you full of performance-enhancing drugs. And we're not talking about a few milligrams of testosterone. I suspect we're talking about a heavy course of anabolics and other pharmaceuticals that can be really unpredictable in the human body. Particularly one that's been through what yours has."

"Seems to be working."

"What about your hair?"

"What about it?"

"When you first came here, it was cut down to about a half an inch. Now you have it tied in a ponytail. Has it always grown that fast?"

"I never paid that much attention."

"Have you noticed that when you're not connected to the machine, your resting heart rate is around sixty? But when you *are* connected, it's around a hundred and ten?"

"So?"

"They're overclocking your metabolism to make you recover faster."

"Whatever. Not the worst thing that's ever been done to me."

"No? How about this, then. You know how when you unhook the tubes from your side, sometimes a little blood drips out?"

"Yeah."

"I don't think it's yours."

"What do you mean it's not mine?"

"Look at the size of those tanks, Fred. And the fact that there's an inlet hose and an outlet hose. There's been some animal research into the therapeutic benefits of swapping out the blood of older specimens with younger ones. I think they might be doing that to you."

The cherry tomato between his chopsticks stopped before reaching his mouth. Still not the worst thing anyone had done to him, but admittedly getting closer. "You're saying that they're draining kids' blood and pumping it into me?"

"I don't know where they're getting it."

He leaned back in his chair and examined her from crinkled brow to white knuckles. "Why are you telling me all this, Lisa?"

"Because I don't want them to hurt you."

"What's it to you?"

"Look, I know you've had a hard life. It's literally written all over you. But you seem like a good person."

He grinned but managed not to laugh.

14

"THAT'S IT," Egan said, pointing through the windshield at the elegant Bordeaux restaurant on the right. The tables on the sidewalk were completely full, as were the ones visible inside. "We only gave Bóchéng the location an hour ago, and we have two people inside. That doesn't guarantee your safety, though. I mean, I doubt he'd light off any fireworks in the middle of a French city, but fireworks aren't the only way to get to someone. We have no eyes on the kitchen, for instance. Better you don't eat or drink anything."

"The last time was a misunderstanding," Jon Lowe said from the gloom of the SUV's back seat. "I'm sure he'll be on his best behavior tonight."

"With all due respect, Jon, a dozen highly trained mercs and a booby-trapped cow isn't a misunderstanding. It's kind of the definition of intentional."

Egan's extraordinarily talented new team had assembled a dossier on the man, and it didn't paint a particularly attractive portrait. Haoyu Bóchéng had been an operative for the Chinese secret police, specializing in tracking down and dealing with dissidents hiding out in Europe. He had a gift for befriending and then betraying his targets, leaving them either dead or drugged and on their way to Beijing. Word was that he sometimes flew back with them to participate in their interrogations. The messier, the better, apparently.

What was less clear was what had caused his rising star to implode. It seemed that Bóchéng no longer worked directly for the Chinese government and hadn't set foot in the country in years. Now he was more of a freelance fixer and broker of information. Rumors were many—including a rather lurid story about a homosexual relationship with a minor—but they had more the feel of smear than truth. Whatever it was, it seemed that his talents were still useful enough to Beijing that banishment, and not death or imprisonment, was preferable. It was a fragile détente that had held together for years but was always just on the verge of collapse.

The general impression was of a man lacking even the most basic humanity. Someone who pursued power and money at whatever cost, then took pleasure in using them to inflict harm on others. Being forced to deal with dangerous pieces of shit like this was one of the many reasons Egan had left the Agency. And now, here he was, lying back down with the dogs he thought he'd left behind.

They pulled to a stop, and he texted one of their advance team. The response was a thumbs-up emoji.

"Okay, Jon, we're a go. But don't make careless assumptions about this prick. He has a history of not always acting in his own best interest, and that makes him unpredictable."

"A good definition of stupidity is the willingness to harm oneself in an effort to harm others," Lowe said as he stepped onto the bustling sidewalk. "Once you understand that, Bóchéng's the most predictable person in the world."

Lowe gave his name to the maître d' and was led toward a booth along the back wall of the restaurant. Diners were packed tightly, their conversations creating a wave of sound with no intelligible component. As usual, Egan had considered everything. The public setting would give some assurance of safety while the bad acoustics would obscure a conversation that was better kept private.

He spotted Bóchéng as they came around one of the building's many columns. It had been little more than three months since they last saw each other, but he'd slimmed down noticeably, and his skin had shed some of its hedonistic pallor. The effect took off a decade, making him appear much closer to his actual forty.

"It's a pleasure to see you again," Lowe said, sliding into the booth. "You look good."

"I feel good. My compliments."

The gratitude, as attenuated as it was, didn't stem entirely from the praise. Lowe had provided Bóchéng access to a number of medical interventions that weren't available to the general public and, because of their complexity, cost, and risks, likely never would be.

These therapies had become an increasingly important area of research for Lowe, and it was the one area in which funding exceeded his ability to spend. If there was one thing that the elite had never been able to abide, it was that they weakened and died just like everyone else. The primary benefit to their desperation wasn't money, though. It was that it provided an extremely effective way to control them. The more advanced the therapies became, the more amenable the ruling class were to enslaving themselves.

"You lied to me," Lowe said as Bóchéng poured him a glass of what was undoubtedly exorbitantly expensive wine. Normally, he'd start the conversation less abruptly, but the truth was that he found the man extremely distasteful. Soonest done, soonest home.

"Based on the adjustments you and your associates made to your business positions, the information I provided was extremely valuable." His English was perfect, a highbrow British that was one of the tools he used to lure the people he later destroyed.

"But not what I paid for."

"I told you what you needed to hear. It's your responsibility to vet the information. Our transaction was beneficial to both parties."

"I can take back what you've been given."

"Don't get too impressed with yourself, Jon. Your little charity is cute . . ." He nodded in the direction of Matt Egan, who had taken a seat at the bar. "And so are your security people. But threats? You may be swimming out to where the water is over your head."

"But there's no reason to test that hypothesis, is there? Why not just give me the information I bought? Accurate information."

Bóchéng poured himself another glass, and Lowe felt an unfamiliar emotion rising in him. Anger. The man traded in human suffering. He created it, reveled in it, fanned its flames. Wealth and privilege were nothing to him unless he could deny it to others.

"My information suggests that Zhu escaped the Chinese government's dragnet. Is that accurate?"

Bóchéng popped a piece of bread in his mouth and chewed slowly. "Yes. Along with some of his followers—mostly scientists and former soldiers. My government's attempts to capture him and the subsequent search have been typically clumsy."

"The documents leaked online include an apology from the woman who released them but nothing about her or Zhu's motivations. Do—"

"You had a personal relationship with the man," Bóchéng interrupted. "Why do *you* think he did it?"

"If I knew, I wouldn't be here."

Bóchéng shrugged noncommittally. "It's so difficult to see into a mind like that. The mind of a genius."

"Do you know how I can contact him?"

He made a show of hesitating before he answered. "No."

"But you can find out."

No response.

"Yichén may well be building a bioweapon. That's not just a problem for the great unwashed, Bóchéng. It's a problem for you."

He seemed unimpressed. Had he become so entrenched in the illusion of his own superiority that he felt immortal? Or was the idea of watching the kind of suffering that Zhu could unleash too delicious for him to resist. Was he *that* stupid?

Lowe leaned back and took a moment to study the man. The transformation really was remarkable. His eyes had cleared, hair was sprouting from where it had once receded, and the thin film of sweat that normally clung to his face was nowhere to be seen.

"You really do look good."

"Are you about to threaten me again, Jon?"

"Not at all. But I wonder if you think that what I've given you is everything."

The man's quiet arrogance slipped a bit, and he caressed the recently installed ports in his side. "What do you mean?"

"I mean every day there's more. Refinements, new protocols, novel compounds. The research just keeps building on itself."

Bóchéng remained frozen for a few seconds before speaking. "Perhaps I could reach out to some of my contacts."

"That would be very generous," Lowe said, raising his glass in a subtle toast. "I'd be in your debt."

15

IT WAS the end of the world, and he'd just barely gotten back.

Fade shut down his phone's news feed and tossed the handset into the grass. The effort almost capsized his air mattress, but he managed to right it and stay dry. On the downside, the ensuing waves carried his smoothie to the other side of the pool. They'd cross paths again soon, though. As much as he hated to admit it, Lisa's vegan, organic, gluten-free concoctions were starting to grow on him. The delicate bouquet of probiotic algae. The bitter note of brussels sprouts that hinted at the loamy soil that had given them life. The palate-cleansing neutrality of yogurt-flavored yogurt.

Ninety-seven points.

He dropped his lower legs into the water and used them to turn the mattress in a lazy arc. Above, widely spaced clouds rotated with him.

During his considerable time online over the last four months, he'd run across more conspiracy theories than he could count. As near as he could tell, the internet was about fifty percent porn, thirty percent kooks in tinfoil hats, and twenty percent irresistible cat videos. As of yesterday, though, news about COVID being engineered by some asshat named Yichén Zhu had pretty much taken over.

The mainstream media was in on the game too. Excited to have a respite from manufacturing imaginary crises, they were behaving like pigs in shit. The subject dominated every television channel, every social media platform, and every newspaper. America's two political parties were gleefully blaming each other in their endless quest for attention and advantage. The conspiracy theorists—once snickered at and belittled—were shouting *I told you so* on the prime-time news programs that had previously refused to give them the time of day. Meanwhile, the Chinese government was rolling out its customary lame denials, significantly undermined by the fact that they couldn't seem to produce the man everyone agreed was some kind of Wile E. Coyote–level super genius.

As was the current custom, though, everyone seemed to be ignoring the actual issue: There was a guy on the loose who seemed both willing and capable of creating a WMD from the building blocks of life. Beyond a growing backlash against anyone who looked Asian and a few independent-minded politicians in safe seats, no one seemed to see this as anything more than a ratings grabber or a subject line for a campaign donation mailing. And that seemed to sum up the problem with the modern era. Everything had become theater. So on the rare occasion that the real world reared its ugly head, no one had any idea what to do.

It had all looked pretty grim until he'd thrown his phone onto the lawn. Now the sun was shining, the birds were singing, and his smoothie was making its way back to him. Screw Yichén Zhu. Screw the Chinese. And screw the politicians and pundits. If this prick wanted to release the plague while everybody shouted nonsense at one another, bring it. No one lived forever.

Fade woke to the sound of a car engine. Not a familiar one, though. Lisa's Outback was parked next to the house, and the weak-ass whine of Christoph's Ford passenger van was identifiable for miles. Besides, he wasn't due to replace the Mystery Machine tank for a couple more days.

Fade turned the air mattress in time to see a red Ferrari Spider barely make the corner that led to the facility's driveway. He'd always been more of a classic car guy, but there was no denying that it was a beautiful machine. A V-8 hybrid with a thousand horsepower, capable of going from zero to sixty in two and a half seconds, if he recalled correctly.

The driver slammed on the brakes, apparently trying to produce a satisfying skid, but found himself thwarted by the sophisticated antilock system. Instead, the carbon-and-titanium work of art came to an abrupt halt dead-straight and without a sound. It was a cruel cosmic truth that only the unworthy managed to get their hands on chariots like that.

Fade considered going back to studying cloud formations but instead watched the driver extricate himself from the vehicle. First to appear was a tree-trunk leg encased in a metal-and-nylon brace. Next was a fire hydrant of an arm, tattooed with an image of an ancient battle-ax. Finally, a rat's nest of long, bleached hair emerged.

While Fade wasn't much on watching sports, it was impossible not to recognize Calvin "Thor" Erickson. An offensive lineman for the Dallas Cowboys, he'd been one of the best in the league until a knee injury had sidelined him.

As good as he was at hitting people really hard, though, he was even better at being a world-class asshole. Most of the press he got wasn't for his performance on the field but for his antics off it. Bar fights, drug use, sexual assault, and a seemingly inexhaustible stream of pointlessly vulgar comments. All smoothed over by an army of lawyers, a top-notch marketing team, and fans who didn't care if he drowned puppies as long as their team won.

The only hope now was that he'd taken a wrong turn and needed directions.

Sadly, that dream was dashed when Lisa came hustling onto the porch.

She tried to speak with him, but he brushed her off. "Great, sweetheart. Now why don't you be a good girl and go grab my suitcase."

She ignored the command, instead coming up alongside and matching his hobbling pace. Her voice was too soft to hear, but his boomed loud enough to flush birds from the surrounding trees.

"Anything to drink in this place?"

A damn fine question.

Erickson stopped suddenly, pointing in Fade's direction and raising the volume of his voice even more. "There's a Haji in my pool. Get him out."

THIS TIME, Fade woke to the sensation of water being splashed in his face.

"I'm sorry, Fred. I meant to talk to you about this."

He was trapped at the pool's edge by the filtration system, and Lisa had taken a seat on the deck next to him.

"About what?"

"My new patient. He wasn't supposed to be here until tomorrow morning. His name is—"

"I know who he is."

"Look, you don't really need me anymore, and this job came up. I know it's not ideal, but it's a major opportunity for me. If I can get Calvin—" She paused to correct herself. "If I can get *Thor* healthy and playing again, it would be huge for my business. So I called your friend, and he said it would be okay."

"Sure. Great. Good for you."

"Obviously, you're welcome to stay, but at this point, it's just wasted money. You're already in better shape than ninety-nine percent of Americans your age, and there doesn't seem to be much point in going further. More risk than reward."

He gazed at her through spattered sunglasses, distracted by something at the corners of her mouth. Powdered sugar. And not one of the subtle hints that he'd occasionally noted during his time there. No, it was caked into the creases for God and everyone else to see.

For some reason, the hypocrisy was endearing. She was just such a . . . human being. A woman who cared. Someone who could utter the words *I want to make the world a better place* and have them come off as sincere.

"I don't know, Lisa. I've been having some pain in my Achilles tendon. We should probably devote some time to it."

The lopsided, sugary smile suggested that she knew it was a lie. "Sure. Better safe than sorry, right?"

He gave her a thumbs-up and pushed off, floating lazily toward the center of the pool.

16

DAWN WAS beginning to penetrate the window as Fade brushed his teeth and listened to the frantic clash of television pundits on TV. He'd thought things had gotten pretty crazy when he was being chased by Homeland Security and every cop in Virginia. Turns out he'd had no idea what crazy really was.

It had been only a week since the Wuhan Papers had gone public, and the politicians were already losing control of the narrative. Partisan attacks were no longer attracting political donations, and idiotic media shouting matches like the one he was watching were losing ratings. At some point over the last twenty-four hours, the public had broken free of the spell they'd been under and realized that this wasn't a game. That there was a nutjob geneticist out there who had already killed seven million people and who might be looking to do better in round two.

Even more interesting was that the saber-rattling between the US and China had spun out of control to the point that two more American carrier groups were steaming east. Russia was throwing gas on the fire, apparently under the delusion that a war between superpowers would leave them to rule the world. Europe was trying to play the peacemaker, but its populations weren't any more immune to panic than anyone else.

Conspiracy websites—though it was hard to refer to them so harshly anymore—were pushing theories that blamed everything from Chinese government bioweapons programs to space aliens to that old standby, the Jews. Demonstrations at China's embassies had reached riot levels in multiple countries, creating dramatic clashes between police and civilians that made for great TV. Antiscientific sentiment was exploding, focused on biology but by no means limited to it. Tens of millions of people who hadn't given two shits about COVID when it was burning across the planet now seemed to think it was the worst thing that had ever befallen humanity. And if they couldn't find a better scapegoat, by God, they'd take their frustrations out on an archeologist.

Fade returned to the bathroom to spit toothpaste before beginning the search for his missing left running shoe. On-screen, the commentators had organized a bit and were now talking with a congressman floating the idea of rounding up Asians and putting them in what sounded a lot like internment camps.

The fevered nature of the coverage had hit new heights overnight because Yichén Zhu had announced that he was going to release a statement. A fucking *statement*. Like some politician who'd gotten caught banging his wife's hairdresser. Or a fast-food restaurant about to release a new nugget sauce.

Outstanding.

The shoe turned out to be hiding under the bed, and once on, Fade began another search—this time for the TV remote. He'd just tracked it down when the pundit-in-charge breathlessly announced that Zhu's statement had been released on Facebook. Fade's thumb hovered over the *off* button as the screen switched to a fortysomething Chinese man standing in front of a blank wall.

"My country has been destroyed."

Good start. Dramatic. Maybe it would be worth hanging around for a few minutes.

Like everyone else, he'd seen pretty much every existing picture of Zhu, but none had captured the full measure of the man. His deep, slightly accented voice, expressive good looks, and intense gaze were a real standout. Scientists with charisma were rare but uniquely mesmerizing. Or maybe that was just bias on his part. He'd always wondered what it would be like to have that kind of mental horsepower. To see the universe through the eyes of Einstein, da Vinci, or Newton.

"My generation and the ones behind have been stripped of all hope. We exist only to serve the old men who have done this to us with their corruption, greed, and insatiable thirst for power."

Fade notched up the volume. Based on everything he'd seen since getting booted out of the coma ward, the man was making a certain amount of sense.

"Youth unemployment is so high in China that the government will no longer release statistics. Our entire economic miracle was built on sand and is on the brink of collapse. China will once again starve. And it will be within the next decade."

Zhu paused, eyes wandering briefly away from the camera.

"Our young people have stopped having children because they see no future for them, adding to the demographic implosion started by the government's one-child policy. And now, after penalizing women for having children and encouraging the abortion and murder of our girls, the government is lecturing about the glory of large families. That these same women are now responsible for breeding a new generation of workers whose only role will be to worship the old men in power."

Man, this was getting depressing.

"And so, as our generation increasingly refuses to participate in our own destruction, Beijing starts their inevitable attempts to blind us with nationalism. They say that Taiwan is a birthright that's been stolen from us." He let out a bitter laugh. "They tell us that our military, with no combat experience and so corrupt that they fill our missiles with water instead of fuel, will secure a quick victory. How stupid do they think we are? Do they believe that we don't know they'll send millions of us to kill and die there, further devastating an economy that already doesn't work for us? For the prize of an insignificant piece of land filled with burned cities and rotting corpses? All while they sit in their mansions and drink imported champagne with their mistresses?"

Fade didn't know anything about Chinese economics or youth culture, but he did know war, and this guy wasn't wrong about Taiwan. An invasion of that island would be a pointless, drawn-out bloodbath that was one hundred percent certain to spiral out of control.

"They put me in prison for trying to use technology to solve the problems they themselves have created. Why? Because they don't want a new era that they don't understand and therefore can't control. They want to continue to grow fat and rich on the status quo while you go hungry. Like I did while they were torturing me. While I was lying naked in a concrete cell being instructed in the greatness and infallibility of our leaders."

Fade finished tying his shoes but didn't make a move for the door. The intensity of Zhu's hatred for China's government amplified his natural charisma, making it impossible to turn away.

"When I finally managed to make them believe that I'd seen the light, they released me and turned me into a slave. Reports were that I was working on a cure for diabetes, but that was a lie. In fact, I was recruited onto a taskforce charged with increasing China's birthrate. The team consisted of generals, propagandists, lawyers, and government officials, among others. My area was medical. I was ordered to find a way to reduce the effectiveness of birth control in our population. To turn our women into breeding stock."

His demeanor changed perceptibly. Some of the hate was replaced by resolve.

"I realized then that I had to act. Our youth have taken to calling themselves the last generation. But it's no different in Washington, Moscow, or countless other countries where twisted old men entrench themselves and block all progress. But we don't have to be the last generation. We can be the first. The leaders of a modern era defined by peace, equality, and environmental responsibility. None of this pain and destruction is necessary. It's not caused by us. Not wanted by us. But we're the ones who have to suffer the aftermath. War. Poverty. Air we can't breathe and water we can't drink . . ." His voice faltered and went silent.

Setting aside the seven million people he'd murdered, it was hard not to sympathize with the man. Fade had experienced some of what he was talking about firsthand. Watching his friends die in Afghanistan knowing full well that the higher-ups had no real goal beyond promotions, reelections, and seven-figure private sector jobs.

"I created COVID," he continued, letting the statement hang in the air for a moment. "It was an attempt to make a pathogen that would target only the elderly. The people stealing our future."

Fade's eyebrows rose. Damn. Did he just say that?

"It was a crude, early version, and the release was unintentional. The result of poor containment protocols at the Wuhan lab. And for that, all I can do is say that I'm truly sorry. But what's important for people to understand is that this had nothing to do with the Chinese government. Very much the opposite. It was intended to target them. So starting World War III won't be necessary."

The screen went dark and then returned to a roundtable of media personalities who were flipping their well-coifed lids.

More and more, the world resembled a clown car blundering into Camp Crystal Lake.

And he kind of dug it.

THE EARLY hour created an unusual calm as Fade walked down the hallway. While genocidal Chinese geneticists were no picnic, Thor Erickson was an unholy disaster. It turned out that he wasn't the god of thunder; he was the god of chaos.

In a mere five days, he'd managed to turn Fade's peaceful retreat into hell's waiting room. He was loud, obnoxious, and spent each of his waking hours on the very edge of violence. Worse, he fought Lisa every step of the way for no reason other than a pathological desire to break her emotionally.

And it was working. She was starting to take on the mannerisms of a rescue dog, hiding when possible and jumping out of her skin at unexpected noises. Subtle chocolate stains and hints of Cheeto dust beneath her nails had been replaced by lazily hidden Twinkie wrappers and peanut butter cup outlines in her pockets.

All this despite the fact that she was Erickson's only hope of ever playing again. Without his ability to plow people down on the field, he'd be just another fat prick with three DUIs and two pending sexual assault charges. You'd think he'd be focused on recovery and not on turning everyone—including Fade—into neurotic pools of jelly.

With very little drama to be had in that idyllic corner of West Virginia, Erickson had decided to treat him as though they were lifelong enemies. Shouted insults and death threats were only the beginning. Yesterday, the dipshit had actually jumped through a doorway and screamed in an effort to scare him. Like some catastrophically swollen eight-year-old trying to startle his sister.

The failure of those attempts at intimidation, combined with Fade's lack of interest in engaging with Erickson on any level, was making the man even crazier. Lisa recognized that the steady escalation could only end badly but had no recourse beyond the seductive, creamy embrace of Hostess snack cakes.

Fade pushed through the door and into air that already felt like bathwater. Setting the timer on his watch, he started out for the easy three-mile run that had been prescribed, crossing the grass and turning up a dirt road that cut through the trees. His data—heart rate, pace, elevation gain, and who knew what else—was transmitted in real time to Lisa for the purpose of refining his training schedule. Undoubtedly, the numbers also went to Matt Egan and his "charity," but for more sinister reasons.

The empty terrain was pleasantly rolling, finally flattening out near a decent-sized pond. He stopped at a white post that was the beginning of a flat mile. Lisa periodically tested him on it, and each time, he put on a convincing performance of a man at his limit. As far as she and anyone else watching was concerned, he could do no better than eight and a half minutes on the course.

Fade turned off his phone and for good measure turned off his watch's Bluetooth connection. After a careful search of the sky for surveillance drones, he took off.

His breathing came up quickly, with an unfamiliar lag in heart rate but no obvious indications that it was going to stop or explode. Though, to be honest, he didn't really know what warning signs to look for.

At the quarter-mile mark, he increased his pace from hard to something that would have prompted Lisa to down an entire pan of Rice Krispies Treats. Finally, he stumbled over the line, stopped his timer, and collapsed to the ground. The wheezing coming from somewhere deep in his lungs didn't sound great but subsided after he vomited what little he'd had for breakfast.

When his vision cleared, he looked at his watch. Five minutes, forty-eight seconds. Not a time worthy of medals or ticker tape parades, but not bad for a guy who a few months ago couldn't stand.

The one thing that definitely still sucked was his recovery. It was a good five minutes before he was able to get back to his feet and walk to a pull-up bar at the edge of the water. The best effort he'd given Lisa was seven, even when she'd goaded him by doing eleven herself.

He jumped up and did a dozen repetitions in rapid succession. The next eight were harder but doable. After that, sharp pain in his elbow prompted him to quit.

The aimless walk back to his phone took more than a half hour. He picked it up and turned it back on but wasn't sure what to do next. With no one direction better than another, he went out into the pond, stopping when the water reached his knees. In full sun, the heat was oppressive, baking his skin and evaporating the sweat from his running shirt.

Remembering the phone, he spoke into it.

"Hey, Google. What now?"

17

IT WAS after 9:00 a.m., but Lisa remained barricaded in her living quarters and Thor was still two hours from finishing his beauty sleep. It was a magic time during which Fade could pretend that no one else existed.

He dragged an air mattress to the pool and climbed on, propelling himself to the middle while engaging in his new favorite pastime, cloud Rorschach tests. The one directly overhead looked like a 1950s toaster. Next to it was a violin. Farther east was a milk jug spilling its contents.

After a few minutes, the sound of an unfamiliar vehicle reached him. An SUV. Foreign for sure. Probably German. A Mercedes?

It turned out to be a BMW with heavily tinted windows, god-awful custom rims, and a gold-plated grill. Had Lisa taken on another rickety lost soul? It probably wouldn't be a bad idea for her sanity, but he doubted it. Not warning him about Thor had sent her on a guilt trip that she wouldn't be anxious to repeat.

The man who stepped out seemed to confirm that hypothesis. He was wearing exactly the tracksuit and jewelry you'd expect from someone who would do things like that to a defenseless Beemer, but he was neither athletic nor injured. Wraparound shades hid his eyes, and his narrow, angular head jerked back and forth as though he were searching for a pack of wolves gathering at the tree line. What made the strongest impression, though, were his tennis shoes. They were almost supernaturally white.

A moment later, the screen door to the farmhouse was thrown open. The sound of it hitting the siding was followed by fast, heavy footsteps on the porch. The child-god of thunder was up early this morning.

When Erickson passed into view, he seemed to be moving pretty well. The brace was still in place, but the limp was barely discernible. Despite his unwavering resistance, Lisa was putting him back together again.

The sooner, the better.

He spotted Fade out of the corner of his eye but didn't engage, clearly more interested in greeting his newly arrived friend. Anxious, even.

No bro hugs, loud greetings, or even smiles. Only a conspiratorial handshake that was mostly blocked from view. They spoke at an inaudible level, with Erickson starting to scan the forest for the same wolves his friend seemed so concerned about.

After thirty seconds, the reunion was over, and the unnamed visitor slipped back into his SUV. Erickson, looking suspiciously cheerful for this hour of the morning, made a beeline back to the farmhouse. As he passed the pool, he pointed in Fade's direction.

"What did I tell you about using my pool, Haji?"

When he didn't get the reaction he was after—or any reaction at all—he came to an abrupt halt. "Did you hear me? Get your ass out of my water!"

Fade slid off the mattress and exhaled, watching the bubbles rise as he drifted to the bottom.

THE SHOWER pounded down on Fade's head, matting his hair and rinsing away the dust of another pointless day.

Near the sink, the phone he'd never made or received a call on was blasting out "Daydream Believer" by the Monkees. He'd always loved the upbeat rhythm, youthful enthusiasm, and sunny lyrics. Now it sounded like a lie.

Lisa had told him about an extensive trail system in the area, and he'd decided to do a little exploring. Somewhere along the way, he'd come across an octogenarian banging away in a pair of elaborate hiking boots and an even more elaborate walking stick. It turned out that she'd been hiking the region since she was a little girl and was the final word on its backcountry. He'd ended up spending the entire day with her, matching her creeping pace and marveling at her determination to keep going.

It turned out they had a lot in common. Her husband had been dead for decades, and her sixty-five-year-old daughter had recently succumbed to a massive stroke. Her friends hadn't fared much better, with most of them below ground, unable to walk without assistance, or suffering from mental decline. But she was fine. Not a thing wrong with her. Never a single fucking thing.

He turned off the shower and reached for the phone. Notifications kept pinging, disrupting the music and putting a damper on what had already been a pretty damp day. He shut them off and threw the phone through the bathroom door, bouncing it off the Mystery Machine.

Yichén Zhu was blowing up on every channel. His attempt at deescalation had turned into one of the biggest backfires in history. About half the people on the planet now thought that the Chinese government was holding him and forcing him to take the blame for their bioweapons program. Many more were expanding the general antiscience outrage into violent demonstrations at universities, medical research facilities, and even tech companies that had nothing to do with any of this. Politicians, facing public backlash for being asleep at the wheel, were rounding up everyone who had even peripheral dealings with Zhu, holding them without charges or evidence. Antigovernment marches were springing up all over the globe, where they were met with unusually harsh crackdowns and even declarations of martial law.

He toweled off and pulled on a pair of boxer shorts before dropping on the bed.

"Fred?"

Lisa was peering through his partially open door with an expression that didn't fit into one of her normal categories. Further, it was nearly 10:00 p.m. Well after her bedtime.

"What's up?"

She stepped inside. "Have you been watching the news?"

He shook his head.

"Yichén Zhu made another video. He says he's going to do it."

"Do what?"

"Finish developing his virus and release it. He says that the reaction to his last video is proof he was right."

Fade pulled up YouTube on his laptop, and not surprisingly, the video in question was first to appear. The simmering rage that had fueled Zhu's first star turn had now exploded to the surface. He railed against entrenched power structures, the inevitable violent collapse of society, and to some extent, human nature itself. The seven million COVID casualties that he'd been so concerned about in his last appearance seemed to have been forgotten.

He finished with a bang, stating that the pathogen he'd been working on for so long was nearly perfected and would soon be released. The fear and uncertainty would end, and a new age would begin.

And that was it. Say what you will about the man, but he understood the subtleties of a good mic drop.

"If he's telling the truth and he really can target seniors," Lisa said, "we're not talking about a few million people this time. I read an article that said there are three-quarters of a billion people over sixty-five. That's ten percent of the human population."

Fade was more interested in why she was telling him this than the actual subject at hand. It suddenly occurred to him that she almost never left the compound, and when she did, it was only for a few hours at a time. She'd never had a personal visitor in the months he'd been there, and he'd never heard her on the phone speaking about anything but business. Was it possible that someone this beautiful, talented, and kind had no one better to talk to?

It was strange that the only two people he'd really interacted with since his most recent resurrection—her and Egan—didn't seem much better off than he was.

"What do you think, Lisa? You've got a PhD, right?"

"I think he can do it. Have you read about him? He's one of the most brilliant people in the world." She lifted her head to meet his gaze. "Do you have people you love? Older people?"

He shook his head. "You?"

"My parents are . . ." She paused for a moment. "Complicated. They were really invested in my athletic career, and when it didn't pan out, we discovered we didn't have anything else to say to each other."

"Friends?"

She smiled sadly. "The people I was close to were all teammates and training partners. Then I got injured."

"And you discovered you didn't have anything else to say to each other."

She nodded. "In school, I was focused on studying, and I had to work to pay my tuition . . ." Her voice faltered again. "It sounds like I'm making excuses."

"Are you?"

"I suppose. I'm good with skis and textbooks."

"And patients."

"It's a simple dynamic."

"You give, and we take."

She seemed to want him to say more, but a sudden beeping from the Mystery Machine broke the spell.

"That's you," she said, making no effort to hide her disapproval. "Time for bed."

The door slammed and listened to her footsteps recede until they got lost in the siren song of the machine next to him. Instead of reaching for the hoses, though, he just lay there. It was becoming an addiction. One of his many masters.

The beeping became increasingly difficult to ignore. Not because it was getting louder, but because he remembered the last time he'd decided to defy it: five hours of staring at the ceiling before he'd finally managed to nod off. Then the nightmares had come. And not the customary retelling of his life's failures and regrets. No, these were more of the giant spider and zombie variety.

He pushed himself into a seated position, determined to kick the machine's plug out. Instead, he inserted a set of earbuds and turned out the light. A quick scroll through the music on his phone turned up a live recording of the Ramones.

Sheena is a punk rocker . . . Take it, dude . . .

Another voice of someone who'd managed to make it to the grave and accomplish the simple task of staying there.

FADE MANAGED to achieve a state between sleep and consciousness that he could more or less maintain. His eyes were open but didn't register the moonlit room around him. And the dreams didn't come. They were out there, though. Hiding under his bed. Peeking through the crack in the bathroom door.

A sound slipped through his barriers, but it was hard to say if it was real or just one of those monsters on the move. In the end, it turned out to be both.

"Hajjiiiiiiiiiii!"

The shout was followed by ham-sized fists hammering Fade's locked door. The handle rattled uselessly, followed by more pounding, this time hard enough for dust to rise off the jamb and hang pale in the air.

"Come out and play, Haji! You're going to die soon anyway! Haven't you heard? All you old bastards!"

Fade frowned. He was only a few years this asshole's senior, and it was almost three in the morning. Apparently, his BMW-abusing dealer had given him the good stuff.

Fortunately, the door was original to the house, lovingly created from solid oak. Back before robots, assembly lines, and particleboard. When craftsmen learned at their fathers' sides and took pride in what they did.

"Thor! What's wrong with you? Go back to bed!"

Fade groaned and muttered to the empty room. "What are you doing, Lisa? Lock yourself in your room."

The pounding went silent.

"Are you high? Have you been taking drugs?"

Heavy footsteps, still slightly off rhythm from his injury.

"Stop it! Go back to bed! Now!"

His response was muted but intelligible. "Oh, come on. You said you'd do whatever it took to put me back together . . ."

Then running. Lighter footsteps with a quicker, more even beat. But the chase was on. It shook the entire building.

Fade swung his feet off the bed and stood, stretching his back and registering once again that it felt good. Probably not good enough to save him, though.

When he arrived at the open door to Lisa's office, she and Erickson were on opposite sides of the desk, staring at each other like the lecherous boss and pious secretary from an old sitcom. When he feinted left, she moved right. When he feinted right, she moved left.

Of course, he could go over or through that piece of IKEA plywood any time he wanted. The question was whether that was really what he had in mind. So far, his violence had been limited to the psychological kind. Would it stay that way?

Best to hang back and wait for an answer. Fade knew his involvement would only escalate the situation. If this was nothing more than a little harmless fun, better to let the god of thunder get bored and end it on his own.

The knee brace was conspicuously absent, exacerbating some residual instability to the outside. It caused him to move right more confidently than left. The power, size, and incongruous grace that had made him famous were all there, though. As was the laser-like focus on destruction.

"Okay, this isn't funny anymore," Lisa said with impressive calm. "It's time for you to go back to bed. If you don't, you could do damage that I can't fix. It could end your career, Thor. Do you understand?"

The discipline necessary to conjure such a serene tone was noteworthy but also a complete misreading of this piece of shit's psyche. He fed off the fear he instilled in others. Denying him that would just cause the fire to burn hotter.

Erickson threw himself forward and managed to get hold of her upper arm. She tried to break free but, despite being a hell of an athlete in her own right, had no chance. Instead, she was dragged over the desk and spun around. With his hand now clamped around the back of her neck, she ended up bent at the waist with her cheek shoved into the blotter.

And so it began.

Fade tore himself from the wall he was leaning against and walked to the doorway.

"Hey, big guy."

Erickson spun, knocking Lisa to the floor. Instead of using her newfound freedom to bolt, she waved Fade off. "Go back to your room! It's okay."

He wondered if she actually believed that she could control this douchebag or if she was willing to take the bullet to keep her first—and unquestionably most charming—client safe. Not that it mattered. Either she had an unwavering faith in humanity or bigger balls than anyone he'd ever met. That made her worth something. If Lisa Thompson existed, maybe the world was actually worth saving.

"Looks like you got a hold of a little too much, Thor. Why don't you and I go outside and walk it off. Let Lisa hit the—"

It was impossible not to marvel at the lineman's charge. It was like getting shot at by a hippopotamus cannon.

Options were limited, and Fade had already considered all of them. Showing up to this fight in nothing but boxer shorts was intentional. Not just because it was becoming a bit of a tradition, but because football players tended to make good use of their opponent's clothing to gain control.

The second decision had been even harder than condemning himself to being beaten to death in his underwear. He'd committed to not retreating into the hallway. While bigger than the office, it was certain death. Outrunning this prick over a quarter mile would be a piece of cake, but not so much over the length of that passageway. Further, there was nothing out there that could be used as a weapon. Going up against this bulldozer empty-handed wouldn't end well. Anything short of an RPG was going to feel light.

Fade slipped into the office, staying on Erickson's weak side and ramming a shoulder into him as they came even. The hope was to nudge him in line with the door and let his momentum carry him through. Then they could barricade themselves inside and wait for whatever he'd taken to wear off.

It turned out to not be that easy. Hitting the guy was like colliding with a sack of wet cement. And the idea that his momentum could be counted on to carry him anywhere turned out to be a complete fantasy. The son of a bitch could stop on a dime.

Erickson spun, swinging an arm that caught Fade in the shoulder he'd used so ineffectively a moment before. The force nearly lifted him off his feet, sending him crashing into—and then over—Lisa's desk. He landed face-first in her chair, which immediately rolled away and dropped him to the floor.

The illusion of having a bit of cover disappeared when Erickson swept the desk away like it was made of papier-mâché.

Admittedly a bad start, but finally, part of Fade's master plan worked. Sweaty, bare skin was hard to hold on to. It wasn't a lengthy reprieve, but it provided an opportunity to throw a magnificent punch directly into the man's groin. Perfect leverage, great technique, propelled by Mystery Machine–enhanced muscles.

The motherfucker didn't even notice.

A moment later, Fade felt himself being lifted. His head penetrated the acoustic tile ceiling, providing him with a brief view of the AC ductwork before he was yanked down again.

The bear hug he ended up trapped in was centered on his lower back, and he expected his spine to fail. It didn't, though. Whoever performed his surgery was due a gold star. No numbness or paralysis from the waist down. Just a complete inability to breathe.

A quick review of his situation uncovered a number of problems, the worst of which was that he was being slowly crushed to death. On the brighter side, he was facing his opponent, and his arms were free. Also, Lisa was releasing a steady stream of obscenities that would have made even his old master chief blush.

Hilarious.

He leaned forward and bit down on Erickson's nose while simultaneously trying to drive a thumb into his eye. Accustomed to having his face protected by a helmet, he was taken by surprise, and Fade once again found himself sailing through the air. This time he landed on the sofa, which wasn't bad until he went over the side and into Lisa's guitar. It shattered beneath his weight, driving a sizable shard through his left triceps.

By the time he yanked it out, Erickson was coming at him, adding his own screamed epithets to Lisa's.

The sofa took the brunt of the collision, but the lineman was still able to get a handful of Fade's hair. Putting up a fight would just waste energy, so Fade allowed himself to be dragged, focusing on keeping hold of what was left of the guitar. Erickson's knee finally started to show signs of weakness, reducing the force with which he was able to slam Fade onto the desk. Still hard enough to loosen a few fillings, but not sufficient to prevent Fade from winding a couple of the guitar's strings around the man's nearly nonexistent neck.

A massive fist connected with his ribs, but Fade ignored it as he tried to fight his way into a position where he could exert some force. Then Erickson made the fatal error of jerking back.

The strings tightened, opening a deep gash that caused his incredible strength to falter. Fade held onto the broken neck of the guitar with one hand and the detached bridge with the other, allowing himself to be pulled to the floor. Erickson kept swinging, connecting repeatedly, confused as to why he was inflicting so little damage.

Lisa appeared from the right, pressing a cloth to his neck in an effort to stop the fountain of arterial blood. A swipe of the man's hand was still enough to send her spinning across the floor.

Fade got a hold of wrists too thick to wrap his fingers all the way around, gaining a certain amount of control.

"You're dying, man! Pay attention!"

Erickson's eyes widened, revealing pupils dilated into manhole covers. Imminent death was a hard thing to process. Fade knew that better than anyone. But it was something to be stared in the face. No one should be cheated out of life's last and most profound experience. Not even this tool.

Erickson finally went still, and Fade tried to stand, using the edge of the desk for balance. He righted Lisa's chair and sat, not sure for a moment whether it was spinning or if it was just his head. He looked down at a desk drawer hanging broken to his right, trying to bring the image into focus. When his vision finally cleared, one of his many suspicions was confirmed. It was refrigerated.

He retrieved an icy Coke and then forced the drawer above, revealing an elaborate junk-food stash. Ho Hos. Twinkies. Chips of various crunch profiles and flavors. The mother lode.

His first sip of Coke in years tasted like blood, so he spit it out. The second was heaven.

"Help me!" Lisa was on her hands and knees, once again pressing a cloth to Erickson's neck.

"You're wasting your time."

"Then do something!"

He opened a packet of Pop-Tarts and took a bite. Cinnamon. What kind of sick taco bought cinnamon? "He's not going to make it, Lisa. Take my word for it."

"Call an ambulance!"

He made a show of searching his nonexistent pockets. "No phone."

She retrieved hers from her sweatpants and threw it at him. He scrolled through her contacts until he found one that said Matt. No last name.

It took six rings, but a familiar voice finally answered. "Lisa? Is everything okay?"

"We've got a problem."

A full second passed before Egan responded. "How big?"

"About three hundred and twenty-five pounds."

The next pause was longer, accompanied by what sounded like fingers on a keyboard. "It's going to be a few hours before I can get anyone there. Can you not screw anything else up until then?"

"Sure. No worries."

Fade disconnected the call.

Despite not being a particularly long conversation, sometime during it, Erickson had expired. Lisa fell back into the blood pooling behind her, blond hair glued to the tears and sweat on her cheeks. Fade grabbed a bottle of chocolate Yoo-hoo and rolled the chair alongside her.

"Here. Drink this. It'll make you feel better."

She grabbed it and removed the lid with a practiced twist, draining almost half before coming up for air.

"Better?"

No response.

"Are you hurt?" When she shook her head, he put a hand under her arm and lifted her to her feet. "Good. Now let's get you cleaned up before the cavalry arrives."

18

"NO, NO, no..."

Matt Egan appeared to be in almost physical pain. Pale, unshaven, and frozen in the door's threshold, repeating that same word over and over again.

His full attention was on Erickson, who was propped over the edge of a large plastic tub that was catching the remaining blood dripping from his neck. The container was about a quarter full, submerging his head in a way that made him look like he was bobbing for apples at Satan's birthday party.

Egan eventually tore his eyes away from the former NFL player and took in the rest of the room. Fade felt like they'd done a pretty good job straightening up. Bodily fluids had been cleaned from the floor with a set of bath towels that now resided in a similar tub by the wall. The remains of Lisa's guitar and a few other damaged items had been stuffed into lawn and leaf bags and piled on the porch. Drawers had been shoved back into the desk, sofa pillows were fluffed, and motivational posters had been straightened. The overwhelming impression—other than the massive corpse in the middle of the floor—was the scent of environmentally friendly cleaning products.

Lisa had insisted on helping, but he suspected that it was only because she needed constant motion to keep her demons at bay. Now she was perched on the arm of the sofa, scrubbed and primped but stiffer than the body at her feet.

"What the hell was he doing here?" Egan said, turning toward her.

She remained silent and mannequin still.

"Lisa! Look at me. What the hell was he doing here?"

"I . . . I don't understand," she said, coming back to life. "I called you. You said it was okay."

"What are you talking about? We never spoke about this."

"We did!" she said, searching her phone with shaking hands. "A couple weeks ago. Where . . . Where is it? It has to be here. We talked! I'm not—"

"Lisa!" Fade shouted through a mouthful of Doritos. "Relax. We know you're telling the truth. We don't need documentation. Right, Matt?"

"No," he conceded. "We don't need documentation."

Fade pulled a beer from the refrigerated drawer and tossed it onto the sofa next to her. "Why don't you go out on the porch and drink that. Let me and Matt talk."

She did as he asked, scooting past Egan and disappearing down the hallway. They waited for the front door to slam before either spoke again.

"What the *hell*, Fade? You can't share a training facility with one guy without killing him? How hard is this?"

"Don't bust my balls, Matt. Do you really think I go around provoking water buffalos into hand-to-hand combat?"

Egan looked down at the body again. "Without him, the Cowboys' passing game is going to go to complete shit."

"His dealer showed up this morning. Some asshole in a tracksuit and blinged-out BMW SUV."

"So Thor was high?"

"Enough to attack Lisa."

Egan nodded, his expression changing to something more familiar. He was mentally cataloging details—the make and model of the damaged desk, the remaining stains on wood and upholstery, the broken bulb in the lamp. He might be a prick, but he was a meticulous, confidence-inspiring prick.

"Fix it, Matt. That's what you do, right? That's *all* you do."

"Fuck you."

Fade cracked another Coke. "And with regard to Lisa. I'll have a talk with her, but no matter what she does or says, she's off-limits. If something happens to her, I'm going to kill you, I'm going to kill that German nurse—"

"He's Austrian."

"—and then I'm going to find that charity you say you work for and kill everyone there."

"I understand."

"Do you? Are you sure?"

He just nodded.

IT WAS late afternoon when Fade stepped out onto the porch and eased into a chair next to Lisa. With the adrenaline long gone, he was starting to feel the effects of the last few hours. Bruises and minor cuts all over his body, a rib that he'd thought was cracked but probably wasn't, and a shoulder that felt like it had been briefly dislocated. He'd put a few stitches in the hole where the wood shard had entered his triceps, but it was almost certain to get infected without the aid of antibiotics. Almost as bad was his stomach. Easing into the junk food probably would have been a better call.

"I know who you are," she said, still clutching the unopened beer.

"Yeah?"

"Arab descent. Scars. Coma. And then there were the performance numbers I was given. Right off the Navy SEAL qualifications list."

"You're not a PhD for nothing."

"So can I assume we're not calling the police? Since you killed a SWAT team and you're supposed to be dead?"

"The cops were an accident. I thought they were someone else."

"I know. I remember when it happened. I remember the news coverage. And what you wrote."

Somewhere inside the house, Egan's muffled voice could be heard barking orders into a phone.

"What about me, Fade?" She turned toward him. "That's what they call you, right? Fade?"

"Some people. A long time ago."

"Who am I now? Not your physical therapist. Just a person who knows too much."

"Listen, Lisa. We committed no crimes here tonight. Thor got hold of some bad drugs and attacked us. I defended myself, and he ended up on the short end of that. Based on his history and the blood work the coroner would do on him, no one would question that story. So instead of going through all that trouble, Matt's going to make this disappear. Better for everyone, right?"

"How does he know I won't talk? It might have been a mistake, but you still killed a lot of policemen. Eight, wasn't it?"

"I wasn't counting. Look, everyone's life would be a lot easier if you just kept your mouth shut. But if your conscience won't allow it, I'll do everything I can to protect you. I'm not sure I'll be successful, though. I don't know much about the people paying my bills, but my impression is that they're not to be messed with."

"Government?"

"Probably."

"CIA?"

"Good bet."

She finally cracked open her beer but didn't drink.

Egan appeared on the porch and leaned against the railing in front of them. "Fred Darwish finished his treatment, and you discharged him two days ago. We'll need to backdate the paperwork."

Lisa shook her head. "He was in the pool when Thor's friend came to see him."

"Doesn't matter. Drug dealers aren't in the business of going to the police with accusations. Now shut up and listen. Last night, you went to bed at your normal time. This morning, you woke up at your normal time. When you did, Erickson and his car were gone. I've got a crew on their way to make sure all the blood's cleaned up, and they'll replace things like your guitar, towels, and desk. Now, tell me. If you got up and couldn't find him, what would you do?"

"Am I allowed to talk now?"

"Yes."

"I probably wouldn't do anything. He's pretty volatile, and I'd assume he got frustrated and needed to blow off some steam."

"How long before you'd contact someone?"

"I don't know. I'd maybe send an email to his coach tomorrow telling him that he's gone and giving him a report on the status of his knee."

"Okay, good. That gives us plenty of time. Plus, I'm guessing his coach is going to come to the same conclusion as you. He'll call around to a few friends and family members to see if they know anything, but it'll be the better part of a week before any alarm bells go off. So basically, all you need to do is forget the events of the last few hours. You went to bed. You woke up. Thor was gone. Period, full stop. Live your life accordingly. Think you can handle that?"

She nodded.

"I want to hear you say it."

"I went to bed. I got up. He was gone."

"Excellent." Egan pointed at Fade. "How long will it take for you to gather up your stuff?"

"Maybe ten minutes. I don't really have anything."

"Do it," he said before going back into the house.

Fade reached out and put a hand on Lisa's shoulder. "You okay?"

"Fine. Things like this happen to me all the time."

He smiled. "Don't overthink it, all right? Matt and the people he works for can make things happen. My death. The Mystery Machine. All you have to do is stay out of their way."

She nodded.

"I hate to sound like Matt, but let me hear you say it."

"Thor Erickson was a complete bastard who has a history of attacking women that goes all the way back to high school, but he's always gotten away with it because of what he can do on the playing field and his rich parents. If it weren't for you, I'd just be another one of his anonymous victims. I might even be dead. You risked your life to help me when you could have just stayed in your room, and I haven't even thanked you." She took his hand and met his eye for the first time since Erickson's death. "So I'm saying it now. Thank you, Fade. And don't worry about me. I'd never do anything to hurt you."

19

FADE WOKE to the hum of transport plane props and the beep of the Mystery Machine. According to the glowing numbers on his watch, he'd been out for forty-eight hours, and the weird sensation in his chest was his heart revving at almost a hundred and forty beats per minute.

He disconnected the tubes from his side with a practiced flick of his wrist but stayed on the cot while his pulse settled. The cavernous fuselage had no windows, relying on a few dim LED strips for illumination. They provided just enough to confirm that he still had no companions beyond the stacks of wooden crates that extended into the gloom. Food, medicine, and clothing, based on the labels.

With no pool to float in, no roads to run on, and no algae-laced smoothies to sip, there seemed to be no reason to get up. Two days after boarding, he could be anywhere in the world. Or off the edge of it.

Still, it could have been worse. The Thor Incident, as he'd decided it would forever be known, had actually cheered him up a bit. The battle had lasted longer than it would have in his prime, but after lying so long in a coma, it was a respectable showing.

And then there was Lisa. Finally, saving the damsel in distress had actually worked out. Far more satisfying than the first time, when said damsel had stabbed him. Or the second time, which had ended with a sniper bullet in his chest. Who knew? Maybe his luck was changing.

The plane hit turbulence, and the motion made him aware that he was lying in a pool of his own sweat. That finally prompted him to ease into a sitting position. The movement was accompanied by a surprising—almost disorienting—lack of pain. A quick probe of his ribs and test of his shoulder turned up no evidence either had ever been injured. There was some residual tenderness in the back of his arm, but the skin had knitted, and there was no sign of infection.

Another miraculous recovery that Lisa would have met with one of her schoolmarm frowns.

Realizing he was starving, he opened a stainless-steel cooler next to his cot to discover that it was full of soft drinks, sandwiches, and rice bowls. Selecting an Italian sub, he smeared it with mustard and washed it down with a root beer before making similar work of a family-sized bag of kettle chips. It all went down pretty well, so he grabbed one of the bowls and took it along for a tour of his new surroundings.

As expected, there wasn't much to be learned. Not a plane used by the US Navy, as near as he could tell—most instructions and warnings were in French. The largest and heaviest of the crates had been pushed up against the cockpit in what appeared to be an intentional effort to prevent him from entering. Doubly effective when combined with his lack of interest in doing so.

Turning up nothing worthy of his attention, he returned to the cot, reattached himself to the Mystery Machine, and sank back into darkness.

WHEN FADE came to again, the Mystery Machine was shut down, and the pitch of the aircraft's engines had changed. Gravity eased, signaling a descent steep enough that it was likely to end on a runway. With no seat belt to fasten or seatback to put in the upright position, he tangled himself in a cargo net and hoped for the best.

They hit the ground hard, bouncing along what his experience told him was a poorly maintained dirt strip. The aircraft had barely come to a stop when the rear began to open, flooding the fuselage with sunlight. He squinted through the glare as an extensive plain surrounded by mountains was revealed.

"This is your stop," a distorted voice said over the intercom. "Take the food and drinks with you."

Fade hesitated for a moment, but then grabbed the cooler and carried it into terrain that looked and smelled completely unfamiliar. There was a shack about twenty yards away, and he started toward it as the plane's loading ramp began to rise. By the time he arrived, the aircraft was already lining up for takeoff.

The tiny building turned out to be constructed of scrap—a single eight-by-eight-foot room under a roof in the process of collapse. There was no electricity, no plumbing, and no communication devices. Only the rusted springs of an ancient mattress and a gas can riddled with bullet holes.

The sun was almost directly overhead, but he managed to find some shade on the north side of the structure. An admittedly spectacular spot. The valley floor was splotched brown and vibrant green, surrounded by rugged peaks all laid out beneath an unbroken blue sky. Other than the airstrip and shack, though, there was no sign of human presence.

The propeller drone became deafening, and Fade closed his eyes to protect them from the dust as the plane passed and took to the air. The sound dissipated quickly, and in less than a minute, the natural silence had reestablished itself.

A pleasant environment in which to assess his situation.

He had no idea where he was or even what hemisphere he was in. Nor did he know why. He was wearing jeans, a T-shirt, and trail running shoes. Beyond that, he had the cooler with a little ice, a few remaining cans of soda, and two sandwiches. A cell phone that likely served no purpose other than to track him rounded out his earthly possessions.

At least it wasn't raining.

THE SUN had set almost an hour ago, but a full moon was doing a good job of filling in. It was notably colder, but given the hint of salt in the air, he was close enough to the sea to moderate further drops in temperature. The cabin contained all the materials necessary to build a fire, but he didn't feel particularly motivated.

The question of what he was doing there became more pressing as the hours passed. The sensation of having been discarded was undeniable, but was it likely? A lot of resources had been expended getting him back on his feet, and if he died there, all would be wasted.

Not that any of it had been a particularly good investment. What good was he to anyone? A legally dead, broken-down former SEAL with a less-than-rosy history with the US government.

Maybe after the Thor Incident, Egan and the people pulling his strings had finally come to that realization. Maybe the shack behind him was their garbage dump. With no obvious source of fluids beyond what was left in the cooler, it wouldn't be long before his skeleton joined that of the mattress inside.

He looked up and focused on a distant mountain to the east. As the valley had gone into shadow, a flickering light had appeared around a third of the way up. Its intensity had grown, but not enough to make out detail. A campsite? House? Well-stocked bar?

Or maybe it was nothing at all. An illusion. Optical or otherwise.

Curiosity eventually got the better of him, and he stood, grabbing a couple of Cokes and a sandwich before starting out across the plain.

20

EVEN WITH the Land Cruiser's high beams and light bar, it was difficult to follow what was left of the road. Egan had already wandered off it a few times, the last landing him grill-down in a dry creek bed. That, combined with a flight delay in Johannesburg, put him well behind schedule. Fade had been parked in the middle of nowhere Madagascar for almost twelve hours now, and Egan was there to collect him. Or at least that was the hope. That, for once in his life, Salam al-Fayed would just sit quietly and not turn a simple situation into an ungodly clusterfuck.

Beyond the halo of artificial light, a hazy valley surrounded by mountains was visible. Temperatures were comfortable enough to keep the windows down, but the bugs were pretty bad. None seemed inclined to bite, but they loved the dashboard gauges so much that they were now unreadable. A good time to take a breath and appreciate that things were more or less under control.

Thor Erickson's body still hadn't been found and likely wouldn't be for some time. His final resting place was at the base of a steep embankment bordering a remote rural road. When he was finally discovered behind the wheel of his wrecked Ferrari, the injuries to his badly decomposed body would be easily explained by his passion for speed and distaste for seat belts.

Lisa had left multiple convincing messages on Erickson's voicemail, begging him to come back, lauding the progress they'd made, and playing up hopes that he'd be able to start next season. Her emails to his coach had received the predicted irritation and promises that they'd try to track him down.

The quality of her performance gave Egan hope that she'd decided to put this behind her. And why not? The cops would see this as an unsurprising—if not inevitable—end to Erickson's life. The media, currently completely obsessed with Yichén Zhu, would relegate the accident to a few lines on the sports page. And with the exception of Cowboys fans, everyone would be better off.

For now, though, all that was thousands of miles away. Out here, there was no radio. No television. No internet. No stories about the increasing desperation of world leaders or speculation about how much destruction they were willing to unleash to save themselves. No lengthy list of elites who had disappeared into hermetically sealed government facilities, private bunkers, and remote country estates. Nothing about China's increasingly violent rhetoric relating to Taiwan as it tried to divert attention from the fact that its leaders had been played for fools.

Egan grabbed his phone from the dash and dialed Fade. It rolled to voicemail just like the twenty times before.

The rough two-track eventually met a graded airstrip that Egan accelerated along. The shack he was looking for was right where it was supposed to be. Fade, on the other hand, wasn't.

He cut the Land Cruiser's lights and stepped out, noting a stainless-steel cooler that still contained some provisions and ice. The cell phone he'd been calling all night was lying in a clump of grass.

Son of a bitch.

He examined the moonlit ground, but its composition wasn't conducive to holding footprints. The local vegetation had a resilience that caused it to spring back into place a few seconds after being stepped on. Walking to the middle of the runway, he scanned the horizon until he came upon a distant flicker to the east. It appeared to be partway up the side of the mountain and, after a minute or so, remained unchanged.

If Fade had gotten bored or decided he'd been abandoned to die, he'd try to find some way to make his last hours entertaining. And that tiny pinpoint of light was the only interesting thing for a hundred miles.

Egan opened the back of his vehicle and pulled out an AR-10 rifle before climbing onto the roof rack. He attached a prototype scope that made everything viewed through it look like a cartoon. It enhanced outlines and color-coded everything it saw—foliage in shades of green, metal blue, humans yellow, and so on. A complete game changer if it hadn't all been wrapped up in a comically heavy package with less than ten minutes of battery life.

Despite the next-gen optics, a sweep of the terrain turned up nothing. With no better option, he climbed back behind the wheel and set off toward the distant light source.

EGAN CUT the engine and lights, standing up through the sunroof to once again scan the landscape. Nothing. The question was, why? Back in the day, it would have been because Fade had already covered thirty miles, using his uncanny sense of direction and smell to find the nearest establishment that served liquor. Not anymore, though. Lisa Thompson was good, but not a miracle worker.

That left the very real possibility that he'd just set off in a random direction with the plan of walking until he dropped. Finally for the last time.

On his scope's second sweep, Egan spotted a sliver of yellow at the very edge of the optic's range. At first, he dismissed it as wishful thinking or an artifact of the beta software, but then it began moving across his line of vision.

Dropping back into the driver's seat, he restarted the vehicle and set all lights to maximum output. It was enough to push thirty kilometers per hour on the buggy speedometer, but no more.

After a few course corrections and what may have been some minor damage to the front suspension, his naked eye picked up something in the distance. A vague shape that transformed into a silhouette and then took on color. The blue of a pair of jeans, the gray of a T-shirt, and finally the intermittent flash of Coke-can red.

He dimmed the light bar and pulled alongside. "Need a ride?"

No reaction at all.

"Fade?"

"What do you think's up there?"

The shimmer ahead was still visible but didn't seem any closer.

"Nothing we'd be interested in."

Fade kept walking. Silent.

"So what's your plan? Find a village? Get a few goats and marry a local girl?"

"Doesn't sound so bad."

"Shut up and get in the car."

AFTER MORE than an hour of bouncing across the valley floor, Egan finally found the mountain pass that would lead them out of it. The occasion was auspicious enough to prompt him to break the silence that had reigned since he'd picked Fade up.

"Not going to ask where we're headed?"

"No."

"I'll tell you anyway. My employer's decided that throwing money around and begging people to act in their own best interest isn't good enough anymore. He wants to build a more convincing capability."

"What's it to me?"

"Seems obvious. He wants you to be part of it."

That got Fade to finally turn toward him. "Why?"

"He sees something in you. No idea what."

"Tell him thanks, but no thanks."

"He'll convince you. He has a weird way of figuring out what people want and giving it to them."

"I don't want anything."

"That's exactly what I told him. But he's not a guy who takes no for an answer."

21

THE WILDERNESS they'd been driving through leveled, with the remnants of irrigation ditches and gates visible to the west. The morning sun spotlighted the mountain they were heading toward, revealing a less jagged, more verdant profile than the ones they'd left behind.

The silence in the Land Cruiser had been nearly absolute for the entire journey. Egan seemed content to focus on his driving, and Fade was equally content to stare through the open window. A while back, a lemur perched on a boulder had answered the question of their location. He'd once seen a documentary about them and recalled that they existed only in Madagascar, an island nation off the coast of Africa. Mozambique, if memory served.

Irrelevant, but interesting. In fact, the country now occupied a unique space in his personal history. It was a bit of a twisted realization, but it was the only one he'd ever been to where no bodies had been left behind. He'd never been the tourist type and thus tended to only travel for work. Afghanistan, Iraq, Belarus, Angola, Lithuania, Ecuador. The list went on. All places he'd been but didn't know anything about. No cathedrals or national parks. No Roman ruins or fancy restaurants. If he'd ever sent a postcard, it would have probably read, *The target walked right out onto his balcony in broad daylight. Great weather. Wish you were here.*

Could this be his moment? If he could catch a glimpse of a baobab tree and find some decent surf, his conversion to a normal human being would be complete. And while he didn't have anyone to send a postcard to, at least the message would be a little more uplifting: *Everyone around me still alive. Great weather. Wish you were here.*

Egan threaded the vehicle through a gap in the trees, and they continued for another few hundred yards before coming to a broad clearing. In a way, it looked like a horror movie version of Club Lisa. The house on the southern edge was about the same size and age but had definitely seen better days. Very little of its original white paint was still clinging, leaving gray, warped boards in various stages of decay. The roof had an alarming bow but looked great compared to the partially collapsed section over the front porch. Window glass was uniformly missing, with plywood substituting on the second floor and dirty plastic sheeting on the first.

At the back of the clearing, a large canvas tent had been set up in the trees. Camo netting was stretched above both it and a dilapidated pickup parked nearby. Probably overkill given the area's remoteness, but overkill was Matt Egan's middle name.

Missing was the barn full of high-tech equipment, manicured lawn, and pool. There was a well that appeared to be in active use, though, and an outhouse that offered further support to the theory that running water wasn't on offer.

"Welcome home," Egan said, turning off the engine.

"Meaning what?"

"I already told you. We're creating an offensive capability. That project started here about a month ago with ten operators from all over the world. Six have washed out. The ones remaining are top-of-the-food-chain. Well trained, well educated, fast, strong, and with extensive psychological testing. And then there's you."

Egan reached over and dug around in the glove box, eventually producing a small plastic box that he held out. "Sleeping pills. A numbered, ten-day supply. The doc tells me you're going to have some trouble without the machine you've been connected to. This'll wean you off. Take them in order and don't take more than one. Apparently, they're pretty toxic."

Fade looked down at the individually packed pills, noting that they got smaller each day. The last one was barely the size of a grain of rice.

Egan laid on the horn for a moment and then got out. Fade followed as people emerged from the tent and surrounding trees. They lined up in the center of the clearing at perfect intervals, spines like ramrods. None spoke, even when he and Egan took positions in front of them.

"Starting on the left, we have Eugene," he said by way of introduction.

They were all likely in their early thirties, but the man, whose name almost certainly wasn't Eugene, looked younger. Tan, healthy, and all-American. Fade guessed no booze, no drugs, and a drawer full of Fellowship of Christian Athletes polo shirts. Probably married his high school sweetheart.

"Good morning, sir."

"Next, we have Ginger."

Red hair, pale skin, reeked of sunscreen. His fatigues were a little less crisp than the others', covering an unremarkable physique. This one was a sleeper. You could tell by the eyes. A man you only got one opportunity to underestimate.

"Good morning, sir." The working-class British accent fit perfectly with the neon sign that might as well have been flashing SAS over his head.

"Second to last, we have Agnes."

"Good morning, sir."

She was more of a challenge. Native-level English with a slight speech impediment that he'd come to associate with Scandinavians. She wore her bland brown hair in a somewhat unruly pixie cut with blond roots. Feminine and attractive in a kind of anonymous way. Her sleeves were rolled up to mid-biceps, showing long, sinewy muscle that accentuated her near six-foot height. A woman who had decided to defeat her male counterparts at whatever game they wanted to play and generally succeeded.

"Finally, we have Duke. When I'm not here, he's in command."

"Good morning, sir."

A second American. Nondescript haircut, beefy, and bearded. One forearm tattooed with something Fade couldn't identify. He looked kind of pissed, but it was hard to say if he actually had something chapping his ass or if it was just a male version of resting bitch face. Not a SEAL. Fade had a nose for his own. And not one of those blockhead recon Marines. Nor a Green Beret. They had sneaky eyes. Probably Delta. The overall impression was of a man who believed in violence as a conflict resolution tool and was good at it.

"I'd like you all to meet Fred. He's going to be joining our little training exercise tomorrow. Questions?"

They stood frozen. It was Duke who finally spoke up.

"Sir, it was our understanding that this isn't so much a training exercise as a final exam."

"That's accurate."

"Permission to speak freely."

"Granted."

"We've been going through hell for weeks now. Most of us didn't make it. But the four of us have. We've trained together, lived together, and bled together. Now, when everything's on the line, you're introducing someone we've never laid eyes on and don't know anything about."

Fade glanced over at his old friend, curious what he'd do. Show some support or throw him under the bus?

"This came from higher up. Not my call."

The bus it was.

22

DESPITE NOT having charged it in days, Fade's unbranded smartwatch was still pumping out data he didn't care about. Time to sunrise: Forty-five minutes. Heart rate: Fifty-one. Temperature: Seventy degrees. Elevation: Three thousand eighty-six feet.

He was sitting in the Land Cruiser's open gate as they bounced across a stretch of grassland north of the encampment. Their fearless leader, Duke, was next to him, with his gear creating a buffer between. Each pack contained food, water, and emergency clothing, and had an MP5 strapped to the side. Egan was behind the wheel, and the rest of the gang was crammed inside.

The pills he'd been given actually worked, and he'd managed to sleep reasonably well. Not Mystery Machine well, but he'd probably spent no more than two hours total listening to the snoring of his new companions. No dreams. Or at least none that had lodged in his memory.

The darkness reminded him of being at sea—his days of being swept along by a current created by DC, his superiors, and his teammates. There was a time when it had all felt so secure. Having every moment of your life planned out for you. Having comrades who would die for you, and vice versa. Eventually, though, he'd started to wonder if that current was pulling him under.

And now, here he was, floating in a much darker version of the waters he'd thought he'd escaped.

The vehicle stopped when the incline became too steep to negotiate. Everyone piled out, shouldering their packs and forming a neat line similar to the one the day before. Fade took a place at one end but was unable to mimic their straight-backed, eyes-ahead enthusiasm.

Egan stared unimpressed at them as his vision adjusted to what was left of the moonlight. "Set me up."

Everyone except Fade went into motion. Duke climbed on top of the Land Cruiser's rack, handing down a cooler, a beach chair, and a large umbrella. The precision of the operation was admittedly impressive—it took them less than thirty seconds to create a comfy little oasis and fall back into formation. Clearly not their first rodeo.

"Straightforward day," Egan said, lowering himself into the chair. "No hostiles or booby traps this time. The mission is simple. Four of my favorite beers are on top of the mountain behind you. I want each of you to bring me one."

He reached into the cooler and pulled out a can of Starbucks espresso, opening it before speaking again. "This was supposed to be a timed event, but now it's not necessary. Four cans. Five people. Easy concept, right? Anyone who comes back with a can gets a job. The person who doesn't gets a ride home."

THE SUN was now in a position to pound relentlessly down on them. The start had been relatively pleasant—cool, open, and not too steep. At the two-hour mark, a carpet of tall, clumpy bushes had presented challenges but also a little shade. It wasn't until they broke back into open terrain that things had gotten interesting. Completely exposed, the land was a combination of loose dirt and shattered stone that caused them to slide back half a step for every one they took forward. Worse, it was scarred with cliff bands that were barely better consolidated and getting increasingly sheer as they continued upward. No clouds were visible in any direction, and the expected breeze at altitude hadn't materialized.

Fade had set a casual pace and was now bringing up the rear. Their implacable team leader was on point, barely visible and going full gas. Agnes was in second position, keeping a solid pace with gazelle-like efficiency. Ginger was third, clearly capable of slamming his fist down on this group anytime he wanted but seeing no reason to do so.

Eugene was a different matter. He was about a hundred yards ahead, looking ragged. His path wandered, and in the loosest sections, he almost completely lost forward momentum. Further, he'd tripped and barely caught himself twice in the last ten minutes. Fade watched as the man started to climb a ten-foot stone wall, lost his grip, and was sent bouncing twenty feet downslope before self-arresting. Once stopped, he managed to push himself into a sitting position, but not to his feet.

"Getting hot," Fade remarked as he came within earshot.

Eugene just looked up at him with eyes that were a little glassy. Clearly, he was in trouble. Maybe he had some kind of low-grade bug. Or the heat was hitting him the wrong way for some reason. Or maybe it was nothing. Sometimes your body just decided to arbitrarily betray you.

Fade grabbed him by the back of his pack and helped him into the shade of the cliff face.

"You all right?"

"Don't worry about me. Worry about you." He was sweating profusely, with salt building up on his forehead and around his mouth. Visible skin had taken on a pale, clammy look, with red blotches around the collar of his fatigues. Reaching out to check his pulse just caused him to jerk away.

Fade dug inside his pack and handed over a gel and some water. "Tell you what. Why don't you wait here. I'll go grab that beer and bring it down to you."

Eugene let out a weak laugh. "You think I'm stupid?"

"Listen to me. I can't stand that prick down there, and I don't want this job. All I want to do is figure out how to move on with my life. But since I'm here, there's no reason I can't help you out."

"My ass."

Fade stared down at him, trying to decide what to do. It was obvious that he wasn't getting across just how deeply he didn't give a shit about Matt Egan, his NGO, or his stupid beer-on-the-top-of-a-mountain stunt. And it was even more obvious that Eugene wouldn't be backing down. Men like him—men like *them*—never backed down. They did their masters' bidding until they went belly-up.

With no better option, Fade dropped his pack, scrambled over the low cliff, and continued up slope at the maximum pace he could maintain. Eugene shouted and tried to follow, but it sounded like he fell again.

The lack of a pack was a significant advantage, but it still took twenty minutes to get close enough to Ginger to make out detail. He'd stopped at the base of yet another cliff band and seemed to be trying to decide whether to go over or around it. When he spotted Fade's approach, he didn't take off, instead watching with bemusement.

"What's up, Freddy?"

His quiet monotone had a weird Zen vibe. Spec ops Gandhi interpreted by David Caruso.

Fade tried to answer but couldn't. Instead, he bent at the waist, gulping air and watching the spit run from his mouth. Is this how everybody else had felt during his military days? Not being Superman sucked.

"Eugene," he panted. "He's in trouble. We need to talk."

"No comms today, mate."

"I know. Can you catch Duke and tell him to come back?"

Asking someone to perform the kind of strong man miracle he'd been so well known for was surprisingly painful. A good lesson in letting go of his ego.

Ginger thought about it for a few seconds and then disappeared effortlessly over the cliff.

"THIS ISN'T a team exercise," Duke said. "It's a race."

Agnes had come back too, and now they were all standing about five hundred yards above the cliff that Eugene had somehow hauled his ass over. He was on his feet and a cursory inspection might hint at improvement. His skin had taken on some color and his eyes tracked whoever was speaking. But anyone not willfully blinding themselves would see the effort he was putting into following the conversation. And worse, he'd stopped sweating.

"Everything's a team exercise," Fade countered.

Agnes looked worried but was sitting this one out. Ginger had his Buddha face on and wasn't one to speak unless addressed directly.

Duke turned to the man in question. "What do you say? Do you want to head down?"

"No, sir."

"How do you feel?"

"One hundred percent."

"Then I don't see the problem," Duke said. "Unless it's with you, Fred. Maybe you don't have what it takes to get to the top and want to lay the blame on someone else."

"Bullshit. All of you know I'm right."

"I don't know any such thing."

"Screw this. Eugene. You and me are starting down. Ginger. Grab two beers. When you pass us on the way back to the car, give him one."

"Happy to do it, mate."

Eugene's answer to what seemed like the greatest plan in the history of plans was to take off up the mountain.

"**SO WHAT** have they got on you?" Fade asked.

The other three had already climbed out of sight because, while Eugene was still putting one foot in front of the other, he was doing so with the speed and agility of a toddler.

"What's it to you?"

"Just passing the time."

The man didn't answer, concentrating entirely on maintaining what little momentum he had. That lasted another five minutes until he stopped to fumble with a water bottle. Fade had to take the lid off for him.

"My older brother," he said, pouring a cautious amount onto his face. "He was in a car accident a few years ago. Got head injured. He can't take care of himself, and my parents are getting old. They can't do what needs to be done, you know?"

"That kind of care's expensive."

"Six figures, man. Six figures to put him somewhere he can live decent. Where the hell is someone like me going to get that kind of scratch?"

"From this gig."

"Yeah. They said they'd put him up for the rest of his life in the best facility in the country. Written contract, everything prepaid."

"Sounds like a good deal."

Eugene stowed his bottle and started up again. "What about you? What do they have on you?"

"I don't know. I'm hoping they'll tell me."

FADE USED a hand to shield his eyes as movement became visible above. With the competition over, it appeared that the winners had decided to descend together.

He and Eugene were propped with their backs against a boulder. It put them in full sun, but the angle of the rays had flattened to the point that the heat was bearable. Fade took a sip from his bottle, swishing the water around to try to free some of the grit clinging to his teeth.

He stayed locked on his new teammates' approach until their distended shadows settled over him. Ginger reached into his pack's side pocket and retrieved a PBR, holding it out toward Eugene.

"Wake up, mate. I got your beer."

"He doesn't need it."

"Why?" Duke asked.

"He's dead."

23

THE TRAIN had officially jumped the track.

Fade had seen Matt Egan mad before, but not like this. The man prided himself on being the icy calculator you wouldn't see coming. Now here he was, screaming like some kind of coked-up baseball coach after losing the big game.

The six of them were among the trees, three at attention in their neat little line, Fade keeping a little distance, and Eugene in a simple pine box. The only illumination was from what little moonlight could filter through the leaves, but it was enough. Maybe too much.

Eugene had taken a beating on the journey down the mountain, suffering no fewer than three incidents that Duke had dubbed *momentary uncontrolled descents*. Blood had soaked through his fatigues, drying to a rusty black, and there was a six-inch gash down the left side of his face. Normally, the dead had some aura of peace around them, but this was an exception. The damage from what Fade more accurately dubbed *getting dropped off cliffs* wasn't the worst of it. That honor went to the rigor mortis that made the body's position in the coffin angular and unnatural.

A shallow hole had been dug, and the sooner Eugene was in it the better. But it didn't look like it was going to be that easy.

"This was your command!" Egan shouted, bringing his face to within an inch of Duke's. "Your man! Your failure!"

"I asked him how he felt, sir! He told me he was one hundred percent."

"Does he look a hundred percent to you?"

"Sir. I didn't—"

"*Does he look a hundred percent?*" The repeated question came at an eardrum-damaging volume.

"No, sir."

Egan turned. "And the rest of you? What was your assessment?"

No one answered.

"Look," Fade started when it became clear that the question wasn't rhetorical. "At this point, it's a little la—"

"Shut the fuck up!" Egan said, jabbing a finger in his direction. "I'm not talking to you. I'm talking to them."

With options waning, Ginger finally spoke up. "Fred's the one who noticed. He was in last position, and then he caught me and had me bring everyone together. He said he'd start down with Eugene and that I should bring two beers and give him one. It was a good idea. But Eugene wasn't having any."

"I'm asking you how he looked at that point."

"Bad."

Egan turned his attention back to Duke. When he spoke, his voice had evened out. Cold, like Fade remembered, but with something lurking just beneath the surface. Not the familiar control. The opposite.

"And what was your reaction?"

"This wasn't a team exercise, sir. It was a race to see who was going to make the grade."

Egan nodded and then swung a foot up between the man's legs hard enough to lift him off the ground. When Duke inevitably pitched forward, he caught a vicious uppercut to the face that sent him toppling backward, with blood gushing from a flattened nose.

Fade and the others watched silently as Egan dragged the semiconscious man to the coffin and deposited him on top of the corpse inside. He then put the lid on and knelt on top of it, dumping a bag of nails.

The sound of them being hammered into place mostly obscured Duke's hands pounding the inside of the plywood, but not so much his shouts. Still, no one interfered as Egan finished the job and then dragged the entire thing into the hole.

"Fill it in," he said, pointing to two shovels leaning against a tree.

No one moved.

He pulled his Glock from its holster and aimed it in Agnes and Ginger's direction. "Was I not clear?"

That got them moving, but with almost comical slowness. It took a good ten minutes for them to cover the box, despite the fact that the lid was only a couple inches below ground. During that time, the pounding and shouting from inside grew in intensity.

"Command is a sacred duty," Egan said when they were done. "Duke's primary responsibility was to his team, and he betrayed that trust for his own ambitions. That cost the life of one of his men. And now he's going to pay the price. Dismissed."

They looked down at the freshly churned dirt, the gun aimed at them, and then to Fade. He nodded subtly toward the tent, and after a short hesitation, they started toward it. Egan holstered his weapon and went in the opposite direction, climbing onto the porch of the dilapidated farmhouse and disappearing inside.

"IS THAT your only glass?" Fade said, crossing the threshold uninvited.

Egan was sitting in a broken chair pushed up to an even more broken table. A battery-powered desk lamp sat next to a half-empty bottle of Jack Daniel's. Other than that, there wasn't much. A rotting sofa with a blanket thrown over it, the skeleton of a kitchen with no remaining appliances, and a hole where the sink used to be. Interior walls were in the process of disintegrating and covered in peeling wallpaper that appeared to have at one time been full of color.

"Yes," Egan responded and then slid the bottle across the table. "They say alcohol will probably kill you if you mix it with those sleeping pills you're taking. But help yourself. That's what you want, right?"

Fade didn't reach for it, instead going for an overturned chair in the corner. He pulled it up to the table and sat carefully, unsure if it would support his weight.

His old friend had bulked up since they'd last spent any real time together. Not fat, though. The way he'd manhandled a coffin containing two men proved that. His dark hair was back in its military configuration, the way he'd worn it before he'd married Elise. The real difference, though, was his eyes. They never seemed to fix on anything.

"So did I get the job?"

"For some reason, you get graded on a curve. Your charmed existence continues."

Fade looked around the dim room. "Yeah. This is great. You and me have the world by the ass."

"Why didn't you do something?"

"About what?"

"About Eugene."

"I wasn't in command."

"That never stopped you before."

"This isn't before, man. I'm not Fade. I haven't been for a long time. I'm just Fred now."

Egan finally looked at him, but it was hard to know what he saw. "It's different when you're not the best, isn't it? Everything was always too easy for you."

"That's not the way I remember it."

Egan just returned his gaze to the glass in his hand, so Fade continued.

"You put them in a tough position. The people you work for figure out what people need—what they're desperate for—and give it to them, right? They weren't going to let that go so easily."

No response.

"What about you, Matt?"

"What about me?"

"What are you doing here?"

"Do you really want to know?"

He wasn't sure, but he nodded anyway.

Egan retrieved his phone, tapping in a few commands before sliding it across the table. Fade picked it up and saw that the screen had a play button in the middle. He pressed it.

The man who appeared was young, naked, and secured to a metal chair. His struggles to escape had caused the rope around his chest to saw through a landscape of bad tattoos. Blood now mixed with sweat, creating a pink film over the lower half of his body.

Somewhere off camera a door opened and footsteps became audible. The kid's head rose, and his eyes found the person who had entered.

"Who the fuck are you?"

Fade's thumb hovered over the phone's screen, knowing he should shut down the video but finding it impossible to do so.

"What do you want?" the young man said, the pitch of his voice rising.

The only answer was the unmistakable hiss and bluish glow of a butane torch being lit. A moment later, Egan entered the frame.

"I want my family back."

And that was enough. Fade stopped the playback, but not before noting that it had almost another three hours of run time.

"The cops knew who did it," Egan said before taking a slug of the Jack. "But they didn't have anything that would hold up in court. No witnesses that were willing to talk."

"So the people you work for got you the name."

"They did more than that. The police knew my background and made it clear that vigilantism wouldn't be tolerated. Hilarious, right? Gunning down a defenseless woman and child for fun doesn't generate much interest from the cops. But if I took it on myself to do their job, I'd end up behind bars for the rest of my life."

"They gave you an alibi."

Egan nodded and looked down at the phone on the table between them. "The cops called me when his mother reported him missing, but I was in Munich and had been for a month. By the time I got back to the States, they'd lost interest."

The fact that Egan had done this wasn't that much of a shock. They'd both involved themselves in worse for nothing more than a meager paycheck and a pat on the back. But keeping the video on his phone? Why? Did he spend his weekends eating popcorn and projecting it on the wall of his living room?

That was some sick shit.

The temperature had dropped significantly by the time Fade exited onto the porch and started across the clearing. As he closed on their newly christened cemetery, he could still hear one of its two occupants. No shouts anymore. Only a weak, intermittent pounding.

The air became denser as he penetrated the trees, carrying the scent of sweat in two distinct flavors. Something that would have been imperceptible to most people.

"Come out," he said quietly.

A moment later, Ginger and Agnes appeared from the shadows.

"We can't leave him like this," she said.

The Brit remained silent, but his presence implied agreement.

"Clear enough dirt off that he can get air. But do it quietly. No shovels, just hands. In a few hours, when Matt's asleep, we'll get him out."

"Matt," Agnes said. "That's his real name? You know him?"

Fade shook his head. "Not anymore."

IT HAD taken a little over ninety minutes for the lights to go out in the farmhouse—about the time Egan would need to polish off the rest of his bottle. At least Fade hoped that was the case. In any event, they now seemed to be as close to the Goldilocks zone as they were going to get. There had been no sound from the building for almost two hours, and it would be another two before they were in any danger of him getting up to take a piss.

Fade watched the front door from the trees while Ginger and Agnes performed the delicate task of removing nails. Silence was critical, making the operation far more time-consuming than expected. Around two and a half minutes to carve out around the heads, then another thirty to ease the nail out.

"Last one," Agnes whispered.

Fade returned to the casket and knelt, helping them lift the lid. Duke looked dazed, but the bleeding had stopped, and he was able to sit up under his own power. They got him on his feet, and Fade ducked under an arm, offering support as they skirted the clearing. The man got stronger with every step, and by the time they reached the pickup truck, he was able to propel himself under his own power.

"Your gear's in the back," Fade said. "The tank's full and the keys are in the ignition. Start it up and floor it out of here. Keep your head down until you're clear of the farmhouse."

His expression was hard to read. Some of that was the result of the smashed nose and dried blood, but not all. A man like him wouldn't be inclined to let a beating like that go unavenged. Or maybe it wasn't that at all. Maybe he needed what Egan was offering so bad that he was thinking about going begging.

"Listen to me," Fade said. "If he ever lays eyes on you again, only one of you is going to walk away. And even if that's you, it's not going to get you what you want. Seek your fortune elsewhere."

Duke stood frozen for a few seconds before climbing into the cab. He reached for the keys, but then paused and looked out the open window. "I may be a prick, Fred, but I'm not an ungrateful one. If you ever find yourself in a bind, look me up."

A moment later, he was roaring across the clearing and into the narrow corridor of trees that would take him out of there.

The farmhouse remained lifeless.

24

LAST TO arrive, Fade crossed the porch and passed through the farmhouse's open door. Despite the gloom, he left his sunglasses on to protect pupils that seemed increasingly unresponsive. Probably a side effect of his quickly miniaturizing sleeping pills.

The members of the team—what was left of it—were just standing around staring at one other, so he set a course for a tiny propane refrigerator he hadn't noticed the night before.

"Nice of you to join us," Egan said.

Fade flipped him off before digging out one of the disgusting Mountain Dews his old friend favored, downing it, and going in for another. Despite the waning medication, he'd managed to sleep reasonably well. The dreams were coming back, though. Mostly Eugene standing in the forest, body stiff and contorted. Watching.

Not particularly alarming in the scheme of things. The dead coming back for a visit wasn't anything new to him. He'd left a lot of bodies in his wake, and sometimes they had things to say. Not this one, though. He just stared.

Silence reigned as Fade dropped onto the sofa. A few seconds later, Egan started talking again. The tone was recognizable even after all these years: business.

"I expected there to be a stronger force in this room today, but obviously things haven't gone as planned. Not ideal, but it is what it is. This is the army we have. And as such, it's probably time to introduce ourselves."

Agnes looked a little uncertain but was the first to wade in. "My real name is Linea Mäkinen. I was a sniper in the Finnish special forces."

That seemed to be all she had to say, so Egan stepped in. "Linea was in command of a team that ran into a group of Russian operatives who'd crossed the border to sabotage a Finnish power plant. There was a firefight, and Linea got four confirmed kills. Three of her men were injured but, because of her, all survived. Despite being outnumbered, they took down all the Russians except two, who they captured. For obvious reasons, no official report was ever made and the Russian government denied involvement."

She gave an uncomfortable nod and looked over at the Brit next to her.

"Daniel Harding," he said, in his customary monotone. "SAS originally. MI6 after. Now here. I've seen action in the Middle East, Africa, Asia, and some other places I won't mention. Straight-up combat, rescue missions, assassinations. Whatever little chore queen, king, or country required."

Now they both fixed on the sofa. Undoubtedly the moment they'd been waiting for. After a month training together, their revelations would be pretty much as expected. But Fade was a wild card.

"You really want me to do this?" Fade said, glancing over at his old friend.

He nodded.

"Fine. It's your party. My name's Salam al-Fayed. I used to be in the navy."

Their eyes widened. Once again, Linea was the first to speak. "I thought you were dead."

"Me too," Harding agreed.

"Since your reputation seems to precede you," Egan said. "We'll move on. For any—"

"Aren't we forgetting someone?" Linea said.

Egan smiled. "You can just call me Matt."

Neither seemed satisfied by the answer, but they reluctantly accepted it.

"For anyone who's curious, we're in Madagascar. While we're protected by the isolated location of this camp, there's a significant amount of guerrilla activity causing problems in other rural areas. A number of NGOs operate here, but they haven't been particularly effective. In fact, it'd be fair to describe some of them as counterproductive. They deliver food to struggling locals, but the moment they leave, insurgents come through, take the food, eat half of it, and trade the other half for weapons. At this point, a lot of innocent people are surviving mostly by eating insects."

He tapped his finger on a map centered on the table he'd been drinking at the night before. Fade couldn't see it from his position lying on the sofa, but Linea and Harding were interested enough to crowd around.

"There's a village not too far from here that's been particularly hard hit. A number of children have already died from malnutrition and related illnesses."

"What's this to us?" Fade asked, since no one else seemed inclined to.

"Tomorrow morning, an NGO is scheduled to make a delivery to the village in question. We're going to offer protection."

"Would we be working for the NGO directly?" Linea asked.

"Not exactly."

"I don't understand," Harding said. "Protection for who? You said the aid workers don't need it. Are we talking about the villagers?"

"Yes."

"But even if the guerrillas scare off easily, time is on their side," Linea said. "We can't stay there forever, and the moment we're gone, everything goes back to the way it was."

"There are other options."

"For fuck's sake," Fade said. "Just say it, man. This isn't a security detail, it's an extermination operation. You want us to hide in the bushes until guerrillas show up and get rid of them."

"Now why didn't I think of that?"

"Hold on," Linea said. "Protecting a food shipment and the villagers it's being delivered to is one thing. But this is something completely different. Whose authority are we working under? Is the local government even aware we're here?"

"You're working under my authority," Egan said. "And no. The local government isn't aware we're here. Is that a problem? Because everyone here is free to leave."

Fade considered taking him up on that offer, but the perpetual question remained: Where would he go? In all the hours he'd spent thinking about trajectories for his new life, he hadn't yet come up with any actionable conclusions. He desperately needed to quit being sucked along by other peoples' currents, but right now there was no shore in sight.

"No one?" Egan said. "Okay then. Let's talk specifics . . ."

25

FADE INSTINCTIVELY wanted to put his hand on the tiller, but there was none. The rubber watercraft they were in was about the size of the Zodiacs he'd used in the navy but with a couple of significant differences. First, it was less than half the weight, allowing his three-person team to easily carry it. And second, the hidden electric motor had no controls. Not even an on-off button.

Apparently, it could be operated with a phone app, but in this case, Matt Egan was piloting both it and a surveillance drone from parts unknown. Fade, Linea, and Harding had forgone the normal water incursion apparel for casual wet suits that conjured the image of a diving trip that had run late. Temperatures were holding at around eighty, and there was only light chop as they paralleled the shoreline. Three hundred yards away, the sand beach glowed pleasantly in the celestial light before disappearing into a palm forest.

All they lacked were a few piña coladas and wood for a bonfire.

"Eighteen minutes," Egan said over their custom earpieces. The clarity was startling—apparently the product of an AI system that recognized his words and tone, then reproduced them as though he was sitting a foot away. Eerie, but effective.

Kind of a good way to describe the whole operation. What the hell were they doing there? Was a onetime intervention really going to set some remote village on the path to peace and prosperity? Was it a test? And if so, of what? The gear? Them? The concept of turning a charity into an army?

Save the Children. Or Else.

No. Wait. *Assassins Without Borders.*

He glanced at Linea sitting near the bow, and then at Harding a few feet behind. If they'd come this far, both felt like they were getting something valuable in return. And that put him in his customary position of odd man out. He didn't have a brother in need of medical attention, a dead wife to avenge, or a desperate desire to save the world. No, he was sitting there catching salt spray in the face because he didn't have anything better to do. In the end, his act three was shaping up a lot like acts one and two. A little flailing around. A little killing. Death. Resurrection. Repeat.

"One minute out," the computer impersonating Egan said. "Thermal on the beach and surrounding area are clear."

Fade put on a pair of flippers and grabbed the dry bag next to him. When as the hum of the electric motor fell silent, all three of them went over the side.

The bags had been set up to work as flotation devices, riding just beneath the surface when held to their chests. Linea and Harding immediately started toward shore, but Fade paused for a moment when he heard air escaping behind him. The raft—their ride—was sinking. According to Egan, it would wait for them a few feet underwater and automatically reinflate when—if—they returned.

Rad.

"I'VE GOT eyes on the NGO truck," Harding said over the comm. "ETA to the village is approximately fifteen minutes."

"Correction," Egan said. "Twelve. Based on historical surveillance, it will arrive in just over twelve."

"Copy that. Twelve minutes."

Fade sighted through the scope of a brand new SIG MCX-SPEAR LT, scanning the rutted two-track rising behind him. The terrain in this part of the island was rugged, with most covered by dry grass growing up to a couple of feet high. Plants that straddled the line between small trees and large bushes grew in random clumps, with the occasional baobab towering above. Wind was currently completely absent and not predicted to make an appearance until well after they were gone. Good for accuracy, but the sun was getting hot.

He turned downslope to study the village again. It consisted of seventeen huts spaced across a dusty two-acre clearing. The dwellings were relatively primitive, made largely of sticks with grass roofs and the occasional clay wall—too thin to stop a bullet. Along the south side was a modernish well and a pen with a few goats. Angular agricultural plots to the east contained nothing but dry, dead plants, victims of a brutal multiyear drought.

At this point, most of the inhabitants seemed to be out in the open. Women were cooking what little they had over open fires, skinny kids were lethargically kicking around a ball made of grass, and men were having feverish conversations in knots of three or four. Overall, he'd counted forty-three people, twenty-five of whom were children. He imagined that there were a few sick or elderly people still inside the huts, but it was hard to say for sure. Neither category would survive long under these conditions.

"Fade, the truck should be visible to you," Egan said.

He rolled on his back, lining his scope up on a vehicle just starting to ease its way over a pronounced crest. It was likely military in origin, with massive tires, a two-person cab, and a fully enclosed cargo area. Its original drab green had been eradicated, replaced by dusty white beneath the red logo of a charity he'd never heard of. Being easily identifiable was critical to its occupants' safety. The local insurgents would consider it completely off-limits. Never bite the hand that feeds.

It picked its way down, finally stopping near the center of the village, where two Caucasian men jumped out. Smiles were strained on both sides, and greetings were muted. Interestingly, the villagers didn't lift a finger to help unload the vehicle. Instead, the aid workers did it all themselves, displaying the lack of precision and speed of people who wanted out of there as fast as possible.

In twenty minutes, their mission was accomplished, both men were tucked safely inside the truck, and it was lumbering back the way it had come. In another ten, they'd cleared the rise and disappeared from view.

If the guerrillas stayed in their well-worn groove, they'd show up in about an hour and a half. Two pickups, each containing four armed men. They'd terrorize the desperate locals for ten minutes or so before forcing them to load the unopened aid crates into the vehicles. Then they'd disappear until the next delivery.

Fade's idea had been to take them out at a beautiful little ambush site about two miles to the north. A couple of RPGs and it'd all be over in a literal flash. Egan, always the buzzkill, had pointed out a few flaws in the plan. First of all, the destruction of the food. The second was that the use of that kind of weapon would point to outside actors and potentially trigger an investigation. Better to make it look like a rival gang.

And that was how simple became complicated.

RPGs had been replaced with weapons using ammunition common in the area, and they'd made the decision to attack the insurgents on their way out instead of their way in. The problem was that shooting at unloaded, descending pickups could carry the fight to the village. Better to hit them when the vehicles were heavy, difficult to maneuver, and on a climb that averaged twelve percent.

Linea also preferred Egan's plan for the reason that she was still concerned about whose authority they were acting under. Killing the men before they'd committed a crime turned the whiff of vigilantism into the stench of murder. It seemed like splitting hairs, but if it made her feel better, what the hell?

The villagers surrounded the crates, and Fade watched as one of the older men began to speak, indicating the fresh supplies and the road they'd arrived on. Then he used a shovel to open the nearest. Everyone rushed forward, snatching up cans, bags, and cardboard containers.

"Matt," Fade said over his throat mic. "They're eating. You told me they never eat any of this stuff."

In fact, Egan hadn't just told him. He'd shown drone footage of the last five drop-offs. The people always gathered around the boxes but did nothing more than stare longingly at them. A few sniveling kids occasionally tried to approach but were held back by similarly teary mothers. He'd seen a lot of spectacularly depressing things over the course of his life, but that footage managed to tick into the top five.

"They never have," Egan responded. "The men coming for it are somehow getting hold of an inventory and know if anything's missing."

"Well, they're digging in now. What's changed?"

"I don't know."

"They may have just gotten so desperate they have no choice," Linea said. "Or maybe the guerrillas decided that if they starve, there won't be more deliveries?"

Fade let out a long breath, keeping his eye to the scope. Like it was ever that simple.

"CONFIRMING TWO pickup trucks," Harding said. "Two men in each cab, two men in each bed. The ones in back are carrying AKs."

"We should assume the same for the men inside," Egan said. "They have been in the past."

Based on their intel, it would take about half an hour total for the villagers to load the food and the guerrillas to get tired of tormenting them. Three minutes after returning to the vehicles, they'd pass Fade's position. At around seven, they'd run into Linea and Harding, who would engage, while Fade was responsible for cutting off anyone who attempted to flee back downslope. The chances of any of those men surviving long enough to run were pretty low, though, making his role in this operation intentionally nonexistent. His new comrades didn't know him well enough to bet their lives on his performance. Egan, on the other hand, knew him as well as anyone and felt the same.

Through his scope, he saw the women start confiscating food from the children while a couple of men carted away the opened crate. Once everything was cleaned up, the kids were herded toward the huts and barricaded inside with their mothers.

That was very much not on the program. Historically, the entire village lined up and waited subserviently for the arrival of the men starving them.

Fade could hear the trucks approaching from behind and flattened himself in the grass as they passed. When he dared raise his head again, the village men had taken up seemingly random positions around the aid shipment. Some were crouching to probe the dirt beneath their feet.

Shit.

"We've got a problem," Fade said, starting to crawl toward the village. "I think they've decided to fight."

"What?" Egan said. "Why do you think that?"

"The women and children have locked themselves away, and the men look like they've buried things around the crates. I'm betting weapons, but I'm on my way to have a closer look."

"Negative. Stay where you are. We're continuing with our plan, or we're aborting the operation."

"I'm just looking," Fade said. "No harm in that."

"Return to your position. That's an order."

Fade ignored him, getting to his feet in an effort to pick up the pace. The trucks were pulling in, and he didn't have much more time before they shut down their engines. After that, it'd be necessary to move more deliberately in order to remain silent.

He made it to the last stand of trees bordering the village and dropped, shimmying forward as the pickups rolled to a stop. The insurgents leaped from the cabs and beds, brandishing their weapons and creating an unintelligible tapestry of what appeared to be unnecessary instructions, threats, and obscenities. Fade kept moving, meandering a bit to remain in grass tall enough to provide cover.

Despite this being an almost monthly affair, the insurgents' operation wasn't exactly a well-oiled machine. First, there was no indication that they'd yet noticed the absence of two-thirds of the population. Even more interesting, the men who'd been riding in the truck beds were swaying in a way that implied drugs or alcohol. The driver of the lead vehicle was the only one without a rifle. Instead, he wore a pistol holstered Old West style, the belt supporting it hidden beneath an impressive stomach. The bored expression and hint of gray hair were consistent with command.

"I'm moving into a position to cover the village," Linea said over his earpieces.

Egan's response was immediate. "Negative. Hold your position."

She didn't acknowledge, leaving her actions ambiguous. Harding remained silent.

"I can see that they're starting to load the crates," Egan said. "Our plan hasn't changed. I repeat. Our plan hasn't changed. We take them on their way out. What does or doesn't happen in that village is irrelevant."

Irrelevant was an easy word to use when your view was a drone feed. On the ground, though, these assholes didn't look particularly tolerant. If they were attacked, there was going to be a bloodbath. And in the very likely event the insurgents came out on top, that bloodbath was going to extend to the women and children. Their stick and grass huts had an alarming resemblance to the ones that hadn't worked out so well for the Three Little Pigs.

But maybe Egan was right. The loading of the crates was going smoothly enough that the guerrillas' short attention spans were kicking in. Guns were largely slung, cigarettes had appeared, and the drunkest of the eight had wandered off in pursuit of one of the village's more attractive goats.

They were almost done when pregnant John Wayne started pointing at the crates and asking questions. Probably about the missing one, but there wasn't time for speculation. He'd unknowingly fired the starting gun.

A few of the villagers attacked straight on, using knives and homemade shivs. Others crouched, grabbing hoes and other farm tools buried just beneath the dusty surface.

"Everyone pull back!" came Egan's voice over his earpieces. "Now!"

Instead, Fade began sprinting toward the fight. So far, the village men were doing pretty well keeping the insurgents confused and close enough to reduce the usefulness of the rifles. The obvious exception was the goat aficionado. He was twenty meters out, clawing the AK from his shoulder and stumbling toward the unfolding battle. Fade stopped and swung his weapon toward him, but before he could line up, the man went face down in the dirt. At first, it just looked like alcohol-induced clumsiness, but then he realized that it was Linea Mäkinen living up to her reputation.

The problem was that she'd exhausted her only viable target. The close-quarters nature of the fighting would significantly reduce her effectiveness. Even with his proximity, Fade didn't have any shots that wouldn't endanger the people they were there to save.

Worse, the tide was turning against the villagers. They had guts for sure, but that didn't change the fact that they were half-starved farmers. Going for surprise had been smart, but the problem with surprise was that it didn't last long.

The first combatants Fade reached were two men struggling for control of a knife. No point shooting when the butt of his rifle would be just as effective. He slammed it into the side of the insurgent's head as he passed, catching the dropped knife and depositing it between the shoulder blades of another.

A muffled gunshot sounded, and for a moment, he thought it might be Linea again. Unfortunately, it turned out to be a report from John Wayne's pistol, muted by the noise-cancellation circuitry in his earpieces.

A farmer went down but didn't seem to have been hit. The guerrilla behind wasn't so lucky. He'd taken his commander's bullet in the small of his back, dropping with an agonized scream. Fade collided with two men locked in battle, and all three of them toppled. As they did, he managed to retrieve his combat knife and draw it across the throat of the insurgent who had landed next to him. The suspension of the pickup a few feet away had been lifted to make it more suitable for the rough terrain, and Fade was able to roll under with an inch to spare. Someone started shooting at the vehicle on full auto, but with zero discipline. By the time Fade came out the other side, the man's magazine was depleted, and he was sprinting toward the huts. A puff of dust appeared just behind his heels, the result of an overly conservative shot from Linea. She had the same problem he did—a stray or penetrating round would go straight through the dwellings beyond. The fleeing guerrilla collided with a wall and did exactly that, disappearing inside.

Fade rose from behind the truck, sweeping his rifle smoothly over the scene and finding no targets. There were two insurgents still alive but on the ground being ruthlessly beaten with farm implements. John Wayne was one of them, his considerable bulk extending his lifespan, but likely not by much.

"Behind you!" Egan shouted over the comm.

Fade spun and dropped as a bullet passed overhead. The man who'd so gracelessly entered the closest hut hadn't been smart enough to keep going through the other side. Instead, he'd decided to rejoin the fight, holding a sobbing woman in front of him as a shield.

"Linea?" Fade said.

"No way. I'm at the limit of this gun's range. The man by the corral was just luck."

Fade held his weapon in front of him, slowly approaching the man and his hostage.

"Danny?"

"I'm still running up the road, mate. Another thirty seconds before I can even see you."

"Stop! I'll kill her!" the insurgent shouted.

The woman was struggling enough to make it impossible for him to steady his rifle, but he also seemed reluctant to point it directly in Fade's direction. Likely he assumed that his opponent would shoot through her if he felt endangered. So instead, his barrel was aimed in the general direction of the farmers who had finished off John Wayne and now appeared to be suffering a postcombat daze. The first time was always the worst.

"Put your gun down!" the man said.

Fade registered that his words didn't track the movement of his mouth. It was like those Chinese martial arts movies he used to watch as a kid. *Your kung fu is strong, but it is no match for my crane technique!*

"Do it now! I want a truck. I'll release her when I get over the hill."

His earpieces. They were translating real time. How cool was that? Even better than the raft.

Fade kept his voice calm, as though he was trying to negotiate a deal. In fact, he was addressing Linea. Hopefully, this prick didn't speak any English.

"I think you can make this shot. You're the best, right? Matt wouldn't have hired you otherwise."

The man just stared at him, confused. So far, so good.

"This isn't my TKIV," she said. "I'm shooting local 762 by 39 through a weapon I'd never seen before today. Don't be stupid."

"You're selling yourself short," Fade said, crouching to put his weapon down. "Go for it. Lob one in."

When he began to rise again the insurgent shoved the woman aside in order to line up a shot. His finger tensed on the trigger, but before he could pull it, a tiny red cloud sprung from the back of his head. He jerked forward and fired but did nothing more than kick up some dust in front of his feet.

Linea's round had barely grazed his skull, and he landed on all fours, unwilling to fully collapse but also unable to lift his weapon. Fade grabbed him by the chin and hair, spinning his head until he heard a satisfying crack.

When he turned to survey the battlefield, he noted that all the villagers were alive and on their feet. Some were a little worse for the wear, and one had a deep gash in his leg, but even he seemed more interested in the stranger in their midst than the fact that he was losing a fair amount of blood.

LINEA STOOD watching Harding bandage the leg of an injured farmer while she typed instructions into her phone's translator. The antibiotics she was going to provide were a little complicated to take, and their earpieces only worked in one direction. She had no problem understanding what the villagers said, but all they heard when she responded was English.

After proving himself to be one of the most reckless combat operatives in history, Fade was now kicking around a makeshift soccer ball with the village kids. He seemed to be able to do just about anything he wanted with it, and despite the carnage around them, the children were having the time of their lives. Their parents watched from the sidelines, adoring expressions more appropriate for a religious figure than a psychotic former SEAL. One started shouting and the others joined in, chanting something over and over again. Their thick accents made it difficult to understand.

"Are they chanting his name?"

"Sounds like it," Harding said, smoothing the bandage and giving the victim a thumbs-up. "Done. We should get out of here."

Her jaw clenched as she handed over a Z-pak and prompted her phone to provide dosage instructions in Malagasy. The man nodded vigorously, and his wife grabbed her hand, shaking it with equal enthusiasm.

"Fade!" Harding shouted. "Time to go!"

Fade struggled to break free from the children clinging to him. They finally relented but joined their parents' chant.

"What part of 'I don't have a shot' didn't you understand?" Linea said when he got close enough to hear.

"Come on, Lin. You made the most badass clutch shot I've ever seen and defeated the forces of evil. How is that not a good day?"

He passed without slowing, and she turned toward Harding for support. He just picked up his rifle and followed.

26

FADE EASED the Land Cruiser around a ditch still running with a trickle of water and angled northwest. A large screen on the dash acted as some kind of next-generation GPS, transparent except for a yellow arrow telling him where to go. Off a cliff probably.

After declining Egan's job offer, he'd been given the vehicle and told that it would take him back to the airstrip he'd arrived on. Linea and Harding had stayed behind to clean up the camp. Based on the distant plume of smoke in his rearview mirror, they were doing a thorough job. Egan had never been a fan of loose ends.

He leaned out the open window, looking up at a cloudless sky through dark sunglasses. Still empty, but that was likely more apparent than real. In this day and age, you rarely got to see death coming. Drones, missiles, landmines. It was a failing of modern warfare in his estimation. Combat should be about blood, adrenaline, and lactic acid. Now, like everything else, it was starting to have a strange sense of simulation.

He'd actually thought the new and not-so-improved Matt Egan might just put a bullet in him back at the camp. Apparently, that was still a little too up close and personal for his taste. While their friendship had imploded spectacularly, the long, intense history was still there.

Or maybe it was just that pumping a round into his face in front of Linea and Danny would be a poor start to their working relationship. When it came to troop expendability, better not to say the quiet part out loud.

So there he was again. The clothes on his back. A cell phone that was probably only useful for targeting. A Land Cruiser with a tank three-quarters full. And a folder full of fake IDs.

He leaned forward, this time looking at the sky through the dusty windshield. Any time now.

Nada.

Better to just kick back and let his mind go blank. The problem was that ever since he was a kid, he'd had an unrelenting avalanche of internal monologue. What would happen if a black hole floated by the earth? Why did popcorn pop when it got hot? Was Elvis still alive? Was plaid in or out?

Death and coma were two of the three things that could quiet it. The third was combat. It made everything disappear except him and his opponent. Fear, pain, and instinct had a way of overwhelming unanswered questions about duck-billed platypus anatomy.

The yellow arrow on the dash began to turn red, and he let the Land Cruiser drift to an idle. Ahead, the glint of an aircraft was just barely visible.

"Hey, Google," he said to the phone resting in the passenger seat. "What now?"

Last time he'd asked, a Rihanna video had come up. This time it spoke: "Keep going."

The plane parked on the dirt runway turned out to be sleek, flawlessly white, and improbably large, without any identifying marks beyond a tail number. He didn't know anything about private jets, but if this one had been a car, it'd be a Lamborghini.

Even more interesting was the man sitting with his back propped against the shack Fade had explored a few days before. He looked to be in his early forties, with unruly hair and a physique that was just shy of muscular. Beyond that, jeans, a logo-free T-shirt, and cowboy boots. When the Land Cruiser closed to around a hundred yards, he turned to watch its approach.

Fade stopped just past the airstrip and stepped out. The man didn't rise, instead reaching into a cooler that looked to be the one he'd left behind. By the sound his hand made, the ice had been replenished.

"Beer?" he said, fishing one out and popping the cap. "Nonalcoholic, I'm afraid. Those pills you're taking—"

"Matt told me."

He just sat there, holding out the beer. Not sure what else to do, Fade took it and a position in the shade next to him.

"How are you feeling?"

"Fine. You?"

"Disappointed that you turned down my offer." He held out a hand. "I'm sorry. I suppose I should introduce myself..."

"Jon Lowe," Fade said.

He smiled and the hand dropped. "You're a secret fan of reclusive billionaires?"

"Only some."

"Do tell."

Fade took a pull on his fake brew. Not as bad as you'd think. "The internet."

"That's your story? The internet?"

"I was doing some reading about coma recovery."

"Understandable. And?"

"And I came across an article about a pharmaceutical company that'd developed a drug for bringing people back. But when they started testing it on animals, there were problems."

"What kind of problems?"

"It only worked twenty percent of the time. The other eighty, it killed them."

"What's that have to do with me?"

"You own the company that did the research."

"Those are pretty distant dots to connect. And I tend not to allow my photo to be included in articles like that."

"It also said you'd backed away from the private sector and started a charitable foundation looking for pragmatic solutions to the world's problems." Fade indicated the landscape with his beer bottle. "And now here we are in Madagascar."

"Bravo," Lowe said, but offered nothing more.

"Is this the part of the island where you grew up?"

"No. The aid agency my parents worked for was based in Antananarivo. But they spent most of their time in the field and left me to be raised by the locals. They were murdered when I was twelve. That's when I was sent to live with an uncle in New York."

"So what we did yesterday wasn't entirely altruistic. It was personal."

"Probably. But not consciously so. It was mostly a proof of concept, and it made sense to do it in an environment I'm familiar with. There was some question of whether it was practical. Or even possible."

"And now that you've proved that it is?"

"The questions are even harder. Can it be scaled? Sustained? Will there be blowback? There's no real precedent to go by."

"What would your parents say?"

Lowe drained the rest of his beer and dug another from the cooler. "Oh, they'd have disowned me after I made my first million. Wealth disgusted them. Their view of the world was . . . simplistic. Rich, poor. Good, evil. In their view, the only way someone could accumulate wealth was by taking it from others."

"I assume you don't agree?"

He shook his head. "Even as a boy, I could see the futility of what they were doing. I thought that maybe it was because I was born here and understood the culture and language in a way that they couldn't. But then I started to suspect they just didn't want to. That a lot of what they did, they did for themselves. They talked about what a sacrifice it was to live here, but I don't think that was true. It was what they wanted."

Fade resisted the urge to look over at the man. It turned out that Jon Lowe was hard not to like. Equal parts charismatic and enigmatic, he was either the most squared-away human on the planet or barely hanging on by a thread. Which was it? "So now that you have more money than God, you're free. You can do whatever you want."

"No. If I were really free, I'd retreat into my tech companies and fool myself into thinking that's the path to salvation. I don't want to be involved in killing. Or bribery. Or threats and blackmail. But that's how things work."

"Or don't."

Lowe smiled. "Exactly. I knew you'd understand."

"Understand what?"

"That humanity's failing. And it's the fault of people like me. At the risk of sounding elitist, the top one-hundredth of the one percent are driving change at a velocity that's tearing society apart. Einstein, Jobs, Darwin, Zuckerberg. We're building a civilization that the average person can't understand or navigate. It's causing them to retreat into tribalism and turn to leaders who promise to protect them and make sense of it all. But that tendency just makes it worse. The people promising answers don't have any incentive to provide them. In fact, the opposite's true. A confused, terrified, and enraged populace will carry you right into power."

"That's always been the case, though, right?"

"Absolutely. But before, it was more isolated. Power had a limited reach and lifespan. Now those barriers are collapsing. Media—whether it be mainstream or social—has the ability to constantly barrage us with everything from dangerous conspiracy theories to the general sense that we're all being cheated and everyone else has more. Even for those with a healthy amount of skepticism, separating real from fake is becoming impossible. Most of the issues people are tearing themselves apart over aren't even real. What happens when these same people can ask a chatbot how to make nerve gas out of ingredients they can buy from Amazon? Or when anyone with a little programming skill can inundate the entire planet with disinformation designed to burn everything down?"

"Seems like the world's governments should get together and make sure those things don't happen."

"I agree. But they're no longer capable. Dictators are only interested in maintaining order in the short term, and voters are turning democracies into circuses. They no longer demand good governance; they demand entertainment. Think about COVID. Seven million people died, and my organization is the only entity who made any kind of serious effort to determine how so many of our systems and health organizations failed so badly. Why? Because the sole purpose of bureaucracies is to deflect and assign blame for political gain. No one showed any particular interest in the report I spent tens of millions of dollars compiling until a week ago. Now my phone won't stop ringing."

"Yichén Zhu," Fade said. "Now that it's the elite's asses on the line, they're paying attention."

"Zhu is another example of what I'm talking about. An unbalanced man who has too much power and is going to use it to impose his solutions on the rest of us."

"But you and all your billionaire cronies won't?"

"What we want is stability. To pull society back from the brink and suppress humanity's most self-destructive instincts. In the past, that's been the responsibility of governments in whatever form they might take. But now, the balance of power is shifting toward people like me. And while we're imperfect creatures, we didn't get where we are by being stupid. Or by birthright, violence, and lies."

"So what you're telling me is that someone has to rule the world, and you're the best of the bad choices."

His grin seemed genuine. "Not exactly how I'd choose to put it, but a fair summary."

"I admire your ambition, Jon. And you come off as a decent guy. But the word *benevolence* doesn't spring to mind when I look at your kind."

"That's because you're not an idiot. But the people I work with can be made to see that accumulating more money than they can ever spend is a waste of a life. There are more important things."

"Things you can give them. Like you did Matt."

"I'm not trying to pass myself off as a saint, Fade. A saint wouldn't survive any longer in my world than they would in yours. Sometimes the difference between good and evil is nothing more than intent."

"What do you want from me, Jon?"

"Have I not been clear?"

Fade sipped his beer and looked out over the landscape. Was he actually considering this? No. Definitely not. That'd be another in a long line of fatal mistakes.

"If you have concerns, let's hear them."

"Okay. Fine. You gave me a drug that has an eighty percent fatality rate."

"Yes. I doubted a syringe would be the thing that finally killed the invincible Salam al-Fayed, but what if it had? Better than lying there for the next twenty years waiting for your heart to give out."

Hard to argue. "Lisa thinks that, along with a lot of drugs, you were swapping my blood out with the blood of children."

"That's also true. It's an extremely effective antiaging and recovery tool."

"But it also conjures a pretty vivid image of pale kids in cages."

Lowe laughed. "Poverty-stricken children from poverty-stricken countries whose families were in the market to sell them into slave labor, arranged marriages, brothels, or whatever. Instead, we pay those families a monthly stipend to have their children participate in what we call medical trials. They're taken to a rural facility in Ghana where they go to school full-time and are extremely well cared for. At sixteen, they're sent back to their home countries, healthy and well educated."

Fade didn't respond. He'd seen way too much during his time in the military and CIA to be easily shocked. What Lowe was doing was unquestionably disgusting, but it was also unquestionable that he was telling the truth about those kids' alternatives. The day the rich white vampires appeared on their doorsteps was probably the luckiest of their lives.

"Not scalable, of course," Lowe continued when it was clear Fade had nothing to say on the subject. "So we're actively suppressing further research as well as anyone advocating it as a therapy. For obvious reasons, we don't want word of the extent of the benefits to go public. Not everyone would be as ethical in their methodology as we are."

"Ethical," Fade repeated.

"Probably not the right word," Lowe conceded. "But you get my meaning."

Loud and fucking clear.

"You okayed Thor Erickson being sent to the rehab facility I was in."

"Worse. I recommended it to the owner of the Cowboys, who I happen to know. But let's not make this one out to be more sinister than it is. I had no reason to think you'd kill him. I just thought you were getting a little comfortable there and that he'd prompt you to make some decisions that needed to be made."

"So you've manipulated me every step of the way. Just like you have Matt and the others."

"Come on, Fade. I gave you options you didn't have lying in that hospital. You can live a life with meaning. You can live a life without meaning. You can step in front of a train. I'm offering the first one, but you're free to choose the others."

"I already told Matt no. I meant it."

"Then the identity is yours, and I'll deposit half a million dollars in a bank account to get you started. The only thing I ask is that if you're ever discovered, you keep our names out of it."

Fade just kept staring out at the landscape, playing with his now-empty bottle.

"Let me ask you a question," Lowe continued. "What do you want?"

"I don't know."

He grinned. "I didn't either. Not for a long time. But how's this for a goal: I want to save humanity."

"From people like you."

"Yes. And from themselves. But I'm only at the beginning of this journey, and I'm not sure where it's going to lead. Nowhere if I can't find the right people."

"You're overestimating me."

"I don't think so. But why don't we find out? Give me a chance. If it's not for you, walk away."

Lowe was really doing it. He was talking him into this. Maybe Fade's brain had been more starved for oxygen during his coma than he thought. But he couldn't just say yes. He should negotiate, right? Ask for shit. But what? A ridiculous salary? 401(k)? Fancy title? Wasn't that what people who got somewhere in life wanted?

"Okay."

Apparently, it wasn't the answer Lowe expected. "That's it? Okay?"

"No. I want Eugene's brother taken care of."

His brow furrowed. "Who?"

"The man who died during training. He had a handicapped brother."

"Oh, of course. His real name was James Land. It's already taken care of. His brother's been admitted to a facility owned by one of my companies. He'll spend the rest of his life there. Is that all?"

"No. I want the Mystery Machine."

"The what?"

Fade tapped the injection ports still present in his side. "You can leave out the kids' blood, though."

"Oh, that. Out of the question. You're young and physically gifted. You don't need it anymore, and it's dangerous over time."

"The sleeping pills, then."

"Also a hard no. You've already been on them too long. They're not just addictive, they're dangerous. No damage done yet, but if you were to continue, your liver and kidneys would pay the price. But don't worry. You'll adapt. Anything else?"

"You haven't given me anything."

Lowe stood and once again held out a hand. "You're wrong. I've given you everything."

Fade shook it this time, but remained seated, pointing in the direction of the Land Cruiser. "Will the GPS take me where I need to go?"

"No. That's mine. I'm going to go see some old friends." He nodded toward the jet. "That's yours."

With nothing more to be said, one of the world's wealthiest and most powerful men got in the car and drove off across the plain.

Fade still didn't rise, instead reviewing what had just happened. After a few minutes of coming to no useful conclusions, he stood and approached the plane. It had windows on both sides, but the shades were closed against the sun. In the movies, the door always seemed to be on the left, so he went that way. With the glare, the fuselage appeared unbroken, but when he got close, a set of stairs lowered. The twentysomething woman leaning from the door was stunning, with Farrah Fawcett hair that somehow worked, a painted-on blue skirt that hit mid-thigh, and a sheer white blouse.

"Welcome aboard!" she said with a smile that also seemed to have been stolen from Charlie's favorite angel. The accent was a thicker version of Linea's.

"Thanks," he said, climbing into the air-conditioned interior. The cockpit door was closed, but another woman was standing mid-fuselage near a sofa covered in what he assumed was rich Corinthian leather. She was a good six inches shorter, probably Thai, and even more gorgeous. Her uniform strained not to split at the seams as she bowed. Not much of a talker, apparently, but the rest of the package compensated.

"Can I make you a drink?" Farrah asked as the door closed and the engines spooled up.

"Do you have tequila?"

"I'm afraid we don't have alcohol on board. How about a lemonade? I make it myself with mint and a bit of coconut milk."

"Sure. Where are we going?"

Blank stares. Either they didn't know or didn't understand the question.

"Never mind. Doesn't matter."

Farrah pointed to a door at the back. "The bedroom is there. Why don't you have a seat and get comfortable for takeoff? When we're at cruising altitude, you can use the shower."

It sounded like good advice, so he squeezed by the Asian girl who seemed purposeful in not giving him much room. Could this get any weirder? Recalling Lowe's good looks, messianic demeanor, and desire to cleanse the world of evil, he was starting to wonder if he'd just joined a cult.

Fade passed through the door, closing it behind him. The room was dominated by a bed with clothes neatly laid out on the comforter. Jeans, a linen shirt, and canvas shoes. No orange pajamas or tambourines in sight.

The shower was even better than the opulent interior of the jet had led him to expect. Spacious, plenty of pressure, and enough expensive-smelling soaps, lotions, and potions to satisfy even the most discerning of former Navy SEALS. He didn't turn off the water until it started to go cold, finally stepping out to dry off and wrap a luxurious towel around his waist. The mirror was steamed up but still reflected a hazy image. It felt more authentic that way. Like a ghost.

When he went back into the bedroom, his two flight attendant friends were waiting. Farrah handed him a frosty glass and made a good effort to ignore the scars that tended to draw people's attention when they first saw him without a shirt. Bullets, knives, scalpels, burns. A road map of where not to go in life.

He sat on the bed and tested the lemonade. Exactly as good as he knew it would be. After downing it, he couldn't bring himself to set the sweaty glass on the polished wood night table. He knew what the builder had gone through to get just that sheen. Instead, he put it on the carpet.

"Would you like something to eat? We have some very nice dry-aged steaks. Or if you prefer, local seafood fresh off the boat this morning."

"Both sound good. But maybe a little later."

"You look tired."

He was. The village op had taken more out of him than it should have. Worse, he'd taken his last pill the night before. A sliver so small it had melted on his tongue before he could swallow.

Her concern was almost certainly professional, but it seemed so deeply held that he felt compelled to explain. "I'm fine. Sometimes I don't sleep that well."

"Maybe we can help," she said, reaching over to undo the zipper on the back of her Asian companion's skirt. The barely perceptible smile she'd worn since he arrived broadened as she shimmied out of it.

27

FADE'S EYES shot open, and he looked down at the foot on his chest. Not one of the severed ones from his dreams, thank God. This one was attached to Lastri, who it turned out was not Thai but Indonesian. A very talented former surfer and swimsuit model.

He eased from under her and her companion before pushing himself into a sitting position. The jet's window shades were translucent with daylight, suggesting that he'd achieved what for him now passed as sleep—a grinding cycle of nightmares so terrifying that the ones featuring Eugene were a welcome break. His late teammate didn't seem pissed, and his stance was a little more casual now that the rigor mortis had eased. For the most part, he seemed content to hover harmlessly at the bottom of the bed, staring down through milky eyes.

Fade padded to the shower and tried unsuccessfully to focus on nothing but the water hitting his face. Man, he needed a drink.

When they hit turbulence, he turned the lever and toweled off. Clothes were hanging on the back of the door, and he put them on before returning to the bedroom. The twins were up but still clad only in thousand-dollar lingerie and million-dollar smiles. Farrah—actually Carina, as it turned out—was holding something that looked like a poncho and indicating a recliner near a window.

He sat and she wrapped it around him before pulling out a case of scissors and razors. Fade closed his eyes while she trimmed his hair and Lastri started in on his nails. Like everyone else in the world, he'd always wondered what it would be like to be one of those guys on TV who hung out on their yachts surrounded by beautiful women. It turned out to be kind of weird. Like jumping out of planes. Exciting and interesting the first few times, but not something you'd want to make a habit.

The bathroom mirror portrayed an image that didn't seem quite real. His shoulder-length hair was perfect—smoothed, trimmed, and otherwise manipulated in ways he didn't fully comprehend. Not enough that a shimmer of gray wasn't visible in places, though. His close-cropped beard had been preserved after a lengthy debate between Carina and Lastri carried out mostly with hand gestures. Combined with the ridiculously stylish wardrobe, the effect was somewhere between Bollywood action star and contestant in the Mr. Taliban beauty contest.

Even stranger was that he felt as good as he looked. Reasonably fit for the ripe old age of thirty-eight.

Or was it thirty-nine?

LINEA MÄKINEN paced in front of the rented SUV, staying in the dim circle of light bleeding from inside. Despite the relatively early hour, everything else—the sky, the endless rolling landscape, and the airstrip twenty-five meters away—was black. The light jacket she wore wasn't quite enough to protect her from the biting wind, but it didn't bother her. In fact, it felt a little like home.

Not that there was much comfort to be taken from that. While she was happy to be finished with Africa, it was all still uncharted territory. Even during her years in the army, there had been some sense of control over her life and destiny. Freedom deferred but not discarded. That was gone now. Her decision was made, and there was nothing left to do but execute.

She glanced at the vehicle behind her but saw no sign of Harding. He'd put the seats down and was now asleep in the back with their gear. Who was he? An exemplary soldier—of that there was no doubt. But why was he there? What motivated him? Where did his loyalties lie? In the military, they were to your team and country. In the absence of those things, what was left?

More uncharted territory.

The runway lights ignited, and she shielded her eyes to protect her night vision. The sound of a plane separated from the wind, its drone gaining strength as it appeared ghostlike from the clouds. She kept it in her peripheral vision as the wheels touched down and began to decelerate. The shades were all closed, but she could see movement through them. Indistinct shadows on their way to the door in its side. The cockpit, oddly, was completely dark.

A beautiful young woman of Asian heritage appeared first, followed by an equally beautiful blond. They stood on the tarmac in short skirts and windbreakers, attention focused on the man silhouetted in the doorway.

Fade had taken on a bit of a rock star quality since last time she'd seen him. His clothes were completely inappropriate for the climate, but he didn't seem to notice as he descended and joined his companions for a lengthy separation ceremony. Hugs. Kisses. Heartfelt promises that they'd soon be reunited. Maybe even a few tears, but it might have just been the glare.

Despite his dramatic history, he didn't seem to be suffering many ill effects. On the mountain, he perhaps would have once been the strongest, but it hadn't mattered. Training was very different from combat, and what he'd accomplished in that village was admittedly extraordinary. She'd always thought the stories about him were just another example of the Americans' tendency to exaggerate. But now she wasn't sure.

Having said that, he was either stupid, mentally unstable, or a combination of both. Her shot had been extremely low probability. The fact that he was there and not buried in Madagascar was nothing more than the outcome of a coin toss.

Was she in a position to criticize, though? It had been him and not her who'd spoken up when Eugene was in trouble. Poor judgment came in many deadly forms.

"Lin!" he called as he strode over and embraced her. "You look great!"

She didn't answer, instead extricating herself and starting toward the driver's door. He went around and climbed in the other side.

"How's it hangin', Danny?"

"Good."

Linea started the vehicle and began pulling away while Fade tried futilely to find something on the radio.

"Where are we?"

"What do you mean?" she said.

"I mean where are we? The US, right? Smells like the West. Colorado?"

"Wyoming."

"Is this where we live now?"

"You haven't been briefed?"

"About what?"

She sighed quietly. Not only had the enigmatic Matt put his unstable friend in charge; he hadn't told him anything about the mission. "We have information that there's a secret Chinese lab set up about seventy miles to the west of here. We're going to check it out."

"I read about those on the net. There was one in Fresno, right? They found a bunch of equipment, dead rats, and shit like malaria and hepatitis. Bankrolled out of Beijing."

She was surprised he knew about that. Salam al-Fayed didn't seem like the reading type. Maybe comic books.

"Correct. But Matt thinks this one might have something to do with Yichén Zhu."

"Okay, but does anyone here know anything about bioweapons?"

Neither she nor Harding spoke up.

"Then shouldn't we be calling Fort Detrick?"

Linea shook her head. "Those aren't our orders."

FADE HAD taken point, weaving through the clumps of sagebrush in order to remain as quiet as possible. The altitude was significantly higher than the airstrip, and there were patches of snow glowing in what starlight could filter through rare breaks in the overcast.

They were dressed as hunters, with rifles hung on packs that hid more potent weapons. Among other things.

The lost hunter angle was apparently the best Egan could come up with on the spur of the moment, and it was fairly thin. An Arab American, a Brit, and a Finn walk into the Wyoming wilderness. It sounded more like the beginning of a bad joke than a workable cover story. Best to stay out of sight.

They'd left the SUV on a dirt road just off the highway and it wasn't likely to get much attention. The steep track was blocked by a gate at around the half-mile mark, but with no fencing to stop foot traffic. They'd gone around and angled into more rugged terrain for cover. Trees weren't abundant, but there were enough deep ruts and rock outcroppings to swallow a force much larger than their three-person team.

The cold was becoming deeper as they ascended, with gusts of probably more than thirty knots. Fade's earpieces did a good job of silencing them but created a weird disconnect between the calm he heard and the swirling snow and dust he saw.

"The wind's causing a lot of problems, but I've got a drone overhead," Egan said over the comms. "I'm still not seeing any sign of human activity. No electricity and nothing on thermal. But that's not a guarantee."

"Copy," Linea said. "ETA approximately fifteen minutes."

They arrived in just over ten, hanging back in some boulders to examine a large metal building surrounded by a chain-link fence. The gate was padlocked, and there were various surveillance cameras visible, but no indication that they were powered up. The structure beyond was reported to encompass seven thousand square feet on a single floor. No known room separation and no connection to the grid. Electricity, to the degree it existed, came from solar panels on the roof and diesel generators out of sight to the west. A smaller building to the north was apparently an outhouse of sorts. According to records that Egan had pulled, the property had served as equipment storage for forest service before being abandoned. Two years ago, a shell company had purchased it and made the security and utility upgrades.

"From above, you look clear," Egan said. "Linea?"

She was scanning the facility and surrounding area through a thermal scope.

"Three antelope on the ridge to the north. But that's all I see."

Fade pulled a set of bolt cutters from Harding's pack and broke cover, moving quickly to the gate and cutting through the chain securing it. His two teammates went through first, one going left and the other right. Both had left their hunting rifles in the boulders in favor of suppressed MP5s. They'd recon the grounds and meet up in the back.

"Watch for booby traps," Egan said.

He'd done a thorough aerial survey of the area, but measures like mines would be hard to pick out in the frozen terrain.

Fade closed the gate and wrapped the chain loosely back around it. A quick scan in the direction they'd come from turned up nothing more than a couple additional antelope.

"We've reached the rear," Linea said. "No contacts, no traps."

Fade followed Harding's footsteps to the rear of the main building, where their gear was already unpacked and reflective tape had been used to indicate the safest place to cut into the building. Egan was concerned that the doors could be wired, so it was best to go through a section of wall that had no structural support, electrical conduits, or pipes.

Harding put a hole saw against the steel while Fade retrieved a canvas bag full of what felt like softballs. The sound and sparks were a little startling in the tranquil surroundings, but he was through in only a few seconds. Fade emptied the bag into the building.

The clatter of the balls landing was followed by the sound of them rolling around on a concrete floor. He didn't fully understand the technology, but the gist was that they would light up in the infrared, swarm the building, and film what they saw. The laptop Linea was staring at would then combine the feeds into a three-dimensional image. Apparently, the system had been created by geologists who wanted to explore cave systems too difficult for humans to access.

"What have you got?" Fade said, pulling a hazmat suit from his pack and starting to put it on.

"It's still low resolution, but definitely a lab," she responded as Harding slung his rifle and began to climb gracefully up a drainpipe leading to the roof. "Tables with containers still on them, equipment, refrigeration. Three cots with blankets but no people."

"Anywhere we can't see?"

"Not that I can tell. The only visible door is the main entrance... Okay, I'm at full resolution and not seeing any threats."

Fade finished suiting up while she attacked the steel with an angle grinder, running it along the tape outline they'd created. More sparks and noise, but the snow was coming harder now, absorbing the sound and light before it could get anywhere near the highway.

The hole she created was only about three feet square, and he went through slowly, making sure not to snag his suit on a sharp edge. Once inside, he turned on his flashlight and swept the beam across the cavernous interior. Linea's report had been accurate, but lacking in detail. The system couldn't see color and its view angle was limited to looking upward from the floor.

He started with the containers on a nearby table, but all were empty and none had labels. Still, he took photos. Maybe their shapes and sizes could tell Lowe's people something. Cubes that had looked solid on-screen turned out to be cages. All uninhabited now, but based on the woodchips and water systems, they hadn't always been. The doors to five incubators were open and similarly empty. Two desktop computers were set up near the south wall, but their hard drives had been removed.

To his right, he spotted a piece of equipment that looked like a steampunk oven—normal sized but with various pipes and wires leading to it. The door was closed, and he examined the entire unit before opening it about a quarter of an inch. No visible threats, but that didn't mean much in the modern technological age. The whole *Do I cut the blue wire or the green wire?* trope might as well have been a thousand years old in an age of lasers, Bluetooth, and microscopic circuit boards.

Still . . . why not?

He opened it the rest of the way, wincing as he waited for an explosion that never came. Instead, he found a bunch of ash that he picked through with a telescoping probe.

"I found some kind of incinerator. It looks like there are a few bone fragments in it. Probably from animals they had in cages. Are you sure we don't want to bag some of this and take it with us?"

"Absolutely sure," Egan said immediately. "We don't have any idea what we're dealing with. It's too dangerous."

"Understood. But if those are the mission parameters, we're done here, and we've come up empty."

"Then get out of there."

Fine with him. The approach through the wilderness had been kind of fun, but the building felt like the inside of an abandoned alien spaceship. And that never went well for the guy holding the flashlight.

He stepped back through the hole and was immediately hit by a chemical spray. Linea was standing a few meters upwind with a wand connected to a tank of disinfectant. He turned slowly with his arms out, giving her access to every part of the suit. After, she helped him out of it and tossed it and a bag of incendiaries back through the hole she'd cut.

"Daniel," she said into her throat mic. "We're leaving."

A moment later, he appeared at the edge of the roof and slid down the pipe.

A dull thud reached them after they were safely through the gate and back among the boulders. Egan had detonated the charges, but they weren't designed to explode so much as to generate an enormous amount of heat. In an hour or so, the building would be a melted heap and anything that might have been lurking inside would be dead.

28

LINEA PILOTED their rented SUV down the town's main street, making sure to stay just under the speed limit. Fade watched the passing buildings, most dark and facing empty sidewalks accumulating snow. A bar near the center was an exception, its large front window revealing an interior packed with dancing young people. In contrast, an old man crossed the street in front of them, hunched against the cold, wearing a Carhartt-branded surgical mask beneath the shadow of his cowboy hat.

The revelry of the world's young people was increasingly common, but this was the first time he'd seen it in person. While some expressed love and respect for their elders, a surprising number seemed to be celebrating their looming demise. Bars were packed, and impromptu street parties were breaking out all over the world—a celebration of youth and invincibility.

Equally surprising was the reaction of seniors like the one he'd just seen. When COVID burned across the US, people had fought tooth and nail against any restriction or requirement, and an extraordinary number had refused inoculation. But that was when they thought God's finger was on the trigger. Now that it was a nefarious Chinese scientist, everything had changed. Mask wearing was nearly ubiquitous in anyone over forty, and seeing someone over fifty working in an office or out in public without good cause was virtually unheard of. Demands for a vaccine were growing even from people with a history of opposition to them, and conspiracy theorists were adamant that the government had already developed one but were withholding it for some reason.

A trait Fade had always found fascinating in his fellow man was that they tended to care deeply about who killed them. If a disaffected white kid strolled into a school with a rifle, it was all shrugs, thoughts, and prayers.

But if someone with his ancestry walked in shouting *Allahu Akbar*, it could change the course of the nation. To him, it had always been more the bullet itself than the owner of the trigger finger.

A Chinese restaurant with an open sign appeared to the right, its spider-webbed front window covered in racist graffiti. There were a few staff members visible inside but no customers. Fade pointed to an empty parking space in front.

"Let's get something to eat."

Linea glanced over at him. "We told Matt we'd rendezvous with the—"

"Pull in."

Her jaw tightened, but she did as he requested.

Fade twisted around in his seat and looked at the man dozing in the back. "What do you think, Danny? Hungry?"

"Sure."

Fade stepped out before Linea even had time to turn off the motor. As he was angling toward the door, two men came out of the steakhouse that shared a wall. They were dressed a lot like the old-timer he'd seen earlier, but as they were still in their twenties, they'd forgone the mask. Both stopped short and the one on the right cocked his head to examine the three strangers congregating on the sidewalk.

"They're closed."

Fade pointed to the neon sign stating otherwise.

The man squinted, unsure why his message wasn't connecting. Finally, he thumbed behind him. "Food's better in here."

"A steak does sound good," Linea said hopefully. Harding remained agnostic on the subject.

"Thanks for the recommendation," Fade said, flashing a grateful smile. "But I have my heart set on an egg roll."

He reached for the door, but the man put a hand out, preventing him from opening it. Inside, the staff were looking on anxiously.

Feeling no reason to prolong the standoff, Fade put a foot into the side of the man's knee, grabbed him by the back of the head, and slammed his face into the brick next to the door. He bounced off, landing on his ass with a deep gash in his forehead. The other one retreated a step, nearly falling due to the icy surface and what had probably been a few too many beers. He didn't seem inclined to get involved, so Fade pushed through the door and into the warm interior.

"Table for three. Something against the back wall, if it wouldn't be too much trouble."

It turned out to be no trouble at all. They settled into a booth while the staff scurried for menus, silverware, and water glasses.

"That was the second stupidest thing I've ever seen," Linea said when everyone moved out of earshot. "Congratulations, you now own the two top slots. Has it occurred to you that it might be better for you to *avoid* getting arrested?"

Fade ignored the comment. "I've worked all over the world, and it can be pretty isolating. Whenever you're away from home for a long time, you start looking for the familiar. Culture. Language . . ." He waved a hand around the restaurant. "Food."

Harding leaned forward across the table. "You think the people working here might know something about the scientists at that lab?"

Fade stood. "I changed my mind about those egg rolls. Order me won tons to start. And then get me the moo shu pork with extra pancakes."

He headed for the bathroom, taking time to peer into the kitchen as he passed. Only one man. Not a lot of work to be done with the new reality that Yichén Zhu had saddled them with.

Chinese voices were audible out back, along with the faint scent of cigarette smoke. He ignored the bathrooms and exited a door that led to an alley. The three Asian men smoking next to a dumpster looked a little confused at his sudden appearance. One pointed at the door in an attempt to get him to go back inside, but Fade answered by pantomiming holding a cigarette. The gesture apparently translated, because a moment later he was leaning one into the flame of a BIC.

"Do any of you speak English?"

"I do," the one on the left said through a thick accent. "Them, no."

"I work for Immigration."

Despite their reported poor language skills, all seemed to understand that word perfectly.

"I'm not interested in you," Fade quickly clarified. "I'm interested in some other Chinese nationals who lived in the area. We think they probably left town around four or five months ago. Tell me about them, and I'll forget all about this restaurant."

The English speaker translated for his friends and got some knowing, frightened, nods. "Yes. Three men."

Interestingly, that matched the number of cots he'd found in the lab.

"Do you know their names? What about pictures? Maybe from security cameras? Cell phones?"

The man shook his head.

"Did they pay with credit card?"

"No. I remember. Money. Cash."

"When was the last time you saw them?"

He asked his companions, and they debated for a few seconds. "Two of them. Haven't seen for long time. As you say. Months."

"Two of them? What about the other?"

"Not sure. Two weeks? More? He live twenty miles."

"Live," Fade said. "You mean 'lived.' In the past."

That generated another hushed conversation in Chinese. "No. Others I think gone. But Gao stays. He has love with Meilin. Our waitress. But she no work here more. Not now."

Fade took a drag off the cigarette and examined the shivering men in front of him. They were dressed to share a quick butt and had now been out in the elements longer than anticipated.

"Let's slow down for a minute so I'm sure I understand. You're saying that two of the three men are gone. But that the other one is right now living twenty miles away with one of your waitresses."

"Yes. That is right."

"So I could go visit him. I could get in my car after I finish my moo shu and drive to his house."

Another brief conversation. This one actually got a bit heated with a lot of furtive glances in his direction. Finally, a decision was made.

"She is . . ." the man's voice faltered and his expression turned frustrated. Fade had been in a similar position a hundred times in Afghanistan—trying to explain a concept too complicated for his Pashto. "She is very beautiful. And very bad. He falls in love. We all do. Even people from city here. He goes to live with her and other people. People from here. Danger . . ." He hunted for the word. "Dangerous people. They all live together on land, yes? Big land. And he helps them now."

"Helps them what?"

He didn't answer.

"Helps them what?" Fade repeated.

"Make money."

There was no need to push further. A scientist helping a group of dangerous locals living in the middle of nowhere make money. Not hard to put together.

"Just one more thing and you can all go back inside. Where exactly can I find them?"

FADE SIDESTEPPED a patch of snow and stayed on the frozen dirt road flanked by pines. Not that silence was all that important—the wind howling through the mountains would cover a reversing dump truck. Better to concentrate on where he was stepping than how. He'd already dodged multiple alarm-connected trip wires.

The darkness behind him was a blank wall, but to the northwest, he could just make out a shimmer of firelight. He adjusted his trajectory toward it.

The turn off the rural highway had been more than five miles farther than the men at the restaurant had estimated, but the landmarks were as advertised. They'd had to be conservative with the SUV, pulling the fuses controlling running and dashboard lights before backing it a quarter mile or so up the dirt track. The rest had to be covered on foot. Fade had taken the straight shot north while Linea and Harding went wide and would come in from the east and west.

It was now closing in on midnight, and the hope had been that everyone up there would be asleep or, even better, passed out. But maybe a campfire would give them a better sense of what they were up against. Egan's drone was out of juice, and there wasn't much off-site research possible at that time of night. It probably would have been better to wait for some background, but Fade wasn't convinced that someone at that restaurant wouldn't call in a warning.

A sliver of their target finally came into view when Fade was about fifty yards out. A few minutes later, he was taking in the entire compound: three trailers, distributed in an arc around a fire pit ringed with chairs. All were currently occupied, with a total of eight men and two women bundled against the cold and incautiously close to the flames. He could see their mouths moving, but the conversation was inaudible over the wind.

Without exception, they were consuming alcohol—mostly beer but a few bottles of liquor were also in view. The pile of empties was impressive but didn't provide reliable information on their level of intoxication because many looked like they'd been there for a long time. Visible weapons were limited to a couple rifles leaned against whatever was available. In all likelihood, there were a few pistols beneath all the clothing and blankets, but they'd be difficult to get to. Further, everyone was staring more or less straight into the fire, so they'd be blind to virtually anything beyond the immediate circle of light.

Most of the men had long hair that could have benefited from the ministrations of the twins. Beards were in favor, with only the men who looked native going clean-shaven. Of the two women, one was probably mid-thirties, wearing the hard exterior of a life poorly led. The other was much more interesting. Young, Asian, and from what was visible between her scarf and hat, quite a looker.

"In position," Fade said, continuing to analyze the details of their operating environment. The trailers had seen better days, with peeling paint, rickety steps, and tires holding down the roofs. A line of vehicles to the east provided a stark contrast. Most were pickups, tricked out to varying degrees and probably each worth upward of a hundred grand. No drug lab in sight, but that was to be expected. You could lose a 747 in this terrain.

"In position," Linea said. Harding followed a few minutes later.

"Thoughts?" Fade prompted.

"I'm not seeing Gao," she responded. "But I see an Asian woman who fits the general description you were given."

"I have good position," Harding said. "If you both do too, we can take care of this pretty quick."

An accurate assessment. Three pros armed with suppressed MP5s against twelve night-blind drunks wrapped up against the cold wasn't going to be much of a fight. They'd be dead before they even knew what was happening.

Predictably, Linea swiped the punch bowl. "I'm not an executioner of civilians. Drug dealers or otherwise."

"I could go either way," Harding said.

As much as Fade hated to admit it, Linea was right. There was no way to know if the man they were after was even in one of those trailers. And if he was, who else had decided to forgo a cold night of drinking in the wind? Other armed adults? Kids? Punching holes in these people on the word of Matt Egan and some restaurant dishwashers was a bridge too far.

"Okay," Fade said. "Let's see if we can figure out something sexier."

TWO HOURS later, there was still one man by what was now just a bed of glowing coals. Fade was starting to wonder if he'd overdosed or frozen to death, but finally he jerked to life and stumbled into one of the trailers.

"And we're clear," Harding said over Fade's earpieces.

The twelve residents were now distributed roughly evenly between the three dwellings, along with whatever other people may or may not have been inside before. Meilin had been one of the first to go, retreating to the westernmost trailer forty-five minutes ago.

"Okay," Fade said. "We'll give them another hour or so to get comfortable. Are you both okay?"

"Fine," Linea responded.

Harding wasn't as thrilled by their situation. "Freezing my ass off."

Fade checked his watch and confirmed that fifty-nine minutes had passed with zero activity. The fire pit was now providing barely enough illumination to see the snowflakes wandering through calmer winds.

As good a time as any.

He reluctantly stripped off his jacket, leaving him in a base layer, insulated hunting pants, and boots. The cold that had been sinking into him for some time attacked, causing his skin to sting briefly before going disconcertingly numb. He pulled a SIG from his pack and stuffed it in his waistband near the small of his back. The silencer was tempting, but would likely be more of a hindrance than a help in the close quarters of the trailer. Besides, if everything went as planned, no shooting would be necessary.

He strode to the edge of the clearing and then stumbled across it, grabbing a discarded blanket from the ground and wrapping it around himself before pausing in front of the fire pit. Someone had left an insulated baseball hat, and he put it on, pretending to stare blankly into the remaining coals.

It was unlikely that anyone was watching, but if they were, all they'd see was the vague outline of a long-haired, bearded man either too high or too stupid to come in from the cold. Probably a pretty good description of half the people living there.

After a couple minutes, he started toward the target trailer, staggering up the rough-hewn steps and entering through the unlocked door.

The interior, illuminated by a single night-light, was as expected. Water-damaged paneling, furniture disintegrating onto a filthy shag carpet, and dishes piled in the sink. People had crashed in whatever space was available—the floor, a sofa, a mattress near the wall. No one stirred, which was good, but there was no sign of the target or his Asian hottie.

That left the closed door at the trailer's west end.

The smell of sweat, urine, and bad breath was overwhelming as he crossed the cramped space. But at least it was reasonably warm. A questionably wired space heater on the kitchen counter had elevated the temperature to what he estimated was the low sixties.

The benefit was that he could actually feel his fingers when he turned the knob and peeked inside at a bed piled with blankets. The man huddled under them fit the description of their target—late forties, with prematurely gray hair and a gaunt, angular face. A bedside table contained a number of syringes and other drug paraphernalia as well as a vial of what Fade assumed they were cooking up in their lab. On the other side of the mattress was Meilin, lying with one long-underwear-clad leg peeking from beneath the covers. Clearly, Gao wasn't getting any. Likely he'd arrived a slave to love and now was just a plain old slave.

And if that was the case, maybe this could go easy. Less a kidnapping than a rescue. A liberation from an unfulfilling relationship that was stifling his personal growth.

Fade clamped a hand over Gao's mouth but got no reaction at all other than causing the woman next to him to stir. Of all the people by the fire pit, she'd seemed the least wasted and the most commanding. It was hard to know if she'd fallen in with this rough crowd or if she'd built it. If he had to bet the farm, he'd guess the latter.

All the more reason not to wake her.

He eased the covers off the man and began to gently lift him. If he could manage a fireman's carry, getting him out of the trailer unnoticed was doable with just a slight assist from Lady Luck. Once clear, he'd make for the trees and disappear.

Or not.

The man started speaking in Chinese, though it was unclear if he was awake or dreaming. Either way, whatever he said caught Meilin's attention. Her eyes sprang open, and she bolted upright.

Fade froze, still holding the scientist like a groom about to cross the threshold. Not part of the plan, but coming out of a semidrunken sleep tended to preclude quick decision-making. It'd likely take her a few seconds to process what was happening.

Or not.

The guy at the restaurant hadn't been kidding when he'd issued his warning about the woman. Her beautiful face twisted into something out of the *Evil Dead*, and she went for a knife sheathed on the headboard.

He was forced to drop the man in order to avoid being run through. Her considerable momentum dragged her onto the floor, but she immediately recalibrated and slashed at Fade's legs. He jumped, allowing the knife to pass beneath his boots and landing to the sound of groggy shouts from the main part of the trailer.

Then she was on her feet, crouched and lining up the blade for another try. As much as he hated the idea of turning his back on this crazy bitch, he had no choice but to dive for the door and lock it. Hopefully, the mechanism wasn't as beat to shit as the rest of the structure.

He managed to flip the latch just as a body impacted the other side. The door bulged at its center but, miraculously, held. The remaining news wasn't as good. The woman was now fully upright and charging with the knife held in front of her like a bayonet. He managed to prevent it from sinking into his chest but felt it slide along his ribs before penetrating the door behind. Fade slammed an elbow down on her arm, causing her to lose her grip on the weapon, but intensifying her rage.

Disarmed, she attacked with fists and then wrapped a hand around the back of his neck, pulling his face toward a shapely mouth full of dangerous teeth. He got a forearm between them, but it wasn't as effective as it should have been. He guessed that the reason she wasn't much of a drinker was that she was on something a hell of a lot stronger.

He managed to create enough space between them to get some

momentum on a left cross, connecting with her temple. She went down hard but came back up on all fours so fast that it was almost as if she'd bounced. Behind him, someone was kicking the door with a level of enthusiasm that pretty much guaranteed success in the next few seconds.

Time to finish this. He swung a boot and connected beneath her chin with enough force to flip her backward. There was a good chance he'd killed her, but no reason to hang around and find out.

"We've got activity," Linea said over the comm. "People coming out of the middle trailer. They don't look too alarmed yet. Just confused."

They probably thought it was some kind of lovers' quarrel and were coming to spectate. That illusion wasn't going to hold any longer than the door, though.

"I'm putting Gao through the west window, Danny. Come and get him. Linea. Head for the car."

The scientist was conscious and using the bed for support as he tried to climb back on it. Fade helped, laying him out and then rolling him in the thick top blanket. His emaciated state made him easy to handle, and Fade threw him through the window, shattering the glass and leaving him to fall into the snow on the other side.

That done, he returned to the door, using his body weight to hold back the onslaught. It felt like an eternity before Harding's voice came over his earpieces.

"I've got him. Heading south, paralleling the road."

Fade kept his back pressed to the door, jerking every time someone kicked it. He was debating how much longer he should stay, but the woman he'd assumed was dead answered the question by starting to crawl toward him.

Launching forward, he jumped on the bed and dove through the window. The door behind burst open as he clipped some glass and then went headfirst into the sagebrush. With no time to assess injuries, he bolted for the trees, chased by three people who had been standing by the fire pit.

The pursuit wasn't particularly organized, and his opponents were in various states of intoxication and undress. That made it possible for Fade to circle around and retrieve his pack before picking his way through the trees toward the road. The darkness and cold were working against him, and no good solutions existed for either. When he heard the sound of Linea reversing their SUV up the dirt track, he decided to risk a head lamp.

None of the people chasing sounded all that close when he crouched to open his pack, but working the zipper with shaking hands and lifeless fingers wasn't a quick operation. When he finally powered up the light, gunfire immediately began pounding the trees to his right.

He sprinted away from the impacts, moving with reasonable speed but also providing a neon sign of a target. The earpieces muffled the sound of the gunshots but enhanced the hiss of them passing by and impacting wood. Not helpful.

"I've got the SUV in sight," Harding said. "Go about another fifty meters and stop."

"Copy that," Linea responded.

Fade could hear the reverse gear straining, and he cut right to escape the trees. It turned out to be a bad call, and he had to reverse himself when people running up the road started shooting. After a few seconds, though, he realized that he wasn't the target. Linea's SUV was. He'd overshot it.

"Linea!" he said, throwing his head lamp into the trees in hopes of drawing fire. "I'm thirty meters ahead of you, moving parallel to the road on the left."

"Copy. Thirty meters on the left."

A car door slammed, and he heard the roar of an engine. His head lamp hadn't fooled anyone and he was still taking fire from the trees. The road would be worse, though.

"Don't stop. Just slow down to about ten miles an hour when I tell you."

"Copy."

"Now!" he said when she was almost even with him. He saw the nose of the vehicle dip, and he exited the trees again, jumping onto a running board and grabbing the gear rack with hands devoid of sensation. She began to accelerate again, and he threw a leg up onto the roof. Normally, it would have been an easy maneuver, but the icy surface and borderline hypothermia added a layer of difficulty.

By the time he got fully on top, a set of headlights had appeared behind. Remembering the gun still hanging on in his waistband, he fired a few clumsily aimed rounds in their general direction.

His chest dropped, and it took him a moment to figure out that the sunroof was being opened. They broke out onto the highway, fishtailing on the snow-dusted surface before Linea regained control.

He slid headfirst into the vehicle, missing the front seat and ending up under the dash with his cheek pressed into the floorboard. Linea closed the sunroof, and he found himself irretrievably stuck, gun frozen in one hand and blood from the cut in his side running into his eyes and mouth.

Once he started laughing, it was impossible to stop.

29

"ARE WE moving too far too fast, Jon?"

Greg Madison spread marmalade on a piece of toast and bit into it, continuing his thought as he chewed. "The POTUS, President of Russia, and leader of China have never agreed on anything in their lives. But if they find out about what we're doing, they're going to agree on coming after us with everything they have. And no one's going to say a thing. What happened yesterday proves that."

He was referring to something that very closely resembled a Chinese invasion of Vietnam. PLA paratroopers had taken control of the city of Pleiku based on what they said were credible reports that Yichén Zhu was hiding there. It was extremely unlikely, in Lowe's estimation, but the troops were now entrenched and carrying out house-by-house searches. Despite understandable protests from Hanoi, the response from the USA and Vietnam's other allies was muted. The message was clear: Beijing had a free hand to do whatever it wanted if there was even a remote chance it could save the world's aging elites.

"I'll admit that your security's impressive," Madison said, waving his hand around absently. "But not when China comes knocking."

He was right on both counts. The island, a mile long by a mile wide, was a mix of white beaches, palm forests, and rugged hills. In many ways, it was a smaller version of Madagascar, the mountains of which could just be seen across the water. When Lowe purchased it, the island was an exclusive resort, encompassing the main building where they were sitting and fifteen luxury bungalows in the trees to the west. Normally, he kept staff in them: a skeleton crew of primarily security and maintenance people. Now, though, that serenity was broken. There were currently no fewer than ten former spec ops people there, armed with everything from pistols to next-generation drones and antiship missiles. Their job at this point was to keep everyone out. With one notable exception—whose arrival was imminent.

Madison, his wife, and two more couples were staying on the island as Lowe's guests. While doomsday bunkers had become very much in vogue for the world's hyperwealthy, they tended to be treated less as an urgent necessity than just another status symbol. That left many either completely impractical or still unfinished. Moats full of fire were impressive at parties, but not particularly useful when you didn't have a functioning water filtration system.

That left the one percenters competing to pay through the nose for remote properties in places like Alaska and Brazil, while others found accommodation with their more forward-thinking brethren. Government officials were somewhat better prepared. In developed nations like the US, top officials had been moved to hermetic facilities designed for just these kinds of scenarios. Less-sophisticated countries saw their rulers moving to isolated palaces protected by loyal forces.

"Nothing's safe," Lowe said finally. "Nowhere."

"Well, you don't have much to worry about, do you? You're what? Forty-five?"

"A little older. But yes. I imagine I'll be fine."

Lowe leaned back in his chair and looked out over the water. A storm system, too far to be visible, was pushing unusually high waves to shore. The rhythmic crashing of them was a rare treat.

"Yichén obviously has a strong political point of view. And he's never been as emotionally stable as people think. The Chinese government was stupid to do what they did. They either should have left him alone or killed him."

"But they didn't."

"No."

"And we all agree he can make good on his threat."

"There's no question in my mind."

"Then I have to ask again if we're moving too far too fast. You've located one of his scientists, and you're keeping that fact from the world's governments. Organizations that are extremely motivated, experienced, and have virtually unlimited resources."

"The scientist you're referring to is named Deng Gao, and he's on his way here. But there's still time to divert him and turn him over to authorities. Is that what you want me to do?"

Madison laughed and put down his toast. "You love being right, don't you, Jon? Society's falling apart on exactly your schedule. Just like you told us it would."

"That's not an answer."

"What answer? You can do what you want, right? My wife and I are here at your pleasure. You can have your storm troopers put us on a boat anytime you want."

"But you know I won't."

"Do I?"

"This is beneath you, Greg. Absolving yourself of responsibility? Playing the victim? I choose my board members better than that."

Madison examined him for a moment and then turned his attention to a fatigue-clad man performing a check on an antiaircraft gun. Finally, he responded. "I've been doing business internationally long enough to know that the Chinese government is built entirely around protecting its leadership. Any attempt to project power outside of their borders or for another purpose is going to be desperate, ham-fisted, and ineffective. But like we're seeing, they'll try. And there's nothing they won't destroy to save themselves."

"Proving Zhu's point, ironically."

Madison nodded. "The Russians, on the other hand, are nothing more than vandals. I can assure you that the old men running that country are all hiding out in bunkers waiting for someone else to save them. Europe has some competent—and generally younger—leadership, but the EU is too fractured and too accustomed to hiding behind America's skirt to put much faith in."

"And what *about* America?"

"What's our good senator say?" he deflected.

Susan Kane was currently sequestered in a Colorado military facility along with fifty of her colleagues, the majority of whom she despised. Her thoughts on the matter had been made clear in a secure phone conversation they'd had earlier that morning: *Under no circumstances should you hand Gao over to the government, Jon. These morons are in full panic mode. They'll start torturing him the second he gets here and wipe any place he even mentions in passing off the map. You have no idea how close we are to the brink. If these geriatric cretins ever start to really believe they're going down, they'll take the rest of the world with them.*

"It doesn't matter what Susan says. What do *you* say?"

"My country." Madison sighed. "You know, I'm a patriot, Jon. You probably think that's quaint, but it's true. I understand what America's done for me. But I also acknowledge that it's falling apart faster than I could have imagined. The president only cares about maintaining her position, and she's surrounded herself with a personality cult of idiots and boot lickers. Ninety percent of Congress are degenerates, too stupid to come out of the rain, or senile. The director of the FBI doesn't know anything about law enforcement and only got the job because he's willing to let the president get away with anything she wants. The head of the CIA is a loyalist who was appointed for the sole purpose of turning the Agency away from foreign counterintelligence and into an apparatus to spy on the president's political opponents. Interestingly, my contacts say that last one's starting to backfire. It turns out that hiring a forty-nine-year-old psychopath with political ambition is a great idea right up to the moment when someone decides to kill all the people standing between him and real power. If he knew where Zhu was right now, I'm not sure he'd speak up."

"And the American people?"

"They're not going to save us. Hell, they're the problem. They've turned into a bunch of sheep who'll elect anyone willing to confirm their dumbass beliefs and feed their rage and victimhood."

"So what I'm hearing is that the risk of handing Gao over to the authorities is greater than the risk of us trying to handle the situation ourselves."

Madison used a glass of fresh-squeezed orange juice to salute the man across from him. "Congratulations, Jon. You've stripped me of all my illusions. Are you satisfied?"

"You can't afford them anymore," Lowe said, looking east toward a helicopter appearing on the horizon. "None of us can."

LOWE LIFTED a hand to protect his eyes from the dust being lifted by the helicopter's rotors. It dropped toward the pad, and Matt Egan jumped out as the skids touched down. He helped the craft's only other passenger to the ground, and Lowe studied him as they moved crouched toward a stand of palms.

Based on a hastily prepared dossier, Deng Gao had done his undergraduate work in Germany and received a virology doctorate from Tsinghua University. Later, he'd worked for a number of pharmaceutical companies in Europe before refocusing his talents on pure research. He was far thinner than in his photos and looked significantly older than his reported fifty years. The hunch in his shoulders went beyond a reaction to rotor wash, instead seeming to be part of him. Not entirely unexpected, given the conditions that Fade had found him in.

Lowe strode toward the two men with a hand outstretched. "Dr. Gao. It's a pleasure to meet you. I'm Jon." He pointed to an armed man in hazmat gear, just barely visible among the trees. "If you could follow this gentleman, he'll take you to your cabin. Have something to eat and get some rest. We'll talk later."

Gao's only response was an expression of stunned resignation. Sweat coated his pale skin, and his mouth clenched in a way that suggested nausea. Perhaps the effects of the flight.

"Fade managed to pull a rabbit out of a hat I thought was empty," Lowe said as he watched the man being led away.

"Everybody gets lucky now and then."

Egan seemed determined to cling to a grudge against his old friend. In truth, what they both desperately wanted was to be brothers again. The question was, would their pride allow it?

"Is Dr. Gao all right?"

"Some minor injuries from being thrown through a window, but we did a quick medical screening just in case."

"And?"

"Fentanyl."

"He's an addict?"

"Physically addicted for sure. Mentally, I don't know. It's possible that he didn't start using voluntarily. It may have just been another form of control by the people holding him. Anyway, he's starting to withdraw. And that's going to create a window where he's going to be extremely cooperative with no effort on our part."

"Understood. What's the situation in Wyoming?"

"Fade roughed up a guy in town, but he's on probation, so the police aren't going to hear about it. Same goes for the people Gao was with. They're going to see this as a rival gang kidnapping their cooker. Not exactly something you report to the law."

"And the woman who attacked Fade?"

"They took her to the hospital. She's in pretty rough shape but they expect her to make a full recovery."

"What are they saying happened to her?"

"That she fell."

"Not particularly believable."

"The cops aren't going to care one way or another. Hospital visits are pretty common with people like that, and no one ever presses charges. Waste of time."

"What about the lab we found?"

"The incendiaries did their job. From the exterior, the building has some visible blackening and warping, but it's not exactly in view of Main Street. Plus, the storm that came in made the road impassable. I doubt anyone will notice the damage until May. Probably later."

Lowe smiled. "So a major win with no repercussions."

Egan still refused to give Fade any credit at all. "Better to be lucky than smart."

"It's better to be both, Matt."

THE BUNGALOW was in the midst of a staging point where food and other supplies arrived and were disinfected. Lowe's lack of hazmat gear meant that he couldn't return to the other side, but there was no reason for him to. It had been convenient to bring Gao to a place where there was no law, but one way or another, their stay would be short.

The structure was an opulent twist on a traditional Malagasy dwelling—wood, glass, and concrete opening onto a white sand beach. No personnel were present, with most prohibited from approaching closer than mid-island. The few whose duties demanded physical presence were obligated to follow strict biohazard containment protocols.

Lowe leaned in through a sliding door but didn't enter.

"Dr. Gao?"

He was sitting at the dining table, looking even worse than before. A gourmet meal sat untouched in front of him.

"Do you mind if I come in? I thought we could talk for a few minutes."

The scientist gave him a short nod and finally spoke in the passable English promised by his dossier.

"They forced me to take narcotics. The woman took me there. She lied to me. I was a prisoner."

Lowe nodded and settled into a chair. Gao had no idea why he was there, but a logical guess would be that it had something to do with his involvement in drug manufacturing. That assumption created two possibilities. First, that his capture had been carried out by the authorities and he'd for some reason been brought to a desert paradise for questioning. The second was that some cartel had heard about his unusual level of expertise and a job offer was on the table.

"Indeed?"

"I just need help. With my sickness. To get off them. Then I'll do what you want."

I'll do what you want. A clever use of ambiguity signaling that he was as willing to turn on his old business partners as to get in bed with new ones. The question was, how far did that pliability go?

"We have medical personnel on the island that can help you, Doctor. But first, I'd like to ask you about Yichén Zhu."

He looked startled for a moment, and then his face went blank as he tried to recalculate his position. While he worked on that, Lowe slid a phone across the table. The screen contained an image of the lab Fade and his team had infiltrated. Gao looked down at it and shook his head violently.

"I don't know what this is."

"You're a brilliant scientist, Doctor. But not a very good liar."

"What do you want?"

"You know what I want."

"To stop Yichén. It can't be done."

"But you know his plans."

"They have changed since he was discovered."

"How?"

"I don't know. He told us that the Chinese government knew about us and gave us instructions to go."

"Where?"

"To meet a plane in Montana."

"But you didn't. You let your companions go without you."

"Yes."

"Because of the woman in the restaurant?"

"Yes."

"What were you working on in Wyoming?"

He didn't respond.

"Would you rather we have this conversation tomorrow? Or perhaps the next day?"

By morning, his withdrawal symptoms would be unbearable—something he knew far better than Lowe.

"Vaccines."

"Not the pathogen itself?"

"No. We developed our first vaccine to fight the original virus Yichén developed. After that, we could often just refine it for more advanced strains. A much faster process."

Lowe leaned back and examined the man carefully. There was no indication that he'd suddenly found a gift for deception. And while Lowe was admittedly not a professional interrogator, much of his success was based on being able to read people.

"So you worked on a vaccine for COVID?"

"Yes. COVID was an early version of Yichén's virus. Very unsophisticated. It relied on the general weakness of older people's immune systems and poor general health to concentrate victims in that group."

"But there are later versions? More sophisticated ones?"

He nodded. "More contagious and longer incubation periods so it can spread widely before anyone is even aware it exists. And much more targeted."

"More targeted how?"

"He's no longer using general health as a selection mechanism. He's found a way to use DNA methylation."

Lowe nodded. Methylation was a way of determining chronological age by measuring chemical tags attached to DNA.

"And that's been more successful?"

"Yes. The last strain I saw was modeled to have mortality rates above ninety-five percent in people over seventy. But those rates drop steeply for people younger. Twenty percent for sixty-year-olds. And it would be extremely rare for someone under fifty-five to even display symptoms."

Lowe found himself in the unusual position of having been left speechless. It was an incredible achievement. Not only the science, but the complete upheaval of society that would result. Mortality in some developed nations would be over thirty percent of the population—concentrated in the wealthiest and most powerful. His own board of directors, so carefully vetted and recruited, would experience upward of a seventy percent casualty rate.

Zhu had always said that he would change the world, and it appeared that he meant it.

30

FADE JERKED, causing the buckle of his seat belt to dig painfully into his lap.

Witches.

And not the fun ones from the Brothers Grimm or Roald Dahl. These women were screaming while they burned. Hundreds of them. Tied to stakes, flung into pits, chained up in dungeons beneath medieval cathedrals. All while Eugene flipped rosary beads with an ever-lengthening thumbnail.

What the fuck? Who dreamed about things that happened four hundred years ago? Not him. Never before that day.

"You're up!" Carina said, appearing from the jet's bedroom. "You seemed so peaceful we didn't want to disturb you."

He was struggling to pull himself back into the present and interpret the strange silence around them. They weren't flying. He turned toward the window and looked past the wing. Blue sky had been replaced by the metallic arch of a hangar.

"How long have I been asleep?"

"Perhaps nine hours?"

Nine hours and he couldn't remember anything before the dream that had woken him.

Was that the secret? Get so tired that his brain overloaded and a breaker tripped? Because the more time that passed since his last sleeping pill, the less productive his efforts at unconsciousness were becoming. The promise that he'd adapt to the loss of the Mystery Machine was turning out to be yet another lie told by yet another liar.

"Where are we?"

She shrugged as Lastri appeared with a tray full of antiseptic and gauze. They helped him remove his shirt and went to work cleaning him up and replacing his bandages. Some had seeped a bit, but otherwise, everything looked scabbed over and infection-free. Carina went to the closet and selected a linen button-down in a red that would camouflage any repairs that didn't fully hold.

"We'll miss you!" Lastri said with rehearsed ease.

"Am I leaving?"

By way of answer, Carina threw the lever on the door. Fade reluctantly approached, pausing at the threshold to study a woman sitting on the hood of a Volvo crossover parked in the shade. The twins descended to the tarmac with him, providing a few gentle hugs that avoided the worst of his injuries. No tears this time, but some exaggerated pouts and a little ear nibble from Lastri. Then they retreated back into the plane and were gone.

When Fade turned, the woman on the Volvo hadn't moved but was staring right at him. She was probably in her late twenties, with chestnut hair about the same length as his but with one side flipped over an ear. Her cotton skirt was just above the knee, showing tanned, athletic legs that matched tanned athletic arms. She slid off the hood and closed the distance between them, taking in every detail as she did. The tiny stud in her right nostril glinted in the sun, as did her teeth during a brief, enigmatic smile. The dimples were irresistible.

"It's a pleasure to meet you, Mr. al-Fayed."

Not Mr. Darwish. Interesting.

She held out a hand. Her grip was firm and dry despite the considerable heat. The accent was light and hard to place. Not Scandinavian. Probably Eastern European.

"Welcome to Greece. I'm Raya."

"Good to meet you, Raya. Call me Fade."

She was fundamentally different from the girls on the plane. Older and less soft in every sense of the word. The playfulness of youth had been replaced with dark eyes that seemed to see the world with all its warts.

"Have we met?" he said. It came out like a lame pickup line but there was something familiar about her that he couldn't put his finger on.

"I don't think so," she said, starting around the front of the vehicle. "Get in please."

The island turned out to be Crete. A nice place to visit, but the timing was less than ideal. The coastal road they'd traversed had been pretty peaceful, but the city of Chania was a completely different animal. Traffic had come to an abrupt halt when a group of a hundred or so people had flowed into a major intersection ahead. Instead of crossing and disappearing into the shopping district, they appeared to have settled in. The growing crowd began to weave through the cars, laughing, shouting, and occasionally jumping on them as frightened drivers rolled up windows and locked doors.

Fade watched as they passed, noting that ages ranged from late teens to mid-twenties. Initially, governments had reacted by sending police and military to break up these disturbances. In more liberal countries, they were largely armed with shields and a little gas. The less enlightened ones rolled out with bullets, nightsticks, and water cannons. That seemed to just exacerbate the problem, though, creating riots that left burned-out vehicles, damaged buildings, and looted shops in their wakes.

Now a more workable solution had evolved. At the first sign of trouble, restaurants, stores, and every other establishment in the area immediately closed and lowered their gates. Another wet blanket on the festivities was the increasing scarcity of booze. It turned out that when old people were forced to self-quarantine, they did so with cocktails. Prices had skyrocketed, and establishments understandably preferred to provide home delivery to wealthy, docile clients than unpredictable, penny-pinching youths.

Raya seemed unfazed by the situation, frowning when the occasional kid slapped the vehicle or pressed their face to the windshield. Most were young men and seemed harmless enough. High on the energy of the crowd and impressed by her beauty. Fade's side of the car got less action. When he was in a less-than-stellar mood, he tended to project a vibe that said something like *I'm going to carve out your mother's spleen and eat it in front of you.* Most people instinctively recognized and respected the message.

A police van appeared ahead, and a blast of its siren was enough to get the column of vehicles moving again. Raya diverted onto a narrow side street, piloting the vehicle at double the speed limit while avoiding pedestrians and keeping both side-view mirrors intact.

They finally escaped the city and began climbing a steep road that led into the mountains. City lights began to come to life below, creating a stunning view that he was content to lose himself in. Attempts to get answers to his questions had failed, leaving nothing but the hum of the engine between them.

Eventually, Raya turned onto a private drive that led to a two-story house with a garage on the first and a broad terrace ringing the second. Constructed primarily of white stucco and glass, the structure merged with the slope in a way that made it feel more modest than it was. Most of the acre-ish lot had been graded flat, and Raya pulled to the end, stopping in front of a three-foot-tall stone barrier that protected the property from the drop-off beyond.

"We're here," she said, shutting down the engine and throwing her door open.

"Where?"

"Home."

She used a remote to open the garage, and they entered through it. A couple of chest freezers, surfboards, e-bikes, and other coastal town paraphernalia took up enough space that a car would be a tight fit. A door at the back led inside, and she turned right to show him a professional-level gym that encompassed half the floor. An awkwardly attached bathroom hinted that the space had once served as a couple of bedrooms and the faint smell of paint pointed to the transformation being recent.

A set of stairs led to an open living area with a glass wall that retracted at the push of a button. He took advantage of it, walking onto the terrace to take in the city and ocean below. Circling around to the back, he found a tiled deck carved from the mountain and arranged with furniture. A decent-sized pool glowed blue in the middle.

Raya slid another glass door open—this time by hand—and they entered a spacious bedroom with an ensuite bath.

"This is yours."

"Great," he said, calculating a bored tone that wouldn't give away that it was the nicest house he'd ever been in.

"Your clothes are in the closet at the back of the bathroom," she said and then pointed to a trunk against the wall. "That's yours too. I'm told that it opens with a thumbprint."

"What's in it?"

She shrugged and then led him into the hallway, indicating left as they headed back to the living area. "My room's over there."

"You live here?"

She nodded, taking a position that put the kitchen island between them. "It's more practical. I'm here to do whatever you need based on the job description you were given."

"Job description?"

Something flashed in her eyes, but it was so fleeting that it might have just been his imagination.

"The document outlining the limits of my responsibilities."

When he just shook his head, she struggled to produce something that would pass for a smile.

"Your friend will be here tomorrow. We can talk about it then. In the meantime, why don't you get settled?"

Apparently dismissed, he wandered back into the bedroom to explore. After testing the mattress, going through all the drawers, and figuring out how to turn on the faucets, he was faced with the trunk. His thumbprint created an electric whir as various bolts pulled back to allow the lid to be opened.

Pretty much as expected. Guns, knives, fatigues, and a few minor explosives.

A little reality to break up the fantasy.

31

EGAN CRESTED the slope and parked in the shade of a structure that looked like the home of a fat British lawyer. The address was right, though, and he stepped out, still wondering what he was doing there. Fade neither needed nor wanted his help, but Lowe seemed inordinately concerned with the man's well-being. Not a responsibility that Egan was particularly interested in taking on, but here he was.

He squinted through the sun at a rocky landscape with a few scattered trees clinging to it. One thing he could say for the place was that it achieved an improbable amount of seclusion. The nearest house wasn't terribly far, but the terrain was rugged enough that it couldn't be seen. Even better, the property controlled the high ground. Literally the end of the road.

When he stopped in front of the door, muffled footsteps were already audible on the other side. A moment later, it opened and he found himself face-to-face with Raya Andris. Her eyes were almost deep enough to distract him from the toned figure, skimpy bikini, and sarong tied at the waist. She looked stunning, but not particularly happy.

"Are you Mr. Egan?"

"Call me Matt."

"He didn't know anything about me," she said, blocking the doorway. "No one gave him my job description."

Egan remembered something about a document she'd created outlining her duties, but only vaguely. Setting up households wasn't really his area of expertise. They had people for this.

"Yeah. I forgot."

"Forgot? You forgot?"

"Look. Fade's not your normal job. Obviously, he's a few sandwiches short of a picnic, but not in a way that's going to cause you problems."

"We have an agreement, Mr. Egan. I live up to my end and you live up to yours."

"Fine," he said, starting to sweat in the heat. "Print it out and give it to him. If you have any issues, message me and I'll straighten it out."

He tried to pass but she still didn't move.

"And by 'straighten it out,' you mean 'enforce it'?"

"For fuck's sake, Raya. Take yes for an answer."

That satisfied her enough to let him inside.

Egan stepped onto the rear terrace and found Fade lying on a recliner in front of the pool. He was wearing only a pair of pink sunglasses and green board shorts covered in black question marks. His collection of scars had been joined by a number of bandages, and the two ports were still visible in his side. Otherwise, he looked healthy. Probably not for long given the joint burning on the deck and the half-empty bottle of tequila next to it.

"What are you doing here, Matt?"

"Don't tell me you can smell me over all that weed."

"I asked what you're doing here."

Egan pulled up a chair and dropped a nylon portfolio between them. "That's the rest of your IDs, Greek residency documents, credit cards, ten thousand euros in cash, and a couple of burner phones. There's also a laptop with a secure operating system. The first time you start it, you'll be able to get in with just your fingerprint. There's a file with passwords. Memorize them and then delete them."

"Okay."

"You're the owner of a security consulting firm with a number of unconnected international clients. You can use the computer to access various things, including your bank accounts. There are five years of deposits and withdrawals, so it looks like you've been actively operating for a while."

"Okay."

"Raya will handle pretty much everything relating to your daily life. She'll interface with your accountant and investment people, make sure bills get paid, taxes get done, and all that. If you have any medical issues, she'll get you to the right people. Whatever you need, she's your first stop."

"What's her deal?"

Egan looked over his shoulder. She was watching them from the kitchen.

"She's smart, trustworthy, and good with languages. Stay out of her way and let her do her thing. If she runs into something she can't handle, she has my contact information."

"She's here to spy on me."

"No. For that, we have your computer, your phones, drones, and a hundred other things. She'd be redundant."

"So now I'm a hired gun for some rich asshole with delusions of godhood."

"You met him, right? Is that how he came off?"

Fade didn't answer.

"Six months ago, you were a sore-covered piece of meat pissing through a tube. Now you're a sore-covered piece of meat pissing in a Greek pool. Seems like a step in the right direction."

"Spoken like a true believer."

Egan stood. "Goodbye, Fade. With a little luck, we won't see each other again for a long time."

"CAN WE talk?"

Fade's eyes shot open. Had he been asleep? It was hard to tell anymore.

"Fade? Are you okay?"

Raya was standing in a position that blocked the sun enough to allow him to look up at her. The bikini had been swapped for a pair of white cotton pants and a blouse buttoned higher than necessary. It had the feel of Mediterranean armor and for some reason made him realize what was so familiar about her. She was perfect. If God Himself had decided to gift him his ideal woman, it would be Raya Andris.

Point, Jon Lowe.

"Can we talk?" she repeated, but it wasn't a question. Despite her obvious discomfort, there was a level of determination in her expression that demanded a couple of Xanax he didn't have.

"Sure."

She held out a sheet of paper. "My job description."

"Uh. Okay. Thanks."

She just stood there with it. Was her hand shaking or was the paper being moved around by the breeze? Either way, it was clear that she wasn't just going to leave it.

"You're doing great work," he said, sliding the sheet beneath his sweating tequila bottle. "Really. Good job."

"I'd appreciate it if you could read it."

"Now?"

"Yes please."

Fucking hell. First Matt, now this. The rest of his joint wasn't going to smoke itself. But it seemed important to her, so he retrieved the page and peered at the neatly typed bullet points.

"I'm here to help in any way I can," she explained.

"Like I said. I don't have any complaints."

"But there are things that aren't part of my duties."

Being quiet, apparently.

"Those are the items that list focuses on. Also, what I expect of you as an employer."

Fade let out a long breath. *Number one: No excessive alcohol use.*

This wasn't starting well.

Number two: No violence.

Getting worse.

Number three: No hard drugs. See appendix one.

Did it really say *See appendix one*?

"On the back," she said, seeming to read his mind.

He flipped it. Meth, heroin, fentanyl, PCP, acid. A few he'd never heard of. Weed, shrooms, and coke were thankfully absent.

He flipped back to the front and moved on to the next category. *Sex.*

No more than seven times per week, which seemed reasonable. It could be refused for cause. No violence, simulated or otherwise, which seemed redundant to the previous section but was likely included for emphasis.

Excluded acts . . . He didn't need to read further to know they'd be enumerated in appendix two. He flipped the page and again found the list to be relatively short and to include things he'd never heard of.

The next section related to nonphysical abuse in the form of demeaning verbal attacks, swearing, threats, and shouting. Also, attempts at bribery. Interesting. He hadn't seen that one coming.

By the time he got to the bottom, he was having a hard time focusing. The Greek weed kind of crept up on you, and his liver hadn't yet adjusted to his renewed ability to consume alcohol.

"Looks good. No problem."

She held out a pen. "Could you sign?"

What was it about organized women that he found so irresistible?

"Turn around."

She did and he pressed the paper to her ass before scrawling his initials on it. After retrieving the contract and pen, she was noticeably more relaxed.

"You know, if you don't want this gig, Raya, you can just quit. You're not my slave."

She smiled in a way that didn't reveal her movie-star-white teeth. "We're both slaves, Fade. You just don't know it yet."

32

FADE CARESSED the glass of spectacular tequila on the table next to him, but it was there more for company than intoxication. It had been over a week since his last magic pill, and sleep was coming harder every night. Experimentation with Ambien, Xanax, booze, and pot—as well as various combinations of the four—hadn't produced much improvement. The Xanax kind of worked but had the odd effect of making his nightmares even more giant-spider-oriented. Kind of clichéd, but he'd hated the creatures ever since his mother had started reading him *Charlotte's Web* against his will. Even at five years old, he'd known that little pig was being set up. When the babies were born, she'd go after him with fangs dripping, leaving him helpless while the family dined on his bacon. Fade raised his glass.

To Wilbur. I barely knew you, man.

Ambien and weed, on the other hand, did precisely nothing. Tequila put him out, but left him exhausted and hungover the next day. He'd texted Egan a few times about getting the Mystery Machine back but hadn't received a response. The subtle ports in his side remained, though. So there was still hope.

That left only sleep deprivation. He was still in the experimental phase, but it seemed that around sixty hours awake was enough to give him ten hours of the oblivion he'd become so enamored of. Not great, but doable.

His hand moved from the cut crystal to a SIG P226 lying next to it. Picking it up, he ran the cool metal of the suppressor against his cheek. Raya was wrong about being a slave. You could always choose to quit the game. Not even Jon Lowe could take that option away. Maybe it was a little twisted, but there was comfort in knowing that a foolproof way to put himself to sleep was out there. Waiting for the moment it was needed.

He glanced at the glowing screen of his watch—4:53 a.m. Forty-seven hours into his marathon. Thirteen to go.

A HUMAN figure appeared from the gloom of the stairwell making no sound at all. Based on his dark outline, he was wearing civilian clothing but with a suppressed bullpup-style assault rifle in his hands. Fade watched disinterestedly from his position in front of a glass wall lit by stars.

Was it real or had he nodded off in the warm silence of the living room? Hard to say. No dripping fangs, and Eugene's putrefying corpse wasn't sitting at the bar spectating. Even more telling was the slight softness to it all. His dreams had taken on a surreal level of clarity. The difference between something constructed directly by the mind as opposed to something being filtered through eyes that weren't quite as sharp as they'd once been.

Another man appeared, hugging the wall, following his comrade toward the hallway that led to the bedrooms. Curiosity finally got the better of Fade and he lifted his gun, aiming at the lead intruder's right temple. What would happen if he pulled the trigger? Would the man crumple to the floor like so many times before? Or would the mutant tarantulas be released?

Only one way to find out.

Fade gently squeezed the trigger, feeling the recoil and hearing the weapon's metallic pop. The subsonic round went where he aimed it, producing the more familiar result. The target went down, leaving a black splatter pattern on the wall behind.

His teammate's reaction seemed just as real. He swung his weapon right, tearing up the bar on full auto before shattering the glass doors leading to the terrace. Fade dove instinctively to the ground and rolled toward a leafy palm that Raya had bought to disguise the house's main support pillar.

Rounds tore through the plant but were easily stopped by the concrete column behind. Fade found himself in a pretty solid defensive position, but it didn't give him much of a line on his opponent. Particularly with him now using more careful single shots to pummel what was left of Raya's tree. That changed when she suddenly appeared at the mouth of the hallway, looking like a ghost in nothing but a white T-shirt and panties.

Spotting her in his peripheral vision, the man reversed the sweep of his weapon. Fade was forced to break cover, firing as he charged. His first round struck the man's torso but the lack of any real effect confirmed the presence of body armor beneath his casual shirt. Raya screamed and crouched, covering her head as the man put a hole in the wall next to her.

Fade collided with him and managed to lift the weapon, sending a few more rounds into a painting that had come back from the framer just that afternoon. Thank God the sofa wasn't being delivered until Thursday.

His opponent drove the butt of his weapon into the SIG, sending it spinning across the floor. Fade closed in tighter, trapping the rifle and causing the man to go for something in his waistband. He wasn't particularly strong, but he was fast and efficient, getting his fingers around the hilt of a combat knife before Fade could stop him.

Pulling away to dodge the blade would be the expected move, but it was better to resist that urge and instead go forward again. It worked and the knife got tangled as they slammed into the wall. The man's back bounced off, and he used the momentum to drive Fade toward the chair he'd been sitting in only moments before.

The fact that Fade was familiar with its shape and weight turned out to be an advantage when they made contact. He managed to stay on his feet while his opponent ended up on one knee in a sea of broken glass. The rifle was still slung around his neck, but he focused on the blade, slashing in an effort to keep Fade at a distance. It worked, giving him enough space to get back to his feet and lunge.

Fade twisted away and got hold of the man's wrist but found himself being driven onto the terrace. The railing hit him in the small of his back, and he began flipping over it. Unable to overcome his momentum, the best he could do was to take his opponent with him. They continued their battle in the air, each trying to get the advantage and pull the other under. It was a solid twenty-foot drop to the asphalt, but whoever was on top might survive with all bones intact.

Fade's opponent hit first, but not the driveway. The impact was too soon and too soft. The roof of a vehicle. Had Raya left her Volvo there last night?

His opponent went still, folded backward over the side with his torso partially covering the driver's side window. In a stroke of good luck, the roof rack had broken his spine. In a stroke of bad luck, Raya's car didn't have a roof rack.

The vehicle reversed violently, sending Fade tumbling down the windshield and jerking to a stop when the waistband of his sweatpants got caught on one of the wipers. Inside, he saw the driver retrieve a submachine gun from the passenger seat.

The vehicle's brakes engaged, causing Fade to slide partway back up the windshield as the driver shifted back into a forward gear. The silence and force of the acceleration suggested some kind of electric vehicle, but it wasn't enough to free his pants. The flash of the weapon lit up the car's interior and Fade swung away from where the rounds were pounding the windshield. A hole appeared in the spiderwebbed glass, and Fade slammed a fist into it, penetrating with less resistance than he expected. That allowed him to get a grip on the hand the man was steering with and pull. The vehicle swerved, this time colliding head-on with the stone barrier that surrounded the property.

Suddenly Fade was free, arcing weightless over the steep slope below.

33

"FADE!"

Color went from black to a deep blue, but there was no other sensation. Just the blue.

"Fade!"

And that weirdly familiar voice calling his name.

He moved his toes. Miraculously, they seemed to work. Even more mind-blowing was that both flip-flops were still clinging to them. Fingers next. All functioned, though his right hand seemed to be wrapped around something he couldn't get free of.

"Fade!"

He lifted his eyelids a little more. Enough to see the beginning of dawn and that he was lying on a steep field of basketball-sized rocks that he'd managed to miss during his landing.

A crunching sound became audible above, followed by a cascade of pebbles rolling down on him.

"Oh my God, are you all right?" Raya's disembodied voice asked. She came into view a moment later, having added a pair of jeans and light hiking boots to her nightshirt. Upon seeing him, her eyes widened and she vomited.

Not a great sign.

He eased his head right, following her gaze to discover that he seemed to be shaking hands with an arm severed near the shoulder. Confusing until he remembered the crash and his death grip on the driver's wrist.

"Are you okay?" Raya repeated, wiping her mouth and dropping to her knees next to him.

"Cell . . ." His voice came out barely a whisper. "Matt . . ."

"You want me to call Matt?"

He nodded, and she dialed, putting the phone to his ear. Egan picked up almost immediately.

"Raya? Why are you calling? Is something wrong?"

"Three-man team," Fade got out. "Pros. Asian. If they came for me, they might be coming for you and the others."

The line immediately went dead.

I'm fine, asshole. Thanks for asking.

"Fade, should I call the paramedics? You need to get to a hospital."

"No. Just help me sit up."

"You're not supposed to move someone who—"

"Do it, Raya."

She lifted gently, one hand on his shoulder and the other cradling his head. Once upright, he did a more thorough check of his condition. Arm and leg joints all moved smoothly and only in the correct direction. His head swiveled side to side with full range of motion, and there were still no discernible issues with his back.

"Can you walk?"

"Probably. How far back up the slope to the house?"

"Maybe twenty meters?"

He rolled on all fours and started to crawl. "Get the arm."

Raya gagged a few times but followed his instructions and stayed right behind in case he slipped. By the time he reached the barrier wall, he was feeling a little better. Not so great that she didn't have to partially lift him over, though.

Daylight had strengthened, allowing him to survey the carnage. A Nissan EV had taken out part of the rock wall, trashing its front end in the process. The now one-armed driver looked like he'd tried to climb out the open side window but had gotten tangled in the airbag and bled out. The man who'd broken in half on top of the vehicle was now in the driveway, piled against a potted tree. The house, on the other hand, looked to be in pretty good shape other than the shot-up glass.

"We need to call the police," Raya said.

He turned and saw her standing at what she seemed to think was a safe distance. The arm had been neatly laid out on the wall behind her.

"No police. We're going to use your car to tow this one back. Then we'll push it into the garage. There are some surfboards in there, and the bags they're stored in will fit these guys. When we're done with that, you're going to have to break the rest of the glass out of the doors and open them. It'll be hard to see the damage with them in that position. While you're doing that, I'll clean off the driveway. The floor tiles in the living room won't soak up blood, but the grout will. And the walls are going to have to be patched and painted. The stonework out here will have to be repaired too. I'll give you a list of what we need, and you can go into town when things open up. Understood?"

BY SUNSET, they were in reasonably good shape. Raya had thrown up a few more times but had otherwise been a trooper. Their three friends were bagged and in the gym with the AC running full blast. The Nissan was in the garage, and Fade had rebuilt the exterior rock wall with mortar that looked a little new but didn't stand out too much. All the glass and debris were gone, the blood was cleaned from the floor, and the walls were spackled. The plaster would have to dry overnight, but they'd be able to sand and paint in the morning.

Even more important, no curious neighbors or cops had come by to inquire about the ruckus. There were no houses with a sight line, and the sound of the suppressed gunfire wouldn't have carried all that far. The crash had been loud, but in the event it woke anyone up, the sound would have been difficult to pinpoint. Mountain acoustics could be tricky.

"Not a bad day's work," Fade said, easing himself into a chair and chewing a few more Greek Aleve.

Raya was frozen in the middle of the room wearing a pair of rubber gloves she refused to take off.

"How about you make us a couple of gin and tonics?"

She nodded dutifully and went to the bar, finding an intact bottle of Hendrick's balancing on a broken shelf.

"Why did they come here?" she said, filling a couple of glasses with ice. "What did they want?"

"I don't know. But Matt'll figure it out."

"Could there be more of them?"

"Maybe. But they won't want to repeat this mess. They'll pull back and reassess."

"For how long?"

His phone rang and he struggled to dig it from his pocket with what was supposed to be his good hand. Matt Egan's number glowed on-screen.

"Yeah?"

"You were right. Daniel got out just in time. They chased him, but he got away."

"What about Linea?"

"Another three-man team, but they were late. She had time to get to one of the sniper positions she carved out of the woods above her place. Took out two. The third escaped."

"Asian?"

"Yeah. All of them. What's your situation?"

"We're pretty well cleaned up, but I've got three bodies that are going to be past their sale date pretty soon."

"Did they have a vehicle?"

"Yeah. It's in the garage. Not drivable."

"I assume you can still fix anything under the sun?"

"I dunno. It's not a real car. It's one of those electric things."

"See what you can do and get back to me."

Once again, the line went dead.

34

FADE USED Raya's blow-dryer to warm the fender before bending it against the frame and securing it with duct tape. Better. Not great, but better.

The temperature in the garage was creeping into three digits and the intoxicating scent of melting plastic, spray paint, and epoxy was overwhelming. After twelve hours of uninterrupted labor, progress was noticeable. It turned out that the Nissan actually still ran, which was a minor miracle. The steering was a little hinky, but it turned okay if you threw your back into it. A replacement windshield was installed and the lights worked but had to be operated by a series of switches connected to a battery in the back. Not sexy, but functional as long as the trip was short.

There was no paperwork relating to where the vehicle came from and nothing that would lead him to believe it was a rental. Also, no trackers or kill switches were evident, though that was certainly not a guarantee. The technology packed into these next-gen cars had left him far behind. Nothing but crap computers, rats' nests of wires, and unnecessary creature comforts. Quiet, though. He hadn't heard it come up the driveway.

The final task was the damage to the front end. Once he'd cut or bent everything rubbing the tires, it was really just a matter of tarting things up enough not to attract attention. On that front, mission accomplished. Not that it would win any awards, but good enough to be overlooked at night. The important thing was avoiding speed bumps and potholes. Tape, superglue, and chewing gum had their limits.

He turned and crawled to a low beach chair near the wall. The cooler next to it was full of beer, but he didn't retrieve one, instead letting the ice work on his swollen hand.

While the battle and falls hadn't done any permanent damage, they'd left virtually every square inch of him dented, bruised, or cut. The fact that he seemed to have no internal injuries and all his bones were in one piece was more evidence that the gods of war still loved him. Or hated him. Sometimes it was hard to tell.

His hand could be hidden in a pocket and his face hadn't sustained any damage that wasn't obscured by his beard. His right knee was a little puffed up and caused a minor limp but nothing anyone would remember. The Neosporin covering ninety percent of his body gleamed a little in strong light but could easily be mistaken for sweat. So while his break-dancing career was probably on hold for a while, there was nothing that would prevent him from moving unnoticed through polite society.

He used his uninjured hand to throw a screwdriver at a switch on the wall but missed by a few inches. On his third try, he scored, and the overhead LEDs died, leaving only the work light in the engine bay. As he settled a little deeper in the chair, a shadow in the far corner of the garage stirred. He grabbed the SIG on the floor next to him but then put it back when recognition set in.

Eugene stepped from the gloom, eye sockets now empty and shriveled face streaked with mold. The stench of decay intensified until it overwhelmed even the Bondo.

"I told you to stop," Fade said. "But you wouldn't listen."

Eugene took a few stiff paces forward, giving no indication that he'd heard.

"I talked to Lowe, man. Your brother's okay. Set up for life."

And then he was gone.

FADE WOKE to a quiet ping. He was still seated, neck craned back and frozen into a position that took a few seconds to get out of.

One thirty in the morning.

He rubbed at his eyes and then reached for the phone next to his SIG. A thumbprint got him into a screen demanding a password. Once he got past that, he was rewarded with a text from Matt Egan.

3 a.m. bring car and cargo. Security cameras will be down. Gate code is 5832.

An included link brought up directions to a slip in a marina about thirty minutes away.

He eased himself to his feet and entered the house, climbing through the semidarkness to the living area. Moonlight was streaming in from the terrace, revealing much-higher-quality work than he'd done on the car. Everything was sanded and painted, there were no lingering odors of death, and damage to the bar had been obscured by flipping the shelves around and adding a few more bottles. The doors were still trashed, but that was going to be a longer-term fix—likely involving various vendors and a lot of YouTube videos on glass replacement.

He continued past a piece of artwork that Raya had found to replace the damaged one and headed toward her room. The light was on and the door open, but he stopped in the threshold. Entering was prohibited by section six of her job description. Or was it section seven?

She was sitting in a chair staring at the neatly made bed. When he spoke, her head turned toward the sound.

"I'm going to get rid of the bodies in about an hour."

"I'll go with you."

"Not necessary. And no need for you to be here when I get back. Matt set up some bank accounts for me. I haven't looked at them, so I don't know how much is there, but it's yours. Should be enough to get you going."

"No. There might be problems. I can help."

He let out a long breath that made his bruised ribs ache. Their relationship hadn't been long, but he'd learned that arguing with her was a losing proposition. And she was right. In the context of this particular half-assed operation, he'd be better off with her than without her.

"Okay. Pack us a couple of small suitcases like we're going on a little vacation. I'll start loading up."

Getting the bodies into the vehicle had almost killed him, but now they looked pretty good. The surf bags were a little lumpy, but not leaking any bodily fluids. An artistic arrangement of tennis rackets, water skis, and tanning paraphernalia provided additional camouflage. Raya appeared with a couple of rollers, and he tossed them on top before settling into the passenger seat.

"You're driving."

The assumption was that this was going to go smoothly, but just in case, he had his SIG beneath the seat and one of his attackers' rifles behind it. A motorcade and some air cover would have been preferable but didn't seem to be on offer. Egan was probably kicked back in his mansion eating nachos and watching football. No corpses in his garage or glass shards in his ass, right?

Raya slid behind the wheel and put her white knuckles at two and ten.

"Okay. I'll tell you step by step how to get to the boat. You just have to follow the rules of the road and keep it around the speed limit. The steering's a little stiff, but you'll be able to handle it. Piece of cake. No traffic. No street parties. Just open road."

"Right. Easy," she said, clearly unconvinced.

He tapped a piece of cardboard containing a series of labeled switches. "I couldn't get the lights to work right, so I'll handle them from here."

She nodded.

"If we're stopped—and there's no reason we will be—the story is that we're going out on a friend's boat for a few days. Just answer whatever questions they ask clearly and concisely. Don't offer extra information."

"Okay."

"The front end's literally held on with tape. Don't hit any bumps."

"No bumps. I understand."

"Are you sure you want to do this? Because my offer's still good."

"I'm sure."

"All right, then. Let's get to work."

35

THE LIGHTS of Crete had melded with the haze and were gone now. From Fade's deck chair on the stern, all that was left were the pinpoints of a handful of distant craft and a few smears representing stars powerful enough to burn through.

Ironically, he'd never liked ships. The ant-farm efficiency. The smell. But most of all, he despised the idleness. His job with the navy had largely been to wait. Lengthy periods of mind-numbing boredom punctuated by brief bouts of chaos.

Obviously, this was a somewhat different scenario. If you had to wait, being one of two passengers on a luxury yacht was a decent way to do it. He closed his eyes and had almost started to drift when footsteps became audible behind him. Rubber soles traveling hesitantly across polished teak, followed by the creak of the chair next to him.

"So what's your story, Raya?"

The sound of her squirming reminded him of the power dynamics inherent in their relationship.

"Don't answer. I'm sorry I asked."

She stood, but instead of leaving took a position at the railing.

"I was born in a small village in Bulgaria. When I was fourteen, a man came through and saw me. A few days later, he met with my parents and told them he could get me a job modeling in Sofia. Then he gave them more money than they would have made in a year."

"But it wasn't really a modeling job," Fade said.

"No."

"Do you think they knew?"

"I don't know. I've never been in contact with them again."

"Because of what they did?"

"I'm sure that's part of it. But I think it's also because my life there came to feel very remote. Like a false memory. Something that never really existed."

"A hard thing to be forced into so young."

"Harder than some, easier than others. I worked entertaining older men in Eastern Europe. Mostly Russians. A few trips to the Middle East, but they prefer blondes. I was lonely and had more time to myself than most people would think, so I decided to educate myself. It wasn't discouraged. In fact, no one really paid attention at first. Eventually, though, it was identified as potentially valuable. You've probably noticed that I'm a very organized person."

"I have noticed that."

"My work became longer term and less narrow in scope. A mistress of sorts. Or . . . is the word *concubine*? I helped wealthy men who were single or away from their families with their lives. I took care of things like housing, food, and travel. I translated. I hired and directed staff. Among other things, of course."

"Was that gig better?"

"Yes. I lived in beautiful places. Some of the work was actually quite challenging and I proved myself. A few of the men were horrible, but most weren't. More, they were distant. Better for me that their lust was focused on power, money, and status."

He wondered where he'd rank in her hierarchy of bosses. Pulling a guy's arm off couldn't help but, to be fair, it wasn't specifically prohibited on her list. An omission she'd probably already remedied.

Section IX: Defenestration and Dismemberment.

"So it's all good as long as everyone follows your rules."

"Yes."

"Do they?"

"Most."

"But not all."

"My job description was created in reaction to one very abusive man. He was in his seventies and not very vigorous, fortunately, but full of rage. Emotionally abusive. Threatening. It never stopped. He even hit me a few times."

"What happened?"

"He got drunk one night and fell down a set of stairs. It was an old, historic house with no railings."

"Died in the fall?"

"No. From the Russian winter. He was either unconscious or unable to get up, and a door was left open."

A door was left open. Such a beautiful use of the passive voice. Was the story intended to answer his initial question or was it a subtle warning?

Nice life you've got there. Shame if something happened to it.

"When did you start working for Matt?" he said, redirecting the subject.

"Only recently. After what happened to Sergey, there was some question about my future. Particularly because I'm so old now."

"How old is old?" he asked, unable to help himself.

"I'll turn thirty in February."

He grinned but still didn't open his eyes. Twenty-nine seemed like another lifetime to him. Probably because it technically was. After his second clinical death but before his third.

"Almost ready for Social Security."

"I think they had less altruistic plans. But then your friend bought me."

"You mean he bought out your contract."

She didn't respond.

"Then what?"

"He gave me the address of the house in Greece and told me to wait. That a man named Salam al-Fayed would be coming. And now I'm here. On the back of a boat next to a car full of dead men."

"Good story."

"Not at all. A life with no arc. A series of anecdotes without significance."

He nodded. "I know exactly what you mean."

They fell silent when footsteps became audible. Unrecognizable to him.

"Sir?"

Fade twisted around to face a man he assumed was the captain. Early sixties, wearing an N95 surgical mask and unwilling to get too close to his younger passengers.

"We've stopped," Fade observed.

"Yes, sir. We're about as isolated and deep as we're going to get before dawn."

"Give me five minutes, then shut off all the lights."

"Do you need help?"

"No."

The man pressed a button on his watch. "Five minutes starting now."

He headed back toward the bridge, and Fade stood, stretching and testing his various injuries for limitations.

"What do we do?" Raya said. "Just put the rails back out and roll the car into the water?"

He opened the stern gate. "No. They don't work that way. The other end needs to be supported by a dock."

"Then what?"

He opened the Nissan's driver-side door and reached for a hammer he'd left on the floorboard. The smell of death had finally penetrated the bags, and it now clung to the interior.

"Fade?"

The power windows had resisted his every attempt at repair, forcing a somewhat-lower-tech solution. He swung the hammer into the glass as Raya looked on. It spiderwebbed on the first blow, and he used the tool's claw to tear it out. Once free, he threw it in the passenger seat.

"I don't think I like where this is going," Raya said.

Fade ignored her, slipping behind the wheel and fastening his safety belt before pressing the ignition button. The vehicle made a few inexplicable noises to signal that it was running but remained completely dark.

"It's a lot longer drop off the back of this boat than it seems," Raya said as he backed the vehicle as far as possible.

"Stop hand-wringing. It'll be fine."

The yacht's lights went out and he stomped on the accelerator. While EVs were unquestionably soulless, there was no denying the torque. It shoved him back in the seat, and then he went weightless for a moment before the impact with the water caused the seat belt to jerk across his injured torso. The vehicle paused nose down long enough for a body to come through the gap between the seats, then started to sink.

The saltwater rushing through the broken window got into every cut and scrape, lighting up nerves Fade didn't even know he had. That, combined with the darkness, made releasing his seat belt more difficult than he'd anticipated. By the time it was free, the car was fully submerged, making depth and direction impossible to discern.

The bagged body that had slipped from the back was now floating sideways across the windshield, interfering with Fade's escape. He shoved it back and reached out, feeling around for the roof rack. Once he got a grip, he was able to pull himself through.

The sudden sense of nothingness took him by surprise. The pain of the salt had melted away, and the inevitable burning in his lungs hadn't yet manifested. It was like floating in a warmer version of outer space. No gravity. No light or sound. Like the calm after a gunshot.

Which way was up? He'd been trained to easily answer that question. The hard part was determining if it was the right direction.

He averted his eyes from the glare of the yacht's lights coming back on. Below, the illumination faded slowly to black.

Beautiful.

A column of bubbles appeared to his right and two arms wrapped around him. A moment later, he'd broken both the surface and the spell. A couple strokes took him to the stern ladder, and he climbed with Raya close behind.

She collapsed on deck, heaving and choking as he looked down at her. After a few seconds, she regained the ability to speak.

"Now we're even."

36

FADE LAID into the Porsche Cayenne's accelerator and felt it react immediately. Not as instantaneous as the EV he'd launched into the Med, but infinitely more satisfying. His preprogrammed GPS said to stay on the main road as it climbed into a rural landscape outside of Granada, Spain. The Sierras had been dusted with snow the night before, creating a stark white layer on the horizon. He had no idea where he was going, but it was hard to complain about the journey.

Raya had been whisked back to Crete shortly after they'd dumped the bodies, but he'd been instructed to stay on the yacht. His cabin turned out to have all the luxuries he was coming to expect along with one surprising bonus: his beloved Mystery Machine. After connecting, he'd spent almost the entire next four days unconscious, waking only for bathroom breaks and to cram himself with protein.

Good times.

The GPS pointed him toward a serpentine road that cut through a forest of widely spaced pines. After a few miles, it narrowed and became gravel, making a number of hairpins before passing through a gate that immediately closed behind him. The house beyond was quite a contrast to the one he'd left a few days before. Far larger, it was constructed from the local stone and looked like it had been there a couple hundred years. A few sections had collapsed and been artistically repurposed as outdoor spaces, while others had been filled with enormous glass patch panels. A weird combination of ancient and modern that somehow worked spectacularly. He knew a lot about construction and design from his time as a furniture builder, and the word *genius* wasn't sufficient to describe whoever had pulled this thing off.

When he stepped out of the vehicle, Raya appeared from a wooden door that must have been ten feet tall and a good eight inches thick. She strode across the stone courtyard and gave him her customary two-cheek kiss before relieving him of his duffle.

"You look good," she said, a bit perplexed. The black eye was nearly gone, as were the countless abrasions and contusions that had covered most of his body. His right hand was no longer swollen, and the only hint that it had been injured was a light layer of gauze still covering his knuckles. Even his knee was normal sized and fully operational again.

"So do you."

In fact, she looked better than good. Form-fitting white jeans, a gray sweater hanging low at the neck, and hair pulled into a ponytail he'd never seen her wear before. The tilt of her head indicated that she wanted to know more about his miraculous recovery but was unwilling to ask. Probably for the better. He'd decided not to give it much thought either.

She thumbed back at the house. "Your behavior seems to have been rewarded."

The interior was even more impressive, with stone arches and hand-hewn beams giving the space a cathedral feel. A state-of-the-art kitchen created yet another seamless contrast, as did a bar with shelves that rose high enough to need a ladder to access.

No booze, though. Whether that was because Spain's allotment had already been slurped up by its panicking senior citizens or because of his recent reunion with the Mystery Machine wasn't clear. Not that it mattered. The sad, dry result was the same.

It seemed impossible, but the back patio turned out to be the highlight. It consisted of a partially covered stone terrace that extended to a pool that seemed to have been built from an ancient aqueduct. At the far end, it hung some twenty feet above the ground and created a waterfall that emptied into another pool below.

A little overwhelmed by the opulence, Fade pointed to a more modest outbuilding visible in the woods to the west. It had been restored with an eye more faithful to its history, leaving two stories of nearly windowless stone fronted by weathered bay doors.

"What's up with that?"

"It's just full of junk."

"Old farm stuff?"

"No. Old car stuff."

His eyebrows rose. "Let's have a look."

With the doors dragged open, he discovered that the *old car stuff* was a nearly-rust-free '69 Camaro in about a thousand pieces. Original parts were strewn about the space alongside more contemporary replacements—a Chevy crate engine that he suspected would make well over five hundred horsepower, state-of-the-art suspension goodies, and a whole lot of gleaming chrome. But that wasn't all. Everything needed to do the work was there too, including welders, an industrial compressor, metal fabrication equipment, and a top-of-the-line lift.

In other words, heaven.

He walked along the vehicle's body, running a hand over the front fender and then leaning through the passenger-side window. A lesser cult leader would have left him the keys to a pristine restoration. Not Lowe, though. He somehow knew that Fade's dream wasn't to drive a car built with the sweat and blood of others. It was to drive one infused with his own.

"I'm working on getting rid of all this stuff, but I haven't been able to find anyone yet. Probably by next week."

He glanced up and saw that she'd stopped in the threshold, unwilling to put her pristine jeans in jeopardy.

"Don't touch a thing."

37

AFTER THREE days, it was difficult to resist the temptation to start grinding on something. That was the soul of a project like this. Hot metal shards, environmentally questionable chemicals, and the clang of hammer on steel. But soul without brains created beauty without the beast. And so there he was. Cataloging, photographing, and tagging.

Fade spun his stool away from the laptop, gazing longingly at the Camaro before scanning the now somewhat better-organized shop. He probably had another week of just figuring out what was there and what he lacked. Then another month of disassembly, bagging parts, and placing orders. After that, he'd be ready to sketch out a restoration plan.

He reached for his phone when Raya's ring tone rose above Bananarama blasting over hidden speakers.

"What's up?"

"A car just turned onto the property and is on its way to the house."

"Hold on."

He picked up an HK416 and danced toward an open window that faced the courtyard. The vehicle turned out to be another Porsche Cayenne, but with the GTS package in red. It stopped at the gate, and Fade centered his crosshairs between the lenses of the driver's Ray-Bans.

"Go ahead and open up, Raya."

He tracked the vehicle as it rolled through and came to a stop.

"It's Mr. Egan," she said.

"I know."

Fade disconnected the call and walked to the open bay doors.

"You look good," Egan called as he approached.

"That's what they tell me."

"Is there somewhere we can talk?"

Choices were plentiful enough to be a little paralyzing. The state-of-the-art gym? Medieval wine cellar? Home theater? Or how about the conversation pit in his thousand-square-foot bedroom suite?

Fade led him through the house's front door, where they found Raya in the kitchen poring over appliance manuals.

"Hello, Mr. Egan. Can I get you something?"

"Thank you, no," he said, taking in the grandeur as they passed through and exited onto the rear patio. Fade motioned toward a dining table near the pool, and Egan sat, dialing his phone as he did. Lowe's voice came on speaker a moment later.

"Fade. How are you?"

"Fine."

"I'm so glad to hear it. I can't apologize enough for what happened in Greece. It was entirely my fault."

"What *did* happen in Greece?"

Lowe sighed audibly. "I got the information about that lab in Wyoming from a man named Bóchéng. He's a former Chinese intelligence operative who now works as a private contractor."

"And a complete backstabbing piece of shit," Egan added.

Lowe's didn't speak up to disagree.

"What's his beef with me? And he sent people for Linea and Danny too, right?"

"I think it was less one thing than a combination of a few. First, I suspect he gave up that lab because he was confident we wouldn't find anything. That changed when you turned up Doctor Gao. Second, he appears to be concerned about my increasing . . ." The phone went silent while he searched for the right words. "Let's just say my security capability. He identified the three of you in Wyoming and saw a way to degrade that capability."

"Where is he now?"

"Underground, it seems. Maybe out of fear of retaliation by me, but I suspect much more out of fear of the Chinese government."

"So if they catch him and question him, they'll find out about you? About us?"

"I imagine so. Also, I think he knows more about Yichén than he's telling me."

"Seems like if that was true, he'd sell it. To you or to the Chinese. Judging by all the dishes they've been breaking around the world, they'd pay a lot."

"That would be too rational. Bóchéng is obsessed with power and only in his forties. He can be a part of bringing down the world's governments and killing more than three-quarters of a billion people. Quite a rush for a man like him. And frankly, quite an opportunity. His business is chaos, and he's good at it."

Fade looked out along the pool to the waterfall at its end. "Did you learn anything from Gao?"

"We did. We learned that Yichén's virus is extremely sophisticated and targeted and that it's all but complete. Gao wasn't working on the virus itself; he was working on vaccines against it."

"Vaccines?"

"Yes. I imagine in case there's an accident along the lines of what happened with COVID, or if the pathogen starts to mutate in ways he doesn't anticipate."

"Did he give you enough information to create your own vaccine?"

"Not entirely. But enough to be able to move quickly once we know exactly what we're dealing with."

"Sounds like you've got this under control. What am I missing?"

"You're missing that the devil is in the details. Yichén's virus will be very contagious and have an extremely long incubation period. Even if we discover it through random testing on people who aren't symptomatic—something we're already doing—we still have to develop the vaccine, produce it, and administer it. The first part won't take much time. One of my colleagues is the CEO of Pfizer, and he's already setting up rapid response teams for this. But the manufacture and distribution of hundreds of millions of doses isn't trivial. Or fast."

Fade smiled. "But plenty of time to whip up a few small batches and hand them out to your billionaire cronies."

"Probably," Lowe admitted. "Look, Fade, I believe I might have the power to deflect the current trajectory of the world. Not reverse it. There'll always be a ruling class. My goal is to make sure it's not made up of the worst of us."

It sounded like more of the same to Fade, but it was also the truth. The food chain would always have apex predators. Maybe the best you could do was make sure it wasn't the hyenas.

"So what's the op, Jon?"

"Op?"

"All of a sudden, the machine everyone says is slowly killing me shows up in my cabin for four days when I would have eventually just healed on my own. It wasn't so I could wander around the Spanish countryside without a limp."

"We're monitoring your well-being very carefully. It isn't—"

"Relax. This isn't new to me. I'm a shooter, and shooters are expendable. Now, what's the op?"

"Bóchéng," Egan answered. "We want to know what else he's got on this."

"And you want to keep him from giving you up to the Chinese government if they get a hold of him."

"Giving *us* up," Lowe said. "But yes."

"How? You said he's gone to ground."

"We might have a way to find him. A mistress. She's his only weakness, and he keeps her existence very quiet."

"But you know about it."

"Only because one of my people runs the cell provider that connects his burner phones."

"You think he'll go see her with all this shit coming down? I mean, I admit that men will go a long way for a piece of tail, but ending up in the hands of Chinese intelligence?"

"A few days ago, he called and asked her to go on the run with him," Egan said. "She declined, but in as slick a way as I've ever heard. Lots of crocodile tears and promises that she'll wait for him until the sun burns out. You know, as long as he keeps paying the rent."

"Evil."

"You have no idea. But she has him wrapped around her little finger. There's a possibility—admittedly small—that he'll try to persuade her face-to-face."

"And if he does, we snatch him."

"Correct."

"Can I assume she doesn't live in some remote country estate?"

"Fourth-floor condo in the middle of Porto, Portugal."

"Tricky."

"But critical," Lowe said. "Millions of lives are at stake, Fade. Maybe more. All these young people throwing street parties might be overestimating how safe they are. The old men with their fingers on the trigger aren't going to go easily. If they contract Yichén's disease, there's no telling what their reaction will be. But take it from a person who knows a lot of them. It won't be benevolent surrender."

Fade considered that for a few moments. "Sure. Why not? I'm in."

Lowe let out a long breath that sounded like genuine relief. "Can I ask you one more favor?"

"Go ahead."

"You're in kind of an ideal position—a large house close to Portugal and owned by a maze of shell companies. Would it be possible for us to use it as a base of operations?"

Fade shrugged. "Mi casa es su casa, Jon."

AFTER A lengthy search, Fade finally found Raya on the second-floor terrace.

"Is Mr. Egan staying?" she asked as he came alongside.

Below, the back of the Porsche was open, and he was unloading luggage.

"For a little while. But you're not."

"What?"

"Things are out of control. We got lucky in Greece, but I feel like our luck's about to run out."

"You seem hard to kill."

"Yeah. But you're not."

"You can protect me."

Fade watched Egan heft a duffle and start for the door. "All this—everything we have—is being provided by a guy named Jon Lowe."

"Who?"

"He's some kind of genius billionaire. A while back, he decided that the world's so messed up he has no choice but to take it over."

"He sounds insane."

"What's even more insane is that I give him a fifty-fifty chance of succeeding."

"So you work for him? You're helping him?"

"Pretty much, yeah. And right now, he's trying to solve humanity's most pressing problem."

Her brow furrowed. "Do you mean Yichén Zhu?"

"Yup. And if the Chinese government finds out we know more than they do—which they probably will—next time, it won't be three guys with guns. It'll be fifty. So I'm going to tell Matt to give you a nice severance and put you on a first-class flight to Montana."

"Montana?"

"Until this blows over—or blows up—probably best to avoid major population centers."

She nodded, watching as Egan reappeared in the courtyard. "He already did."

"Who did what?"

She fished her phone from the back pocket of her jeans, scrolled through the screen, and then held out a text from Egan.

Very sorry about what happened. Paperwork is done for your permanent residency in USA. $250k deposited in your account. If you're not sure how to get started, text me. Have people who can help.

"I'm a little confused," Fade said.

"About what?"

"Why you're still here."

"It's complicated."

"Explain it in terms I can understand."

"You saved my life."

"And you saved mine, remember? I think you even said something along the lines of 'We're even.' And you were right. We are."

Her expression took on a hint of frustration. "Who do you have?"

"You mean in my life?"

"Yes."

"No one. I'm an only child, and my parents are dead. I never knew the family we left behind in Syria, and after the war there, they're probably dead too." He pointed down at Egan. "But you want to hear the really pathetic part? That asshole used to be my best friend."

"I don't know if my parents are dead," Raya said. "But they are to me. I haven't had a real friend since I left my village. A few years ago, I got sick while I was working as a companion for a man in Riga. I went to the hospital alone, and by that afternoon, I'd been replaced. I was there for two weeks and almost died. No one ever came to see me or advocate for me. When I was released, I just got in a cab and told the driver to take me to the nearest hotel. Finally, that night, someone came to see if I was still pretty and able to work. No one's ever done anything for me, and I've never done anything for anyone else. Not until a few days ago."

"You're setting the bar too low, Raya. Go to Montana. Marry a nice guy with cows. Make normal friends. Have a normal family. You'll be a lot happier, and you'll live a lot longer."

"But how would I explain who I am to normal people? How could they understand my past and help me find a future?"

"I'm not sure that surrounding yourself with people who are as broken as you is the way to go. At best, it's a cop-out."

"What about you?" she said, unmoved by his amazing advice. "Who will you tell your story to? Where will you find someone who won't judge you? Or be afraid?"

"This isn't about me, Raya."

She nodded toward Egan, who was closing up the Porsche. "Your former best friend. Do you trust him?"

"No."

"And this other man. Lowe?"

"No."

"Can I trust you?"

"That's a hard question to answer."

"It's an easy question to answer. We don't have anyone, Fade. Neither of us. But what if we could have each other? Just for a while. Until we get on our feet. What is it you Americans say? I'll have your back if you have mine."

He stared down at her outstretched hand for a few seconds before finally reaching for it.

38

FADE WAS still a little groggy when he entered the dining area. One of the short-term side effects of the Mystery Machine was a case of semi-narcolepsy that he'd learned to take advantage of. Three hours of hard sleep wasn't an easy thing to come by these days.

Raya was at the front door talking to a delivery man in Spanish, which she seemed to have picked up over the last few days. He gave an unintelligible response and started toward the kitchen, looking around with the same disoriented amazement as everyone else the first time they entered.

"Are you feeling better?" she asked, angling across the stone floor in his direction.

"Yeah, thanks."

"Can I get you anything?"

He rubbed eyes that didn't seem to want to fully open. "I'd take a beer."

She shook her head. "No alcohol for seventy-two more hours. Mr. Egan said it's because of the medication they gave you for your injuries."

"Yeah. Right."

"How about one of Carina's lemonades? She told me you liked them."

Fade felt a pang of embarrassment. It hadn't occurred to him that Raya would know the twins, but of course she did.

"Sure."

"Everyone's waiting. I told them they couldn't wake you." She pointed. "Están en el teatro."

"Thanks, Raya."

"De nada."

It turned out they'd gotten the whole band back together. Egan, Harding, and Linea were standing near the massive video screen, talking conspiratorially.

All looked in his direction when he entered, but only Harding approached for a quick handshake and embrace. "Thanks for the heads-up on that team, mate. Could have gotten hairy."

Linea gave him the expected icy nod. Not a barrel of laughs, but admittedly confidence-inspiring when the shit hit the fan. Egan just frowned in irritation. It was all he knew how to do anymore.

"Nice of you to join us."

"Fuck you too," Fade responded, dropping into the nearest chair.

"I guess we can start now."

The other two sat, and the screen behind Egan lit up with the image of a puffy Asian man in his mid-forties.

"Our target. Haoyu Bóchéng. Since this picture was taken, he's lost about twenty pounds of fat and put on ten of muscle. He's definitely behind the attacks on you, probably for his own account and not on the orders of the Chinese government. His relationship with them has always been complicated, but we're pretty sure it's taken a serious turn for the worse. Our best guess is that they're after him for the same reason we are—they have reason to believe that he knows more about Yichén Zhu than he's letting on."

"Or because they're desperate," Linea said.

"Possibly," Egan admitted. "But remember that he's the one who told us about the lab in Wyoming. It's a pretty good bet he didn't give us everything."

"Is that true? Or is he just our *only* bet?"

"Doesn't matter at this point."

She shrugged and settled back in her seat again.

The screen darkened, and the photo was replaced by one of an Asian woman in her twenties. "This is Bóchéng's favorite mistress, Shuchun. We know that because he's now contacted her three times asking her to come with him on the run. So far, she's refused."

Fade examined her, noting that these Asian femme fatales seemed to be popping up a lot in his life. This one was completely different from the psycho bitch who'd tried to kill him in Wyoming, though. She was perfect. Flawless skin, flawless hair, designer everything. Her annual grooming costs looked like they probably exceeded the GDP of some developing nations. It worked, though. A woman to die for.

"And you think he'll try to go make his case personally?" Linea said, sounding skeptical. "That seems overly stupid."

Fade smiled. Not having a penis, women could just never understand the organ's power to cloud one's judgment.

"He could have her snatched," Harding pointed out.

"Unlikely," Egan said. "Based on their conversations, he's afraid of her. Like I said earlier, he's had quite a physical transformation recently, and he'll want to show it off to help persuade her. Also, one of the things that got Bóchéng to where he is today is an insatiable appetite for risk. In this case, that plays in our favor."

The screen changed again, this time depicting an old building with blue and white tiles covering part of its facade.

"This is in the center of Porto, Portugal, on an unrestricted two-lane, two-way street. It's been renovated into luxury holiday flats that are listed on various websites. Four stories total, with one small elevator and a set of stairs. The first two stories have two apartments each, while the third and fourth each have one large apartment. Bóchéng has rented out the top floor flat long-term for Shuchun."

He clicked through a series of Airbnb ads for each of the building's units. The one in question was basically the twin of its neighbor below, with a sizable entry flowing into an open layout living area and kitchen. The rear wall had a sliding glass door that led to a modest terrace overhanging a narrow pedestrian street. A hallway passed a powder room, eventually arriving at two large ensuite bedrooms with custom closets. Furniture was Euro-posh and identical in both apartments, right down to the artwork and fake plants.

"If he's coming, will we know in advance?" Harding asked.

"Unlikely. Based on their conversations so far, she'd probably tell him not to. If he shows up, my guess is it'll be unannounced."

"Can we assume he travels with a security detail?" Linea said.

"Typically, four former soldiers. Competent but not all stars."

"Can we just pay off the girl?" Fade asked.

"Too risky. He's set her up pretty well, and she's smart enough to know what he's capable of. There's no reason for her to turn on him in favor of an unknown."

"Then this is a pretty heavy lift, Matt. The building's right in the middle of a crowded tourist city on a heavily used street. In all likelihood, he'll be dropped off right out front with either his entire detail or three of them with the other circling until he's ready to leave. Could we get him on the way into town?"

"There's no telling how he's going to arrive. Train, car, private plane, airline. And for the most part, those places are just as populated."

"On the way out, then?" Linea said.

"It's something to consider, but we run into the same problem. What route is he taking to get out of the city, and how's he leaving the country?"

"We could cover every port of entry and figure it out when he arrives," Harding suggested.

"That assumes he's leaving the same way he came," Egan countered. "And while that's a reasonable bet, it's not a sure thing."

"I wonder if it's even a reasonable bet," Fade commented. "I mean, after seeing the girl, I feel better about the possibility that he's going to make a play for her. But he knows the risks, and he'll be cautious to the point of paranoia."

Based on the murmurs that rose up in the theater, his teammates agreed.

"Mission impossible," Linea said.

Fade grinned at the reference. "Exactly. Mission impossible."

39

FADE PEERED past his cab driver and through the front windshield. They were driving through Porto's popular central district, but it had a bit of a post-apocalyptic feel. Despite being barely eleven at night, there were few signs of life beyond an occasional sliver of light escaping the houses lining the street. Shops and restaurants were closed, streetlights were dark, and sidewalks were empty. The vehicle's headlights mostly washed across barred windows and walls full of fresh graffiti.

"You know of this, no?" his driver said. "The curfew? It starts at ten o'clock. We had much trouble. With the young people."

"I heard," Fade said, rolling down his window to exchange the stench of stale cigarette smoke for cold, damp air. Temperatures had dropped into the high fifties, significantly lower than they had been in Spain. Not that he'd had any time to enjoy his new pool or even assemble the enormous grill Raya had ordered. Duty—such as it was—called.

"They are stupid," the man continued. "They don't think. All have family. Friends. Like me. Like you, no?"

"Sure," Fade lied.

"They think it is a game. That they will get everything . . . Inherit, yes? Inherit without having to work. But this isn't how things are."

Fade leaned his head a little farther out the window, enjoying the wind against his skin and in his ears. The calm before the storm.

His strategy of bingeing the first few seasons of the *Mission Impossible* television series had been met with skepticism at first. After a few hours, though, Linea and Harding had joined in. First out of curiosity, and then because the exercise actually seemed to be producing some interesting ideas. Egan had been largely consumed with logistics, enlisting Raya to help him plan transportation, gather equipment, and identify the thousand other details that he was so good at nailing down. When they hit a lull, he'd drift in and critique their half-baked plans, demonstrating that his edge hadn't dulled as much as Fade thought.

In the end, they'd cobbled together an operation with way too many moving parts and a shameful reliance on luck. But you went to war with the plan you had, not the plan you wished you had.

"This is it," his driver said, pulling to the curb. "Good location. There are still restaurants here, and you are not too far from the water. There is also a supermarket ahead. The corner to the right."

"What about alcohol?" Fade said.

"A little harder. Particularly for tourists. The people are . . ." It took him a moment to come up with the right sentiment. "Taking it for themselves."

Undoubtedly true, but likely not insurmountable. Particularly when in the company of a cab driver. If you wanted something in any city in the world, they were the people to talk to.

"Maybe you'd know someone who can help," Fade said, passing a hundred euros between the seats.

The man looked at the banknote, examined Fade in the rearview mirror for a moment, and then handed him a card containing nothing but a handwritten phone number.

Fade got out and walked to the rear of the minivan, his flip-flops smacking audibly. The sound of the world saviors since AD 30.

The driver helped him with a bike box and two rolling duffels, finally leaving Fade in the building's empty lobby. The tourist industry across the world had collapsed as older travelers hunkered down and businesses were forced to close or to provide limited services with their younger staff. With the exception of Shuchun's penthouse, the place was vacant and would stay that way. Egan had booked the other five flats for the entire month.

As expected, the elevator was out of service, and he was forced to carry his bags up the narrow stairs one at a time. Apartment 1-1 had a keypad, and he entered the code to open the door.

It was a nice place. Smaller than the ones on the floors above, it comprised a similar living area and terrace access but only one bedroom and bath. He tossed his duffel on the bed before walking over to examine the interior of a spacious closet.

Everything more or less as advertised. So far, so good.

He returned to the kitchen and started his laptop, opening an application that connected to cameras set up a few hours before. The tiled feeds confirmed that everything was functioning within expected parameters. They covered the elevator, lobby, and stairwell, as well as the facade from Harding's fourth-floor apartment across the street. Fade clicked on another tab, and the feeds from the apartment above appeared. It was dark, but the camera's night mode compensated, giving him every room and the terrace.

Outstanding.

Next was an app that had been loaded on his phone before he left Spain. It was still in active development and hadn't been working on the plane, but after an update, functionality improved. The interface was pretty straightforward but was still going to take some practice to operate confidently.

He returned to the main camera feed tab on his laptop and watched absently as the occasional car cruised by. Twenty minutes passed before a minivan similar to the one he arrived in glided to a stop in front of the building. Linea stepped out and went around the back to retrieve even more luggage than he'd arrived with.

Fade swiped through the app on his phone until he found the screen that, in theory, would give him control of the elevator. It actually worked, and he watched Linea remove the out-of-order sign and start stuffing luggage. After a quick glance behind her at the hidden camera, she pushed the button for the fourth floor—the location of the apartment where Bóchéng kept his mistress.

Fade pressed a lightbulb icon with the number four in it and she gave a thumbs-up to indicate that the correct button on the elevator's control panel had lit. That done, he pressed an icon with the number three, sending the elevator to that floor instead of the one above.

Linea got out and entered the apartment, piling her luggage on the floor while Fade switched to interior cameras. He watched her pull out a rug and various other items that Shuchun, based on her many social media selfies, had upgraded. Not that Bóchéng seemed like the kind of guy who would notice decorating details, but it paid to be thorough.

Fade closed his laptop and returned to the bedroom to unpack the bike box he'd stored there. It contained building materials and various tools, all neatly arranged in bubble wrap. Nothing that plugged in, though, because of the noise. Not a big deal. He'd always preferred hand tools anyway. Not as fast or accurate as twenty-first-century machinery, but a hell of a lot more satisfying.

40

FADE GRABBED the remote off the bed and turned up the television. Not that it was going to do much good. While the soccer match's commentator was more colorful than most, Portuguese was a completely unintelligible language. Worse, the picture was compressed, taking up only half the screen while video of the building took up the rest. With virtually no tenants, though, there wasn't much to see.

Linea had turned off the feeds to the apartment she was occupying, but they now had Shuchun's flat fully wired. That, too, was less entertaining than it should have been. It turned out she didn't do much. Outside, a surveillance team kept tabs on her shopping, coffee drinking, and gym attendance. As near as they could tell, she had no friends, no other lovers, and no job. When at home, she was even more dull. She ate the same things every day, watched TV, posted selfies to social media, and oddly, was a bit of a gamer. He hadn't bothered to turn on her feeds for days. Her activities were largely irrelevant to the operation, and it was depressing to be reminded that someone that hot could be so soul-crushingly dull.

He walked to the closet, examining his handiwork for what had to have been the thousandth time. Transforming the space to the left into a secret compartment had initially been an exercise in speed over precision. No more, though. Being trapped in the flat for days on end had left him with nothing to do but go back over every detail. He'd even ordered some handmade Japanese chisels for the fine work. Now it was perfect. Even the owner of the property would be unlikely to notice that the closet was smaller by a third. It'd probably stay that way for years until an overpacked vacationer complained that it wasn't as spacious as in the ad.

He ran a finger down the invisible joint between plaster and wood, wondering if it was maybe *too* invisible. Contrasted with the shoddier work of the rest of the flat, it might stand out. Maybe he should trash it a little to make it more consistent. And to push back the boredom for a few more hours.

The excitement in the TV announcer's voice began to build, and Fade flopped back on the mattress in time to watch a barely deflected shot on goal. He took a measured sip of his beer as the howls of the young crowd filled the bedroom.

It was just after 9:00 p.m., with the score holding at three to two, when the ping of an incoming text sounded. He grabbed his cell and looked at the screen.

Three blocks out

Shit. The hope had been that they'd get a reasonable heads-up before Bóchéng arrived—that Egan's surveillance teams would spot him at the airport or train station, or he'd call Shuchun to tell her he was on his way. Learning of his arrival a minute before he stopped in front of the building wasn't a great start.

Fade responded to the text with a thumbs-up emoji and then opened the now much more capable building control app. After running a quick diagnostic, he took command of the elevator and intercom. Finally, he switched the soccer match to the video feed from Linea's apartment. Once again live, it found her in frantic motion.

She'd stripped off the sweats she'd been living in for nearly a week, leaving her in only a pair of black lace panties and bra. Her skin had been dyed to match Shuchun's, and her short hair fit easily beneath a dark wig. Bare feet brought her a little closer to the right height, an illusion that was enhanced by putting the entryway credenza on blocks and raising the artwork three inches. Makeup had been used to try to alter her features to the degree possible, but they were counting more on backlighting and the fact that no man in his right mind would be looking at her face in the scenario they'd created.

"He's pulling up in front of the building," Harding said from his vantage point across the street.

"I'll be ready," Linea responded, donning a sheer robe that she didn't close at the front. The shimmery material broke up her more athletic outline.

"I'm all green on the app," Fade said.

"Confirming that it's Bóchéng. He's on the sidewalk. Four guards like we expected. Three got out with him. The driver's pulling away."

There was some debate as to whether their target would have a key to the front door. Fade and Linea were the only ones who guessed no. This woman was all about control.

It turned out that they were right. Bóchéng buzzed, but the call went to Fade's laptop instead of Shuchun's intercom. Subtitles of the man's less-than-romantic greeting were generated automatically.

It's me. Open the door.

"I'm letting him in," Fade said as he buzzed the lock.

"Two men coming with him," Harding said. "The other's staying outside, moving to the north edge of the building. One's staying in the lobby near the stairs. Bóchéng and the last guard are going for the elevator."

Fade managed to get the timing exactly right, lighting the button to the fourth floor just as the guard touched it but sending them to the third.

"They're on their way up, Linea. ETA twenty-four seconds."

"I'm ready," she responded.

The cameras in her entry provided a good view of both her and the front door. Lighting was working as intended, providing a provocative outline but not much detail.

"They're exiting the elevator," Fade reported.

"Copy."

Bóchéng approached while his guard retreated to the far side of the landing, doing his best to disappear as his client knocked.

"Come in," Linea said in Chinese good enough to sound fluent through the door.

He did, stepping through and pausing for a moment to admire her before pushing the door closed.

"Looking good so far," Fade said.

In his experience, people saw what they expected to see. What they wanted to see. Not what was real.

Linea moved forward, her gait a practiced approximation of Shuchun's. Bóchéng remained motionless, enraptured by the approaching figure. She was within six feet when his brow finally furrowed.

The speed and force of her charge surprised him, and by the time he thought to resist, a syringe was already being emptied into his neck. Linea clamped a hand over his mouth and held him close, locking them into something approximating a lover's embrace as she lowered him to the ground.

"And he's down," Fade said as she began dragging the unconscious man toward the terrace. "Nice work, Lin."

He exited the bedroom and started toward his own terrace but paused when Harding's voice came over his earpieces.

"We've got a white cargo van coming up the road fast."

"And?" Fade said.

"Okay, it's stopped in front of the building. Back doors are opening, and people who look a lot like Chinese spec ops are jumping out. All are wearing body armor, and all are carrying assault rifles."

"How many?"

"Looks like all of 'em, mate."

"A number would be better," Fade said, exiting onto the terrace and leaning over the rail to look up.

"Working on it, but it's chaos down there. They just busted through your building's door . . . Call it thirteen? But now you've got another van coming from the other direction. Looks like it's going to stop too. Bóchéng's exterior guard just took off. The van's stopped. Same drill."

"You're saying we have twenty-six Chinese operators out front?"

"I'm saying you've got thirteen Chinese operators out front and another thirteen running up the stairs. Bóchéng's lobby guard is down. The one in the hallway outside Linea's door has dropped to his knees and put his hands on his head."

Bóchéng appeared on the terrace above as Linea folded him over the railing. There was a harness around his chest, and she connected it to a belay device in preparation for lowering him.

"They popped the third-floor guard and are coming up on Shuchun's apartment," Harding said. "Now they've broken through the door. She's in the kitchen, and they have her. Men are flooding in to search the place. They're screaming at her, but it's too much for the translator."

Linea pushed Bóchéng over the railing, and he started to descend. Fade reached up and got hold of one of his feet to guide him onto the terrace, but it was pretty clear that the operation had—as Harding was fond of saying—gone a bit pear-shaped.

"They're tearing the place apart searching for him. Two of 'em are literally ripping out the kitchen cabinets."

The sound of the destruction was drifting down along with Bóchéng, confirming the report.

"Someone who looks like he's in charge is out in the hallway giving orders. Still can't get a translation, but it looks like they're about to start a wider search."

A rhythmic pounding became audible, adding to the cacophony.

"That's them knocking on your door, Linea."

"I've got him," Fade said.

She dropped the rope and belay device, causing Bóchéng's limp body to come down on top of Fade. He slid out from under and stood as Linea dropped into a hang from the lower part of the railing above. She swung forward and made a moderately graceful landing just beyond where their target lay.

"They're at your door, Fade. And I don't think they're going to bother to knock."

The sound of a boot colliding with wood echoed through the apartment. The doors were solid, with several dead bolts penetrating into a frame—strong enough to thwart that kind of attack. It took the Chinese soldiers only a few seconds to realize that and start shooting the locking mechanism. How long before they were through? Ten seconds? Maybe twenty if God, Santa, and Krishna all decided to simultaneously intervene?

Screw this.

Linea was about to grab Bóchéng and drag him to the secret compartment Fade had built, but he shoved her backward onto her ass.

"Get in the bedroom!" he shouted over the bullets impacting their door. "Now!"

She hesitated for a moment but then did as she was told. He pulled a knife from his pocket and cut the harness from Bóchéng before unceremoniously tossing him over the railing.

Fade ran into the living area, stuffing the rope system beneath a chair cushion and grabbing a lamp as the door finally swung open. He held it threateningly as five men flowed across the threshold, three shouting in Chinese and aiming their weapons at him while the other two spread out. A few seconds later, Linea, still in her expensive lingerie but now wigless, had been thrown on the floor next to him and was doing her best to sob hysterically.

It seemed that one man was now deemed sufficient to cover them and the other four started a destructive search of the flat. The bed was flipped over, carpets were moved to look for trap doors, and the closet doors were yanked off their hinges. From his position, Fade could see a man about to drive a rifle butt into the wall of his handcrafted secret compartment, but the blow never came. The soldiers all suddenly stopped and the man covering them lifted a finger to his earpiece. It appeared that someone had discovered Bóchéng's untimely suicide.

And then they were gone—pounding down the steps toward the lobby.

"Looks like our new friends are leaving with Shuchun," Harding said over the comms. "There are three police cruisers out front, but they're not blocking the road and they don't seem keen to engage."

Partially self-preservation but also an example of the increasing trend of countries allowing the Chinese to carry out violent operations on their soil without repercussions. What were a few dead civilians and a violation of sovereign rights when weighed against the well-being of the geriatric assholes who ran the world?

"What did you do?" Linea said, running into the bedroom where there was a change of clothes for her in Fade's suitcase.

Harding came on before he could answer. "They're getting back in the vans. Police are still hanging back."

She pulled on a pair of jeans as Fade dug her shoes from beneath the overturned bed.

"We'll talk about this later. Let's go."

She put them on, and then they ran together down the steps.

"The vans are pulling away, and the cops have decided to move in. A few civilian spectators, but they're keeping their distance. No vehicles on the road."

The lobby was empty when they passed through, but a number of uniformed police officers were converging on the shattered front door. Their weapons were finally out, and one shouted something at them in Portuguese.

"We're tourists!" Fade said, raising his hands. "This is an Airbnb!"

The man switched to English and pointed to one of his colleagues. "Keep your hands up and go there."

Getting interrogated by the locals wasn't on Fade's agenda.

"Danny. A little help?"

A moment later, an unsuppressed burst punched through the windshield of the closest cruiser. The cops all spun, some raising their weapons while others went for cover. Linea let out an Oscar-worthy screech and sprinted across the street toward an alley to the west. Fade was right behind.

41

THREE IN the morning was the best time on the island. The temperature, breeze, and silence were perfect. No phone calls, no texts, and none of the trivial problems of day-to-day life. Even the oppressive presence of security melted into the darkness enough to be temporarily forgotten.

Jon Lowe stayed close to the water, giving his running shoes a firm surface and maximizing the sound of lapping waves. His pace was purposely slow—the ten-minute mile that he found optimal for reflection. Just hard enough to clear his mind but not so hard as to intrude on his thoughts.

The moon was almost full, making a head lamp unnecessary even in the fifty meters of rocky technical terrain ahead. He didn't slow when he reached it, navigating partially by the pale celestial light and partially by well-worn memory. Behind, the sound of his bodyguard stumbling became audible but then just as quickly disappeared.

Lowe began to push the pace, savoring the sensation of a pounding heart and struggling lungs. He wasn't on the customized therapies he provided many of the people he surrounded himself with. His youth had been active, and the benefit of that was still with him as he approached fifty. Not that he'd ever been a competitor. The opportunities for organized sports had been limited in Madagascar. But he and the local children never sat still. Running, climbing, swimming, exploring. In so many ways, his youth had been a privileged one, though most of his peers wouldn't see it that way. What was undeniable, though, was the intoxicating simplicity of it all. Even he—a man whose rise had turned on his ability to understand and manipulate complex systems—still felt the pull of those years.

His shoes hit sand again, and he slowed, letting his mind return to the present. The operation to capture Bóchéng had been a massive failure that left the man dead. Fade and his team could hardly be blamed, though. Their plan had been creative and detailed, and their execution flawless. The arrival of the Chinese at that moment had been an unresolvable problem. In truth, it was a minor miracle all three had survived.

And so the mystery persisted: What had the man known?

Lowe shook off the thought. It didn't matter. The only question worth asking was, what was his path forward?

The world continued to fall apart at a rate even he wouldn't have predicted and one that he hoped Yichén Zhu was taking note of. The old men he was threatening were becoming increasingly authoritarian, lawless, and violent. On the other side of that scale, the world's youth were getting a taste of power and not handling it much better. He would have liked to clamp down hard on the social media aspect of the situation, but the systems necessary to manipulate those platforms on such a grand scale were still in their infancy.

Antiscience sentiment was still on the rise and reaching a fevered pitch. It had always been there, simmering in churches, political back rooms, and the internet, but now it was out in the open. Clashes between Luddite protesters and university students were becoming commonplace, as were attacks on top scientists around the world.

In a way, it was hard not to feel sympathy for the agitators. A lone actor had decided to kill three-quarters of a billion people. Probably not for the first time in history, but what *was* unique was that Yichén had the power to succeed where entire countries run by men like Adolf Hitler and Genghis Khan had failed.

The terrifying power that technology put in the hands of individuals was one of the reasons Lowe had embarked on this enterprise. But was it delusional to think he could really make a difference? Perhaps self-destruction was a fundamental trait of his species—baked in by evolutionary pressures that no longer existed.

His thoughts turned to the scientists who had been attacked over the past weeks. Many were acquaintances, some even friends. But maybe they deserved the beatings they'd received. All were members of the intellectual hyperelite who had created a world that seemed to be on the verge of collapsing. In truth, it was an unusually controlled tantrum on the part of the public—never lethal and targeting only top minds. Despite the victims being elderly and sometimes even infirm, the most serious injury to date had been a broken wrist.

Lowe slowed, wandering from his line and finally stopping when the water began lapping at his ankles.

Top minds. Elderly. Minimal injuries.

How could he have been so stupid?

The wail of an alarm erupted from the other side of the island. Lowe turned and saw the dark outline of his bodyguard sprinting toward him across the sand.

"Pirates?" Lowe said when he came within earshot.

A little more than a year ago, they'd been attacked by three rafts overflowing with armed insurgents. Initially, he'd forbidden the use of deadly force, instead warning them off with the island's powerful PA system. Sadly, they hadn't been so easily dissuaded. When they landed, he'd had little choice but to turn the matter over to his security chief. The battle had lasted only a few minutes and left no survivors on the Malagasy side.

"Not pirates," his man said. "The attack's coming from the air. Can you hear it?"

In fact, he could. What he'd initially mistaken for the wind had taken on the signature of an aircraft engine. Maybe more than one.

Flashes became visible over the inhabited part of the island, followed quickly by the sound of gunfire. His guard pointed to the sky, and Lowe followed his finger, making out various shadows against the stars. He counted nine, descending quickly toward not only the beaches but also the island's rugged, forested interior.

"I'm with Sailfish now," his guard said into his radio, using the code name for him they insisted on. "Understood. Escape point Charlie. I repeat. Charlie. Roger that. Out."

As they ran for the trees, Lowe's instinct was to ask for more details about what was happening. But the truth was that he already knew.

Bóchéng.

There was no other answer. He hadn't been killed in the fall and was now in the hands of the Chinese. A man like him would immediately give them everything, starting with what he knew about Yichén and eventually getting around to Lowe.

The sound of gunshots increased in frequency and volume, overpowering the slap of leaves as they dodged through the dark forest. The snap of a paratrooper dropping through the canopy became audible to the east, and they were forced to angle away from it.

"Tell our people to surrender," Lowe said to the man leading him.

The island's defenses were formidable but had been designed to repel raids by local thugs, not Chinese special forces. Continuing to fight wouldn't result in victory, only a bloodbath on both sides.

His man relayed the message, and gunfire became more intermittent. The protocol was to get guests and nonsecurity personnel to the relative safety of the main building's storage area. If their defenders retreated there and laid down their arms, it would almost certainly defuse the situation. The Chinese would want everyone alive for questioning but would quickly discover that the island's staff knew nothing about his activities. Only his two board members would be of any interest to them.

Another paratrooper dropped through the trees a short distance away, getting hung up a few feet from the ground. Lowe's bodyguard fired a single round from his pistol and the man went limp.

They increased their pace, bringing back the pounding heart and burning lungs from earlier. Despite that, progress was slow. They were constantly forced to adjust their trajectory to avoid the men now coming down around them like rain. The only real advantage the Chinese had over the rest of the world was superior numbers, and they knew how to leverage it.

Finally, they came to the tree line, stopping just short of a beach that sloped gently for about fifteen meters before disappearing into the sea. His man—a former member of Israel's elite Sayeret—had brought them exactly where they needed to be. He swept foliage and dirt from the lid of a buried container and opened it, revealing the hidden treasure inside: scuba gear and an underwater scooter.

"I'll try to draw them away," he whispered. "Good luck, sir."

"You too, Caleb. Thank you."

Lowe secured two scuba tanks to his back, hung a pair of flippers over one arm, and grabbed the scooter with the other. He looked both directions along the open beach but saw nothing. Not far away, a burst of gunfire erupted, followed by shouting in Chinese. Running footsteps became audible behind him, and he waited for them to recede before breaking cover.

More shouts rose up as he crossed the sand, burdened with equipment and a scuba mask that had begun to fog. He looked back to see two armed men burst from the trees in pursuit.

He made it to the water, lifting his feet high as he navigated the increasing depth. A deafening burst of automatic gunfire lit the waves, bullets impacting twenty feet left. Lowe finally dove, feeling a hand clamp around his ankle as he went under. He kicked violently and started the scooter, but the grip was unbreakable.

After getting the regulator in his mouth, he turned the electric motor to what passed for full power. In the process, the man got his other hand around Lowe's knee and was pulling himself forward. Despite what was left of his childhood athleticism, it was clear that he was no match for a professional soldier, so he focused on tracking the seafloor. Soon they were deep enough that the moonlight could no longer penetrate. There was a violent jerk when the man got hold of one of the tanks, but his movements were increasingly desperate and clumsy. Lowe continued to hug the bottom as it fell away and took them farther into the darkness.

A few seconds later, he was free. Starved for oxygen, the soldier kicked for the surface and allowed Lowe to set a course for Madagascar's main island.

42

I'LL HAVE your back if you have mine.

Fade pulled the stolen car into the trees and turned it off, letting the darkness envelop him. After the clusterfuck in Portugal, he, Linea, and Harding had split up, each responsible for making their own way back via different methods. Being the insomniac of the group, he'd taken the overland route with the goal of dragging the nine-hour drive into a day or two by hitting a few seaside villages. Pretty country, good food, and a little extra time for Linea to cool off. She'd busted his balls hard for dumping Bóchéng over the railing and remained unwilling to admit that there were no better options.

And then, right when it seemed impossible, the situation had taken a turn for the worse. He'd been eating a surprisingly good taco in Lagos when his news feed picked up a story about the Chinese military invading a small island near Madagascar. Very little official information was available at that point, but some rich guy named Greg Madison had uploaded a panicked blow-by-blow to his social media accounts. Fifteen minutes later, Fade had converted all his bank accounts into untraceable cryptocurrency, tossed his phone in the ocean, and was jacking the first of a number of cars.

His initial plan had been to head down to Algeciras and take a ferry to Tangier. From there, he could go overland to Jordan, where his native-level Arabic would allow him to disappear for long enough to figure out his next step.

He'd been tantalizingly close to the Spanish coast when he reluctantly turned the vehicle north. It seemed almost certain that Lowe had been captured, and if that was the case, he'd likely already spilled his guts. While tougher than the average billionaire, he wouldn't last long once the pliers came out. Unfortunately, that meant the Chinese would know about the Granada house and pay a visit. That left Raya twisting in the wind.

She'd probably already been transported to Beijing for questioning, but there would be a team still stationed there in the unlikely event he was stupid enough to return. And it turned out he was. Without Lowe and Egan to point him in the right direction, stupid was about all he had left. The only thing that came to mind was to roll in blind and see if he could drum up some intel. Then, if he survived, an impromptu rescue mission to China where he would wage a one-man war against the largest internal security apparatus ever created.

Hooyah.

Fade stepped out into the cool evening and went around the back of the vehicle. A quick search of the trunk turned up nothing more deadly than a tire iron. Europe was unlike the US in that you couldn't just walk into a department store and outfit yourself with enough military-grade weaponry to assault the Kremlin. If he wanted a gun, the only thing he could think to do was mug a cop. But that plan just piled more stupid on the existing stupid, so he'd decided to pass.

Besides, automotive tools were underrated as weapons. Quiet, easy to use, and impervious to water and dirt. Multifunctional too. Once he'd used them to take out the heavily armed operators dug in at his house, he'd be well equipped to tighten any lug nuts loosened during the battle. Try that with an HK.

He started down a steep slope, weaving silently through widely spaced trees. No rush at this point. The end result of the evening was likely to be the same no matter when he got there.

The glow from his property was stronger than he'd imagined, suggesting that pretty much every exterior light was burning. Was it possible they'd sent the entire team from Portugal? It seemed like overkill, but they'd been in the neighborhood and, after missing Bóchéng, probably weren't too anxious to go home.

As he eased closer, he came upon a complex mechanism strapped to a tree. It didn't seem to serve a purpose yet, with various wires hanging loose in an empty battery chamber. He continued in a crouch, pausing every few seconds to take in his surroundings. Eventually, a lone man became visible downslope. Armed with a rifle, he was kneeling next to a backpack awash in the red beam of his head lamp. He didn't seem to be patrolling but instead working on a mechanism similar to the one Fade had seen before. Probably a component in some kind of sensor array. The Chinese really were desperate if they were willing to expend these kinds of resources to capture a nobody like him.

The man messed with the wires for a few seconds before connecting a battery and installing a faceplate. Fade retreated back to the tree with the first partially installed sensor and climbed about ten feet into the branches.

The technician took his good, sweet time, but finally strolled up and started making connections. He glanced upward when Fade dropped, but it was unclear if he even registered the falling shadow before catching a wrench to the forehead. Not hard enough to kill him, but hard enough to put him out for a while. Depending on how all this went down, he might be more useful alive than dead.

Fade freed the man's HK416 and used the night vision optic to get a little more detail on his surroundings. Other than amplifying the glow coming from his still-distant house, there was nothing of interest.

No news was good news.

Interestingly, the man turned out not to be Asian. In fact, when Fade pulled off his skull cap to get at his comms, a head of blond, military-cut hair was revealed.

The fact that his earpiece was custom-formed made it hard to insert, but Fade finally managed to get it in far enough to pick up chatter. Everyone was speaking English but with a broad array of accents. The subject matter was mostly logistical—food, equipment, quarters, and fortification. After a few seconds of eavesdropping, a familiar voice came on to ask about when the SAMs would be online.

Fade grimaced and looked down at the unconscious man before activating the earpiece's microphone.

"What are you doing to my house, Matt?"

"Stefan? What are you talking about?"

Fade was confused for a moment but then remembered that Lowe's next-generation technology picked up what the user was saying and mimicked their voice to enhance clarity.

"This isn't Stefan."

"Shit. Hold on. I'm isolating this frequency."

Fade used the rifle to scan the trees again while Egan cut out the other listeners. Was he being blamed for botching the job in Portugal, and his old friend was there to dole out the punishment? Unlikely, but not impossible.

"Fade. Are you still there?"

"Yes."

"We figure that Bóchéng survived the fall, and he's talking to the Chinese. I assume you heard that Lowe's island was attacked, but what you don't know is that he escaped. We didn't have a lot of options for a place to regroup, and your house is still the most practical."

Fade nodded in the gloom, considering what he'd heard. It rang true, but what was truth anymore? Basically, the mathematical average of a hundred lies. Not a calculation anyone in their right mind would bet their life on. Right?

"I need a medic two hundred yards due north of the pool."

It turned out that there really were SAMs.

Hidden beneath netting and surrounded by wooden crates, they sat at the very edge of his courtyard. Nearer the gate, Fade spotted an area where drones painted to match the cobblestones were waiting to take to the air. Personnel were even more plentiful than expected, all wearing camo that matched the specific microenvironment they were operating in. Apparently, they'd learned from the attack on Lowe's island and weren't looking to repeat the same mistakes. Still, it had the feel of a last stand.

Egan was at the center of it all but stopped what he was doing when Fade emerged from the trees.

"The medic says the man you attacked is conscious and talking. They're taking him to Granada for a CT scan."

"I barely tapped him. Now, what are we doing here?"

"Chasing our tails. Jon's fine and inbound, but after your screwup in Porto, we don't have much left to work with. We're trying to find other secret labs, tracking equipment that Zhu might need for his work, and looking into the people he escaped with. But I'm not expecting to get anywhere."

"So the better part of a billion people are about to drop dead."

Egan watched a man on an ATV drag something into the woods. "We're going to keep swinging, but yeah. Checkmate."

Inside the house, the impression of military occupation was even stronger. Large pots were crowded onto the stove and manned by mercenaries taking a turn feeding their comrades. Food and other supplies lined the walls, and the living area had been taken over by electronics. Banks of processors were cooled by purpose-built fans, cables snaked across the floor, and tables had been set up to hold monitors and video game controllers. It looked like something that would take an army of techs to handle, but apparently not. One heavily inked young woman seemed to have everything well in hand.

On the combat side, various Kevlar and steel blinds had been set up in the event the building was breached. Also, a number of boxes had been attached to the walls and painted to look like bad modern art. Based on their height and locations, he suspected some kind of antipersonnel charge. One of the drones he'd seen outside was partially disassembled on his dining table, its rotors extending beyond the edges and a rifle barrel protruding from its underside. The general vibe was of a prehistoric insect that had evolved to prey on dinosaurs.

Crazy.

It turned out that his expansive bedroom was one of the few parts of the house that hadn't been pressed into service. He was about to fall into bed fully clothed when it registered that the bathroom light was on. And that on the other side of the half-closed door, someone was quietly humming an off-pitch rendition of "Despacito."

It turned out to be Raya, decked out in flannel pajamas and brushing her teeth with exactly the level of precision that he would have expected.

"Are you lost?"

She leaned forward and spit toothpaste into one of his hand-painted Italian sinks.

An answer wasn't really necessary. The bathroom was covered in beauty products, and his once sparsely populated closet was now packed.

"My room is full of bunk beds, sweaty men, and canned food. You had space."

She pushed past and climbed into bed, perching a pair of glasses on her nose and a laptop on her knees.

"I'm going to take a shower," he said, knowing that resistance was futile. "Why don't you go scrounge me up a bottle of tequila."

She examined him over wire rims. "I take it your trip didn't go well?"

"What makes you say that?"

"There are missiles by the pool."

"Nothing that a bottle of Cierto Extra Añejo won't fix."

"I have some bad news."

"I'm not currently accepting any."

"All the liquor is locked away."

"Again?"

"A lot of people with guns. It's not a good combination."

They'd have to agree to disagree on that point, but again, there was nothing to be gained by arguing. Instead, he showered, pulled on a pair of Bugs Bunny boxer shorts that for the first time did nothing to lighten his mood, and dropped onto the other side of the bed.

"Are you ready to go to sleep?"

"I'm always ready."

She closed the laptop and turned out the light.

"Mr. Egan said you were never coming back."

"Really?"

"He said you'd drained your bank accounts, destroyed your phone, and abandoned your car."

"Yeah."

"But you did come back."

"Yeah."

"Why?"

"I ran out of clean socks."

She didn't speak again for long enough that he thought she might have fallen asleep.

"Thank you," she said finally.

"You're welcome."

He heard her rummage around in her nightstand and a moment later a joint and lighter were hovering above him in the darkness. "Sorry about the tequila. But I set this aside for you."

He lit it and took a drag before holding it out. She shook her head. "Not with them here."

"Why not?"

"Because sometimes it makes me cry."

"Me too," he said, stubbing it out on a dish that was probably priceless.

"Can I ask what happened?"

"We should have a party," he said, ignoring her question.

"A party?"

"Yeah. When all this is over. I'll make paella."

"You cook?"

"No. But I can learn. Everyone likes a good cook. No one likes a killer. They pretend to because they're afraid or they think you can protect their money and power. But they don't really."

"Then I'll make the bread."

"You bake?"

"No. But I can learn. Everyone likes a good baker. No one likes a call girl. They pretend to because of lust or insecurity, but they don't really."

Sleep crept up on him faster than normal, just closing its grip when someone started pounding on the door. He opened his eyes and saw that Raya was already fully awake, her ramrod-straight outline visible in the gloom. The knock didn't sound again. Instead, the door opened just wide enough for Jon Lowe's head to pass through.

"Get up. I've been an idiot."

43

LOWE HAD managed to remove enough food and weaponry to carve out a little space in Fade's basement theater. The screen was running a loop of footage depicting various attacks on scientists over the past few weeks. One, labeled as coming from an ATM camera, showed an elderly woman walking along a sidewalk in broad daylight. She passed by a storefront, looking idly toward the window as two men ran up behind and knocked her to the ground. One held her by the legs while the other threw a few flailing punches. A moment later, they took off, sprinting up a side street without ever showing their faces.

The screen went blank for a moment before coming to life again with the image of an MIT professor getting beat up in a public park. Taken by a not-so-good Samaritan, the quality was significantly better—capturing the shock and pain in the man's expression before he flung an arm protectively over his head. A golden retriever, not a human, finally came to the rescue.

Many academics had started refusing to venture out in public, but a rash of home invasions had brought the efficacy of that strategy into question. About all you could say now was that maybe it was slightly preferable to get your ass kicked in the comfort and privacy of your den rather than on the six o'clock news.

"Nine attacks in total," Lowe said, pacing in front of the screen. "They've happened all over the globe but they all have common elements. The ambushes are carried out by between two and four young men who use fists and feet, but never weapons. They leave their victims, all of whom are over sixty, hospitalized but with relatively minor injuries."

"Why is this important?" Fade said, settling into a seat behind Egan, Linea, and Harding.

"Don't you find it strange that they never kill or even seriously harm their victims?"

Fade shrugged.

"Are you saying these attacks are linked in some way?" Linea said. "That there's some group coordinating them and dictating parameters?"

"That's the FBI's theory. They're searching chat groups and conspiracy sites for suspects, but I think they're missing a critical piece. Another commonality between all these incidents."

"What commonality?" Egan said.

"All the victims are brilliant."

Fade squinted at the man. His triumphant expression seemed a bit smug for such an underwhelming observation. Maybe Lowe was finally starting to feel the enormity of what he'd taken on. His calm, philosophical demeanor came off as genuine but also a little thin. Like a coat of waterproof paint on a crumbling dam.

"So?" Fade remarked when it became obvious no one else was going to speak up. He was still feeling the effects of Raya's weed, and the sooner they got this over with, the sooner he could go back to bed.

Lowe frowned like a disappointed grade school teacher. "Can I assume that everyone's familiar with Planck's principle?"

Their blank stares were rewarded with a face palm.

"Planck's principle states that science moves forward one funeral at a time. Yichén is very much a believer in the theory—that most scientists' important work is done early in their careers, and then they spend the rest of their lives standing in the way of further advancement."

"This isn't helping me," Fade said.

"The critical concept here is that there are exceptions. People who are doing creative, cutting-edge work despite being older. People Yichén admires."

He turned and watched the video behind him for a few seconds before using a remote to slow it down. "Look carefully. The right hand of the man in the sweat shirt."

Fade leaned forward, watching him land a few half-hearted punches on the gray-haired woman beneath him before slamming the side of his fist down on her ass. Then he leaped to his feet, gave her an even more half-hearted kick to the thigh, and took off. The video replayed a few more times before freezing at the point of contact between the man's hand and the woman's butt.

"He's holding something," Lowe said.

Everyone squinted at the screen. There might have been something, but it also could have been an artifact.

"What?" Egan said.

"I hypothesize a syringe."

They all considered that for a few seconds with Fade being the first to make the connection. "You think those knuckle draggers work for Zhu?"

"Exactly! We know from the man you captured in Wyoming that they've been creating vaccines concurrently with their pathogens. My assumption was that it was a safeguard in case his virus escaped prematurely like COVID did or mutated out of control. And that still might be part of it, but now I think that the other reason was to inoculate the few seniors he still thinks are important to society's progress."

Lowe clicked a few buttons on his remote and the on-screen video was replaced by a tiled view of seven people who looked like academics straight out of central casting. "I've identified these men and women as likely future targets. All are at the forefront of their fields and still producing science that could have worldwide impact. In fact, I provide research funds to three of them." He clicked again and the screen filled with a photo of a man standing behind a lectern. He was a well-preserved seventysomething, with shaggy salt-and-pepper hair and a severe expression partially hidden by half-moon glasses.

"This one is the most interesting. Dr. Carl Becker of Stanford. He's still one of the most productive biologists in the world and, more important, Yichén's mentor. It wouldn't be going too far to say that Yichén sees him as a father figure."

"I think I've seen reporters chasing him on the news," Egan said.

"Indeed. Their relationship is well known, but he's been adamant in refusing to talk to the press about it."

"Could he be involved?" Fade asked.

"The FBI's investigated and couldn't find any evidence of that. I read the transcripts of their interviews with him, and he seems genuinely upset about his role in training Yichén. I also know him personally and don't see him being involved."

"But you knew Yichén personally too," Fade said.

"That's true. And while I admit I didn't predict this, I'm not all that surprised. But I'd be floored if I found out Carl participated."

"Okay," Fade said. "How do we use this information?"

"Good question. What I'm proposing is that we stop one of these attacks before the injection. With an intact syringe in hand, we could learn a lot about the virus Yichén's created and maybe even start vaccine production."

"Do we have enough manpower to watch that many scientists around the clock?" Linea asked.

"No," Egan responded immediately. "But we could hire it. There are competent surveillance experts and private investigators we can get hold of. People with experience and track records."

Fade stood, feeling a little unsteady on his feet. The Hail Marys seemed to keep getting longer, but what the hell. Lowe could spend his money on whatever blew his hair back.

"Let me know what you figure out."

44

THE CLOCK in the old Subaru's dashboard ticked over to 9:00 p.m., indicating one more hour in Bradley Miller's lengthy shift. As near as he could tell, he was one of a team of at least five human surveillance operatives giving an assist to an enormous number of remote cameras, listening devices, drones, and all the other shit that would soon put him and everyone else out of work.

Not yet, though. That night—and every other night so far that week—he was being paid five times his normal rate with the possibility of a quarter-million-dollar bonus. A far cry from his salary as a cop and, with the ink on his divorce finally dry, out of his money-grubbing ex's reach. She was going to get a chance to stand on her own two feet and see how easy life was without him to suck dry.

The overcast had come in as predicted, leaving the street illuminated only by the porchlights of the houses lining it. None of them were particularly spectacular, but you could smell the money in Menlo Park like a fart in an elevator. The smooth, spotless asphalt. The carefully groomed yards and late model crossovers.

Location, location, location. That's what his realtor sister loved to say. A bunch of rich assholes with fancy degrees roll into California, kick out the riffraff, and put up a wall. Not a physical one, but a wall was a wall. People like him knew when they weren't welcome.

Across the street and two houses up, a stylish front door opened and a man exited onto the porch. Dr. Carl Becker was nothing if not punctual. Every night at the same time, he appeared in a formless gray sweatsuit to power walk around the neighborhood. Unlike virtually everyone else his age, he didn't wear a surgical mask against the virus his protégé was threatening to release, and he took no precautions to protect himself against the young men who'd set their sights on people like him.

That was Miller's job. His orders were to stop an assault before it happened by whatever means necessary and to search the attackers—or their corpses—for a syringe. If he found one, he could exchange it for a cool quarter-mil.

In a way, it was kind of a shame. If it weren't for the bonus, he'd be tempted to drag his feet a little. Let the old bastard take a few shots. A little dose of reality before getting saved by someone he'd spent his life looking down on. No one elected these pricks. He sure as hell hadn't. But that didn't stop them from telling everyone what to do. Become a vegetarian. Put solar panels on your roof. Announce your pronouns. If you don't, you're nothing more than an idiot caveman.

Not so much an idiot caveman that he'd ever believed the Chinese government wasn't behind COVID. Or that putting his six-year-old son in a dress and giving him a Barbie to play with was good parenting. Or that NASA sent men to the moon a decade before you could buy a VHS.

He got out of the car, zipping his light jacket against the cold and stuffing his hands in his pockets. When Becker had a bit of a lead, he started after him, resenting the fact that the seventy-three-year-old's pace got him huffing.

Traffic on the residential street was nonexistent, but that changed when a van from one of the security companies active in the area appeared from a side street. The passenger leaned out the window to say something and Becker paused his relentless march to approach.

Miller slowed to maintain a fifty-yard interval between them. He was pretending to check his phone when the side door of the van slid open and Becker was yanked inside. A moment later, the vehicle was gliding smoothly up the road.

45

FADE'S HAND brushed past the pistol lying on the table in favor of a bottle of Clase Azul that Raya had tracked down for him. He took a more delicate sip than was his tradition, downing just enough to enjoy the promised notes of oak and vanilla as he gazed out from the rooftop terrace.

At half past two in the morning, the grounds were completely dark. Egan had done an impressive job of obscuring his NATO-level security, refining equipment and protocols to the point that they would be invisible to distant neighbors and even drones. If a Chinese spec ops team tried to throw their weight around like they had in Portugal, it would be quite a show. By the time the local cops arrived to investigate reports of an illegal fireworks display, there wouldn't be much left but scorched earth and charred remains.

To the southwest, he could see the glimmer of Granada, with its maze-like streets and ancient Arab fortress. The Muslims—his ancestors—had ruled the region for centuries. It had been an era of unprecedented change in Europe and the world. Technology, politics, religion and warfare were all suddenly transformed. A violent shift in what before had always been plodding evolution.

The plague had killed more than half the population—an event with a scale that was hard to imagine in the present context. Entire families wiped out, the permeating stench of the dead, terrified survivors desperately trying to understand what they'd done to deserve such wrath from their gods. In the end, though, it weakened the hereditary ruling class's grip, allowing the poor to rise up and usher in the age of art, science, and philosophy that had been suppressed for so long.

The Roman Empire. The World Wars. The Industrial Revolution. What was the theory Lowe had told them about? The idea that science advanced one funeral at a time? Maybe society was the same. Chained to the past until some great tragedy broke it free.

Fade reached for his drink and took another sip, this one less conservative. Too much perspective. His ability to discern between reality and dream was getting better every day, but it turned out not to be as much of an improvement as he'd expected. There were giant spiders in the real world too. They were just cleverly disguised and hidden in shadow.

Footsteps on the stairs became audible and, a few seconds later, identifiable. Jon Lowe had two gaits: the steady, plodding one that accompanied depression or boredom, and the quick, uneven one that denoted excitement and hope. Surprisingly, the rhythm on the steps belonged in the latter category.

"It's been a productive twenty-four hours," he said as he exited onto the terrace.

Fade didn't turn around, continuing to enjoy the distant city lights as Lowe dragged a chair over.

"Matt's people managed to intervene in an attack on a scientist outside Paris."

"And? Were you right?"

Lowe nodded. "They retrieved a syringe. Undamaged and unused."

"Congratulations."

"Thank you."

"Is it a vaccine?"

"We don't know yet for certain. It's been sent to the Pfizer team led by the man you captured in Wyoming. They're doing the analysis now."

"If it is, does that mean you'll be able to copy it?"

"Almost certainly. It's just a matter of time."

"Lucky for you and your people."

Lowe waved a hand around indicating the luxurious house and grounds. "Your people too now. If you were in danger from Zhu's pathogen, you'd be near the top of the list."

Fade wasn't sure how to respond to that uncomfortable truth, so he just took another pull on his tequila.

"But that's not the best part."

"No?"

"Remember Carl Becker? Yichén's mentor?"

Fade nodded.

"He wasn't attacked and vaccinated. He was kidnapped."

"Why?"

"I can only speculate, but I suspect that Yichén wants an opportunity to explain himself in person. Becker's probably the only person alive whose opinion he cares about." The breeze kicked up and Lowe leaned forward so he didn't have to raise his voice. "We had a team watching him and now we know that he's on a container ship bound for Asia."

"Not the fastest way to travel."

"No, but the most secure. Planes are easy to track. There are flight plans and radar, and they have limited ranges and places they can land."

"Don't ships have the same problems?"

"Yes. The difference is that you can get off them. The ship's scheduled to dock in China, a place that I can almost guarantee Yichén isn't. That's not Becker's destination."

"So you think they'll wait for a moment no one's watching and pull him off. By helicopter or boat, or even by throwing him overboard and picking him up later."

"Exactly."

"And you still don't want to get the government involved?"

"I don't."

"So it falls to you."

"I think we're in the best position to succeed. And that's critical because there won't be a second chance. The vaccine is clearly done, and now it's just a matter of time. I imagine Yichén will wait for the doses he's administered to reach maximum effectiveness, and then he'll release the virus."

"How long?"

"Two weeks." He reached for the tequila bottle. "Maybe less."

46

FADE HAD landed on a lot of ships in his lifetime, but this was unquestionably the nicest. Dull gray steel and deck armor had been replaced by a gleaming white hull and polished teak. The scale was smaller, of course, but not as much as he would have thought. The yacht they were descending toward had to measure a good three hundred feet.

Even better was the welcoming committee. No sweaty sailors or scowling cigar-chomping officers. Instead, two women in microscopic bikinis were waving excitedly with their right hands while holding broad straw hats in their left.

It had been widely reported that the world's yachts were currently all at sea—man-made islands that provided quarantine experiences befitting the status of their owners. No moldy bunkers, hazmat suits, or remote Alaskan cabins for these assholes. It was all teenaged underwear models and champagne. A good way to take the edge off the looming end of their world, but also fuel for the overt glee and sincere sense of hope being displayed by the younger generations.

Maybe the privilege of this boat's owner had been won by eighty-hour work weeks and genius. Maybe it had been inherited or stolen. Maybe it was time for them to step aside and let someone else take a shot. Maybe their successors would be even worse.

Maybe, maybe, maybe. Nothing was certain anymore, including where Fade fit in. Was he still the guy who'd barely graduated high school, fought for his country, and been discarded when he was no longer useful? Or was he the guy who lived in a European mansion and hobnobbed with the people whose hands were on the levers?

Neither.

That was the problem. The answer was always neither.

The skids hit the deck and he jumped out, shouldering his duffle as he jogged toward the twins.

"Did you miss me?" he shouted over the noise of the chopper taking to the air again.

By way of an answer, Carina leaped onto him, wrapping her legs around his waist while Lastri relieved him of his gear.

No crew was evident as they led him below deck. The deeper they traveled, the more inappropriate the comparison to a naval vessel seemed. More like a combination of Noah's ark and a Vegas casino. If humanity was wiped out, not to worry. It would soon be repopulated by young hotties and old douchebags.

Oh. And him.

"YOU'RE STARTING to look less and less like a disaster."

It was as close as Matt Egan would ever get to a compliment, Fade knew. But it was a fair assessment. Despite the gentle rolling of the deck, Fade moved with steady grace toward a bar at the far end of the dining area. His balance was nearly back to normal, as was his strength. Endurance and speed were lagging, but those were time-consuming abilities to improve.

Best of all, after one of the twins' patented massages and happy endings, he'd actually slept reasonably well. Dreams that had been hyperrealistic horror shows were now more jumbled vignettes that quickly dissolved. Breakfast had consisted of chilaquiles, hash browns, and a quarter bottle of hot sauce with no complaints from his digestive tract. The sense of being trapped somewhere in reality's twilight was still there, but was no longer accompanied by the overwhelming desire to crawl back into a coma.

He crouched on silent knees and dug around for the ingredients to make a Michelada.

"The cargo ship carrying Carl Becker will pass seven miles to the east of us early tomorrow morning," Egan said.

"Are you sure he's still on it?"

"To the best of our knowledge."

"How good's your knowledge?"

"The weather's been clear with mostly calm seas since they set out. We have decent satellite coverage and we're regularly overflying with surveillance drones. No indication that anything or anyone's gotten on or off . . ."

Fade abandoned the lime he was juicing and turned toward his former friend. "I hear a *but* in there somewhere."

"We're heading into some weather. Heavy overcast, intermittent rain, and wind around twenty knots."

"Ideal conditions for sneaking him off that thing."

"Our thoughts exactly."

"So, good, right? Then we can follow him, and maybe he leads us to Zhu."

"Not likely. The conditions aren't going to allow us to keep eyes on him. Particularly without being spotted. They'll bounce him around, mix him with decoys, and who knows what else. Even with our resources and technology, the chances of us losing him are pretty high."

"What then?"

"We need to get to him on the boat."

"And by *we*, why do I think you mean *me*?"

Egan turned on a TV that depicted a 3-D model of the ship in question, including the containers stacked on its deck. He used a wireless controller to rotate it into an overhead view and then zero in on a midship gap—hole really—in the cargo.

"There are containers stacked five high here with no access to this empty area in the center." He clicked a button on his controller and three of the bottom containers were highlighted. "Have you ever heard of storage container houses?"

"Sure. Companies cut windows and doors and then sell them cheap."

"That's what these bottom three are. You just can't see the windows because they're packed in so tight."

"You're saying he's being held in one of them?"

Egan nodded. "They were put on the ship in this configuration for a reason. We're fairly certain that Becker is in the one toward the stern, and the people guarding him are in the facing two. The empty space between is about twenty feet square and used as outdoor space. A drone flight two days ago showed three men out there with chairs they'd dragged from the containers."

"Living large."

"Yeah."

"What about the crew? To make this happen, they'd have to be in on it."

"A few of the officers is all they'd need. We're guessing that everyone else is in the dark."

"No chance they're part of Zhu's cult?"

"Never say never, but it's unlikely. All are professional sailors with loose relationships to one another. The exception is what appear to be four Asian security personnel who patrol the deck in shifts. We've got video of them, but there's no documentation showing they exist."

"Where are they sleeping?"

"With the crew."

"No one would think that was suspicious?"

"All the captain would have to say is that the company hired them. High-value cargo, fears of piracy. Whatever. Why would anyone question that?"

"How many more shooters down in that hole with Becker?"

"We've been able to identify four from drone flyovers, and that seems like plenty to nursemaid one aging academic. But I wouldn't bet my life on it."

"Would you bet mine?"

He didn't answer.

47

FADE EXITED onto the stern wearing the camo wet suit that had appeared in his cabin that morning. Face paint was courtesy of the twins, an artistic collage of muted greens, blacks, and grays, with a touch of rust that Lastri felt highlighted his cheekbones. His hair was pulled back into a ponytail secured with a piece of black Gorilla Tape that was admittedly hard to get out but foolproof in all conditions. A SIG was strapped to one thigh and on the other a knife and compact set of bolt cutters.

The weather had deteriorated slightly, with intermittent stars visible in only about half the sky. Seas still weren't bad, but the movement of the deck was becoming more pronounced. Carina was already starting to feel it, and if the forecast was right, she'd be spending some time hanging over a highly polished railing.

Egan, on the other hand, looked typically solid as he stood next to something that resembled a photon torpedo from *Star Trek*. About ten feet long, it had a slightly squashed capsule shape and the velvety gleam of titanium.

"What's that?"

"Your ride."

Egan swiped his phone and the thing opened like a giant clam. Inside, there were no visible controls, no glass to see out, and no computer screen or switches. At least none visible beneath the seawater it was full of. The only indication that it was designed for human transport was a scuba regulator attached to a hose that disappeared into the bottom.

"I'm supposed to get in?"

Egan nodded. "Don't worry about the water. It's just there to give it a more neutral buoyancy and somehow plays nice with the electric motors. Engineering stuff. Not my area. What I do know, though, is that it's preprogrammed to take you alongside the freighter and hold there."

"Where'd it come from? Has it ever been used in combat?"

"It's a prototype. The navy's done some initial tests, and it's passed with flying colors."

Fade frowned deeply. Navy equipment tests tended to consist of floating gear around in a heated pool for a few minutes. The primary goal was to make sure that no problems surfaced that could reduce contractor profits and jeopardize the local admiral's chance of getting a sweet postretirement board position.

"If there's a problem, the water automatically evacuates, causing it to surface. Then we pick you up. But that's not going to happen."

Fade wasn't convinced. And slowly sinking to the bottom of the ocean trapped in a titanium coffin wasn't how he wanted to go.

"You know who loves this kind of techy crap and never complains? Danny. Riding around in something like that is dead in his wheelhouse."

"I made that exact point to Jon. But he overrode me."

Fade let out a long breath and stared into the opaque reflection of water inside the craft. "What happens when I get alongside the ship?"

"Glad you asked," Egan responded, opening a plastic case at his feet. It contained a device about the size of a grapefruit that he attached to the harness integrated into Fade's wet suit. After connecting a thin rope, he dug out a grappling hook launcher and tossed it into the incursion vehicle. It immediately sank from view.

"Shoot that over the ship's railing. You've got enough compressed air for three tries, but you'll likely only need one. The hook was designed specifically for this op, and as long as you clear the side, it'll anchor. Then flip the switch on the unit at your waist. It'll winch you to just below the railing. Like we talked about, you shouldn't have any crew to worry about. Just the two-man patrol."

"When I'm done, how do I get off?"

"No idea. But I'm sure you'll come up with something. Once you're in the water, we'll swing by and get you."

Fade looked at the sky and then out across the sea. Considering the stakes, the plan had kind of a half-assed feel to it. He'd been involved in similar operations in the past, but they'd been accompanied by the full force and proceduralized chaos of the US Navy. A team, gear checks, strategy meetings, backup plans. Maybe it had been overkill, but it had been confidence-inspiring overkill.

"You sure about this, Matt?"

"What?"

"That we shouldn't be calling in the cavalry?"

"Jon is."

"I'm not asking Jon. I'm asking you."

By way of an answer, Egan motioned with his head toward the craft. "Your chariot awaits."

After a lengthy hesitation, Fade climbed in, put the regulator in his mouth, and donned a pair of swim goggles. It took a few seconds to make a space for himself among the gear, but as soon as he did, the lid came down. Inside, the darkness was broken only by the glow of his wristwatch. A countdown timer started and was now taking up most of the display. A much smaller number at the bottom showed his elevated heart rate. Normally, tight spaces didn't bother him, but this floating tomb was an exception.

He felt lateral movement and then a brief drop before hitting the waves. The water in the capsule actually helped soften the impact but also added to his disorientation by muting the sensation of up versus down. The motor started, generating a hum that was nearly imperceptible over the rush of the jets. Speed, direction, orientation, and depth were unknown.

28:14 to intercept.

The first fifteen minutes were among the worst of his life. In the past, he'd always loved insertions. Madagascar had been a perfect example. The vibration of the raft beneath him. The spray of the ocean against his face. The silhouettes of his team. The way God intended. The way it had been since the time of swords and hats with horns. Not alone in the dark, unable to move, and increasingly convinced he was being shuttled straight to Davy Jones's locker.

Worse, he'd already had to pull the regulator from his mouth twice to throw up. It reminded him of a story an old-timer had once told him about landing on the beach during D-Day. He and his guys had been so seasick, leaping out into withering German fire had been an improvement.

The timer on his watch seemed to move in slow motion but finally reached zero. Once again, there was no sensation of slowing or changing direction; only the muffled sound of the lid releasing and a little welcome illumination. He spit out the regulator and lifted himself on his elbows, taking a deep breath of sea air that helped settle his stomach. The ship loomed to his left, throwing a wake that the capsule was navigating with impressive ease. The sickening sway of it had been replaced with improbable stability, allowing Fade to retrieve the grappling hook launcher and rise to his knees beneath the skyscraper of a hull. The hiss of compressed air was accompanied by a light recoil and the hook was airborne. It arced out over the deck, working as promised.

He activated the winch and started to rise, dangling well away from the hull at first and then closing in on it as he neared the top. Also as promised, he came to a stop just beneath the railing—close enough to reach it, but not so close that he could be seen by someone on deck.

Zhu's enforcers had fallen into a bit of a rut since boarding. They always patrolled clockwise, maintaining the maximum interval between them and following a well-worn path through the stacked containers where possible. Routine was the enemy of good security and would make them relatively easy to avoid.

Fade did a partial pull-up, bringing his eyes even with the deck. No sign of human activity, but the visual chaos created by the ship, its cargo, and the intermittent electric lights was considerable. Reasonably satisfied, he hooked his right heel over the railing and disconnected the cable. It fell through the intensifying wind and was swallowed by the ship's wake.

One more quick scan of his operating environment turned up nothing, so he pulled himself up and scrambled for a shadow big enough to swallow him. After a minute's pause, he was convinced that he was alone and took the opportunity to climb up a level to the main cargo deck.

There wasn't much space between the containers and the railing, but he was able to skirt along them for about twenty yards before ducking into a narrow corridor. The system that anchored the containers was relatively easy to climb, and he covered thirty feet quickly, slipping over the top and then slithering into a position that would be invisible to anyone looking down from the bridge. A light mist was reducing visibility, but it made sense to be cautious. As near as he could tell, all of Jon Lowe's eggs were in this one loosely woven basket.

Certain he was hidden, Fade rolled on his back and let the rain fall on his face. He was still feeling a little queasy from the insertion, and there was no particular hurry. Now and ten minutes from now were equally good.

Between the cold droplets against his skin and the relative stability of the ship, his recovery was quicker than that. He pushed himself to his feet and began weaving across the tops of the containers. Gap jumps were longer and more frequent than he would have liked, but the rising storm covered the clang of his landings.

He made it to the edge of Carl Becker's improvised prison courtyard and dropped to his stomach again, easing his eyes out over the precipice. The bottom was in deep shadow, but not so black that he couldn't see raindrops exploding in shallow puddles. Nothing else, though. Just walls of colorful containers and a few hoses snaking to the three that Egan said were occupied. Likely electricity, water, and propane. All the comforts of home.

He circled to a position above where the guards were thought to be living and began descending a set of slick vertical bars. With only ten feet remaining before he reached the deck, the sound of grinding metal floated up to him. A moment later, a door in the container directly below opened, spilling light from within.

A disembodied voice yelled something in Chinese as a man in a rain slicker appeared and closed the door behind him. The muscles in Fade's forearms felt like they were on fire, but he held on and watched the guard retrieve a pack of cigarettes. One last smoke before the storm came to full force.

Fade was starting to shake from the effort of staying in place, but the asshole below refused to turn his back. Instead, he lit up facing the door, staying close enough to protect his match from the swirling wind.

Strength waning, Fade had no choice but to drop, pushing off enough to land just behind the man and drag him down. The maneuver generated a fair amount of noise, but a locked-in choke hold limited it to the thud of them hitting the deck. Fade did his best to keep strangling the flailing guard with one arm while pulling his pistol and aiming it at the door. The man slapped at his hand, still able to breathe enough to fight but not enough to shout. Fade wrapped his legs around him from behind, gaining marginally better control. After a five count with no one coming to the rescue, he dropped the gun and reached for his knife. The man was throwing elbows now, connecting each one, but with a lot of the impact absorbed by Fade's wet suit.

Time to finish this.

He released his grip and heard the man take a deep breath in order to warn his companions. Before he could, Fade drew the blade across his throat. One more adrenaline-fueled burst of strength preceded him going limp.

Fade snatched up the gun again, sweeping it between the containers housing the guards and keeping the bleeding body on top of him as a shield. Nothing. Just the rain.

Back in the day, there would have been little chance their struggle would have gone unnoticed. Now, though, no one had any idea what was going on around them. Saved by God's grace and the invention of the AirPod.

48

FADE SLID out from beneath the body as blood dispersed across the wet deck. Egan had made it clear that everything had to go perfectly. Any screwup meant the immediate end of the operation. But did this really rise to the level of a screwup? Or was it more of a glitch?

He grabbed the corpse by the collar and dragged it to a container on the other side of the makeshift courtyard. This one was secured with a simple bolt placed where a padlock would usually hang.

It came out easily, and he pulled the body inside before closing the door behind him. Despite the blocked windows, it wasn't completely dark. A dim light was glowing somewhere in the back, providing enough illumination to take in his surroundings. The space was cramped, but surprisingly luxurious, with wood floors and cabinets, stone countertops, and quality upholstery. There was even a fresh flower arrangement centered on the dining table. Lowe was right. Zhu really did have a thing for this guy.

"What do you want?"

The voice that emanated from the back was unafraid. Maybe even a little angry.

Fade moved toward it, finding Carl Becker sitting up in bed. Shadow obscured his face, but his posture and tone suggested he was unharmed.

"Who are you?" he demanded.

Fade put a finger to his lips, but the man ignored the gesture.

"Is this supposed to be some kind of rescue?"

"Not exactly," Fade replied quietly. He sat next to the bed and leaned in toward the man. "I'm here to ask you to rescue *us*."

"I can't—"

"Listen. We only have a couple of cigarettes' worth of time. Do you know where they're taking you?"

"To see Yichén."

"Physical location?"

Becker shook his head.

"Okay. They're almost certainly going to pull you off this boat and move you around to make sure you're not being followed. We need to be able to track you." Fade pulled out a cylinder about four inches long and three-quarters of an inch in diameter. "I need you to shove this up your ass."

"Is this a joke?"

"Sorry about the size, but we needed the battery life and a solid GPS connection."

He didn't appear to be impressed by the plan.

"It's not as bad as it looks. We even prelubrica—"

"Yichén is the most brilliant person I've ever known," Becker started.

"Seriously, man. We don't have time—"

"He sees everything in logic. Identify the problem, then formulate the most efficient solution. He believes in what he's doing. And a lot of other people do too. More than you think."

Fade closed his hand around the cylinder and pulled it back. "Does that include you?"

"One of Yichén's weaknesses is that he sees most people as unremarkable. Not necessarily evil. Just . . . irrelevant. Unless someone has what he believes to be extraordinary intellect, he considers people interchangeable."

"Look, this is all really interesting, and we should talk about it over a drink sometime. But right now I've got a dead guy bleeding in your kitchen."

"That seems like an insurmountable problem."

"Depends on how far you're willing to go to help me."

Becker nodded slowly. "I married my high school sweetheart. We've been together for over fifty years. She doesn't have a Nobel Prize or even an advanced degree. But I can tell you that I find her quite remarkable."

FADE PULLED himself onto the top container and turned to look over the edge. Thirty feet below, the body of Zhu's guard was lying in the rain next to a steak knife from Becker's stylish kitchen. The scientist squinted up through the rain to confirm he was clear and then slammed a foot into the steel wall next to him. The deep clang and his unintelligible shout rose above the rumble of the weather.

For an interminable fifteen seconds, there was no reaction, but the continued disturbance finally got the remaining guards off their asses. As a door opened, Becker ran to the far side, feigning an attempt to climb the bars that Fade himself had just ascended.

An Asian man in a sweatshirt and jeans sprinted toward the scientist, shouting in Chinese as he pounded barefoot through the puddles. The door of another container opened as he grabbed Becker from behind and pried him from the bars. They both stumbled back, and Fade grinned when the academic managed to catch the man with an off-balance right cross. Both ended up on the deck as the remaining guards bore down. A moment later, they'd regained control, but with the expected kid gloves. Zhu's disciples would rather die than harm his science daddy.

Fade pulled back from the edge of the container. Mess made, mess cleaned up. Put that in your pipe and smoke it, Matt Egan.

He ran across the slick metal surfaces, staying in shadow until he reached a gap where he could descend to the main deck. That part of his escape plan went pretty smoothly, but the rest posed challenges. First was the sheer height of the vessel. He'd once thrown a Marine off a battleship—a nearly career-ending event prompted by way too much Fireball whiskey—and the guy had suffered a broken pelvis from impacting the water.

The second problem was that this wasn't a sunny afternoon, and they weren't in dock. The ship was moving along at a pretty good clip, creating a significant wake in dark, high seas. The hydraulics were impossible to predict and had the potential to pull him under, send him into the propellers, or just suck him along in something resembling an old-timey keel haul.

With no way to control any of those factors, there was no choice but to retreat as far as possible and run. He reached the edge at a full sprint, diving over the rail and then somersaulting into a position that would allow for maximum penetration.

The fall was disconcertingly long and the impact wrenching enough to make him regret what he'd done to that Marine. He was pretty sure he was in one piece, though, and this time didn't feel the temptation to stay under. If he had a therapist, the word *breakthrough* would undoubtedly be bandied about.

He activated the CO_2 cartridge on his life vest, and it pulled him to the surface. The ship was startlingly close, giving the impression of some prehistoric beast indifferent to the speck of a creature at its side. Fade rolled on his stomach and swam as hard as he could away from the hull, but it was impossible to know if he was moving forward or getting pulled back. At that moment, it didn't matter. Just go full gas like he'd been taught. No past. No future. Just that moment.

By the time the ship went clear, he was more choking than breathing and the taste of blood from the effort was strong enough to overpower that of the seawater washing it down. He slowed and finally stopped, bobbing in the waves. After a few minutes, the vessel's lights were swallowed by the rain, and he was left in blinding darkness.

49

FADE SLAMMED a foot into the pickup's brake pedal, raising a cloud of dust and barely avoiding a series of wild boars darting through his headlights. It felt good to be on the move and back on dry land again, even if it was in middle-of-nowhere Laos.

The yachting life had turned out to be better in theory than in practice. Admittedly, the twins were a better-than-average diversion, but there was only so much fun in the sun a person could take before boredom set in. He'd been on the verge of heading down to the engine room to see if anything needed overhauling when an unannounced helicopter came to collect him.

Why? He had no idea. But for now, it didn't matter. The air flowing through the open window was a perfect sixty-five degrees, the mountains were silhouetted against a star-filled sky, and Olivia Newton-John was playing on the eight track stuck in the dash. It felt a little like freedom, but probably wasn't. The sense of possibility was real, though. Hovering somewhere just out of sight.

In the end, Google Maps didn't take him to the promised land. Instead, the ever-narrowing dirt road finally just dead-ended into the trees. Once parked, his phone gave him a new track to follow—five miles of bushwacking through dense rain forest. Not entirely unexpected given the hiking boots, backpack, and machete he'd been provided.

A quick internet search for backcountry dangers pulled up an article enumerating twenty-two deadly snakes and had various shout-outs to tigers. How sweet would it be to see a tiger in the wild? A flash of orange, black, and ivory, and then it was all over.

NO TIGERS.

But also no snakes. Just a lot of sharp branches, slick roots, and muddy river crossings. Two hours punching through dense, undulating terrain had led him to a primitive camp that was just taking on a predawn glow. Fade crouched at its edge, taking advantage of the cover provided by the forest. A Land Cruiser modified to handle the terrain was parked just ahead, its matte-green paint blending nicely with its surroundings. Two large canvas tents had been wedged into the trees, with a table surrounded by six chairs set up between. Various plastic tubs were strewn around, but there was no practical way to discern their contents.

Matt Egan exited one of the tents, glancing down at his phone and then in Fade's general direction.

"Are you out there?"

Fade squinted against the interior glare as he entered the tent. It was even more spacious than it looked from outside, but not exactly luxurious. A couple of cots were pressed against the walls and a table like the one outside dominated the center. Chairs were absent, but Lowe, Linea, and Harding were all present.

A few nods of greeting were all he got from the combat contingent, but Lowe strode over and embraced him. "It worked!"

"What worked?"

"Come to the table. I'll show you."

There was a topographical map spread out on it. Lowe tapped one of a number of hand-drawn circles. "We're here." He slid a finger west to a red X. "This is where they took Carl."

"So the signal was actually strong enough to track?"

He nodded. "And it was critical. With the weather and the number of times they moved him, we would have lost his trail."

"What is that place?"

Egan held out a stack of eight-by-ten photos. "A colonial-era farm owned by a Chinese shell company. The main building was recently restored, and a number of metal buildings were brought in. They're scattered around in the trees."

Fade flipped through the pictures, admiring the architecture of the house, though the image clearly predated its renovation. The remaining photos were all overheads—likely just Google satellite views. The outbuildings were sizable but would have been difficult to make out if they hadn't been marked with a highlighter.

"What do we know?" Fade asked.

"That Becker's inside the main building," Linea answered.

"And Zhu?"

"Uncertain," Lowe said. "But if he isn't already there, it seems likely that he's on his way. They went through a lot of trouble to get Carl to this place."

"And risked a lot," Egan added. "It's always the human connection that gets you when you try to disappear. Bóchéng paid for that weakness. And now Zhu's giving us an opportunity."

"A weakness we can all aspire to," Lowe said.

"Your sentiment. Not mine."

"Can I assume from the quality of the photos that none of you have been down there?" Fade asked.

"We haven't. But it seems like a pretty good bet that this place was Zhu's backup plan. Living quarters and probably lab space in case things went south in China."

"Agreed," Lowe said.

Fade tossed the eight-by-tens back on the table. "So we're not sure how many people are down there or if Zhu's one of them. We've got five buildings in total spread out over what looks like about a hundred-yard radius with dense trees between them. Based on what we saw in Wyoming, the metal buildings will be windowless and easily secured at the first sign of trouble. And finally, there's the virus, right? What do we know about that?"

"If they're vaccinating, it's almost certain to be in its final form," Lowe said. "There's likely at least a sample here, with others spread around the world. I'd guess that Zhu has protocols in place to release it at a moment's notice if it becomes necessary."

"Great. Any other bad news?"

They all looked at each other.

"Shit. That was meant as a joke. There's more?"

"The Chinese Navy boarded the ship that was transporting Becker two days after he was taken off," Egan said. "It looks like they've quietly taken control of the vessel and everyone on board."

"Do we know how they found out about it?"

"That's another problem," Lowe admitted. "We don't. Likely something they learned from Bóchéng, but because my involvement in all this is now known, my last remaining contacts in China have stopped taking my calls. The world's other intelligence agencies are suspicious, but the Chinese are being typically tight-lipped about why they raided my island, so fortunately I've been able to maintain most of my Western contacts."

"Does Zhu know about the ship?"

"Open question," Egan said. "But if he doesn't now, he will soon. And that leaves us in an uncomfortable position. Usually, we have better intelligence than everyone else. Now we're working in the dark."

"And with a lit fuse," Fade said.

Lowe nodded. "Burning fast."

50

IT HAD been a long, pointless day of planning and logistics. Egan, Lowe, and Linea just couldn't help themselves. At the core of their being, those three were data analysts. The more they could weigh, measure, and manipulate, the better. Watching them flail around with a few crappy photos and Google overheads had been equal parts distressing and hilarious. Three Supermen trapped in a kryptonite mine.

Now the sun was going down and there was finally something to do. Fade stood near the outdoor table, checking the contents of a pack and going over his rifle while Egan stared at the tree line. Into the unknown.

"Stay out of sight," he said, rubbing both hands repeatedly through his hair. "That's the mission. Get what intel you can, but invisibility is the priority."

Fade remembered the nervous gesture from years past. His old friend was overwhelmed. He'd reached his limit and was now leaving it behind.

Ironically, the thing that had made him the perfect team leader also made him the wrong man for the job. He took everything to heart. Every failure—from obvious miscalculation to just shit luck—was his and his alone.

Fade survived on nihilism and black humor—two things that couldn't be stripped from him. Egan had gotten through his days because of his family. And they weren't coming back.

"You doing all right, Matt?"

"Yeah."

"No reason to tear yourself apart over this."

"Over what?"

"All these politicians and dictators and old ladies who cut in front of you at the grocery store. You and Jon are doing everything you can. More than any country or government could, right? You've proved that."

"But what's the end game?"

Fade didn't respond, unsure what Egan was referring to.

"Kali was still at the age where everything was shiny and new. And Elise always saw hope. She believed humanity was moving toward perfecting itself. It was just a matter of finding the right combination of artists, philosophers, and leadership. In the end, she even started to believe people like you and me had a role."

"Really? I'd have bet good money she'd always see us as part of the problem."

"I wonder if they suffered," he said, running his hands through his hair again. "I think about it a lot. Not so much physically, but if in that last split second, they saw the world for what it really is. I didn't know until they were gone that my only purpose in life was to protect them and keep those illusions alive. I failed on both counts."

Fade put on the pack and picked up his rifle. "Then why do you keep doing it?"

He had to think for a moment. "Habit."

FADE SWITCHED on the unfamiliar scope like he'd been taught and was met with an image unlike any he'd seen through night vision gear. The ungodly weight and Egan's warning about battery life suggested a lot of fancy electronics, but they turned out to be worth it. Instead of the hazy green of light amplification or the even hazier grays of thermal, the landscape took on the look of a low-budget Technicolor movie.

He'd found a spot in the trees that kept him hidden but allowed for a decent view of the colonial building they were targeting. An iron fence surrounded the grounds, probably eight feet high and with stylish spikes at the top. Some of it might have actually been original, but numerous enhancements were apparent, including bracing that would likely withstand anything lighter than a small bulldozer and a hefty sliding gate that had replaced the more elegant one of days gone by.

No cameras were obvious, but that meant precisely zip. They could be the size of a pinky nail now and installed almost anywhere. Four dogs were roaming freely, as were two armed guards who moved like they knew what they were doing. No fixed weapons or fortified positions were apparent. Certainly nothing like what Egan had done to Fade's place in Spain.

He began to circle, focusing on remaining completely silent and stopping often to listen for exterior patrols. None appeared. The overall impression was that the people inside weren't expecting much in the way of trouble. Probably because all the world's armies, spies, and electronics came off as an antiquated joke when compared with Yichén Zhu's test tubes and incubators. Overnight, thousands of years of power dynamics had been turned on their head.

It took another two hours and three scope batteries to reach the back of the mansion. There, the structure had two levels of exterior space—a stone patio and a long, deep balcony that hovered over it. The fire pit, dining table, and plush furniture looked inviting and played into the illusion of normalcy. Even the guards could have been mistaken as a security detail for a rich celebrity taking a break from the rat race. The fence bracing and windowless outbuildings, though, were harder to explain away.

Fade was about to continue when one of the French doors opened onto the balcony. He froze and focused his scope on the two men who appeared. One was Carl Becker, motioning violently with his hands as he spoke. The words were inaudible, but based on his body language, he wasn't happy. The man behind seemed much calmer, nodding sagely and holding a drink. Fade zoomed in on his face, feeling a rare surge of adrenaline.

Yichén Zhu.

51

IT WAS still dark when Fade broke from the trees and walked back into camp. He was soaked with sweat despite predawn temperatures in the sixties, but the difficult two-mile ascent had felt a little less like an insurmountable chore and more like old times. His body and mind seemed increasingly resigned to the idea that being alive might turn out to be a long-term condition.

The canvas of the main tent was thick enough to be completely black, but not so thick that muffled voices didn't betray its occupants.

"Coming in," Fade said before slipping through the flap.

Everyone was present, with the three operators standing around the table at the center and Lowe sitting on a plastic trunk in the corner. Photos uploaded from Fade's scope had been printed and pinned to the walls.

"Thoughts?" Egan asked.

Fade stripped off his pack and rifle before grabbing a plastic bottle of water. He downed it in one long pull and crushed it in his fist. "Same as yours. We're fucked."

"That's it?" Linea said. "That's your professional opinion?"

She was decked out in custom camo, ready to save the world. But sometimes you were just dealt a losing hand.

"What do you want me to say, Lin? That we should surround the place, take out the dogs and guards without anyone noticing, and then just walk through the front door?" Fade twisted the lid off another bottle. "You want to bet the lives of a billion people on there being no security inside, nobody in those outbuildings, and that Zhu's the only person on the planet with access to the virus?"

"He's right," Harding said reluctantly. "Everything we know says he's going to attack when the vaccines he's given out reach full strength. That's a few days at most. He's ready to go, and there's no way he's planning on a single release in rural Laos."

"If we can get him quietly," Linea said, "we can interrogate him. Find out who else has the virus and how to get to them."

Fade shook his head. "You're talking bullshit and you know it. Zhu will have it set up so if his people don't hear from him—or if they hear from him in a way that isn't exactly how he said it would be—they'll release."

"I'm hearing a lot of problems," Egan interjected. "But not a lot of solutions."

"Call in the cavalry," Fade said.

"So they come in here and make all the mistakes we just talked about," Linea said. "But with more men and equipment?"

Fade glanced back at Lowe, but he didn't even seem to be listening. Hopefully, his not-so-tightly-bolted-on wheels hadn't finally come off.

"Yeah, but *they* make the mistakes, Lin. The Chinese know about Jon's involvement in this, and we've got no path forward. I say we turn everything we know over to them, the CIA, FBI, MI6, SVR, and whatever other three-letter agencies we can think of. Let them take the blowback on this, not us."

"He's right again," Harding said, speaking up for a record-breaking second time. "We found this bastard, which is something no one else could do. Maybe they have a plan that we don't know about. Whatever it is, it can't be worse than what we've got up our sleeves, which is nothing. Also, it might get us off the hook. Because if we don't say anything and the situation goes pear-shaped—which is what's going to happen—we're going to get crucified. And rightly so."

Lowes phone rang and everyone turned to watch him pick up.

"Hello? Yes, I understand. That's right, but almost certainly not the only one. I see. Can you stop them? You're sure? How long? All right. Thank you, General."

He disconnected and stared down at the screen for a few seconds before speaking.

"It's too late."

52

LOWE STOOD, eyes darting around the interior of the tent. "Fade, you're with me. The rest of you, gather up the weapons and any personal items. Then get in the car and go directly to Luang Prabang. Leave everything else behind."

"Who was on the phone?" Egan said.

"It doesn't matter. You're wasting time. Go!"

They hesitated for a moment, but then went into motion, scooping up Fade's rifle along with a number of other weapons before disappearing outside.

"Fade. Take me to Yichén's compound."

"They just walked off with my—"

"You won't need it."

Lowe followed the others outside, and a moment later, Fade could hear him penetrating the trees to the west. Much more inviting was the sound of gear being tossed into the SUV. Luang Prabang. Good food, cool tourist sites, and a complete lack of people trying to kill him.

He sighed quietly and pushed through the tent flap, starting downslope at a reluctant jog.

LOWE FELL again, and this time Fade couldn't grab him before he started to roll. After about ten feet, a downed tree stopped him pretty abruptly, but he got right back up. The fatigue was starting to show, though.

"We're only about ten minutes out," Fade said. "Back off a little."

Lowe answered by accelerating.

By the time they reached the edge of the clearing containing Zhu's compound, the sun was up but hadn't yet cleared the mountains. Fade yanked Lowe back before he burst into the open, pulling him to the ground in a place that had a view of the gate. At this time of morning, the contrast between sun and shadow would work to their advantage.

"There's no more time!" Lowe protested a little too loudly. One of the dogs in the yard stopped and looked in their direction.

"Surprising people carrying assault rifles never ends well, Jon."

"Then what?"

They traversed north, exiting the forest along a sweeping curve in the road leading to the property. It put them just out of sight but still within a few minutes' walk. Lowe was increasingly agitated, but Fade managed to keep him from running, limiting him to the awkward gait of a Miami Beach power walker.

When they came into view, the dogs rushed the fence, barking with the abandon of creatures finally about to get to do what they were bred for. The guards arrived a few moments later, aiming their weapons through the bars and shouting in what Fade assumed was Chinese but also could have been Lao.

"Easy, Jon. Let's go with a lost tourist vibe, here."

"You're wearing camouflage."

It was a valid point.

When they got close enough for a human voice to be audible over the dogs, Lowe held his hands up and spoke calmly.

It turned out the asshole spoke Chinese. And not just *I'll have the Peking duck*. He seemed to be pretty conversational. What he said was a mystery, but it was clear that he was going for the direct approach. The name *Yichén* was repeated multiple times.

A moment later, Zhu appeared at the front door followed by Carl Becker. He barked a few orders, and two guards took control of the dogs while another unlocked the gate. On the second floor, a rifle barrel appeared from an open window. It didn't track Lowe as he strode toward Zhu, though, instead staying steady on Fade.

The two men embraced before beginning a rapid-fire conversation in hushed tones. Less than a minute later, Zhu was shouting orders at his men, and Lowe was walking back toward the gate. He pointed to a white SUV parked near the north fence line, while the guard not dealing with the dogs ran into the house. Becker just looked on with a dazed expression.

"Fade, could you pull the car up, please? I'm told that the keys are in it."

Fade ran over and slid behind the wheel. It started with no problems, and he threw the passenger door open as he skidded up alongside Lowe. Lowe climbed in while Zhu and Becker waited for four guards to cram into the third row. Once everyone was aboard, Lowe motioned toward the still-open gate.

"We're leaving. Faster is better."

Fade accelerated, hovering at around fifty miles an hour on the arcing dirt road.

"Faster, please," Lowe said.

He did his best to accommodate, but the surface was too rutted to push much harder.

"Look, Jon. If the Chinese are sending paratroopers, it doesn't matter how fast we go. They'll see us when they come overhead, and there's only one road in and out."

"They're not sending paratroopers," Lowe responded. "The road's straightening out. Could we go a little faster?"

Fade leaned out the open window and looked at the sky. Nothing but a few fluffy clouds.

"What? Bombers? Missiles? The biggest thing the US has is probably a

MOAB, and I doubt the Chinese can do much better. It has a blast radius of about a mile, and we're clear of that. No reason to end up in a ditch."

"The most powerful *conventional* weapon is the MOAB," Lowe corrected.

Fade slammed the accelerator to the floor.

53

LOWE WAS consumed by the screen of his phone, but it didn't have anything to do with communication.

"Two-minutes, forty-seven seconds to detonation."

"Not helpful," Fade said over the roar of the wind rushing through the window.

"But accurate, I think. The Chinese gave a very precise warning to the US, Europe, and a number of other countries about the launch so that there wouldn't be any misunderstandings."

"Did they warn Laos?"

"I don't think it was on the list."

Fade glanced in the rearview mirror, taking in the stoic faces of Yichén Zhu and Becker, the confused expressions of his guards, and the road receding in slow motion. He'd been a Discovery Channel junkie for much of his life, but for some reason, he was blanking on all the Manhattan Project shows he'd watched. When the shit hit the fan, it turned out that all he could remember was the wildlife documentaries.

"One minute twenty-four."

The road steepened, but this was one of those rare occasions when the high ground created exposure instead of advantage. Distance was good, though, right? Distance was always good.

"Fifty-nine seconds, Fade."

A bridge came into view ahead, spanning maybe fifty feet over a muddy river. He'd once seen a space travel series that talked about how water was a good radiation shield. Or was that one of the *Star Wars*?

With forty-three seconds left on the clock, there was no point in bogging down in minutia. Leaving aside his doubts about radiation shielding, there was no question that water worked against flame and intense heat. He yanked the steering wheel right, taking out a number of young trees before dropping down a slick embankment and sinking the front end in the river.

"Everybody out!" he said, throwing his door open.

"Nine seconds," Lowe commented.

"Get in the water and stay down as long as you can!" Fade shouted before jumping in and submerging. He managed to find a root on the riverbed and used it to hold himself down.

Four, three, two, one...

Nothing.

The flash came a moment later, bright enough that he instinctively turned away. It was around another ten seconds before a deep roar penetrated his ears and chest. Unable to resist, he tilted his head back and squinted through the muddy water at the hurricane of dust, smoke, and pulverized foliage passing overhead. Everything turned dark, and he lost sense of time, clinging ever tighter to the root.

The air cleared a bit, and he allowed himself to float within inches of the surface. His lungs were burning from lack of air, but he barely noticed. The hazy mushroom cloud rising in the distance was too mesmerizing.

He kept his grip on the bottom, content to let someone else surface first. It turned out to be Becker. The old man burst from the water, gulping air that apparently hadn't been vaporized or ionized or any of those other deadly sounding *-ized* words.

Yichén was next. Then Lowe. And finally, the guards. When Fade was satisfied that no one's face was melting, he rose just enough to expose his eyes. It was a little hotter than he expected, but still cooler than an average summer day in Virginia. A few more inches brought his nose above the waterline. The scent was standard forest fire with notes of something more exotic. Something he suspected not many people had smelled and lived to tell about it.

TURNING THE key in the vehicle's ignition elicited no response at all. The electronics appeared to be fried. Phones were also all nonfunctional. They turned on but had no signal or GPS.

The humans had fared better. No one had suffered any injuries beyond a few scrapes and bruises. Wind coming from the northeast had largely cleared the air and would hopefully keep the fires from advancing too quickly in their direction. Setting aside the possibility of cancer later in life, a better outcome than Fade would have guessed. The others were on the riverbank, all maintaining a solemn silence until Lowe broke it.

"Look what you've done, Yichén."

"What I've done? Did I build that weapon? Did I panic and launch it? Do I spend my days stealing everything I can even though I have more than I could ever need or want?"

Both stood and for a moment looked like they were about to start throwing punches.

"That's a pretty carefully curated list, isn't it, Yichén? You left out the genocide part. The part where you killed seven million people and have threatened the lives of hundreds of millions more."

"People who have never paid a price for their crimes. Now, for the first time in history, they will."

Zhu turned and said something to his men in Chinese. Fade didn't understand the words, but he understood that the guards all suddenly turned their attention to him. He bolted for the opposite bank, losing the cover of the SUV as they went for their rifles. The muddy slope was probably only ten feet long, but it felt more like a mile when accompanied by the sound of automatic fire and rounds slapping the foliage around him.

"DR. BECKER?" LOWE said. "Are you all right?"

The man coughed and wiped at his eyes before giving a weak nod.

"Then you'll excuse us for a few minutes. Yichén. Let's walk."

They started upstream through sunlight filtered in a way that made the scene a bit surreal. Beautiful in its own postapocalyptic way.

"Not exactly how you saw it playing out."

Zhu shook his head. "It would have come and gone like a storm. According to my modeling, no more than twelve weeks from the first fatality to the last. Deaths are quick and painless, and eventually investigators would have traced the outbreak to a bat colony in Yunnan. There would have been no politics or ideology. No one to blame. Only a world ready for reinvention."

"The best laid plans, eh, Yichén? But this isn't a natural phenomenon anymore. It's an attack. A generational war. How did the youth you have so much faith in react? Parties. Racism. Riots. And remember that all the people you find so destructive—the ones you despise so much—were young only a few years ago."

"Maybe you're right, Jon. Maybe you're not. But we're going to find out." He pointed in the direction of the mushroom cloud rising lazily into the sky. "Because this won't change anything. It's just another desperate, stupid act by desperate, stupid men."

"But maybe not the last. If the people in power contract your disease, what do you think their reaction will be? To go quietly?"

"You're too used to getting your way, Jon. Save your proselytizing for the weak minds you surround yourself with."

"You're making a mistake, Yichén. What the Chinese government did to you has left deep scars. It's understandable, but not a luxury someone as powerful as you can afford. Try to think objectively for a moment. How much of this is you looking to perfect society, and how much is revenge?"

Automatic gunfire erupted somewhere in the distance, and Zhu tilted his head to listen. "Don't psychoanalyze me, Jon. And don't try to dictate. You're not in a position to."

"Perhaps."

They walked in silence for almost a minute before Zhu spoke again. "Someone had to act. Before we destroy ourselves. Empty, hypocritical gestures toward the future aren't enough anymore. And neither is starting a charity."

Lowe smiled at the thinly veiled insult.

"I was surprised by that, Jon. It seems naive, and that's not a word I would have thought described you."

"I'm going to use it to take over the world."

"Excuse me?"

"Sorry. It sounds so grandiose when you say it out loud. But it's something I've been thinking about for most of my life."

FADE CROUCHED and scooped up a handful of forest floor, smearing it across his face and through his hair to enhance his camouflage. There was a temptation to tie the bandanna in his pocket over his mouth and nose, too, but what was the point? It'd filter out some of the smoke and pulverized forest but would do precisely zip about all the angry little atoms.

One of his opponents apparently had also forgone a mask and coughed somewhere to the southwest. Fade picked up a rock and threw it in the direction of the sound. It traveled silently for a moment before clattering off a tree trunk. A burst of automatic fire followed, the muzzle flash giving him a reasonable idea of the shooter's position.

So good news. These guys were decent but not A-listers. They'd missed him on the riverbank, and at least one guy was willing to expend a lot of rounds without a clear target. On the other hand, he was outnumbered by a factor of four, and they'd been smart enough to bring guns.

He heard shouting as the men formed up on the shooter and some excited dialogue as they tried to figure out if he'd hit anything.

So what were the available options?

Charging them with his combat knife was actually kind of tempting. The terrain would let him get pretty close before he burst into view, and if they were bunched up, he could take out two before they even knew what was happening. If they panicked and he was able to get hold of one of their sidearms, it could theoretically work. Plus, it had the benefit of being quick. Hanging around ground zero until he started to glow wasn't all that appealing.

After further consideration, it seemed that something a little less kamikaze would increase his chances of survival. He crossed the river at a wide point, penetrating the trees for a few yards before reversing himself in the same footprints. The fallout from the blast had turned the water even more murky and filled it with debris—two things that would work in his favor. He submerged next to a clump of severed branches snagged on a tree trunk and grabbed a broad leaf as it floated past. A small stick pinned it to his hair, and then it was just a matter of sinking to his nose and waiting.

The passage of time tended to wander in these kinds of situations, but on that day, it got completely lost. Sunlight was being bounced around in a way that robbed it of direction. There was no birdsong or insect drone gaining and losing volume as the day wore on. Even the distant crackle of fire had dissipated. All that remained was the monotonous flow of water and occasional impact of floating debris.

At some point in all that, one of Zhu's people spotted his carefully created trail of footprints. Fade would have bet the farm that they'd descend as a team, but it didn't happen. A lone man approached the river edge, locked on the far bank with an intensity that would seriously degrade his situational awareness. A trick? Were the others dug in just out of sight? Or was this guy just way out over his skis?

He spoke at length into his throat mic, providing additional evidence that he didn't have cover, then he waded into the water.

The depth around the snag was around three and a half feet, which was enough to force him to hold his rifle up and at an awkward angle. Either way, though, it wasn't a great close-quarters weapon.

He chose to go left around to the snag, which was ideal—downstream and on Fade's dominant side. Fade took a quiet breath and sunk to his eyeballs, waiting for the man to come alongside. There was still no evidence of anyone in the trees, but after the radio transmission, backup was undoubtedly on the way. Best to make this quick. Keeping his arm beneath the surface, Fade reached out and slid the razor-sharp knife upward into the man's stomach. His expression was more one of confusion than pain or fear. A couple of choking coughs brought up some blood, but instead of squeezing his weapon's trigger, he just sank.

Letting the body float downriver was a solid option, but instead, Fade decided to tangle it in the snag and submerge again. Things were going to be trickier this time, but he still liked his chances. Surprise and the fact that bullets didn't travel well through water were advantages he wasn't anxious to trade for the vagaries of a running fight.

The team's point man emerged from the trees a few moments later, immediately dropping to one knee and sweeping his weapon. He yelled something, and another man appeared to his right, hanging back a little. The third was likely somewhere just out of sight. It was hard to say if that was because he was reluctant to break cover or simply due to Fade's unwillingness to move his head and widen his field of vision.

Satisfied that no threat was imminent, the lead man entered the water. His dead companion was hung up in a way that would make his wound invisible, and the water was muddy enough to obscure any residual bleeding. That would make his cause of death impossible to determine without closer inspection. It was possible—though admittedly unlikely—that he'd just been hit by a fallen tree and drowned.

The approaching man was taller and able to hold his rifle more at the ready than his comrade. Fade took a breath and sank, positioning himself beneath the corpse. He had just enough visibility to see the outline of his opponent as the man rolled his former teammate over.

The upward thrust of Fade's blade once again caused his victim to freeze for a moment. This time, though, his finger clenched, and the roar of his gun was quickly joined by others—likely shooting blindly in the same general direction. Fade pulled a pistol from the man's thigh holster and stood, giving it a quick shake and using his opponent's body as a shield. His first round hit the man crouched on the bank, pitching him forward into the mud. The other shooter was indeed still ensconced in the trees, and he immediately redirected his fire in Fade's direction. By then, though, he'd already slipped back beneath the surface and was skimming the bottom on his way downstream.

"IT'S NOT just old people, Yichén. It's all of us. We come from the same evolutionary tree as other primates, and maybe we're not as different from them as we'd like to think. Violence, sex, submission. Those things have been built into us over millions of years. We're not prisoners of culture; culture's a prisoner of us. If you cut a branch, the sprout that appears isn't going to suddenly change direction."

Zhu didn't respond.

"You say that the people in power are stupid, immoral, and power hungry. I agree. Where we part ways is the idea that the next generation—the people reveling in what you're about to do—aren't exactly the same."

"But not you. You're different."

"Yes. I'm different. And so were you before the reeducation camp. Your experience there has blinded you."

"To what?"

"To the fact that the elites wear their cravings and biases on their sleeves, and that makes them easy to manipulate. The time of governments, militaries, and nations is over. Technology is power now. Me and the people who've joined me control space, medicine, transportation, energy, computing, and social media. Not dictatorships. Not democracies. The world's rulers just want the limelight. To feel superior. The fact that they're puppets won't matter to them. Handled skillfully, most won't even notice. And neither will their subjects."

"To what end?"

"To your end, Yichén. Peace, prosperity, and stability."

The geneticist nodded. "I've always admired you, Jon. As a man of vision. But I wonder if in this case your reach exceeds your grasp."

"I thought the same. But now I'm worried about the opposite."

"Oh?"

"I've been more successful more quickly than I planned. The fact it's me here and not someone from one of the world's intelligence agencies is an example of that. I'm not sure I have all the checks and balances in place yet. They say that absolute power corrupts absolutely for a reason. Do I think my people and I are immune to that? No."

Zhu turned without warning, starting back. They'd almost reached the Land Cruiser when a rustling became audible in the trees to their left. It turned into footfalls and ragged breathing just before one of Zhu's guards burst from the trees. He nearly made it to the water's edge before a gunshot struck him in the back of the head.

Fade appeared a moment later, hair matted with mud and sweat. He ignored them, crouching next to the river and dunking his head.

"It's time for you to stop what you started, Yichén. I can maintain the illusion that you died in the blast, and I can fund whatever research you want to pursue. More than that, I can give you a seat at the table."

"And if I refuse?"

Lowe looked around him through the haze. "Then you never leave this place."

Epilogue

THE MIDDAY sun was pounding down without a breath of wind to diminish its effects. In the distance, the imposing Sierra Nevadas were topped in a white blanket left by a storm system that had moved through two days before. Everything a late fall day in southern Spain should be.

A hint of steam coming off the pool shimmered in the glare as Fade paddled toward a mojito floating a few yards away. Raya had found a brand of elaborate inflatable armchairs that allowed him to navigate the pool without actually getting wet. In his estimation, an invention on par with V-8 motors and antibiotics.

He reached the cocktail, but went for the phone beside it instead. WhatsApp was already on-screen, and he typed a brief message to Raya.

Lazy river through the woods. Call contractor.

It appeared beneath a number of other ideas she'd ignored.

Learn to ski. Buy equipment necessary.
Floating fire pit? Check viability.
Does Penélope Cruz live nearby? Investigate.

This one got a little more action. Raya's voice floated down from an open second-floor window.

"We're not cutting down perfectly healthy trees to expand a pool no one but you uses!"

A woman lacking in vision.

He glanced at the news alerts clogging his screen but then swiped them away and went for his drink. He already knew what they said.

Other than the Lao government and the people downwind of them, no one seemed particularly concerned about the dropping of the first nuke since 1945. In fact, the world's news agencies—largely run by grateful people over sixty—were giving it about as much press as the average celebrity love triangle. No need for everyone to get their panties wadded up. Christmas sales were just around the corner!

A few days after the blast, the Chinese government had miraculously managed to crack Zhu's encryption, and that led to various raids preventing the release of the virus, once again making the world safe for the golf cart set. Young people whose excitement had reached such a fevered pitch at the prospect of getting their hands on the reins of power quickly went silent, partially out of well-warranted fear of retaliation and partly, it seemed, out of some genuine shame for their behavior.

It was an interesting facet of human nature that Fade had first become aware of in the Middle East. People tended to mistake underdogs for good guys. In his experience, that was very much untrue. Most underdogs had no interest in peace, justice, or equality. They just wanted to be the hammer and not the nail.

He polished off the mojito, noting that his cocktails were getting progressively weaker as a result of Raya's concerns about his drinking. They'd have to have a talk about that.

Unintelligible voices reached him a few moments later. Friendly greetings based on the tone. He paddled his chair to face the back door just as Jon Lowe came through.

"How are you, Fade?"

"Good. You?"

"Can't complain. Do you mind if I join?"

Fade pointed to an identical chair leaning against a wall. Lowe put it in the water and boarded carefully, managing not to splash his jeans or sweatshirt. Seconds later, Raya appeared and handed him a can of the IPA he favored.

"While you're up, why don't you make me another mojito."

Based on her expression, there was a roughly zero percent chance of that occurring.

Lowe seemed content to drink his beer in the sun, and they floated for quite a while before Fade spoke. "I've got two words for you, Jon: Lazy river."

The man craned his neck toward the trees. "Through the woods there? I like it. You could continue the aqueduct theme."

"Right?"

They floated for a few more minutes.

"I was afraid your two words were going to be *I quit*."

Fade ignored the comment. "How goes the subjugation of humanity?"

Lowe grinned and took another pull on his beer. "Almost there."

"And Zhu?"

"He destroyed all the samples of his virus and gave me the locations of the labs. I put that information somewhere Chinese intelligence could find it. The raids made for good television, and people feel safer."

"It would have been kind of anticlimactic otherwise," Fade agreed.

"Exactly. It's nice to have a sense of closure."

"Do you trust him? Do you think he really got rid of all of it?"

"I do. I gave him something better in return."

"A position on your board and unlimited funds to play Doctor Frankenstein for the rest of his life?"

"He didn't come quite that cheap."

Fade turned to fully face the man. "There's more?"

"Yes."

"Do tell."

"It's a little complicated, but you remember how he was making vaccines to protect people he admired?"

"Sure."

"Well, in the course of creating them, he had a few failures. One was effective at eradicating the virus but also caused a fatal immune response."

"I'm not following."

"One of the raids the Chinese kept confidential was on the laboratory where that failed vaccine was developed. There were about a hundred doses still left in the freezer."

Fade thought about that for a few seconds. "There's no way for the Chinese government to be sure they got all the labs. They'll pass that vaccine out to the hundred most powerful people in the government just in case."

"That's Yichén's theory."

"So you're telling me you just wiped out the entire Chinese government?"

"The upper echelons, probably. We'll know in a couple weeks. But technically, they'll have wiped *themselves* out."

"So Zhu gets his revenge on the people who sent him to that reeducation camp, but everyone else survives."

"Correct."

"And you get off the hook too. The Chinese know about your involvement in all this, but with their leadership dropping dead, you'll get lost in the shuffle."

"It's a fringe benefit that I considered."

"What about the other intelligence agencies? They'd have to be suspicious of you."

"The Chinese government was becoming increasingly belligerent, authoritarian, and in the case of Taiwan, outright dangerous. I don't think anyone's going to look too deeply into their deaths. Particularly when the late Yichén Zhu is such a convenient scapegoat."

"You can't keep a good billionaire down."

"That's what they tell me."

They floated for a few more minutes.

"Can I ask you a personal question, Fade?"

"Sure."

"What's it like to be dead?"

"Like you were never born."

Lowe closed his eyes and tried to imagine it for a moment. "So are you still with me?"

Fade let out a breath that tasted like rum and mint. "It's something I've been thinking about."

"Any conclusions?"

"You're on a dangerous road, Jon. That village in Madagascar. Zhu and now the Chinese. And that's just the tip of the iceberg, isn't it? Just what I've caught a glimpse of."

"I'll show you anything you want."

"Pass."

"Why?"

"Because you're manipulating the entire world to chase something you think is the greater good. And maybe it is, what do I know? But it's a lot to keep your arms around, Jon. Taming the monsters you create isn't easy. Neither is altruism. It always seems to get twisted. You said it yourself. Why did your parents do what they did? To help people? Sure. But they were also dealing for their own account."

"We can learn from the mistakes of the past."

"All evidence to the contrary," Fade said, sitting a little straighter in his chair. "You and your brilliant washboard-abbed, seven-minute-mile-running billionaires are having a great time being our saviors, right? Towing the PC line and telling yourselves that you're just helping out people who were dealt a worse hand than yours? But deep down, you don't believe it. In a year or two, you'll start seeing the rest of us as your dim cousins. Then pets. Then bugs. Do you read H. G. Wells?"

"You're about to bring up *The Time Machine*, aren't you?"

"Hell yes I'm about to bring up *The Time Machine*. The elites literally evolved away from the masses. But you don't need evolution, do you, Jon? You don't need a time machine either—you've got the Mystery Machine and Yichén Zhu."

"*You* have the Mystery Machine," Lowe said, pulling up his shirt to display his lack of injection ports. "Not me."

Fade fell back against the air mattress again. "Fuck you."

Lowe laughed. "This is why I need you, Fade. Not for your gun. For your cynicism. Your unique moral compass."

"But why do I need you?"

"The lazy river?"

"Not good enough."

"How about the opposite then? How about I strap us to a missile, and we close our eyes and light the fuse?"

Fade tilted his face toward the sun.

There was no denying it. The man was good.

Acknowledgments

After almost fifteen years of writing for Robert Ludlum and Vince Flynn, it's been quite an adventure to be out on my own again. I've been particularly lucky to begin my journey alongside my publisher, Authors Equity. It's a lot of fun to be included in something new and creative, and I'm grateful to the entire team for their ideas, hard work, and enthusiasm. So a big thanks to Madeline McIntosh, Don Weisberg, and Nina von Moltke for inviting me to their party; David Highfill for the eagle eye and great advice he shared during editing; Carly Gorga, Sarah Christensen Fu, Ilana Gold, Kathleen Schmidt, and JoliAmour DuBose-Morris for putting their marketing expertise to work for me; Craig Young and Deb Lewis for selling my vision to bookstores; Andrea Bachofen, Rose Edwards, and Scott Cresswell for producing a striking book and audiobook any author would be proud to call their own; and Diana Simmons for keeping the ship's finances on track.

James Abt and his crew at Best Thriller Books—a group I've worked with for a decade now—deserve a round of applause. They've never failed to make me laugh, and they're committed to ensuring thriller readers know about my books.

Rod Gregg has been there for me since my first Rapp novel and has never fumbled even the most esoteric firearms question. So if I ever refer to a magazine as a clip, it was undoubtedly over his strong objection.

Sam Lightner helped me sort out who's who on an NFL team and what they do.

My appreciation goes out to Simon Lipskar for finding me the perfect new home for my next act.

As always, thanks to my mother for her endless support and for eagerly agreeing to read and provide notes on the word salad that is my first draft.

Lastly, and mostly, thank you to my wife, Kim. So much of the nuts and bolts of what it takes to get a book out into the world falls on her shoulders. And while it is my life's goal to not be the temperamental artist, I sometimes slip into that role. For more than thirty years, she's managed to talk me down and refrain from throwing a dish at my head.

About the Author

Kyle Mills is the #1 *New York Times* best-selling author of twenty-four political thrillers, including nine in Vince Flynn's Mitch Rapp series and three for Robert Ludlum. He initially found inspiration from his father, an FBI agent and former Interpol director, and still draws on his contacts in the intelligence community to give his books such realism. Avid outdoor athletes and travelers, he and his wife split their time between Jackson Hole, Wyoming, and Granada, Spain. Visit his website at KyleMills.com or connect with him on X, Facebook, and Instagram @KyleMillsAuthor.